KT-195-509

FORFEIT

By Barbara Nadel

The Inspector İkmen Series
Belshazzar's Daughter
A Chemical Prison
Arabesk
Deep Waters
Harem
Petrified
Deadly Web
Dance with Death
A Passion for Killing
Pretty Dead Things
River of the Dead
Death by Design
A Noble Killing
Dead of Night
Deadline
Body Count
Land of the Blind
On the Bone
The House of Four
Incorruptible
A Knife to the Heart
Blood Business
Forfeit

The Hancock Series
Last Rights
After the Mourning
Ashes to Ashes
Sure and Certain Death

BARBARA

NADEL

FORFEIT

HEADLINE

First published in Great Britain in 2021 by
HEADLINE PUBLISHING GROUP

1

Cataloguing in Publication Data is available from the British Library

ISBN 978 1 4722 7348 2

Typeset in Times New Roman by Palimpsest Book Production Ltd, Falkirk, Stirlingshire

Printed and bound in Great Britain by Clays Ltd, Elcograf S.p.A.

Headline's policy is to use papers that are natural, renewable and recyclable products and made from wood grown in well-managed forests and other controlled sources. The logging and manufacturing processes are expected to conform to the environmental regulations of the country of origin.

HEADLINE PUBLISHING GROUP
An Hachette UK Company
Carmelite House
50 Victoria Embankment
London EC4Y 0DZ

www.headline.co.uk
www.hachette.co.uk

To all the storytellers, the crafters of tales,
the magicians of thin air, the skryers of souls.

Cast List

Çetin İkmen – former İstanbul detective
Çiçek İkmen – İkmen's eldest daughter
Bülent and Kemal İkmen – İkmen's sons
Berekiah Cohen – İkmen's son-in-law
Samsun Bajraktar – İkmen's Albanian cousin, a transsexual
Dr Arto Sarkissian – police pathologist, İkmen's oldest friend, an ethnic Armenian
Inspector Mehmet Süleyman – İstanbul detective
Sergeant Ömer Mungun – Süleyman's deputy
Inspector Kerim Gürsel – İstanbul detective
Sergeant Eylul Yavaş – Gürsel's deputy
Selahattin Ozer – police commissioner
Yusuf (aka Patrick) Süleyman – Mehmet's son
Dr Zelfa Halman – Mehmet's ex-wife
Nur Süleyman – Mehmet's mother
Murad Süleyman – Mehmet's brother
Edibe Süleyman – Murad's daughter
Gonca Şekeroğlu – gypsy artist, Süleyman's lover
Rambo Şekeroğlu – Gonca's son
Asana Şekeroğlu – Gonca's daughter
Rambo Şekeroğlu senior – Gonca's brother
Sinem Gürsel – Kerim's wife
Pınar Hanım – Sinem's mother
Emir Cebeci – Sinem's brother
Pembe Hanım – Kerim's transsexual lover

Madam Edith – Pembe's friend, a transsexual
Betül Gencer – wife of deceased TV psychologist Erol Gencer
Sibel Gencer – Erol's first wife
Hürrem Gencer – Sibel's daughter by Erol
Filiz Tepe – Erol's boss at Harem TV
Berat Tükek – fan of Erol Gencer
Samira Al Hussain – Syrian woman in prison for attempted murder of Erol Gencer in 2018
Wael Al Hussain – Samira's husband
Rima Al Numan – Samira's sister
Rauf Bey – traditional seller of herbs and spices
Belkis Hanım – Rauf's wife
Genç – a pornographer
Lagun – a prostitute
Kiyamet Yavuz – friend of Betül Gencer
Sami and Ruya Nasi – stage magicians
İbrahim Dede – a dervish
Harun Sesler – Roma gypsy godfather
Serkan Sesler – Harun's son
Wahıd Saatçı – a drug dealer
Neşe Hanım – a witness
Fahrettın Bey – magic shop owner
Hafiz Barakat – Syrian refugee
Eyüp Çelik – celebrity lawyer
Kurdish Madonna, Virjin Maryam, Matmazel Gigi, Bear Trap Hanım, Sucuk Hanım – trans prostitutes
Zenne Kleopatra – male belly dancer
Sıbel Akşener – a meddah or storyteller
Müslüm Bey – a kapıcı
Mevlüt Aktürk – a landlord
Dr Emir Doksanaltı – a psychiatrist
Nabil Nassar – a Syrian bookseller
Abbas – a Syrian refugee

Pronunciation Guide

There are 29 letters in the Turkish alphabet:

A, a – usually short as in 'hah!'
B, b – as pronounced in English
C, c – not like the 'c' in 'cat' but like the 'j' in 'jar', or 'Taj'
Ç, ç – 'ch' as in 'chunk'
D, d – as pronounced in English
E, e – always short as in 'venerable'
F, f – as pronounced in English
G, g – always hard as in 'slug'
Ğ, ğ – 'yumuşak ge' is used to lengthen the vowel that it follows. It is not usually voiced.
As in the name 'Farsakoğlu', pronounced 'Far-sak-orlu'
H, h – as pronounced in English, never silent
I, ı – without a dot, the sound of the 'a' in 'probable'
İ i – with a dot, as the 'i' in 'thin'
J, j – as the French pronounce the 'j' in 'bonjour'
K, k – as pronounced in English, never silent
L, l – as pronounced in English
M, m – as pronounced in English
N, n – as pronounced in English
O, o – always short as in 'hot'
Ö, ö – like the 'ur' sound in 'further'
P, p – as pronounced in English
R, r – as pronounced in English
S, s – as pronounced in English

Ş, ş – pronounced like the 'sh' in 'ship'
T, t – as pronounced in English
U, u – always medium length, as in 'push'
Ü, ü – as the French pronounce the 'u' in 'tu'
V, v – as pronounced in English but sometimes with a slight 'w' sound
Y, y – as pronounced in English
Z, z – as pronounced in English

Chapter 1

Truth, my friends, truth!

One name is like another, the same is true of orphans and of neighbourhoods. A tale of the past is told, a lie is heard as truth, and thus the time is passed.

And so, my friends, to a tale of a poor boy, a powerful paşa and a woman of enormous wit . . .

'Did you feed him?'

Gonca Şekeroğlu took off the old dress she'd put on to answer the front door and threw it on the floor.

'I opened the fridge and told him to help himself,' she replied.

She'd been in bed with her lover, Inspector Mehmet Süleyman, for several hours before her son Rambo had knocked on her front door and put an end to his mother's sexual congress. Naked, she got back into bed.

'What's he doing here?' Süleyman asked as he cupped his hands around her breasts. 'I thought he was doing something in Bulgaria.'

Gonca arched her back in pleasure as he began to lick her nipples.

'Oh who cares?' she said. 'He's a grown man, he makes his own decisions. Now, baby, I am hot for you . . .'

Her breathing came short and laboured. He moved a hand down her body, over her hips and between her legs. She groaned. He lifted his head from her breasts and said, 'My fantasy is for you to go on top . . .'

She laughed as she swung one of her legs across his body and mounted him. He moved his hips beneath her and she said, 'Oh baby . . .'

He gripped her waist, digging his fingers into her flesh.

'Gonca . . .'

Then his phone rang.

'Really!'

He put a hand out to the bedside table and picked it up.

'Süleyman.'

'Mehmet Bey, I am sorry to disturb you,' a familiar voice said.

'Kerim Bey?'

Kerim Gürsel was another inspector working in the homicide division of the İstanbul Police Department.

'Yes. Look, I'm out in Sarıyer, and if I tell you that this incident has taken place on Değirmendere Ayhan Sokak . . .'

That road name made Süleyman sit up, much to the discomfort of Gonca.

'Ow!'

'I worked on that attempted murder up there last year. Erol Gencer,' Süleyman said.

'I know,' his colleague replied. 'That's why I called you, Mehmet Bey. Because this time Erol Bey did not have the benefit of his wife on the premises.'

'So he's . . .'

'Oh yes, quite dead,' Gürsel said. 'And he's not alone . . .'

The boy was clearly shaken. He had, after all, found the bodies. Or rather he'd seen them through the trees and shrubs that surrounded the villa. Kerim Gürsel had tried to see the poolside area from where the boy said he had been positioned, but could make out little beyond a wide tree trunk and a portion of wall. He strongly suspected seventeen-year-old Berat Tükek had actually been trying to get into the property when he found the bodies. He wouldn't be the first star-struck mentally unwell young person to do that.

Erol Gencer, one of the dead men, and owner of the villa, was a media phenomenon. He'd apparently trained as a clinical psychologist many years before, although nobody seemed to know whether he'd actually practised. What he *had* done was get involved first with radio, then as a consultant on psychological matters on TV, eventually hosting his own highly successful show. Some people said he'd fucked his way to the top of the talk-show media tree, but however he'd done it, most people in the country knew who he was, and many of them claimed to love him.

Dr Erol, as he was styled, was not only handsome and urbane but also, apparently, really caring. People displaying varying degrees of insanity or social dysfunction or both appeared on his show. Some would lose control and fight, others would weep, and a lot of women with husband trouble would express suicidal ideation. But whatever was wrong, Dr Erol, with his broad shoulders, deep, calming voice and seemingly genuine love for his fellow beings, would try to do whatever he could to help. Young people particularly adored him. By contrast, he had always made Kerim Gürsel's skin crawl.

Berat Tükek broke through Kerim's reverie. 'This doctor who's coming, is he a psychiatrist?'

'No, a pathologist,' Kerim replied. 'Apart from anything else, he's required to formally pronounce life extinct. Not sure a psychiatrist could do that. Why?'

'Oh, nothing, it's all right . . .'

The kid was probably on a sack of medication. Although in spite of being shocked, he seemed all right for the time being, sitting next to one of the local cops who had been first on the scene. Even if the boy was mentally ill, he appeared far from being in any sort of crisis. But then whatever state he was in, that didn't mean he wasn't a suspect. There was a convention that a person who found a body or bodies, unlawfully killed, was most likely to have committed that offence. Young Berat was going to have to endure a lot of unwanted attention in the days to come. Maybe psychiatric support would be needed?

As scene-of-crime officers secured the area, Kerim stepped to one side and called his wife. Now that he knew that the pathologist, Dr Sarkissian, was on his way, as well as Kerim's own sergeant, Eylul Yavaş – who was bringing Erol Gencer's wife from the couple's apartment in Nişantaşı – he could finally let Sinem know he was all right.

Of course had he been alone with his wife in the apartment when he had been called to the scene, he could have simply left her sleeping and written her a note to explain his absence. But his mother-in-law, the redoubtable Pınar Hanım, was staying with them, sleeping in the next room. As soon as his phone had beeped, Pınar had been in their bedroom demanding to know what was happening. Kerim and Sinem's baby was due imminently, but he knew the old woman would stay on after the birth for God knew how long. How he would endure it, Kerim didn't know.

As soon as Sinem picked up, he said, 'Are you all right?'

'Yes.' But she didn't sound it, she never did. Sinem Gürsel suffered from rheumatoid arthritis. Usually the pain that resulted from this was dulled by medication, but now that she was pregnant, she had to limit her drug intake.

'Can you take anything?' he asked.

'Not yet. Where are you?'

'Sarıyer,' he said. 'It's going to be a long night.'

'Oh.' Sinem had been Kerim's wife for long enough to know what this meant. Someone – maybe more than one person – had died.

'Did your mother go back to bed?' he asked.

'Eventually . . .' There was a pause, and then she said, 'I wish she'd go home.'

'You know she won't.'

'Oh Kerim, I am so sorry!'

'What about?'

'My mother,' she said. 'If she wasn't here, things could get back to normal. I know you—'

'Sinem, it's all right,' he said. 'I'm fine. Just look after yourself and our baby. That's all that matters to me.'

'Yes, but—'

'Inspector Gürsel.'

Suddenly a short, portly individual wearing thick round glasses was at his side.

'I have to go,' Kerim said and ended the call. 'Dr Sarkissian.'

'Ah, Inspector Gürsel,' the pathologist said. 'So what dark deed has dragged us from our beds this time?'

He didn't have to be driving over to Sarıyer in the middle of the night. From Gonca's house in the Old City, the smart Bosphorus village of Sarıyer was hardly just around the corner, and he was officially on leave. Only for two weeks, but they were crowded ones, and hot. August in the city was living up to its unbearable reputation, and his son, visiting İstanbul for the first time since he was a toddler, was finding it challenging.

In spite of having fallen out of love with Yusuf's mother many years ago, Mehmet Süleyman had always made sure he supported the boy. His ex-wife had been a dual Turko-Irish national, and so when the marriage had ended, Yusuf – or Patrick, as he preferred to be called – had gone with her to live in the Irish Republic. Every year Mehmet spent most of his annual leave staying at a hotel in Dublin so that he could see him. Now sixteen, Patrick had come to İstanbul to get to know his father and his family *in situ*. So far it hadn't gone well.

Seemingly horrified by his father's small flat in Cihangir, Patrick had gone to stay with Mehmet's brother Murad, his daughter Edibe and the Süleyman family matriarch, his grandmother Nur, in the old woman's mansion in Arnavautköy. Outwardly unimpressed by his father's family's connections to the deposed Ottoman imperial family, the boy nevertheless seemed to prefer to reside in a building with some class. Back in Ireland, he lived with his psychiatrist mother in a large Georgian house just off O'Connell Street. He also went to one of the best schools in the city, Gonzaga, and spoke, for some reason, in a sort of exaggerated drawl. In spite of having a Turkish father and a half-Turkish mother, he purported to speak no Turkish at all, and had declared himself bored to tears by most things as soon as he'd arrived. Physically, he was tall and looked mature for his age. He was also, like his father, extremely handsome, and when they'd spoken on the phone prior to his visit, Mehmet's ex-wife Zelfa had admitted she was having trouble with Patrick and girls.

In a way, Mehmet felt slightly guilty about palming the boy off on his brother, but only slightly. Even before Patrick had arrived, Mehmet hadn't seen Gonca, his Roma mistress, for several weeks due to work commitments. And although he also had a girlfriend, in the very pleasing shape of Çiçek İkmen, he had yearned for the older woman's somewhat wilder approach to sex. When he'd left her to go out, voluntarily, to Sarıyer when Kerim Gürsel called him, she'd lost her temper, and as he'd disappeared into the night, she'd called out after him, 'I'll never suck your cock again – bastard!'

She would, and they both knew it. But that was what made her so hot to him – her never-ending sexual passion. Unlike dear Çiçek, who was beautiful, kind and also sexy, just not *that* sexy . . .

But women and children lived in one part of his mind, his

work in another, and what Kerim Gürsel had told him had piqued his interest. The previous September, Süleyman had been called to an incident at this very same property in response to a request from the wife of TV psychologist Erol Gencer. Betül Gencer had an unnamed woman at gunpoint in the bedroom she shared with her husband. The woman, who turned out to be a Syrian national called Samira Al Hussain, had apparently been besotted with Gencer and had turned up to kill him when he wouldn't acknowledge her. She was now serving time for attempted murder in Bakırköy women's prison.

It was easy to see which house was Gencer's by the number of police cars parked outside, together with a black Mercedes S Class he knew belonged to the pathologist, Dr Sarkissian. Once out of his car, he walked towards the entrance to the property and showed his ID to the officers who admitted him. As he walked inside the vast white house, he could still smell Gonca's deep rose perfume on his skin, and it made him smile.

'Mehmet Bey!'

Kerim Gürsel looked pale underneath the spotlights in the ceiling of Gencer's hallway. Süleyman knew that his colleague's wife was pregnant and also that she had a long-term illness. Kerim was probably not getting a lot of sleep. And now this . . .

The two men shook hands and then briefly embraced.

'What's the story?' Süleyman asked as they walked out of the house and into the garden. Scene-of-crime officers were measuring, bagging up and collating evidence, while Dr Sarkissian, a small but wide figure in white plastic coveralls, was leaning over a body on the ground. Body number two was about two metres away, face down, on the edge of the swimming pool. The water was threaded with thin tendrils of blood.

'Well, there are two victims, both male,' Kerim said. 'One easily identified as Erol Gencer, although no formal ID will be made until his wife arrives. The other . . .' He shrugged. 'Slim, looks middle aged to me. Can you remember what the circumstances were surrounding that attempted murder of Gencer last year?'

Süleyman told him what he knew and added, 'The woman involved was Syrian. Worked in Fatih selling scarves, I think. In the past, when she first came to the city, she'd worked the streets. She had, she claimed, serviced Gencer on several occasions. But there was no evidence for that. She was fixated on him. His wife maintained that she'd stalked him, although that was never reported to us. The woman, Samira Al Hussain, had several psychiatric assessments. There was a lot of trauma in evidence, as there so often is with Syrian refugees. Of course she's in Bakırköy now . . .'

He saw Arto Sarkissian hold up a hand in greeting, and waved back.

'Not the psychiatric hospital?' Kerim asked.

'No.'

'But if there was a question mark over her sanity . . .'

'She had a . . . I suppose you'd call it a cover story that just didn't make sense,' Süleyman said. 'While she held to that, progress was difficult. But then she changed her story and admitted to the charge of attempted murder. She said she *had* stalked Gencer.'

'You said there was no evidence for that.'

'Until her confession, no, nothing solid,' he said. 'Neighbours reported seeing a woman about, but whether that was Samira or not they couldn't say. I don't know precisely what caused her change of heart. But the fact remains that when the local cops broke into this house, they found Betül Gencer holding a revolver and Samira Al Hussain with a knife to Erol's throat.' He called over to the pathologist. 'Doctor!'

'Hello, Inspector Süleyman. I thought you were on leave,' Sarkissian said.

'I am.' Süleyman smiled. 'Sort of.'

'Ah.'

'Cause of death?'

'Don't know,' the doctor replied. 'Certainly no idea about the TV star as yet, though he's vomited quite spectacularly. Cursory look at the other man, but that one's pretty obvious.'

'In what way?' Kerim Gürsel asked.

'Stomach slit open,' the medic said. 'Terrible mess. Good job he's lying on his front.'

'It makes me despair,' Çetin İkmen said as he lit a new cigarette from the smoking butt of his last one. 'Conforming to a stereotype is so lazy and also, I think, insulting. As if the old Turkish teyze isn't bad enough, poking her nose in everywhere in the real world, now we have the old bags on social media.'

His wife Fatma, who was dead and existed only in ghost form, said nothing.

Even though it was three o'clock in the morning, ex-homicide detective Çetin İkmen wasn't able to sleep, and so he'd come out onto his apartment balcony to talk to his wife. Famed for his impeccable clear-up rate when he worked for the İstanbul Police Department, İkmen was a skinny sixty-two-year-old with a massive cigarette habit and a bit of a drink problem. He was also the son of a once-renowned Albanian witch whose ability with things not of this world, including ghosts, he had inherited.

August in İstanbul was as hot as a hearth and so he wasn't the only one struggling with sleep. As he looked down onto the thoroughfare known as Divan Yolu, the Sultanahmet Park beyond and the great mosque itself beyond that, he saw that a lot of people were milling about aimlessly in the dark. For a moment he wondered where his children and his friends might be. Was Mehmet Süleyman, as he suspected, having wild sex over at

Gonca Şekeroğlu's quirky house in Balat? He went back to his original subject.

'Bülent spends half his life on Facebook, Twitter and Instagram as far as I can see,' he continued. 'Supposed to be blocked by the state, I think, but of course our son can get round most things. In fact most people can – hence old women wearing tights that could withstand nuclear attack fixated on pouring bile into the ether. Some of these old harridans are "influencers", whatever that may mean. Just hope they're not influencing people to kill "bad girls". And as for bloody husbands—'

'Whose husband?'

İkmen looked up into an elderly, heavily made-up face and said, 'Ah, Samsun. Good night?'

Samsun Bajraktar, İkmen's transsexual cousin, threw herself into the chair she knew Fatma wasn't using.

'Desperate,' she said as she lit up a cigarette and then leaned back. Ever the diva, she was wearing a long red cocktail dress and impossibly high-heeled shoes, which she now took off. 'My feet are howling.'

'Apart from that . . .'

'Oh, the club?' She shrugged. 'Usual nonsense. Loads of silly little things dancing around a couple of bears. If any of them get off with those, they'll end up with black eyes – if they're lucky.'

İkmen said, 'Cynical.'

Samsun worked on the bar at a gay and trans pub in Tarlabaşı. She'd seen it all.

'Just heard you talking about "bloody husbands" . . .'

'Bemoaning social media,' İkmen said. 'As if the stereotypical Turkish husband didn't already have enough scope to persecute his wife, now we have the rumour mill that is online. A place where anyone, even if they've never set eyes on you, can tell you they saw your wife with another man in the bazaar and you will believe them.'

Samsun snorted. 'Well, I'm not Turkish . . .'

'Oh, Albanians are no better,' İkmen said. '*Men* are no better!'

'I'm not a man.'

'I know. I'm just . . .'

'Just what?'

'Bülent came round today and regaled me with his stories from his social media addiction. It depressed me.'

'Did you tell him to leave?' Samsun asked.

'No, he's my son and . . .' İkmen shrugged. 'The only work I have on at the moment is on behalf of a client who works in the Mısır Çarşısı and thinks his wife is stealing his bloody useless herbal Viagra to give to her lover.'

Now retired from the police force, Çetin İkmen made a little money and kept himself amused by working as an ad hoc private investigator. Sometimes the cases he worked on were very interesting, and sometimes they weren't.

'Wouldn't mind if the wife was some kind of siren,' he said.

'A vision in muted colours and headscarf?'

'Oh that's dressing up for a party for this woman!'

They both laughed, and then Samsun said, 'Çiçek in bed, is she?'

'Hours ago,' İkmen said. 'Waitressing's hard work in this heat. She was exhausted. She's off tomorrow.'

Although forty-three years old, Çetin İkmen's eldest daughter still lived at home with her father and Samsun. Divorced and purged from her job as a flight attendant in the wake of the attempted coup of 2016, she now worked in a café in the funky district of Cihangir.

Samsun said, 'She told me she's out with Mehmet Bey and his son tomorrow.'

'They're going to Arnavautköy, yes.'

Samsun leaned forward. 'Have you seen Prince Mehmet's son yet, Çetin?'

'I went with Mehmet Bey to pick him up from the airport, yes. Very handsome young boy; very bright too, apparently. But he doesn't speak any Turkish, which upsets his father.'

'Handsome?' Samsun shook her head. 'If the kid behaves like his father . . .'

İkmen wanted to defend his friend against what he knew his cousin was about to say, but he couldn't.

Samsun lowered her voice. 'I'll be honest, Çetin, I worry about our Çiçek and him. I mean, I thought that was all over in the spring . . .'

'There was some sort of falling-out, but now they're back together again. I don't get involved,' İkmen said.

'Well maybe you should . . .'

'She's a grown woman!'

'Word is that Prince Mehmet is fucking the gypsy again,' Samsun said. 'And no, Çetin, that isn't just old-lady gossip. I have it on very good authority from a girl I know who lives in Balat who's seen him going into Gonca Şekeroğlu's house. She, this girl I know, she knows a woman who lives over the back, and she says they fuck openly, in the garden!'

İkmen sighed. Having his best friend dating his daughter was not ideal, but when Süleyman had started seeing Çiçek he had promised himself that he wouldn't listen to gossip. That said, his much younger friend was well known to have little self-control when it came to women. And women, it seemed to him, had very little self-control around his friend. It was well known that Süleyman had been in a passionate on/off relationship with Gonca for years.

Eventually İkmen said, 'What do you want me to do? Keep her in?'

'No!'

'Then what?'

Samsun shrugged. 'I don't know. Warn her or something.'

'Warn her? She's not an idiot!' İkmen said.

'Oh, well then . . .' Lost for words, she looked to where her cousin's wife's ghost had been sitting and saw that she was gone. But she said what she was going to say anyway. 'What Fatma Hanım would make of all this, I don't know!'

Sinem Gürsel lit a cigarette. If Kerim knew she'd had one, he'd go mad. But he wasn't coming home for hours yet, by which time the smell would have gone. She had all the bedroom windows open. And she was in pain.

Tonight it was her fingers that were the worst afflicted area. She had suffered from rheumatoid arthritis since she was a child. As the years had passed it had only got worse, and now that she was pregnant, at the age of forty-two, it seemed to be less under control than ever. This was partly because there was a limit on the strength and frequency of painkillers she could use in her condition.

As she smoked, she looked out from her bed into the darkened streets outside her window. She and Kerim had lived in the down-at-heel district of Tarlabaşı for twelve years. With its multicultural population of refugees from the Middle East and Africa, its Roma contingent, and its shifting population of gay men and women, trans girls and prostitutes, it wasn't the most obvious place for a police officer and his wife to live. But it was perfect for the Gürsels. It was convenient for the pharmacy where Sinem obtained the medication that prevented her from screaming in agony, and it was also close to the room that Kerim's lover, a trans woman called Pembe Hanım, rented from another trans girl down by the Syrian Orthodox Church of the Virgin Mary.

Kerim Gürsel had told Sinem Cebeci that he was homosexual when they were both fifteen. In common with a lot of girls at their school, Sinem had been secretly in love with Kerim. He was so thoughtful, kind and handsome, and he was good fun. However, unlike the other girls at school, Sinem was Kerim's best friend, and so when she told him that she was queer too, their relationship blossomed. They went everywhere together, with Kerim in the role of Sinem's dashing protector. Only after they married, to provide cover for each other's sexual preferences, did Sinem tell Kerim that she was in fact bisexual, and that had been all right. But things had changed.

Firstly Kerim had met and fallen in love with Pembe Hanım, who later also became Sinem's carer, helping her with the housework, personal care and shopping. The transsexual had moved in, and most nights Sinem had to make sure she took sleeping tablets so she didn't have to listen to her beloved Kerim and Pembe making love in the next room.

At the end of the previous year, however, Sinem's condition had worsened, and her mother Pınar had insisted upon caring for her. As Pınar Hanım moved in, so Pembe Hanım moved out, and Kerim was obliged to sleep with Sinem to keep up the image of a normal marriage. But he still went to Pembe for sex, in spite of his mother-in-law's near-constant berating of him for not getting her daughter pregnant.

Kerim and Sinem had tried to have sex early on in their marriage, but had soon given up. Sinem had felt hurt, but she'd had to hide her feelings. However, when her mother came to live with them, she managed to persuade her husband that maybe trying for a baby wasn't a bad idea, to put her mother off the scent.

And so they'd tried. Sinem had attempted to hide how aroused she felt when her husband touched her. Not that he was fooled. Although he never accused her of lying to him about her sexuality, he now knew that she was heterosexual and in love. Then one night, at the right time in her cycle, he'd impregnated her, and now she was so much in love with him it hurt. She ached to have him back with her and prayed that the incident he'd gone out to attend to was not dangerous.

*

Of course, Erol Gencer's wife was beautiful. No male TV star had a wife who was anything less than perfect. Although Betül Gencer was, it seemed, more heavily reliant upon plastic surgery than most. Süleyman wondered how old she was. He also wondered why he was in no way attracted to this type of woman. Most men seemed to be. But then a lot of men were also very attracted to older, naturally beautiful if physically flawed women, like Gonca. In his experience, those women had fewer inhibitions.

Kerim Gürsel greeted the woman with his condolences. Sitting beside him on a vast white sofa in what was now solely her living room, she said, 'How did it happen? How did Erol die? I don't understand.'

'I'm afraid we don't yet either,' Kerim said. 'Betül Hanım, do you know whether your husband was due to meet anyone here tonight?'

Her eyes were dry, but they possessed a staring quality that Süleyman had seen in those undergoing shock many times before.

'No.' Then she said, 'Was he with a woman?'

'Would you have expected him to be with a woman?' Kerim asked.

Erol Gencer had been the sort of man women threw themselves at. Were Süleyman a betting person, he would have put money on the TV psychologist having one mistress at the very least.

Betül Gencer said, 'No! No, we were happy! We were in love! What will I do without him?'

Kerim Gürsel was a deeply compassionate man and Süleyman could tell that he wanted to comfort this woman in some way. But he was too professional to put an arm around her, even though in his case there could be no ulterior motive involved.

'You don't know how he died?' she reiterated.

'Not yet,' Kerim said. 'But our doctor is investigating. We will find out. As you can see our forensic team are also working hard. It will be necessary, Betül Hanım, for them to take a DNA cheek swab from you for elimination purposes. I trust that is all right?'

'Yes. . .Yes, of course.'

'Now, Betül Hanım, is there anyone I can call for you?'

'There's my mother. But she's in our village.'

'Anyone here in the city? A friend?'

'My brother Levent,' she said. 'He lives in Kadıköy.'

'All right. Would you like me to call him for you?'

'Oh no. No, no, I can . . .' She took her phone out of her bag and dropped it on the floor. 'Oh fuck it!' she said. 'Fuck it! Fuck it! Fuck it!'

Then she dissolved into tears as Kerim Gürsel picked up her phone and waited for her sobs to subside.

Chapter 2

Erol Gencer's death dominated the news. In print, on TV, on the radio and especially on the Internet. As he watched Kerim Gürsel and his sergeant Eylul Yavaş gown up prior to accompanying him into his laboratory, Dr Arto Sarkissian pondered on what US President Donald Trump called 'fake news'. Not that the doctor believed the American leader would know what 'fake' was if it hit him in the face . . .

So far the online conspiracy mill had peddled some really impressive theories. Firstly there was the one that could yet be true, that Gencer had committed suicide. After that came numerous variations on the theme of murder. Various criminal mobs were alluded to, as was the state, guests on his show, the CIA, magic, aliens and the Queen of England. All of these theories could be justified, albeit by specious if not insane evidence, and those who believed in such things were filled with a passion Arto could barely comprehend.

As he opened the door into the laboratory for his colleagues, he said, 'I've decided to start with our man in the street.'

Kerim Gürsel said, 'Why?'

'Because he's the easy one,' the doctor replied.

Kerim nodded. He could understand that. The sight of Dr Sarkissian's assistants lifting that body and trying to slip it into a bag without its stomach contents falling into Erol Gencer's swimming pool was a sight he would not easily forget.

*

Süleyman's alarm clock buzzed into life and he looked at its face. Two hours' sleep. Terrific. But he had to meet Çiçek at 10.30 and he needed a good long shower before that could happen. First, however, he needed to speak to Gonca. She was accustomed to him leaving her suddenly during their trysts, but the previous night's example had been particularly rapid and brutal.

He rang her number, and when she picked up he said, 'I'm so sorry about last night.'

She didn't answer for a few moments, and then she said, 'You left me hot and horny, you bastard. I had to drag Adem Bey out of his bakkal to finish me off!'

Süleyman laughed. Adem Bey, the owner of the local grocery store, was famously in his nineties.

'Did you kill him?' he asked.

She laughed too. 'Are you coming back, baby?' she said. 'I know I said I'd never suck your cock ever again, but I was angry. Now I want it, badly. I'm a woman, I can change my mind.'

'Believe me, there is nothing I would like more,' he said. 'But I have to go to Arnavautköy to pick up Yusuf. My brother is a patient man, but with our mother demanding to be treated like an empress in one corner and Yusuf being a brat in the other . . .'

'Ah, you are excused,' she said. 'But then if you're picking your son up, I don't suppose you'll be back any time soon.'

'No,' he said. 'But look, it's only a week and a half.'

He heard her scream and it made him laugh again.

'What am I going to do without you for a week and a half?' she said. 'Baby, I will go mad! I will tear my clothes in grief, I will not wash and I will exist only in darkness!' She laughed again. 'But of course when I do see you, I will fuck your brains out.'

Then in typical Gonca fashion, she put the phone down.

Once washed and dressed, Süleyman looked up the latest news

on his tablet. The sudden death of Erol Gencer was the headline in most of the tabloids. He knew without looking that social media was going into conspiracy theory meltdown over it. He also felt his own whole metabolism go up a gear as he anticipated the thrill of the unravelling of the mystery to come. But then he reminded himself that it wasn't his case. It was Kerim Gürsel's, and in spite of the younger man seeking his counsel in the middle of the night, it was now Kerim Bey's business and not his.

Süleyman frowned.

Was her Turkish up to it? It was, even though her confidence was not. She'd managed to read the damned newspaper headline, hadn't she!

Rima Al Numan put down the bag of groceries she'd just bought from some little bakkal in the streets bordering the Grand Bazaar, and sat on a bench in front of the Sultanahmet mosque. She often did this on her way from her first job of the day, cleaning in a leather shop, to her second, cleaning in a back-packers' hostel in Cankurtaran. She loved the huge circular fountain that shot high into the air in Sultanahmet Park, the fantastic gardens between the mosque and Aya Sofya. It was 10 a.m. and already tourists were beginning to mass around the ancient monuments of the Old City, but it was still possible to find little oases of calm, like Rima's bench.

That Erol Gencer was dead brought her neither joy nor closure. He, poor man, had been the proposed victim last time there had been trouble at that house in Sarıyer. Or so it was believed. What she couldn't accept, even with her sister banged away in Bakırköy prison, was that Samira had been telling the whole truth. She had, she had eventually admitted, intended to kill Erol Bey, but only because she had been desperate and because she had been asked. The police had only heard the first part of her statement: she had intended to kill.

This time, however, not only was Erol Gencer dead, poor man, but nobody could pin it on Samira. Yet Rima still had to speak to the police, because she knew who had done it. Or did she? And were her Turkish language skills up to it? The last time they hadn't been. But almost a year had passed . . .

'The body is of a man, approximately forty years old, weight sixty-four kilograms, height one-point-eight-three metres. Distinguishing marks: a vertical facial scar three-point-two centimetres in length down his right cheek; a tattoo of a mythical creature with the head of a man and the body of what appears to be a lion on the outer plane of his upper left bicep. He has black hair, going grey at the temples, and green eyes. His penis is circumcised, probably in childhood. His ethnicity I would venture would most easily conform to the southern European stroke Middle Eastern type. In view of his circumcision, I would place him as most probably of either the Islamic or Jewish faith. While being underweight for his height, the subject would appear to have been in good health at the time of his death. The clothing he was wearing when he was discovered was of a cheap, probably market-purchased variety. Personal effects were removed at the scene and will be described at the end of this report.'

Dr Arto Sarkissian switched off his voice recorder and then looked at his two assistants and the two police officers, Inspector Kerim Gürsel and Sergeant Eylul Yavaş, who were attending this post-mortem.

'Any questions?' he asked.

'These personal effects,' Kerim Gürsel said. 'Do we have a name?'

'Yes, although I would rather we keep to the physical details right now, Inspector. All in good time.'

'Understood.'

'Anything else?' the doctor asked.

Nobody spoke, and so the doctor switched on his recorder once again. 'On first examination it appears that the subject has been slit down the front of his torso from between the collarbones to half a centimetre above the pubis. I will now begin my examination of this feature, beginning at the commencement of the wound, between the collarbones . . .'

Çetin İkmen saw his daughter wave down into the street from the balcony, and as she flew across the living room and out of the front door he called out, 'Give Mehmet Bey my love!'

Çiçek was off to spend the day with her boyfriend and his teenage son at the house of Süleyman's mother in Arnavautköy. She said she was looking forward to speaking English with Yusuf or Patrick or whatever the sixteen-year-old boy was calling himself. But İkmen knew that she'd mainly gone to be with her lover. And although he dared not even really admit it to himself, he knew that his cousin Samsun had been right about Çiçek's relationship with his friend. It was not exactly healthy. İkmen, like Samsun, had no doubt that Mehmet was still besotted with Gonca, the gypsy artist of Balat. But he wasn't going to get involved.

What he had been involved with that morning had been his client, Rauf Bey, who had a shop in the Mısır Çarşısı, the spice bazaar. A traditional seller of herbs and spices, Rauf Bey had for very many of his seventy-five years been making up potions and mixtures to cure all sorts of ills. It was no surprise that he should have eventually lighted on the lucrative herbal Viagra market to help pay his rent. Sellers of herbs and spices had been coming up with aphrodisiacs for centuries. No empirical evidence existed for their effects. However, Rauf Bey was convinced that his seventy-year-old wife, Belkis Hanım, had been stealing his secret recipe to give to her lover.

As İkmen had suspected all along, there was no lover, just

like there was no truth in the efficacy of Rauf Bey's Viagra. Poor Belkis Hanım rarely left their small apartment in Fatih, and when she did, it was simply to go to the local bakkal to buy food. The truth of what was happening in this case was that Rauf Bey had his eye on a buxom fifty-something widow who worked in an olive oil and caviar shop on the other side of the market. His eyes lit up every time he looked at the lovely Nazlan Hanım, who smiled back very prettily. Working in her brother's shop, this lady probably wanted to be her own boss, and saw the old man as one possible way to achieve dominion over some very valuable herbs and spices. Unfortunately, poor old Belkis Hanım was in the way, and so, thinking that private detective İkmen would fall in with his plans to smear his wife, Rauf Bey had offered him really quite a lot of money, which he had refused. While knowing that this was how so much of the world worked, İkmen nevertheless had always stuck to his principles when it came to being bought. He didn't go there and he was fiscally poorer for it.

As he sat back in his chair on the balcony, he pondered about his standards in his professional life and in his marriage. He had not once been tempted to cheat on his beloved Fatma. She had been the love of his life, and he smiled as her ghost came back into view in her chair beside him. If only his Çiçek could find a man who loved her as completely as he had loved her mother. He knew Çiçek hoped that man was Mehmet Süleyman. He also knew that she was aware deep down that it wasn't.

But in the meantime, İkmen had another problem. He looked at Fatma. 'And so here I am again with no work on, and I am, of course, bored.'

His dead wife just smiled at him like she usually did.

'I know, I know I should go out to the coffee house and watch football on TV with all the other old bastards past their usefulness. But I hate football, as you know. I also hate old bastards, and anyway, you can't smoke in coffee houses any more. You have to go outside, and you know me, I really can't be bothered. Oh, and apparently some chat show host has been murdered, that Dr Erol you always liked.'

'Hypovolaemic shock means that he basically bled out,' Arto Sarkissian said.

Upon completion of the post-mortem on the man, whose ID indicated that he had been called Wael Al Hussain, the doctor had taken the two police officers to his office. There they had thrown away their disposable laboratory coveralls and were now having tea.

He continued. 'Whoever killed him thrust the murder weapon into his chest and pulled it downwards, crucially damaging the liver, which generally means that the chances of survival are minimal.'

'He couldn't have killed himself?' Sergeant Yavaş asked.

'No. Not in my opinion. The cut is too deep. One could not, I think, exert enough force to do that to oneself.'

'So what about interaction between this man and Erol Gencer?' Kerim asked.

The doctor was due to perform a post-mortem on the TV psychologist with the same officers in attendance after their short break.

'Gencer's clothes have been subjected to blood spatter,' he said. 'I would probably lay money, if I did that sort of thing, on some involvement on his part. But until I can find out his cause of death and get back some of the forensic test results I have requested, I won't be able to determine that for certain. And even then, a direct case of cause-and-effect may be impossible to establish.'

Kerim Gürsel knew from experience that science didn't always provide the answers people wanted. But he saw the look of confusion on his deputy's face and said, 'I've learned over the years that even so-called hard evidence can be open to interpretation.'

'And can sometimes escape through a legal loophole,' the doctor put in. 'I know, Sergeant Yavaş, that you are a woman of faith, but I am sure Inspector Gürsel will reflect my own observation that when one works with unexplained death, even one's most deeply held beliefs may be tested.'

Eylul Yavaş was one of a new intake of female graduate police officers who chose to wear hijab.

'Luckily, you're up to it,' Kerim said to his deputy, and she smiled.

When they arrived at the Süleyman family's old wooden konak in the stylish Bosphorus village of Arnavautköy, Mehmet Süleyman took a moment to look at his phone.

Çiçek peered over his shoulder. 'What's that? Erol Gencer?'

'Yes,' he said. 'Kerim Bey called me out to it last night.'

'But you're on leave,' she said.

He shrugged. 'Seems the wife, Betül Gencer, is pressing for a funeral as soon as possible.' He shook his head. 'Good luck with that. PM today, then we'll see.'

He took her hand and led her through a rickety gate into the back garden of the property. Although hardly of the manicured variety, it was a lovely large area with a very ornate ornamental pond, complete with fountain, and a swimming pool.

A pretty young woman was splashing about in the pool with an older man Çiçek knew to be Mehmet's brother Murad. Ten years her lover's senior, Murad was a long-time widower who had sad, gentle eyes and a much thinner and shorter frame than Mehmet. It was clear from what the young woman was saying to Murad that she was his daughter, Edibe.

When she saw Süleyman arrive with Çiçek, she got out of the pool and flung herself into his arms.

'Uncle Mehmet!'

They had always been close, and Çiçek had to sit on a tiny bit of jealousy as the girl hung on Mehmet's neck.

Murad Süleyman yelled from the pool, 'Edibe! You're making Uncle Mehmet wet. You know this pool is full of algae.'

The girl laughed as her uncle looked down at the patches of water on his suit.

'Oh Dad!' she called back. 'You do make such a fuss about nothing.'

'Mehmet, I'm sorry about her,' Murad said.

His brother laughed. 'It's no problem.' He grinned at the girl. 'Not this time. But do it again and you'll pay for the dry-cleaning.'

Edibe looked at Çiçek. 'Hello,' she said. 'You must be Çiçek.'

'Yes.'

The two women kissed. Then Edibe said, 'She's very beautiful, Uncle.'

Çiçek felt her cheeks go red.

'Yes, she is,' Mehmet said. 'Where are Yusuf and your grand-mama?'

The girl rolled her eyes. 'Inside,' she said. 'On a lovely day like this!'

'What are they doing?'

'I think Grandmama is sleeping,' she said. 'Patrick? God knows. I don't know anything about Ireland, but if he's typical of boys over there, it must be a very strange country.'

'Oh, he's not typical of anywhere,' Mehmet said.

He led Çiçek through a set of ancient French windows at the back of the house and into a dark, dusty salon. Every window was festooned with thick velvet curtains; they were open, but still their very presence seemed to soak up light. The furniture, of which there appeared to be enormous amounts, was huge and seemed to be made mostly of black wood.

Reading the look on her face as one of shock, Mehmet told

Çiçek, 'Unfortunately when my family moved here, they brought their furniture from a much bigger property. This place was basically a small summer house, while the furniture . . .'

'Came from a palace,' she said. Çiçek knew the story of how the Süleyman family had gone from being aristocrats to nobodies when the Turkish Republic had been declared back in 1923.

He put his arm around her and was about to kiss her when they both saw the pale figure of a boy walk soundlessly in from the hall. He struck Çiçek as almost a carbon copy of his father, albeit a much younger one.

'Ah,' Mehmet said in English. 'Good morning, Patrick.'

'So now you're telling me that you actually entered the property?'

The boy said nothing.

'That's not what you told Inspector Gürsel last night.'

Sergeant Ömer Mungun didn't usually work alongside Kerim Gürsel. His own superior, Mehmet Süleyman, was on leave, but with the potential murder of a celebrity on the horizon, every available officer was needed.

The boy, seventeen-year-old Berat Tükek, had found the bodies of Erol Gencer and the other man out beside the former's swimming pool. At the time, he'd told Kerim Gürsel that he'd seen the dead men from the street. But when Gürsel had put this to the test, it had proved impossible. Now the boy said that he had actually gone into the garden, which was more like the truth.

Berat Tükek looked at his father, who, because of the boy's age, had accompanied him to police headquarters to make his statement.

'Well go on then, tell him!' his father said. He was a stout and apparently perpetually furious individual who smelt strongly of cheap aftershave and might be a little bit drunk.

Berat said, 'I really liked Dr Erol. Some of the stones in the wall round his garden move and so I'd got in a few times.'

'To do what?' Ömer asked.

The boy shrugged.

'You know, Berat,' the policeman said, 'that kind of behaviour can be construed as stalking.'

The boy lowered his head. His father, ever furious, said, 'Well he's a nutter! Don't know what to do with him! Don't know what to do with you, do I, boy?'

Ömer wanted to tell the man to leave but knew that he couldn't.

The boy said, 'No, Dad,' and then addressed Ömer again. 'I know it looks like that. But Dr Erol, he said a lot to us kids who suffer with depression—'

'You're not depressed, you're idle!' his father roared. 'I was working when I was your age, not poncing around in college—'

'Mr Tükek,' Ömer said, 'whatever you may think about how your son lives his life is irrelevant to what is going on here. I need to know why your son was in Erol Gencer's garden last night and how he came to discover two dead bodies. Berat?'

The boy swallowed and looked at his father.

Ömer said, 'Don't look at your father. Pretend he isn't here. Look at me.'

The older man made angry huffing noises at this, but Berat did as he was told and found himself looking into a pair of slanted green eyes in a dark, slim face that probably appeared more Arab than Turkish. But then Ömer Mungun did come from the very far south-eastern province of Mardin, near to the border with Syria.

'I've not been well lately,' the boy said.

'Do you have a psychiatrist or psychologist that you visit?' Ömer asked.

Berat lowered his head. 'Dad doesn't believe in it.'

'Load of bloody nonsense!'

Ömer held a hand up to the boy's father to silence him. 'Berat?'

'I watched Erol Bey's show every day. It made me feel better. I felt that if I could just get to talk to him . . .'

'He'd be able to help you?'

'Something like that,' the boy said.

'How did you find out where he lived?' Ömer asked.

'Rezan told me.'

'Rezan?'

'My idiot daughter,' Tükek senior put in.

'How did she know?'

'Some girl at her school lives in Sarıyer.'

'Her school?'

'Notre Dame de Sion,' he said. It was one of the most prestigious and expensive schools in the city. Berat's father explained this apparent anomaly. 'That's down to my wife,' he said. 'She has pretensions.'

Ömer ignored him. 'So when did you first go to Erol Bey's house, Berat?'

'Couple of months ago,' he said. 'But he was out. He was out a lot, which was how I managed to move those stones so that I could get in the garden. I didn't go into his house, though.'

'Did you ever speak to Erol Bey?'

'No. When he was at home, I was too frightened.'

'Why?'

He paused for a moment and then said, 'Because he wasn't like how he is on the TV.'

'In what way?' Ömer asked.

'He was really nasty to his wife,' the boy said. 'He called her all sorts of bad names.'

It was difficult to discern what Patrick made of her. Like a lot of sixteen-year-olds, he was a sulky kid. Çiçek had brothers; she knew. But then Mehmet's mother appeared, a tiny, still stylish woman in her eighties, who looked at Çiçek, made a noise in her throat and then said to her son, 'I'm going outside. That strange boy won't leave me alone; keeps sitting about and staring at me.'

'I'm sorry,' Mehmet said. She walked into the garden.

He turned to his son. 'Grandmama says you keep staring at her. Can you please stop?'

The boy said nothing. He looked so unhappy it hurt.

'Go out into the garden and talk to Edibe,' Mehmet continued. 'I'm going to show Çiçek the house.'

Patrick sloped off. When he'd gone, Çiçek said, 'Poor kid.'

'Poor kid?' He shook his head. 'Spoilt kid. Goes to one of the poshest schools in Dublin, has a mother who dotes on him. Skiing every winter, Caribbean every summer . . .'

'He seems lonely,' Çiçek said as she followed Mehmet up the long, dark staircase to the first floor. The large carpet-strewn landing led to three rooms.

Mehmet indicated the one on the left. 'This is my mother's room,' he said. 'I won't take you in there. Not without her permission.'

'Of course not.'

He seemed more worried about his mother than his son, which Çiçek didn't understand. Her own father would have been minutely interrogating Patrick if he were his, trying to get to the bottom of his misery. That was just what he had done when her brother Bülent had been behaving badly because he had been worrying about doing his National Service.

'This room, however,' Mehmet said, taking her hand and pulling her towards the room behind him, 'is mine.'

Again it was jammed with heavy furniture, its windows shrouded in metres of ornate net curtain.

'It's—' she began.

He kissed her. 'I've missed you.'

Earlier in the year she'd fallen out with him over his apparent need, from time to time, to just force himself on her wherever they happened to be. In one way it was flattering, but in another way she always ended up feeling used.

'Mehmet . . .'

He unzipped her dress and cupped his hands around her breasts. As he held her close, she could feel that he was hard.

'I thought we might take a little time for ourselves,' he said.

'You know I don't—'

'You're so beautiful,' he said. Then he kissed one of her nipples.

When they'd argued about this, he'd gone straight to his mistress, Gonca. Did she know that he was back with Çiçek again?

He sat on his bed and then pulled her down so that she was sitting on his lap.

Chapter 3

There wasn't enough credit on her phone to make anything but the shortest call, and Rima had no money.

Sitting on her greasy bed in her tiny room in the bustling district of Tahtakale, she looked at her empty wallet and then considered the fact that her İstanbul Kart, the city's essential travel pass, also needed topping up. Police headquarters, which was where she now knew she had to get to somehow, was several kilometres away in Aksaray, and she was exhausted.

Rima knew that a lot of Syrian refugees like herself would kill to have a room of their own, even if it did mean working three jobs. She was lucky not to be out on the street. But then she had skills. She could speak English and French, both of which she'd taught at high school back in Aleppo. Her whole family had worked in education. Her sister Samira had taught at the university. Her sister Samira, who was in prison . . .

Erol Gencer was dead this time and Samira had nothing to do with it. Rima had tried to contact Wael, but his phone just rang out. She wasn't sure she wanted to talk to him anyway, after what Samira had told her. They hadn't spoken since Samira's trial.

It seemed she had no option but to walk however many kilometres it was out to police headquarters. She remembered from the newspaper she'd seen that morning that an Inspector Gürsel was dealing with the case.

*

His old man didn't talk much. From what Patrick could gather, some TV star had got himself killed and so his father was busy following that on his computer in the kitchen and making phone calls, even though he wasn't at work. One of the few things his mammy had told him about Mehmet Süleyman was that he was a workaholic. She'd not said too much about sex, though, only that his father had women.

His father and his girlfriend must have thought they'd closed the door behind them when they'd started fucking in that creepy old bedroom his scary grandmother had put him in the previous night. The girlfriend had her back to the door, naked, when he saw them sitting on the bed, her on his lap, doing it. His old man had his head in her tits and they were making sex noises. It was disgusting. But he'd had to watch. Afterwards, when they'd taken him to that really cool mall and his father had bought him trainers and her, the girlfriend, some handbag, he'd smelt it on them, the sex. But he hadn't said anything.

Now here he was stuck in this tiny flat with a man he hardly knew, and Patrick didn't like it. If he were honest – and though it pained him to admit it – he actually liked Çiçek more than his father. She was very fit but she was also kind, and it had been fun hanging out with her. What she saw in *him* was beyond Patrick. But then he was fucking her and so maybe it was that. Maybe he had a big dick.

He was due to phone his mammy in just under an hour, and he wondered whether he should tell her about the sex.

If anything, the couple's Nişantaşı apartment was even bigger than the house in Sarıyer. Being a TV star was lucrative.

The maid placed glasses of tea down in front of the officers and then left. Her mistress, Betül Gencer, already had tea, and anyway she was chain-smoking. A tall, attractive red-haired woman in her fifties, she looked much older than when Kerim had first seen her in the early hours of that morning. Now more accustomed to her husband's sudden death, and without any make-up, her face had a pouchy, unhealthy look underlined by a strange grey pallor.

'Erol had a stent fitted three years ago,' she said.

Kerim remembered Dr Sarkissian showing him this device inside Erol Gencer's dead body. To him it had just been yet another structure covered in blood.

'Our pathologist identified coronary heart disease,' he said.

She sighed. 'We didn't make a fuss about it in public,' she said. 'Erol just took some time off as annual leave.'

'Had your husband been unwell lately?' Eylul Yavaş asked.

She'd seen the way the very secular-looking Betül Gencer had looked at her, almost pitying her in her headscarf. What she didn't know was that Eylul lived in an apartment very like her own, but in Şişli, with her parents.

'I know he was tired,' Betül said. And indeed, when speaking to some of Gencer's colleagues earlier, the sergeant had discovered that the psychologist had not been in good spirits for some time. He'd also lost weight.

Betül Gencer leaned forward and looked into Kerim's eyes. 'Inspector,' she said, 'was it a heart attack that killed my husband?'

'I'm afraid our pathologist is still uncertain,' he said.

'Uncertain?'

Although in reality Kerim knew what at least one of Dr Sarkissian's suspicions or fears about Erol Gencer's body were, he did what he often did and hid behind assumed ignorance of anything medical.

'I don't really understand,' he said. 'But I know he wants to perform some more tests.'

'So I can't bury my husband?' Her eyes filled with tears.

'I'm sorry, no.'

Eylul, the devout Muslim who could fully understand why it was so vital for a member of the faith to be buried as soon as possible, said, 'İnşallah it will not be long.'

Not that the sergeant saw Betül Gencer as one of the faithful. Eylul had also told her boss she thought Betül Hanım was not really that upset when she'd been informed of her husband's death.

Kerim Gürsel took his phone out of his pocket and looked at the screen.

'Betül Hanım, do you know a man called Wael Al Hussain?' he asked.

'Why?'

'A Syrian refugee,' Kerim continued. 'I believe he was unemployed. Please answer the question.'

Eylul slid her eyes sideways towards her superior. Other officers said Inspector Süleyman had a poker face when it came to interrogating suspects. But Gürsel wasn't far behind. What would this woman say?

Çiçek put her new handbag on the coffee table. Predictably, her father said, 'Another handbag? I thought you didn't have any money?'

'I don't,' she said. 'Mehmet Bey bought it for me.'

'Did he?' He groaned. 'I didn't think he had any money either.'

'He bought Patrick a pair of trainers. We went to the mall in Nişantaşı. I think he was trying to impress the boy.'

'I see.' He smoked. Then he said, 'Have you seen the news story about that TV psychologist?'

'Yes,' she said. 'Mehmet went out to the scene last night.'

'I thought he was on leave.'

'He is. Kerim Bey is investigating. Mehmet went to talk to him about the murder attempt on Erol Gencer he investigated last year.'

'Oh yes, I remember,' İkmen said. 'Did he say whether Kerim Bey suspects foul play?'

'No. He was tight lipped about the whole thing. But he was also on his phone a lot.'

İkmen shook his head. 'If it is murder, he'll be anxious to get back to work.'

'Just like you.'

She sat down.

'You know, Dad, Patrick seems to me like a bit of a lost soul,' she said. 'He's quite withdrawn, but if you can engage him in conversation, he's a really nice kid. Just needs someone to take some notice of him.'

'Well good luck with that. His mother spends all her time with her patients, or so Mehmet Bey tells me, and he's no better. He should completely forget work now and spend some time with the child.'

'Like you did?'

He gave her a look that told her he was displeased but nevertheless acknowledged the truth of what she was saying. He'd rarely been at home when his children were young.

'So,' she said, 'have you been busy, Dad?'

'No. Only had one client and he was a toxic idiot, so I dispensed with him.'

'Hence the long face,' Çiçek said.

He smiled. 'How well you know me, my very beautiful daughter.'

She laughed. 'Mehmet Bey called me beautiful today too.'

'Oh, then it must be true,' he said.

She got up, kissed the side of his face and then took her new bag to her room. As she was leaving, she said, 'What you need is some murderous puzzle to entertain you.'

She was right. İkmen was bored, and when he was bored, he started thinking about things he shouldn't. Like what he should do about Fatma's ghost, and whether Mehmet Süleyman was cheating on his daughter. He loved Mehmet, but his behaviour with women was uncontrolled to say the least. And he'd had sex with Çiçek that very day. She thought he didn't know, but he did. He could see what remained from the glow of passion still on her face.

Betül Gencer lit another cigarette. She said, 'That was a terrible time in our lives, as you can imagine, Inspector.'

'My colleague Inspector Süleyman has told me,' Kerim Gürsel said.

'Ah yes, I remember him,' she said. 'You know when Samira Al Hussain was sent to prison, I thought I'd never hear that name again.'

'It must be a shock,' Kerim said. 'Do you have any idea why her husband might have been with your husband last night?'

'None at all.'

'You've not been in contact with Wael Al Hussain since his wife's trial?'

'No. Why would we?' she said. 'My husband was ill for quite some time after that incident. The woman was deranged. We were both sorry for her husband, but we couldn't do anything for him.'

'Why were you here at your apartment and your husband at the house in Sarıyer last night?' Eylul asked.

She smiled, sadly. 'As you can imagine, Sergeant, my husband's heart condition meant that he was no longer in the business of going to clubs and restaurants very often. I, on the other hand, have a large group of friends and colleagues with whom I socialise on a fairly regular basis. Last night was one of those occasions.'

Kerim looked at his notes. 'And you were at the Ulus 29 in Beşiktaş.'

'Yes. I don't often go out to nightclubs, but it was a friend's birthday.'

'Yes,' he said, 'a Mrs Elif Dönmez. She has verified that you were with her and Mrs Kiyamet Yavuz and Mrs Emine Uzun until approximately one a.m.'

'We had a meal in the restaurant first and then went into the nightclub area.'

'You danced?'

'Yes. We had a few drinks.'

'Did you meet anyone?' he asked.

He saw her face fall. Both Kerim and this bereaved woman knew what he meant.

'You mean men?' she said.

'You must know that I have to ask, Betül Hanım,' he said. 'We do not yet know how your husband died. It is a legitimate question.'

She sighed. Then she said, 'No. And no, Inspector, there is no other man apart from my husband in my life. I went out with my friends last night. We had a nice meal, we danced, we had a few drinks and that is all.'

He had riled her, but then that had been unavoidable.

She said, 'How did Wael Al Hussain die?'

Kerim sat back in what was a very handsome leather chair. 'I am not yet at liberty to give out that information,' he said. 'But we believe he was unlawfully killed.'

'By my husband?'

'We cannot yet be sure,' he said.

'So it's a possibility?'

'Anything is possible,' Kerim said.

'He's called Gürsel,' she said. 'I read his name in newspaper.'

They'd only just let her past the guards at the front entrance. Now Rima Al Numan had this disappointed-looking middle-aged cop to deal with.

He looked down at her, in every possible interpretation of that phrase, and said, 'He's busy.'

'Then I will wait,' Rima said.

'No.'

She was confused. She was speaking in a language not her own and she was exhausted. She'd asked this officer whether he could speak either English or French, in which she was way more fluent, but he'd just ignored her. Should she try Arabic? She looked into his blank, resentful face and thought not.

'Inspector Gürsel,' she repeated, as if this person's name might act like some sort of spell giving her access to another, more understanding dimension. But it didn't.

'He's working,' the cop said. 'Out.'

'I need speak—'

'You probably do,' the man said as he took her by the arm and began to pull her back towards the front entrance.

'Ow!'

'You lot always want everything now,' he said. 'Gürsel's out.'

He opened the door and attempted to fling her unceremoniously into the cooling evening air. But Rima wasn't easily brushed away.

'I have information,' she insisted.

'No you don't!' he said.

'What's going on here?'

Both Rima and the officer turned at the same time. A young man with sharp, dark features stood at the bottom of a staircase.

'What are you doing, Constable Sak?'

'This woman,' the cop said. 'Syrian. You know, Sergeant . . .'

Fearing that this other man could be even more frightening than the front-desk cop, Rima thought better of coming to this awful place. Pulling her arm free, she ran. Horrifyingly, she saw the younger man come after her, and put on a turn of speed she didn't know she had in her. The one time she turned to look at him, she thought she heard him say something in her native language, but she couldn't be sure.

*

When they finally left Betül Gencer's apartment, it was dark. Kerim Gürsel and Eylul Yavaş talked as they stood beside their respective cars.

'You know, sir,' she said as she took her keys out of her pocket, 'I don't think I realised just how strange that incident Inspector Süleyman investigated last year actually was until this evening.'

Kerim shrugged. 'I think its oddness had a lot to do with the perpetrator's seeming instability.'

'That she changed her story once she'd been in custody for a while isn't something new,' Eylul said. 'No, I mean the story she initially told about her involvement with the Gencers.'

'There was no evidence for that,' Kerim said.

'It was like something out of a fairy tale.'

'Which is where our judicial system decided it belonged. And of course, as you say, by that time she'd changed her tune.'

'I saw Inspector Süleyman at the scene last night,' she said. 'Did you talk about that?'

'Only on a very basic level,' he said. 'He's on leave.'

'Mmm. But you know what he's like, sir. I'm sure if he can help us, he will.'

'I know, but what—'

'Sir, we need to pin down the relationship, or however you'd categorise it, that existed between Erol Gencer and this Al Hussain man,' Eylul said. 'I mean, I don't know about you, but I'm not buying that they didn't contact each other after Samira Al Hussain's trial. There must have been some kind of contact.'

'Unless Al Hussain simply broke into the house?'

'There was no sign of forced entry.'

'Except by Berat Tükek,' Kerim said.

'You think . . .'

'No stone, if you'll excuse the pun, will be left unturned,' he said. 'But you make a very good point about Mehmet Bey, Eylul.

I had only the bare bones of a conversation with him last night. I'll give him a ring before I go home.'

She nodded. 'I'd like to find out more about the Gencers, sir, if you think that's a good use of my time.'

'You don't believe Mrs Gencer's story about her whereabouts?'

'Oh, I think she was at the club,' Eylul said. 'What I do have a problem with is her perfect marriage. Berat Tükek was a fan of Dr Erol and was disappointed when he heard him speaking disrespectfully to his wife. Why would he, a fan, make something like that up?'

'OK, see what you can find,' he said as he took his phone out and scrolled down to find Süleyman's number. 'I'll call Mehmet Bey.'

She left, and Kerim placed his call.

Her sister, Hülya, lived over in Balat and so she had an entirely legitimate reason for being there. But Çiçek still felt guilty when she turned a corner as she was leaving her sister's house and came face to face with Gonca Şekeroğlu. A tall, statuesque figure wearing a full-length gown made of, by the look of it, gold silk, with her hair hanging down to the ground, the gypsy looked like an evil queen from a fairy tale. But that could have just been Çiçek projecting negative feelings onto a rival.

In spite of herself, Çiçek smiled. 'Good evening, Gonca Hanım.'

The other woman bridled almost imperceptibly, but then said, 'Çiçek Hanım. How are you? How is your wonderful father?'

Of course she knew Çetin İkmen. With her unsettling collage art, her spells and her fortune-telling, she was his kind of person. He had even employed her once, to read fortunes at Hülya's wedding. Çiçek knew she had at one time been one of her father's informants.

'Dad is very well,' she lied. İkmen could never be said to be 'well' in the normal course of events.

'Good. And you?'

Çiçek didn't know whether Gonca was aware that she was involved with Mehmet Süleyman. She wasn't sure whether that would even make a difference. The gypsy had a somewhat elastic sense of what was acceptable in her relationship with Mehmet Süleyman. Çiçek didn't actually know whether her lover and this woman were still having sex. Because that was all it was. The gypsy liked rough, loud, mad sex, and Mehmet was entranced, and had been since he'd first met her.

Çiçek forced herself to smile. 'Well, good evening, hanım. I must be getting home.'

She began to walk away, aware that Gonca's black eyes were burning into her back, her large, half-exposed breasts heaving up and down underneath her gold bodice as she struggled to maintain her dignity. Oh she knew all right! If looks could kill . . .

'Çiçek Hanım!'

And now she'd called her back. Oh God, what for?

Çiçek turned and saw her rival pull herself up to her full height.

'Yes?'

'I want you to know that it isn't what you think,' she said.

'What isn't?'

The gypsy lowered her head. 'You think it's all just sex, but it isn't.'

She didn't have to say his name.

'Oh?' Çiçek knew that she sounded sarcastic and glib, and regretted it, but there was nothing to be done.

'I love him,' the gypsy said. 'I've always loved him. Even when he's cheated on me with you and all the women who came before you, I loved him. I will always love him.' The tears that came into her eyes then were either those of rage or hurt as she finished with, 'I will have him. Me.'

And then she ran off down the road towards her house, and if Çiçek wasn't too much mistaken, she was openly crying.

With the sensible part of her brain, Çiçek knew she should see what had just happened as an example of manipulative behaviour. It was well known that Gonca Şekeroğlu would do just about anything to keep Mehmet Süleyman with her. But there was also a genuineness Çiçek had picked up. Like her father, her instincts were often uncannily correct, and she wondered whether she was right about Gonca now. Far from being just an intriguing sexy older woman, the gypsy was also a creature suffering the pangs and pains of true love.

Could Çiçek claim the same depth of emotion when it came to Mehmet Süleyman? In spite of herself, she followed the gypsy.

Chapter 4

Ömer Mungun stood up and the two men embraced.

'What are you doing here?' Kerim Gürsel asked his colleague.

Süleyman came back into his kitchen and offered his guests drinks.

'I put the samovar on when Ömer Bey arrived,' he said. 'But I've also got Efes in the fridge. Also we have every kind of juice and soda known to man.'

This probably had more to do with the young boy the two officers had glimpsed in the hallway than to a sudden desire on Süleyman's part to drink sweet, sticky cordials and juices.

Kerim sat down at the kitchen table opposite Ömer Mungun.

'In answer to your question, Kerim Bey, I saw a face from the past tonight,' Ömer said. 'From when the boss and I were working on the Gencer case last year.'

'Oh?'

Süleyman cut in. 'Gentlemen,' he said. 'Come along. We will discuss these matters once we've all got drinks and I've lit a cigarette.'

'OK,' Kerim said. 'Efes for me. I can walk home from here, so with your customary generosity, Mehmet Bey, I'd like a beer.'

Süleyman smiled. Like his father before him, he had a reputation as a good host, especially when it came to alcohol. 'Ömer?'

'I'll wait for tea, thank you, sir,' he said.

Süleyman was just about to open the fridge when his son entered the kitchen.

'Ah, Patrick.'

The boy just looked at him. Süleyman said, 'Gentlemen, this is my son Patrick. He doesn't speak Turkish, so English if you please . . .'

'Hello,' Ömer Mungun said to the boy, who looked almost exactly like his father. 'I am Ömer, your father's sergeant.'

He held out his hand to the boy, who took it and said, 'Hello.'

Kerim said, 'Good evening.'

'It seems the gentlemen need my help this evening,' Süleyman said to the boy.

'Oh,' Patrick said. 'Can I have some Coke, please?'

'Of course.'

He poured the boy a glass of Coca-Cola and then, wordlessly, the young man left.

When he'd gone, Süleyman said, 'I've set him up with computer games. I doubt he'll be in again. Now, gentlemen . . .'

Kerim Gürsel had always liked Mehmet Süleyman. He'd been a good colleague and was scrupulously honest and generally fair. But his dismissal of his own son made Kerim's skin crawl. Of all the fears he had about his own unborn child, one he knew he didn't possess was the possibility of it being overlooked. For all sorts of reasons, he and Sinem would treat that child like a precious jewel. Because in a way, that was exactly what it would be.

Samsun had called him to say that she wasn't coming home until the morning. Whether this meant she had some sort of romantic assignation, İkmen didn't know and didn't want to. Çiçek was still with Hülya in Balat; no doubt they were gossiping about the men in their lives. He knew his children well.

And so İkmen was in the apartment alone, save for the ghost of his dear wife Fatma and the awful djinn in the kitchen. Most of the time he wasn't uncomfortable or even in the slightest bit bothered by these beings from another dimension, or his mind or wherever. He actively encouraged his frequent audiences with his wife. But tonight he wanted to be around human beings, and so he took the unusual decision to leave the apartment.

The streets of Sultanahmet were alive with the usual mixture of tourists and locals at leisure in restaurants, the old pub up by Aya Sofya and various outdoor nargile joints. İkmen nodded his head at a couple of carpet dealers of his acquaintance and smiled at an old man known as Hilmi who had in his youth been a very reliable drug dealer to the bands of hippies that used to patronise the Pudding Shop. The usual beggars were in place on their accustomed pitches along Divan Yolu, and an abundance of flashing multicoloured lights emanating from souvenir shops, an orange juice stall and a bookshop vied for his attention with the overpowering smell of bubbling grilled lamb.

The Old City wasn't a bad place to live. To İkmen it was the only place to live. Although he'd been born in Üsküdar, on the Asian side of the Bosphorus, he'd lived most of his life in Sultanahmet. His father had bought what was now Çetin's apartment for almost nothing back in the 1960s. It had been handy for the old man's work at İstanbul University. It had also represented a clean break from their previous life with İkmen's mother back in the dark wooden house of his childhood. Sometimes he looked across the Bosphorus towards Üsküdar, seeing whether he could still pick out their old place just to the left of the great Selimiye Barracks, where British people often went to see where the famous nurse Florence Nightingale had once worked. Sometimes he'd spot the house and sometimes he wouldn't. But then that was in the tradition of the shifting nature of İkmen's past. Sometimes the magic worked and he could see where he had been, and sometimes it didn't.

Although he wanted to be around warm human bodies, he didn't really want to interact with any of them, and so he took himself across Divan Yolu to Sultanahmet Park. Some people were still sitting on the seats that surrounded the round pond, and the fountain was still splashing away even though it was dark. İkmen found an empty bench, sat down and lit a cigarette. Maybe if he could relax out in the open, he could forget about not currently being employed.

Did the gypsy know she was there? Probably. Like Çiçek's father, and like Çiçek herself to a certain extent, Gonca Şekeroğlu knew many things that most people didn't. One of the myths about her was that she could see through walls. But Çiçek ducked down anyway so that her head wouldn't be seen above the stone wall that surrounded the gypsy's garden.

Now no longer crying, Gonca was sitting on the ground making something using a frame and some dull brown yarn. She was talking in the Roma language either to herself or to someone Çiçek couldn't see. When she held her handiwork up to the light, Çiçek could make out that it appeared to be a piece of weaving.

She had been a fool to think that Gonca hadn't known about her. She probably knew what Mehmet Süleyman did before he actually did it. It wasn't a comfortable thought. What was also far from comfortable was why Gonca Şekeroğlu had been so fixated on Süleyman for so long. The gypsy had always, famously, loved men. She'd been at the top of the Turkish art scene for decades and had taken many men of all sorts to her bed. Some had been young and beautiful, some old and fascinating, and there had even been one, so her father had told her, who had come all the way from Spain just on the off chance Gonca might fall for his charms. A Roma himself, and an exponent of flamenco dancing, he had loved the Gypsy Queen for one insane, violent and sexually explosive month. Where he'd gone afterwards wasn't known. Maybe she'd eaten him . . .

Gonca had told Çiçek that her relationship with Mehmet

Süleyman wasn't just about sex. But what else did they have in common? She was, Çiçek had to acknowledge, weirdly beautiful, but she wasn't young and her face was sometimes frightening. But she did know things, and she was clever. Her collage art could command tens of thousands of dollars. She'd also raised twelve children, all now grown up. She heard the voice of one of them now, saying something sharp and spiky to his mother, who replied in Turkish, 'Fuck off!'

Çiçek peeped over the wall to see if she could see his face. She did, briefly. He was, like his mother, tall and handsome. He left her and went inside the house.

It was easy to see what Gonca saw in Süleyman. It wasn't just the way he looked; there was also his desire, often against his own judgement, to do what was right. He was basically a flawed man trying very hard to be good. And there was the sex. Naturally selfish, he nevertheless understood what pleased women, and that was a rare thing even in the twenty-first century.

Just then, the gypsy looked in her direction. But she didn't say anything. Instead she took the piece of cloth she had woven and plunged it into some liquid. Then she held it up as if for Çiçek to see. Instead of looking brown, the thing now glowed gold.

'Rima Al Numan is Samira Al Hussain's sister,' Ömer Mungun said.

Süleyman placed a glass of tea down in front of his sergeant. 'She came to headquarters earlier tonight?'

'Yes. But she got short shrift from the cretin assigned to the front desk,' Ömer said. 'All he saw was an Arab woman, so he dismissed her. I asked him what she'd wanted and he said she'd asked for Kerim Bey. No point telling him that he should at the very least have taken her details. I tried to catch her, but she disappeared into some knot of tiny streets.'

'How would she have known to ask for me?' Kerim said.

'You're named in most of the papers,' Süleyman said. He turned back to Ömer. 'I don't actually remember much beyond the fact that Samira Al Hussain had a sister. I don't think I'd be able to recognise her.'

'I interviewed her,' Ömer said. 'She reiterated the same story her sister told until she had a change of heart.'

'Remind me,' Kerim said.

Süleyman drank some rakı and then lit a cigarette. 'When we arrested Samira Al Hussain, she told us a story about how she'd met Betül Gencer,' he said. 'Remember we were called to the Gencer house by Betül, who said that she'd caught an unknown woman in the process of, she thought, slitting her husband's throat.'

'Mrs Gencer was armed when we arrived,' Ömer said. 'Basically it was a stand-off. Samira Al Hussain with a knife to Erol Gencer's throat, Betül Gencer holding a gun to her head.'

'But Samira gave me the knife as soon as I asked for it,' Süleyman said.

'When we arrived, it was almost as if some sort of spell had been broken,' Ömer continued. 'The boss only had to ask her once and she just gave him her weapon.'

'Then she cried,' Süleyman added. 'When we cuffed her, she screamed.'

'Screamed?'

'It was Arabic,' Ömer said. 'We thought at the time she had little or no Turkish. Betül Gencer claimed she'd seen her before, hanging round outside the house. I translated for Samira while this was going on. Later we found out she could speak Turkish adequately.'

Ömer Mungun was famously multilingual, mainly in the languages of the Middle East, although his English was passable too.

'When we did manage to interview her, not only did we discover that she could speak Turkish, but she also had a very strange tale to tell,' Süleyman said.

Kerim Gürsel smiled. 'Excuse me, Mehmet, Ömer,' he said, 'but this is beginning to feel like a ghost story.'

Süleyman looked at his sergeant and Ömer looked back at him.

'In a way it is,' Ömer said.

'Really?'

'Yes,' Süleyman added. 'And that is because it concerns a lot of people who do not exist.'

'Dad?'

İkmen looked up. 'Çiçek,' he said. 'Did you have a nice time with your sister? How is she?'

Çiçek sat down on the bench beside him. 'She's fine.'

'Timur and Berekiah?' he asked, naming his daughter Hülya's son and husband.

'The kid's a bit of a brat, but he's entering his teens,' she said. 'I tell you, Dad, looking at Timur and at Mehmet's son, I wonder how you did that with nine of us. Nine sets of teenage tantrums, crazy hormones, exam anxiety . . . Anyway, what are you doing out here? Fresh air isn't usually your thing.'

He shrugged. 'I needed to be around the living,' he said. 'Samsun's staying out tonight and I didn't know about you . . .'

'Coming home now?' she said.

'Mmm.' Then he said, 'Fancy a drink at the Mozaik before we retire? My treat?'

It was his favourite bar, in part because it was in the same street as his apartment.

'All right,' Çiçek said.

İkmen got to his feet. 'I think the cat may well be waiting for us there,' he said.

Ever since Çetin İkmen had brought his new wife Fatma home to live in his father's apartment, there had always been a cat on the premises. Always large, male and feral, successive cats just simply moved in on him. And because İkmen could never be bothered to learn new names for his cats, all of them had the same name: Marlboro.

When İkmen and Çiçek got close to the fairy-light-illuminated tables outside the Mozaik bar, an enormous ginger and white cat with a scarred and tattered face approached them.

'Ah, there he is!' İkmen said as he herded the animal towards the table he had chosen. 'And what have you been doing today?'

He talked to the cat like he was an extra child. Çiçek sat down and said, 'He's been doing what he usually does, making everything round here pregnant.'

The cat jumped up onto the chair next to İkmen, and when the waiter came over to take their order, it consisted of a large gin and tonic, a very large brandy, and a plate of fish for Marlboro Bey.

When they'd all settled down – the cat was eating, İkmen and Çiçek drinking and smoking – he said to her, 'So. What's on your mind?'

Even though Çiçek knew that her father rarely needed telling much, she said, 'Ah, so you know.'

'I wouldn't say you're an open book, Çiçek . . .'

She shook her head. 'Dad, you've known Gonca Şekeroğlu for a long time, haven't you?'

'Yes.'

Now it was her turn to read the signs. Did her father suddenly look a little wary?

'Why?'

She leaned forward so that only he could hear. There were a couple of men at the table behind them who might or might not have been listening to their conversation.

'Well I know that you have this sort of way you categorise things in your head,' she said. 'Magic things.'

'Yes. There's stage magic, there's real magic, and then there's where those two arts meet,' İkmen said. 'Which, as I've always told you, is a place I can't really name.'

'Tonight I saw Gonca Şekeroğlu do something that confused me,' Çiçek said.

'Gonca? She doesn't live near your sister.'

'No.'

Her whole demeanour made it plain she wasn't going to say anything more about why she'd been watching Gonca Şekeroğlu, although İkmen was pretty sure he knew.

'So?'

Çiçek said, 'She was making something with some sort of yarn. Sitting on the ground. I think she was weaving it. It was a sort of mud colour, not exactly pretty.'

'Right. I think I know what you're talking about, but go on,' her father said.

'So look, Dad, she took this stuff and dipped it in something – liquid, I think. And when she took it out, it shone. Not just in an ordinary way – it was like the sun coming out. It glittered and made me have to look away. I mean, I know a little chemistry, but to me it looked just like magic. The intensity of it.'

'Well it is chemistry, but it's also magic too,' İkmen said.

Çiçek looked at him and shrugged. 'Uh?'

He leaned towards her. 'Gonca has been weaving for what I believe is a very select client for some time,' he said. 'As you've seen, she isn't just weaving any old yarn.'

'So what is it?'

'It's called sea silk,' İkmen said. 'It's made from the tendrils put out by the giant byssus mussel when it attaches itself to rocks in the sea. What you saw her do was plunge the material into lemon juice, which makes it turn from brown to a gold colour that never fades.'

'Really?'

'Really. Sea silk was used in the clothing of the Byzantine emperors, the mummy wrappings of Egyptian pharaohs, the sultan's robes. It's very, very rare these days. It's the most expensive material on earth, and that includes precious metals and stones. And no, I've no idea where Gonca gets it from and I won't be asking any time soon. I would suggest you follow suit.'

Çiçek frowned. 'You think she's dangerous?'

'I think I don't know enough about what skills she may or may not possess to make any sort of judgement,' he said. 'And anyway, Çiçek, we both know why you have an interest in Gonca Şekeroğlu . . .'

He watched her gaze drop.

He said, 'I don't know whether or not she is seeing Mehmet Bey . . .'

'Oh, she is,' Çiçek said. She looked up. 'She as good as told me.'

'Ah. And she was telling you the truth?'

She looked away.

'Unless you confront him, you can't be sure,' İkmen said.

'She told me she's in love with him.'

He sighed. 'That, I fear,' he said, 'is probably true.'

'Do you think he loves her?' Çiçek asked.

'I don't know. I'd describe it as more of an addiction myself.' Then he said, 'Do you love him?'

'I don't know,' she said. 'I idolised him when I was younger. He was like some sort of movie star. Then when I began seeing him . . .' She shrugged. 'That whole protective manner he has with women . . . You brought all of us girls up to be independent, and so I always feel a bit of a fraud. I am a fraud, I suppose. I fall for that gentlemanly thing he does every time. He makes me feel special. Were I younger, maybe it would be different.'

İkmen took one of his daughter's hands. 'As you know, Çiçek, I love Mehmet, he is a good friend. But you are my daughter and so I love you with all my soul. I've not interfered in your relationship and I won't now, unless you want me to. But I must tell you that in my opinion, with this information you've had from Gonca herself, you are within your rights to question him. Whatever you have with him, where is it going? And if that destination is nowhere, you must ask yourself whether you want it to continue.'

'According to Samira, she met Betül Gencer at a coffee house in Fatih,' Ömer said. 'I say a coffee house, but more accurately it was actually an empty apartment.'

'As I'm sure you know, Kerim,' Mehmet said, 'the area around Malta Çarşısı Sokak is somewhere a lot of Syrians have settled. Even now that many of the illegals have been told to leave the city, it's still a sizeable number. Many shop signs are displayed in Arabic, many goods and services are aimed at Arabs. Last year the number of migrants in that area was considerable. Both legal like Samira Al Hussain, and illegal.'

'And that was part of the problem when we came to try and check her story out,' Ömer said. 'This "coffee house", though thoroughly described to us by Samira, was somewhere we could get no information about.'

'It's what I meant when I said that Samira's story concerned people who did not exist.'

Kerim Gürsel looked at Süleyman questioningly.

'Basically we could find no one who would corroborate her story,' Ömer said. 'Even when I used my best Arabic. As a Turk, I couldn't get through that closed community wall. And anyway, what would someone like Betül Gencer be doing in a coffee house patronised by Syrians?'

'Curiosity?' Kerim said.

'In Samira's account, there was a storyteller,' Süleyman said. 'Like our meddah.'

Kerim looked confused.

Süleyman said, 'They tell traditional tales in coffee houses during Ramazan. Quite rare now. I've never heard one in public. My father engaged one for my sünnet celebrations, but of course I was really young and had other things on my mind.'

Most Turkish men could remember their circumcision ceremony, which took place when they were six or seven years old. Not many, mercifully, in detail.

'I had a clown,' Kerim said miserably. 'He was terrifying.'

'Storytellers are called "hakawati" in Arabic,' Ömer said, dragging the older men away from their memories. 'This one, according to Samira Al Hussain, was of the traditional Arabian variety, inasmuch as he travelled. In the old days many hakawati were itinerant, moving from town to town, city to city, telling their tales and lodging in hans or guest houses. Professional hakawati were still working in coffee houses in places like Aleppo and Damascus right up until the beginning of the war. I believe some have gone back to work more recently. Samira had a name . . .'

'Ahmad Al Saidawi,' Süleyman said. 'An elderly Syrian no one we could find had even heard of. As far as we could discover, Betül Gencer couldn't speak Arabic and so how would she even know where to go to see a hakawati, let alone why.'

'What we could corroborate, however, were Betül Gencer's accounts of how Samira Al Hussain had stalked her husband,' Ömer said. 'A woman matching her description had been spotted by neighbours hanging around the Gencers' house. Gencer himself was aware of her, although he denied Samira's allegation that she had slept with him.'

'Why didn't he report her?' Kerim asked.

'The story was that he and his wife were simply trying to ignore her. Apparently this had happened several times before with overenthusiastic fans. That boy you picked up last night I imagine is a case in point.'

Kerim frowned. 'So Samira alleged she met Betül in a coffee house in Fatih. The significance of that being . . .'

'Samira told us that they fell into conversation,' Süleyman said. 'She claims they got on. Samira Al Hussain was a professional person back in Syria, an art historian. They talked about the art of storytelling. Then the topic changed to their personal lives.'

'One thing that turned out to be a fact,' Ömer said, 'was that Wael Al Hussain beat his wife. We gathered that from the couple's neighbours and from her sister. However, quite why one would tell a stranger such a thing, I don't know. Samira alleged that Betül Gencer opened the subject. She told her that Erol Gencer was violent towards her. She said that if only she could get away with it, she'd kill him. That was when Samira shared her own story.'

'And so enter Alfred Hitchcock,' Süleyman said.

'The Hollywood film director?'

'Yes.' Süleyman smiled. 'Or rather one of his most famous films. Not that Betül Gencer alluded to *Strangers on a Train* at any point. All she said, allegedly, was that it would be very useful if the two of them could swap murders. Do you know the film, Kerim?'

'No,' he said.

'Very basically, it's about two men who meet on a train. One has an inconvenient ex-wife, the other an unpleasant but rich father. The man with the rich father is also a psychopath. He suggests to the other man that maybe they should kill these people who are messing up their lives but that he should kill the wife while the other man kills his father. With no connection to their respective victims, it would mean that they should be able to commit two perfect crimes. Of course it doesn't work, but it is a plan not without merit if one is so inclined. Samira Al Hussain said that when she was found in the Gencers' bedroom with a knife at Erol's neck, she was upholding her part of the bargain.'

'So she admitted she tried to kill Gencer?'

'Yes. She said she had been desperate for her suffering at the hands of her husband to stop.'

Ömer said, 'When physically examined, Samira Al Hussain showed signs of having been subjected to repeated abuse, which had resulted in broken ribs, bruised internal organs and so on.'

'However, we could find no evidence whatsoever of any abuse perpetrated by Erol Gencer on his wife Betül. In fact, at that time he was in rather frail health, having just had heart surgery,' Süleyman said.

Kerim crossed his arms. 'So what was Wael Al Hussain's take on all this?' he asked.

'Wael Al Hussain told us he thought his wife was insane,' Süleyman said. 'I disagreed, as did the two psychiatrists who examined her. She was – is – a desperate woman, clearly abused by her husband, who entered a fantasy world involving a television star.'

'An elaborate fantasy,' Kerim Gürsel said.

'Oh yes,' said Ömer. 'One worthy of the best hakawati who ever played the coffee houses of old Damascus.'

Chapter 5

And so it was that in this great bazaar here, in our very own city of İstanbul, there lived and worked an imam of great wisdom. Though sadly widowed, the imam had a son, a dark, slant-eyed, Arab-looking boy, whose love for great knowledge was only overshadowed by his love for the face of a beautiful woman . . .

Çiçek İkmen looked across at her father. He had assumed his usual position out on the sunlit balcony, sitting next to the ghost of his wife, smoking.

'Where are you going today?' he asked her.

This was the second of the two days' leave she'd taken from work to be with Mehmet Süleyman and his son.

'Büyükada,' she said.

'Very nice.'

The largest of the group of islands in the Sea of Marmara called the Princes' Islands, Büyükada was picturesque, historically fascinating and had a no-motor-vehicles rule. A playground for the elite in Ottoman times, it was still somewhere only the rich could actually afford to live.

'Wouldn't have thought it would be the sort of place a teenager would want to visit,' İkmen said. 'Bit quiet.'

'Patrick is quiet,' his daughter said. 'So different from our boys.'

All the İkmen children had been loud, the boys particularly. During their teenage years, they had seemed to fight each other on a daily basis.

'So the basis for your visit is . . .' He looked over his shoulder apparently at something or someone down in the street.

'Family history,' Çiçek said. 'One of Mehmet's aunts had a house there. He wants to show Patrick. What are you looking at, Dad?'

'A couple of women having an argument,' he said. 'I keep thinking I hear my name.'

'Maybe they're arguing over you,' Çiçek said.

Her father pulled a face.

'Or not,' she said. She picked up her new handbag.

İkmen said, 'You know that Mehmet Bey's ex-wife lived on Büyükada, don't you?'

'I didn't,' she said. 'But so what? That was all over decades ago.'

'I'm just saying. Anyway, how will you get about on the island? No cars, remember.'

She smiled. 'We're hiring bikes.'

Çetin İkmen laughed. 'I take it that was the boy's choice,' he said. 'Somehow I can't see Mehmet Bey on a bicycle. You must take a photograph.'

Wael Al Hussain had lived in a rented apartment in the old, as yet un-redeveloped area of Tarlabaşı. For years this district, close to the central Taksim area, had been the preserve of artists, prostitutes, gay and trans people and a fair sprinkling of drug dealers. Students wishing to be edgy often chose Tarlabaşı. But with the coming of gentrification in the form of new Ottoman-style houses for the ruling elite, the area was slowly crumbling and people were moving out to make way for, albeit temporary, homes for poor rural migrants and refugees. Although not quite at the level of some of the unofficial brothels that Ömer Mungun had been into in the course of his work, Al Hussain's apartment wasn't much of a step up. What passed for the bathroom was particularly pungent. His fellow officer, Eylul Yavaş, pulled a face when she stuck her head round the door.

'That is disgusting!'

Ömer shook his head. 'It's not bad for round here,' he said. 'Some of the places the boss and I have been in would blow your mind.'

Although she was an observant woman who wore a hijab, Eylul Yavaş came from a wealthy secular family from fashionable Şişli. Rackety Tarlabaşı was not the sort of place to which she was accustomed.

The building's landlord, who had showed first the scene-of-crime officers and now the two detectives in, stood in the main doorway into the apartment. It was on the fourth floor and gave off a narrow corridor at the top of a rickety staircase.

Watching the officers look around what was an almost empty space, the landlord said, 'He had nothing, the Arab. Even when his wife was with him, the two of them had very little. And they rowed.'

'What about?' Ömer asked.

The old man shrugged. 'I dunno. Don't speak Arabic.'

The Al Hussains had come into Turkey as illegal immigrants but had soon applied for settled status, which had been granted two years before. They had both been educated people: both art history fellows at Damascus University. Both multilingual, they had taken a variety of menial jobs until Wael had apparently lost the plot and opted to do nothing. Samira, meanwhile, had worked in a small Syrian-run textile business in Fatih. There she had advised the owners on which designs she believed would make their products, scarves, sell more. She also acted as translator for English- and French-speaking buyers.

'Anyway,' the landlord continued, 'I told all that to some posh policeman back when the woman was accused of trying to kill Erol Gencer.'

'My boss,' Ömer said.

'I should've thrown the Arab out on the street when his wife went to prison,' the landlord continued. 'Normally I'll have no criminals here. But I didn't have the heart. The poor man probably didn't know he was marrying a lunatic when he got with her. I mean, what was the woman doing offering herself to Erol Gencer like a prostitute?'

Ömer said nothing. What could he say? Samira Al Hussain had been convicted of attempted murder.

Eylul Yavaş, who had walked into the room the Al Hussains had used as a bedroom, called out to her colleague.

'Sergeant Mungun, can you come here, please?'

Ömer excused himself to the landlord and joined her in a room that was dominated by a vast, ancient bed. Actually dirty as opposed to simply untidy, the bed was characterised by a tangled mass of greasy, stained bedclothes. Ömer wrinkled his nose.

'I wonder who he's had in here,' he said.

'If anyone,' Eylul said as she passed a copy of a photo magazine very gingerly to her colleague.

He looked at it and shook his head. It had been many years since he'd seen an old-fashioned sex magazine. Most people got their pornography online these days. But then this – what Çetin İkmen called a 'fuck book' – was titled in Arabic. Probably from Syria, which had lived under a repressive regime for decades. Ömer couldn't see the Assad family approving of the Internet somehow.

He very carefully turned the pages. It was tough stuff. The women involved looked as if they were in pain.

He looked at his colleague. 'Non-consensual?' he asked.

'If he treated his wife like that, no wonder the poor woman retreated into fantasies about murder,' she said.

'Where was it?'

'In the bed,' she said. 'Maybe scene-of-crime didn't have the stomach for it.'

'I doubt that,' he said.

Without either of them noticing, the landlord had joined them in the bedroom. Now, looking over Ömer's shoulder, he said, 'I never let any of the men in my properties have women in here, you know. Certainly not bad women like those.'

How did two psychologists live together? How did that work? Would they be forever analysing each other? Or would they never, ever talk about what might be going on in each other's heads?

Kerim Gürsel cradled his chin in his hands and scanned through the list of websites about Erol Gencer. He'd just turned sixty-one, apparently. Kerim had imagined he was a lot younger than that. But then maybe he'd had plastic surgery.

Erol had married Betül, now fifty-six, back in 1990. His second wife, she'd met him while studying his part-time psychology course. She had been an assistant on TV game shows back then, employed as the pretty face and sexy body that presented prizes to bewildered peasants from Central Anatolia. Kerim remembered such shows well. Full of embarrassed covered women, their fat feet bursting out of cheap sandals, the men unable to take their eyes off the scandalously unfettered breasts of women like Betül Gencer. Erol had still been in academia in those days. Had it been Betül who had got him involved in television?

He put his pen in his mouth and leaned back in his chair with one foot up on his desk. After he hadn't come home the night Gencer and Al Hussain's bodies had been discovered, his wife had hoped he'd be early the following night. But he'd spent hours and hours at Mehmet Süleyman's apartment talking about the case. Then on the way home he'd come across Pembe Hanım.

He hadn't seen his transsexual lover for over a month and the alcohol he'd had in Süleyman's kitchen had made him reckless. They hadn't made love, but he'd pulled her into a shop doorway and they'd kissed. A long, sweet, passionate kiss. Then when he'd got home, he'd become obsessed by the idea that Sinem knew. She'd been angry and in pain and he'd cradled her in his arms until she fell asleep. He loved her so much, and he was already in love with their baby, but he also ached for Pembe. When he'd left home that morning, he'd kissed his wife and wished her a good day, but he'd looked out for Pembe everywhere on his way to work.

It was said that Mehmet Süleyman still went to see his gypsy mistress in spite of his relationship with Çetin Bey's daughter. Kerim didn't know whether that was true and hoped it wasn't. Çiçek Hanım was a nice woman, and when he saw them together, Kerim could see that she and Mehmet were happy in each other's company. But he also knew that Mehmet Bey was a man who liked to be adored, and Çiçek Hanım wasn't the adoring type.

His phone rang.

'Gürsel.'

'Good morning, Inspector,' Dr Sarkissian said. 'I hope I find you well?'

Kerim took his foot off his desk and let himself rock forward. 'Yes thank you, Doctor,' he said. 'And yourself?'

'The aches and pains of increasing age aside, I am fine,' Sarkissian said. 'I have some toxicology test results on Erol Gencer for you.'

'Good.'

'Ah, you say that . . .'

'Yes?'

'Let me preface what I'm about to say by telling you that cause of death was myocardial infarction – a heart attack.'

'Gencer had heart disease.'

'Indeed,' the doctor said. 'But what caused this particular

event was more to do with the ingestion of a poisonous substance than the mere progression of a pre-existing disease.'

'He was poisoned?'

'It would seem so, although I have ordered some further, more specific tests for the substance I suspect he came into contact with. I've never come across it before and so, as well as wishing to provide you with as much evidence as I can, I am also fascinated.'

Kerim frowned. 'What is it?' he asked.

'Something called sodium monofluoroacetate, otherwise known as Compound 1080. It's used as a pesticide, although not in this country as far as I am aware.'

'Why's that?'

'There is no antidote,' the doctor said. 'So if a human being ingests this substance, he or she is dead. Depending upon the dosage, symptoms can begin to occur thirty minutes after ingestion. It acts by blocking the Krebs cycle . . .'

'I don't know what that is.'

'. . . and results in cell death,' he continued as if Kerim hadn't spoken. 'Odourless, colourless and tasteless, it's fascinating stuff. Used a lot in Australia, I believe, mainly to kill off non-indigenous species like the millions of rabbits that were introduced by European colonisers. As I say, I'm not absolutely certain yet, but . . . Makes you wonder where it came from, doesn't it?'

'To say the least,' Kerim said. 'And the other man? Al Hussain?'

'Positive for a small amount of alcohol, but that is all,' the doctor said.

Kerim thought for a moment. If one of the men had been poisoned and the other killed with a knife, then who had done that? Had they killed each other, and if so, how?

'Al Hussain was in court for the entire duration of his wife's trial,' Mehmet Süleyman said into his phone. 'Whether he met

Gencer during that time, I don't know. So saying that they knew each other is a stretch, unless we get more information to that effect.'

He turned away from them. Çiçek stifled a disgruntled sigh and then said to the boy standing beside her, 'Come on, let's get an ice cream. Your father needs to talk to his colleagues.'

Çiçek and Patrick walked across the road to the Roma ice-cream stand. Because they'd got to Büyükada early, the island wasn't yet heaving with people and so they had time to choose what flavours they wanted in their waffle cones. The usual amount was four or five, and although the boy knew what some of the flavours were, Çiçek translated those he couldn't work out. Eventually he settled on milk, Nutella, fig and walnut, and melon. Çiçek, because she was flustered and frustrated by Mehmet's behaviour, had the same.

While Süleyman talked, grave faced, on his phone, Çiçek took Patrick to a bench beside the ferry stage with a view out across the sea to the other islands. It was a beautiful day, and although Çiçek imagined that the boy wasn't used to a lot of sun in Ireland, his skin was already turning pale brown. He had his father's colouring. In fact he was in almost all physical ways the image of Mehmet.

'So do you remember İstanbul from when you were little?' she asked him.

'Not really,' Patrick said. 'Not much.'

'I remember you.' She smiled. 'You were such a beautiful little boy.'

He blushed.

'You were!' she said. 'Sometimes your mama would bring you to our apartment and we all spoiled you. How is your ice cream?'

'Good.'

'Which flavour do you like best?'

'Nutella,' he said. 'Back home, I sometimes have it for my breakfast. On bread, like.'

'It's nice,' she said.

They both looked over at the boy's father, his phone still jammed against the side of his head.

Patrick said, 'I do remember your flat, Çiçek. I wish I was staying with you and your family now.'

Süleyman ended his call and walked across the road towards them.

Çiçek said, 'Is everything OK?'

He sighed. 'I am going to have to go into the office tomorrow to speak to Kerim Bey. He needs to discuss with me whether there are similarities between his case now and the one I investigated involving Gencer last year.' He looked at his son. 'Will it be OK for you to come with me? It will be only for a couple of hours.'

The boy looked crushed, as well he might. Çiçek knew he hadn't flown all the way from Dublin to sit in a stuffy office listening to his father speaking in a language he didn't understand.

'Patrick? What do you think?'

Çiçek intervened. When it came to children, Mehmet was clueless. 'Unless you would prefer to come to us in Sultanahmet, Patrick.'

The expression on the boy's face told her everything she needed to know.

'If your father approves, maybe you can come home with me tonight and stay over,' she continued. 'My little brothers Bülent and Kemal are coming for dinner. You can join us.'

It was clear that Patrick wanted to do that, but both Çiçek and the boy waited to hear what Süleyman would say. He was a little put out, but he hid it well.

'Um, I suppose if you would like to . . .'

'I would. Yes.'

'And I am sure you can join us for dinner too tonight if you wish, Mehmet,' Çiçek said.

But he didn't say yes or no, just smiled a little weakly.

Sibel Hanım still used the name Gencer even though she'd been divorced from Erol since 1989.

'We have a daughter together,' she told Kerim Gürsel. 'Why should I have a different name from her?'

She'd arrived at headquarters just after he'd got off his call from Dr Sarkissian. The ex-wife was on his to-do list and so it was convenient that she had come to see him.

She was upset. 'I never stopped loving him, you know,' she said. 'There has never been anyone else. Do you think he suffered, Inspector?'

The bereaved often asked this question. Kerim imagined that the unusual poison must have caused pain, but he didn't know. What he did know was that death had not been instantaneous.

'I'm sorry, Hanım,' he said. 'Our doctor is still looking into Erol Bey's death. I don't know.'

'Oh.'

Sibel Gencer was probably about the same age as her ex-husband. A small, very slim woman, she had none of the costly sheen that seemed to cover Betül Gencer's expensively maintained flesh. Her hair, though well cut, was grey and her face was clear of any signs of Botox.

'I called my daughter as soon as Betül Hanım called me,' she said. 'She lives in Rome. She's on her way now.'

So Betül Gencer had contacted her predecessor. Kerim considered how thoughtful that was, and also how organised.

'As I am sure you will appreciate, Sibel Hanım, I will have to ask you about your movements on the night your husband died.'

'Of course.' She wiped some tears from her face.

This woman was, Kerim felt, extremely fragile. He modulated his voice downwards.

'And so . . .'

'I was at home, in Moda,' she said. 'I have an apartment on Yusuf Kamil Paşa Sokak. I was alone. It was a normal evening. I telephoned Hürrem – that's my daughter – as I usually do at about eight. She works for the Turkish Embassy to Vatican City; she's a diplomat.'

She was obviously very proud of her daughter and smiled when she spoke of her.

'Then I watched some television, after which I went to bed,' she said. 'I knew nothing about Erol's death until Betül called me the following morning, yesterday.'

'Mmm.' Kerim breathed in deeply. 'You are on good terms with Betül Hanım?'

'Oh yes,' she said. 'I have been divorced for a very long time, Inspector.'

'And yet you never stopped loving him.'

'Love isn't a tap you can just turn off,' she said.

That was very true. Kerim felt sorry for her and for himself.

'We had to keep seeing each other because of Hürrem,' she continued. 'He might have fallen out of love with me, but he was always a good father to her. He never missed an access visit when she was young, paid for her to attend the best schools. They were always close, and to be fair to her, Betül never interfered with that. Not that she had much to do with Hürrem. Betül is a career woman. I don't think she ever wanted children of her own and so I think she was probably happy to let Erol have his daughter to himself.'

'Do you know how your husband met Betül Hanım?'

As soon as the words left his lips, Kerim could see pain clouding the woman's features. But it was a question he'd had to ask.

'In 1988, Betül enrolled in a new part-time psychology degree course Erol had developed at Boğaziçi,' she said. 'It was, he told me, love at first sight.'

'That must have been hard for you.'

She shrugged. 'It was. But if you love someone . . . I would have done anything for Erol,' she said. 'I was prepared even to be the spurned wife as long as he stayed with me. He could go to her with my blessing.'

'But he divorced you.'

'He did. She got him on the radio and then she made him a television star.'

So Kerim had been right in assuming Betül had 'discovered' Erol Gencer.

'It was Betül who nursed him through his heart operations, put him on the diet he had to stick to if he wanted to stay alive. I've had an easy time in comparison,' she said.

Could he buy into this understanding, almost saintly woman's story? Kerim knew he couldn't, even though he could relate to it. When one allowed one's life to be pushed in an unlooked-for direction, there was a price to be paid. In this woman's case it was her entire romantic life; in his own it was his relationship with Pembe.

It was so hot. If he'd had his wits about him first thing in the morning, Çetin İkmen would have got himself organised to go over to Büyükada with Çiçek, Süleyman and his son. Out in the Sea of Marmara, away from the stifling city, he was sure the humidity would drop.

Asleep for much of the morning, he was vaguely aware of the door buzzer going. But he knew that Samsun was in and so she'd get it. She'd already started preparing the ingredients for their evening meal. His sons Bülent and Kemal were coming over to eat with them and Samsun wanted to put on a bit of a culinary display.

He was about to let himself drift off again when she shook him awake.

'There's a woman to see you,' she said.

'Who?'

'I don't know. Sounds foreign. I told her to come up,' Samsun said. 'You'd better wipe the drool off your chin.'

He took a handkerchief out of his pocket and dabbed his chin. These days whenever he went to sleep in his chair, he tended to do so with his mouth open. He also snored.

Getting out of his chair somewhat stiffly, he walked into the living room and lit a cigarette. Çiçek, to her credit, had tidied up the books and newspapers he had left all over the floor before he'd gone to bed. But the place still looked awful. No one cleaned in the same way Fatma had done. When she'd been alive, the rugs had been beaten almost to death to remove any dust, and the furniture, though old, had always been free of dirt and decorated with freshly washed cushions. She would rather have died than let a stranger into her home like this.

Samsun came back accompanied by a small, thin woman who İkmen reckoned looked about forty. Although he was sure that Samsun had made sure she took off her shoes in the hall, he was still surprised to see that her feet were bare. In his experience, women who wore headscarves usually wore socks.

'This is Rima Hanım,' Samsun said. 'I don't know what it's about.'

'OK. Thanks, Samsun. Can we please have some tea?'

She pulled a face. 'Yes, efendi.'

The woman watched her go. God alone knew what she made of her.

İkmen offered the woman a seat and she sat down, but only on the very edge of the chair. She was nervous.

'So, hanım,' he said, 'how can I help you?'

She took a breath. 'Some women I know, they tell me you help people.'

There was an accent and her Turkish was slightly halting.

'I try to,' he said. 'I used to be a police inspector. If people need my help, I try to accommodate that. Do you have a problem, hanım?'

'Yes.'

Samsun came in with two glasses of tea, which she put down in front of İkmen and Rima. Once she'd gone again, the woman said, 'It is about my sister.'

'All right,' İkmen said. 'Let us go back to the beginning. I can tell you are not Turkish, hanım . . .'

'From Syria,' she said. 'Aleppo. Me, my sister, her husband, we come here to escape the fighting.'

'As refugees.'

'Legal,' she said.

'OK.'

'We do many jobs. Sister and her husband have very good degrees but here they clean and work shops.'

It was a familiar trajectory. Syrian refugees, unless medically qualified, usually had to do menial jobs when they arrived in the Republic.

'Everything is all right until Samira, my sister, she meet with this rich Turkish woman.'

Had this poor woman been ripped off by a con artist? To İkmen it sounded as if that was what the story was building up to.

'They meet at Syrian coffee house,' she continued. 'For hakawati.'

'Hakawati?'

'Mmm.' She looked down at the floor. 'You speak English?'

'Yes,' he said.

A trace of a smile touched her lips. 'Storyteller,' she said.

'Ah yes.' İkmen nodded. 'Would you like to continue in English now, Rima?'

Her smile broadened. 'Yes. It's easier for me,' she said. 'That was my subject at the school.'

'One of mine, too,' İkmen said. 'Please do drink your tea or it will get cold.'

She took a sip, then said, 'My sister had a lot of trouble with her husband at the time. He was very unhappy and he took that out on her. He beat her. She was in despair. I don't know how she came to go to see the storyteller on that day . . .'

'When?'

'Last year, April. The place was in Fatih, around the Malta Market, you know? Many Syrians are there.'

'Yes,' İkmen said. 'I know it.'

'I don't know how, but in that place she got talking to this Turkish lady. Then three month later my sister is arrested by police when she try to kill a big television star. You know Dr Erol?'

'Oh, yes,' İkmen said. 'So your sister is Samira Al Hussain.'

'Yes.'

'Rima, your sister confessed to attempted murder,' İkmen said. 'One of my old colleagues worked that case. Samira is in prison.'

'She is. But now you know that Erol Gencer has been killed for sure,' she said. 'People are talking about murder. But that couldn't be my sister, because she is in prison.'

'No, that's true, but she did admit to attempting to murder him . . .'

'Because she was keeping her side of the bargain she made with Betül Gencer!'

He'd heard about it from Süleyman. If there had been any truth in Samira Al Hussain's story about how Betül Gencer had encouraged her to swap murders in order to kill both their husbands, Mehmet would have found it. At the time, Samira's story had seemed fantastic, but to his credit, Süleyman had attempted to engage with the Syrian refugee community in order to check its veracity. But he'd found nothing.

'And now my sister's husband, Wael Al Hussain, is dead too,' Rima said. 'It was his body that was found with Erol's.'

'And so you're saying . . .'

'Betül Gencer has finally got rid of them both,' she said. 'Now you must find the hakawati, who can tell everything.'

'My colleague told me that with no proof that this coffee house even existed, there was no way he could go looking for an itinerant storyteller,' İkmen said.

'Oh, he would never find him unless he is like you,' she said. 'People say you can see things . . . From other worlds, from . . .'

He looked out towards the balcony at the ghost of his wife. Now the back of his neck was tingling. He felt Rima's hand on his arm.

She said, 'The hakawati travels between worlds. Not all can pursue him there.'

Chapter 6

'Was your auntie a princess?' the boy asked.

The old house on Yirmiüç Nisan Caddesi was still nominally owned by the Süleyman family, and so when they arrived, Süleyman let Çiçek and Patrick in. None of them had really enjoyed their bicycle ride. The machines they had hired had been old, and Süleyman had nearly thrown his into the sea in frustration.

'I don't know whether rats and mice worry you,' he said to his son as they stepped into a small dust-choked salon, 'but I suspect there are a lot of them here.'

Patrick Süleyman just shrugged. Then he said, 'So was she a princess?'

'Princess Bulbul,' Süleyman said. 'Your grandpapa's sister.'

'Did people ever call Grandpapa a prince?'

'Yes,' his father said. 'Old people. He always said he didn't like it, but I think he did.'

Süleyman flicked a light switch and they looked around. Not all the old Princes' Island villas were gloomy, but this one was. Arranged around a large central hallway leading to a grand staircase the İzzet Süleyman Efendi Pavilion was an example of late-nineteenth-century over-elaboration. Intricate wallpaper covered in dusty paintings enclosed rooms crammed with black or brown furniture, taxidermy, mirrors and depressing onyx clocks. Curtained with vast spider's webs, its surfaces carpeted with dust, it reminded Patrick of one of the books he'd been required to read at school.

'It's like Satis House,' he said.

'Where is that?'

Çiçek, who was much more knowledgeable about literature than her lover, said, 'Miss Havisham's house in Charles Dickens' *Great Expectations*. The old lady keeps her house the same as it was on what would have been her wedding day.'

'Her man jilted her at the altar,' Patrick said.

'Well this house has just been neglected,' Süleyman said. 'My aunt died in 2005.'

Çiçek walked over to look at a painting on the wall and commented on the way the floor creaked beneath her. 'It's not going to collapse, is it?' she said.

Süleyman smiled. 'No. These old houses always creak. We had it inspected for, you know, damage and such last year.'

'Do you own it, then?' Patrick asked.

'Me? No,' his father said. 'Or rather I don't own it alone. It belongs to our family.'

'So could you come and live in it?'

'I suppose I could ask my brother and my cousins and of course my uncle Selim. He is the last of grandpapa's brothers still alive. If they all agreed, then I guess it might be possible. Why? Do you like it here?'

'It's cool,' Patrick said.

It was the highest expression of praise he could give and it made his father smile.

'There is a library on the first floor,' Süleyman said.

Patrick's eyes lit up.

'Some of the books are in English,' his father continued. 'Princess Bulbul married a diplomat. Uncle Fahrettin worked in France and then New Zealand for many years. They may be dusty, but there are a lot of books in his library. Go and see. I am sure that if you want to borrow one, that will be fine.'

The boy walked upstairs smiling. When he'd gone, Süleyman turned to Çiçek. 'Aren't you back at work tomorrow?'

'Yes,' she said. 'But Patrick can spend the morning with Dad and the boys.'

'They're staying over?'

'Yes. Samsun is cooking tonight and so there will be alcohol. Why don't you come for dinner?'

He put an arm around her. 'I could,' he said. 'But why don't you come home with me? In the morning you can walk to work.'

'I could.' But she didn't want to. When she was with him, Çiçek found that she always fell in with his plans. And given what Gonca Hanım had said to her, she didn't want to do that. If the gypsy really was in love with him, that was serious. She needed time to think about the implications. She said, 'But I can't just dump Patrick on the family.'

'They won't mind.'

She felt one of his hands pull her close while the other one slipped underneath her skirt.

'I can't . . .'

He kissed her.

'Mehmet! The boy . . .'

Now caressing the flesh at the top of her legs, he said, 'Not my fault you're so sexy.'

When they'd made love in his mother's house, she had initially resisted. But she found it was difficult to do. He took over, as he was doing now, making her do what always left her feeling uncomfortable and bad about herself. Because she wanted him.

He pulled her into what had once been the reception salon and closed the door behind him.

According to Berat Tükek, who had found the bodies of Erol Gencer and Wael Al Hussain, they had been on opposite sides of Gencer's swimming pool. This was how the police had also seen them. Gencer at the back, nearest the house; Al Hussain nearer the road. Unlike Gencer, Al Hussain had been close to the swimming pool and had to some extent bled into it. Forensic officers were confident the bodies hadn't been moved.

The offices of Harem Medya, the TV company responsible for *The Dr Erol Hour*, were based on the fifth floor of an office block on Uğur Mumcu Caddesi, at the far northern end of the district of Beşiktaş. The company occupied the whole of the fifth floor in the form of a vast open-plan office. Light and clean, it was nevertheless, to Kerim Gürsel's way of thinking, sterile.

He'd been met at the lift by a young man who had introduced himself as Mustafa, assistant to Filiz Hanım, the director of production. Mustafa showed him to the only dedicated single office the place had. When he entered, a woman got up to shake his hand. Probably in her fifties, Filiz Tepe was tall, slim and groomed to perfection. She wore a very flattering asymmetric tea dress, over which her long black hair hung in great glossy swathes. The heels of her Manolo Blahnik shoes made her taller than Kerim.

Once they had got the niceties out of the way and been given tea, Kerim quizzed the woman who had effectively been Erol Gencer's boss. When she spoke of him, she smiled.

'He was a lovely man,' she said. 'A devoted husband and father. Everyone here loved him, and of course our viewers did too.'

The 'devoted husband' part seemed rather at odds with what Berat Tükek had told him.

'Did he get a lot of attention from fans?'

'Oh yes! Erol Bey was enormously popular and highly respected,' she said. 'He was one of our most precious assets. We are all devastated by his death.'

'Do you know of any instances where Erol Bey may have been the subject of unwanted attention?' Kerim asked.

'Apart from that incident last year? Although I have to say that woman never came either here or to the studios. My understanding is that she stalked him at his home. But she went to prison, didn't she?'

'Yes.'

'Well . . .' She looked up at the ceiling. Kerim casually observed that her neck was a lot older than her face. 'Of course as you can imagine, Inspector, some members of our studio audience can prove problematic from time to time. Erol Bey always handled them very well, and we do have security. But things happen. The only significant episode I can recall is when an audience member threw a punch at him. About eighteen months ago, I think. I can send you a copy of our incident record.'

'That would be very useful. Can you tell me what happened?'

'Do you watch the show, Inspector?' she asked.

'No,' he said. 'I am aware of the format. My wife watches.'

'The point of it is to help people solve their problems,' she said. 'Every week we cover a different topic: child marriage, pornography addiction, drugs, infidelity. This particular show was about polygamy. As you know, this is always an issue for Muslim countries, and in spite of the legal ban on multiple spouses, it happens.'

He nodded.

'So Erol Bey has these two brothers on the show. Between them they have seven wives. In order to put the discussion into context, Erol Bey begins by defining what polygamy means, where it fits into the practice of Islam, how the Mormons in America do it. He also mentions the Shia practice of mut'a marriages.'

Kerim, who knew very little about religion, said, 'This is where a man may marry a woman on a temporary basis?'

'Yes. They do it in Iran,' she said. 'It's basically so unmarried men can have sex with women without feeling they've sinned.'

'Mmm.'

Just from that one little murmur she realised that he didn't approve, and she smiled.

'Anyway, one of the brothers from . . . I can't remember where, a village somewhere,' she said, 'he gets the idea that Erol Bey is equating this Shia heresy with what he does with his four or however many wives permitted by Islam. Erol Bey tried to explain, but this man wasn't in the business of listening. He threw the punch before security could take him down, and Erol Bey was left with a black eye. We were all for pressing charges, but Erol wasn't like that. He even went and spoke to the man. I mean, I would have put him on the first flight back to the middle of nowhere. But Erol had real compassion.'

'Erol Bey was an attractive man, as well as being a media star,' Kerim said. 'Any trouble with women in that regard?'

She frowned. 'Not really. I think some of the older ones – the grandmothers, the ancient teyzes – wanted to mother him. Dr Erol was an attractive man, but he wasn't a sex symbol. Although some of the guests and the studio audience could sometimes get hysterical, Erol Bey was essentially there to help. He was your kindly uncle, your therapist, your big brother and your mother all rolled into one. The fact that he was married to a very glamorous woman was only to be expected, but that had little to do with his professional image on our show.'

'Do you know his wife, Filiz Hanım?'

She smiled. 'I worked with Betül many years ago on a show called *Büyük Risk*. I don't know whether you remember it?'

'Yes.' It was the Turkish version of the American show *Jeopardy*.

'She was so glamorous I really thought she'd get snapped up by a movie star or a politician. But, you know, she came from a very poor background and was very interested at the time in improving her education. I knew she'd enrolled on a psychology course at Boğaziçi University. She didn't say much about it. Then the next thing that happened was she'd moved in with this academic, Erol.'

'How did Erol Bey become involved in television?'

'Oh, that was my predecessor, Celal Bey.'

Celal Koca had been at the helm of Harem Medya until his death in 2012. Rumour had it, or so Ömer Mungun had told Kerim, that Filiz Hanım had been his mistress.

'I believe the recruitment of Erol Gencer happened after one of Celal Bey's parties,' she continued. 'He and Mrs Koca would hold wonderful Şeker Bayram celebrations at their house on the shores of the Bosphorus. I am not a religious woman but I love the end of Ramazan. So colourful and exciting. Anyway, Betül and Erol were married by that time, and so they came as a couple. I think it was probably sometime in the late nineties. I can send you a copy of Erol's employment contract if that will help.'

'Thank you.' Kerim looked down at his notes. 'So . . .' he said, 'your friendship with Betül Gencer . . .'

'Oh, we aren't friends,' Filiz Hanım said. 'Not now.'

He looked up. 'Why?'

'When I took over from Celal Bey in 2012, one of my first tasks was to look at our existing shows and decide which ones were viable and which ones were not,' she said. 'Erol's show was doing well and so that stayed, but we also ran a show called *Devil Brides*, which was fronted by Betül. The basic premise was that she toured the country seeking out spoiled and petulant brides-to-be.'

Kerim remembered it. 'Is that the one where the bride is fooled into believing her dress has been ruined or her honeymoon cancelled and then the hoax is revealed and the couple have some sort of fairy-tale wedding on the network?'

She laughed. 'I love your turn of phrase, Inspector,' she said. 'But yes, that was it basically. Anyway, viewing figures were right down by that time, and so I axed it. Purely a commercial decision on my part. But Betül took it personally and has never spoken to me since.'

What sounded like a bowl or jug breaking on the kitchen floor smashed into İkmen's consciousness as he sat zoning out in his living room.

'Crap!'

Samsun was cooking and now she'd broken something.

İkmen called out, 'Are you all right?' But he didn't get up. She had to come to him.

Her face red with fury, she said, 'Yiğit!'

'The djinn?' He laughed. 'I thought you were used to it?'

Ever since just before Fatma's death, the İkmens' kitchen had been haunted by a djinn, an Islamic creature of smokeless fire and malice. Not everyone could see this creature the family had dubbed Yiğit, or 'brave', but those now living in the apartment saw it all the time. İkmen himself believed that it wouldn't leave the property until his wife's ghost faded away. The fact that his interaction with her kept her in view meant that the djinn was going nowhere.

'I am,' Samsun said. 'But I still get caught out when it rears up behind me. That's a perfectly good bowl gone forever.'

She went back into the kitchen and slammed the door. İkmen continued his reverie.

The story Rima Al Numan had told him was intriguing. He recalled the attempt on Erol Gencer's life, and how Süleyman had wrestled with the notion of a Syrian coffee house no one could name, remember or identify. As Mehmet himself had admitted, there were so many secrets locked within the traumatised Syrian community it was very hard for outsiders to work out what might or might not be true. What had been beyond reasonable doubt was that Samira Al Hussain had attempted to kill Gencer and was now serving time for it. But now that Samira's husband had been found dead – at Gencer's house – her sister was reviving an idea that had seemed fantastical when it had first been mooted and was just as fantastical now.

What was more, Rima hadn't actually been to the coffee house in question herself. Beyond being aware that her sister had met Betül Gencer there, all she had known was the name of the storyteller who'd given a performance that day. İkmen had googled the name she'd given him, Ahmad Al Saidawi. His search had come up with information on an eighteenth-century hakawati who had once apparently strung out the tale of the legendary Egyptian Sultan Bayburs for three hundred and seventy-two nights. More willing than most people to believe that a lifespan could possibly be elongated by magic, İkmen was nevertheless of the opinion that this Ahmad Al Saidawi was not three hundred years old. Whoever he was, and in spite of what Rima had said about him living between worlds, İkmen was more inclined to believe that this apparently itinerant storyteller traded on and in some cases lived behind his famous name. If indeed it was his name at all.

Also, what had a Turkish woman like Betül Gencer been doing at an event organised for Arabs in Arabic? A quick look at her Wikipedia page had told İkmen that she'd been born Betül Ozcan in a village outside Adana on the south-eastern Mediterranean coast. She'd got out of there as soon as she could and become a model in İstanbul before she was twenty. Her own career in TV had been followed by her husband's even greater success. She had studied psychology, but later on in life. Unless she had Arab relatives, İkmen doubted she could speak the language. And that was what had been so strange about the whole story. Samira Al Hussain was an educated woman who would know, surely, that it was unlikely that a woman like Betül would even know where a Syrian coffee house was. And anyway, why had

Samira been there? She did, admittedly, work in that area, but how had she found out about the storytelling event?

Genç was old and his sight was going due to cataracts. When he put his glasses on to peer at the magazine, they made him look like an owl. After a moment's contemplation, he said, 'Vintage.'

'Vintage?'

'A vintage example of my art,' the old man said.

Photographer, pornographer, maker of filthy films, Genç was as much a Tarlabaşı institution as the local drug dealers, trans bars and once elegant houses that lined its streets.

Ömer Mungun took back the magazine inside its transparent evidence bag.

'Any idea what vintage?' he asked.

'It's colour,' the old man said. 'I never worked in colour until the nineties.'

'So the nineties?'

'Late,' he said. He pointed to the woman on the cover. 'She didn't turn up until the late nineties.'

'So this is an old magazine.'

'Oh yes. Made for the Arab market. I don't do none of that leather straps stuff no more. But see, the nature of those men who buy my stuff means that they hang onto it. Furtive. That's what men are in this city. All lovely and lovey with the wives until the women go shopping, and then it's out with the fuck books.'

'I think most men amuse themselves online these days,' Ömer said.

'Youngsters, yes. But there's still a market for what I do. Online they can trace you.'

'Who?'

'The authorities. Good value, a decent fuck book.'

Ömer showed the old man a picture of Wael Al Hussain.

'Know this man?' he asked.

More peering, then Genç said, 'No. Why?'

'That magazine was found in his bed.'

'So?'

'He's dead,' Ömer said. 'Murdered.'

'Not for that fuck book he weren't! I know men pass them around . . .'

'He was called Wael Al Hussain,' Ömer said. 'A Syrian.'

Genç drew in a whistly breath. 'Don't get involved with them!'

'You make magazines for them.'

'That's business. Used to have a translator from Iraq, I think. But since all this trouble in Syria . . . Wouldn't touch them.'

Ömer looked down at the magazine. 'It's pretty strong stuff, you know, Genç.'

The old man shrugged. Then he laughed.

'You don't think none of that was real, do you, Sergeant?' he said. 'Most of them women was too old to get into positions like that. And him, that Georgian lad I used to use, he couldn't get it up half the time. Smoke and mirrors, my friend, smoke and mirrors.'

Coming back from the islands on the ferry, Çiçek made sure that Patrick sat between her and Mehmet Süleyman. On the tram up from the ferry terminal to her father's apartment, she thought about what had happened earlier.

So far the part of her that wanted sexual adventure had always won out, in one way or another, against the part of her that felt cheap and used. But Mehmet had promised he wouldn't put her in that dilemma again. He'd broken that promise twice, one day after the other. In that dusty old reception salon back on Büyükada he'd caressed and licked her body until she was so hot for him she let him take her up against an old cupboard, which creaked and cracked as they had sex. The boy upstairs must have heard. It made her feel ashamed. But for a while, afterwards, she hadn't felt ashamed. She'd felt satisfied and sexy, and when Mehmet had signalled that he wanted more, she'd been happy to comply. But then Patrick had called down to them.

'Can you tell me where the bathroom is?' he'd said.

His father had told him, and although he'd tried to take her back to where they'd been before, she'd refused and that had been that.

Her brothers had arrived when they got to the apartment. Bülent, looking so much like their father, plugged into some game on his phone; Kemal tall and groomed and handsome. She kissed them both and then went into the kitchen to ask if she could help with the cooking. But when Samsun saw her she just shouted, 'Out! Out!' She often did that when she was cooking, particularly when she was brewing up what turned out to be culinary disasters.

Her father was outside on the balcony talking to her mother. Çiçek walked past her brothers, who were now chatting to Mehmet and Patrick in English, and joined him. As soon as he saw her, Çetin İkmen stopped talking and stood up to kiss her.

'Did you have a good day?' he asked.

They both sat down.

'Yes. Yes, we did,' she said.

'You look glowing, I must say.' He offered her a cigarette, which she took, and then took one for himself. 'Glowing' was an odd word for him to use. Did he know what she'd done? He often did. Çiçek chose to ignore it.

'Dad,' she said, 'Mehmet has to go to work tomorrow.'

'I thought he was on leave.'

'He is, but something's come up, for Kerim Bey. The death of Erol Gencer, I understand.'

Çetin İkmen's eyes lit up. 'Ah,' he said. 'Is he here, Mehmet? I need to talk to him myself.'

'Yes . . .'

Her father stood up.

'Dad . . .'

'What?'

Clearly he was itching to get to his old colleague.

'Dad, because Mehmet is going to be out tomorrow morning at the very least, I wondered whether Patrick could stay with us. We could all have dinner together, then he could stay over and—'

'Yes, yes, that's fine.'

And then he was gone, back into the living room, and after a cursory greeting to the young Irish boy, he took his friend to one said and Çiçek heard him say, 'About this Erol Gencer affair . . .'

Çetin İkmen was a strange man. That funny little girl at the hostel, where Rima cleaned, had told her about him. She'd said that he could do anything, that he was powerful and that he had magic. Rima's mother had believed in magic and it was from her mother that she'd learned the tales once told by Ahmad Al Saidawi. He'd had magic too, according to her mother, and had never died but had continued to live in Aleppo. All gone now, old Aleppo. The great souq, those vast mansions that dated back centuries, the old Baron Hotel, the coffee houses. There was nowhere in the city for Ahmad Al Saidawi to tell his tales these days, and so it made sense that he wandered.

What did it say about her that part of her mind could accept that a teller of tales could be three hundred years old? It said that she was a product of a country pulled apart at the seams, a brutalised place where only stories made any sense. And why not? If the leader of her country could destroy his own people in order to stay in power, what wasn't possible? The world Rima had grown up in had been hard, but it hadn't been like this. Never in her wildest dreams had she thought she'd ever be a refugee, lost and alone in a country she didn't understand.

And anyway, the girl had told her that Çetin İkmen had magic, and so, if that were correct, he would know whether or not the story was true. Because he had taken her case, he must've decided that it was. He'd also agreed to track Ahmad Al Saidawi down for absolutely no charge.

He'd said, 'I know some people who live on the edge of . . . I don't know, reality? Whatever that is. It will be a challenge.'

And when she'd asked him, finally, whether he thought he could find the storyteller, he'd said, 'Oh, hanım, I will find something, I can assure you. Whether it's what you want me to find or not, I cannot say.'

Chapter 7

They couldn't even eat together in peace! Pınar Hanım, who did admittedly cook for the three of them, was giving a lecture on child-rearing.

'People these days will tell you that swaddling a newborn is a bad thing,' she said through a mouthful of bulgur and chicken. 'But you were swaddled, Sinem, and all your brothers.'

Sinem Gürsel knew that her mother believed that children who were swaddled benefited from straight limbs, though it hadn't done her much good. But she said nothing, ditto her husband, who was now wiping pieces of bulgur his mother-in-law had inadvertently spat at him off his face.

'And draughts,' Pınar Hanım continued. 'I don't care if it's forty degrees, a newborn in an apartment with open windows is vulnerable to chills. And the Eye . . .'

She left to go back to the kitchen to tend to the yogurt soup she made her daughter drink every day. Kerim put his head in his hands. Sinem massaged the back of his neck.

'She means well.The Evil Eye is very real for my mother. '

'I know, but . . .'

Although he knew that Çetin İkmen, whom he respected enormously, was very in tune with what Kerim considered superstitious nonsense, he himself had never been able to believe in things for which he didn't have empirical proof. Also he knew that the older man agreed with him when it came to things like swaddling, even if he did apparently have a djinn living in his kitchen.

'She'll go when the baby is born,' Sinem said.

'You say that . . .' He shrugged.

'She will! Nurettin's wife Zeynep has just become pregnant,' she said. 'Her mother died years ago. Mum won't be able to resist going over there and giving her the benefit of her experience.'

Kerim hoped that Pınar Hanım would indeed go to stay with her youngest son and his wife, but he doubted it. As far as he was aware, she knew nothing about his sexuality; she just didn't like him, she never had. Busy at work and driven crazy by the old woman at home, he was beginning to feel he didn't know himself.

He was a bad man. As soon as he'd left Çetin İkmen's apartment, Mehmet Süleyman had driven straight to Gonca's house in Balat. Now, having kissed his girlfriend goodbye and dumped his son on her, he was in the gypsy's bed again. Admittedly she wasn't with him; that bloody kid of hers, Rambo, had called her downstairs just as things had started to get interesting. He'd given her a love bite on her breast, like a bloody teenager, he'd been so turned on! But of course she'd gone to her son because that was what she did. As far as Mehmet could tell, Rambo was a dishonest little shit, but his mother loved him.

He sat up in bed and lit a cigarette. Both his women were stunning in their own way. Çiçek was beautiful, kind, and bright like her father. Men had used her badly in the past and he knew he was no different, though he'd never set out to hurt her. The same was true of Gonca, who was beautiful, clever and, behind all her attitude, kind as well. He'd been with the gypsy for years, on and off. Other men had come and gone, but he had remained in her life. He didn't know precisely why, although sometimes as they lay together after sex, she'd told him that he was hers, that she was addicted to him, and that she would die without him. Did she say that to all her men? He doubted it. And anyway, there were no other men in her life now. He hoped she wouldn't be long. Gonca did things to and for him that no one else did, and just thinking about her made him hard.

He put his cigarette out in the ashtray beside the bed and was about to close his eyes and try to sleep for a while when the voices he heard downstairs suddenly became shrill. Gonca and Rambo always spoke in their own language, and so he couldn't understand a word of what was being said. But then she started screaming, and so he jumped out of bed, put his trousers on and grabbed his gun.

It was a strange but nevertheless worthy exercise for the whole family to be speaking English. Çetin himself and Çiçek were the most fluent, Samsun the least. His boys were adequate and were very good at understanding Patrick Süleyman's games and movies references even if the kid did speak with a strange accent. İkmen had known his mother and she'd never spoken like that, drawling and whatever. Maybe it was some youthful affectation in Ireland?

While the boy talked to his sons about something called 'Fortnight', İkmen sat out on the balcony watching the sun go down. Fatma was nowhere to be seen, but he was glad to be on his own for a while, to think. Çiçek and Süleyman had been odd around each other earlier, but he had resolved to keep out of that even though he knew that Süleyman was cheating. After dinner, his daughter had gone to her room while Samsun had left to go who knew where. Their household was made up of a strange selection of waifs and strays these days.

Süleyman had told him little about the attempt on Erol Gencer's life in 2018. He remembered Samira Al Hussain and was, of course, intrigued that her husband should have now been found dead at the Gencer house together with the man his wife had tried to kill. But, as he had done at the time, he gave Samira Al Hussain's coffee-house theory short shrift.

'If one person had come forward in support of it I would have given it some credence,' he had said. 'But no one did.'

İkmen had asked, 'Did you try to find this storyteller?'

'How? If I remember correctly, the name she gave us was of some sort of mythical figure. And anyway, all of that hinged upon the woman having met Betül Gencer at this event, and that clearly didn't happen.'

İkmen had asked him how he could be so sure, and Süleyman had told him that Betül would have been recognised by someone in the area. Her face was famous. İkmen wondered whether that was so. Was Betül Gencer well known in the Syrian community? And had Süleyman taken into account the fact that maybe the Syrians just didn't want to get involved with the police. He said he had, but . . .

İkmen knew he wouldn't have much more success with the Syrian refugees. But signposts along the esoteric trail were another matter, and he knew exactly where to start.

Süleyman pressed the muzzle of the gun hard up against the boy's head and took the safety off.

'Breathe in a way I don't like and I'll blow your brains out,' he said.

Gonca, curled up in a corner of the kitchen, her head covered in dust, screamed, 'Don't hurt him! Don't!'

Rambo Şekeroğlu was a slim, good-looking boy of twenty. Dark like his parents, he was covered in tattoos that might or might not have been gang related, and he had a fierce temper and a sharp tongue. But he wasn't a fool and so he threw his hands up as soon as Süleyman put the gun to his head.

'Mehmet Bey . . .'

'What's going on?' Süleyman asked. 'I come in here and find your mother cowering away from you. Tell me!'

The boy said nothing.

'Well?'

A look that he couldn't interpret passed between mother and son, and then Gonca said, 'Oh, it's nothing.'

'Nothing? You were screaming. I thought someone was trying to kill you.'

'We had a disagreement,' she said.

'What about?'

This time Rambo spoke. 'Romany stuff,' he said. 'You wouldn't understand.'

Süleyman pushed the gun harder against the boy's head. 'Try me.'

'Mehmet, don't hurt him!'

'Then tell me what this is about!' he yelled. He glared at Rambo. 'I'm sick of you looking at me like I'm a piece of shit.'

'I'm sick of you fucking my mum!'

'Rambo!' she screamed.

The boy fell silent.

Süleyman looked at Gonca, who said, 'It's just about money, Mehmet.'

'What? He wants you to give him some and you say you're not going to – again? Oh, I understand that, mainly because whenever he comes here he always seems to manage to get money out of you!'

'He's my son!'

'He's a little shit!'

Süleyman breathed in hard and then put the safety back on his gun and replaced it in its holster. Rambo visibly slumped. Gonca ran to her son and took him in her arms.

Süleyman took his wallet out of his trouser pocket. 'How much do you want?'

'Oh Mehmet, leave the boy alone,' his mother said.

Süleyman ignored her. 'Well?'

The boy looked at him with cold, hard eyes. 'How much you got?'

'Two hundred dollars and you fuck off for the rest of the night.'

Gonca, horrified, began to speak, but her son pushed her away and stood in front of Süleyman.

'US dollars?' he asked.

Süleyman handed over some notes. Rambo nodded and began to make his way towards the back door. Just before he left, Süleyman said, 'If you ever threaten your mother again, I will fucking kill you. Are we clear?'

Tarlabaşı was coming alive for what Ömer Mungun called the night shift. This was when the markets, the hordes of kids and all the little mum-and-dad shops in the district shut up or moved inside and gave the quarter over to the drug dealers, the drag queens, the massage parlours and the bars. Had Wael Al Hussain ever patronised any of the prostitutes, the masseuses, the trans girls or maybe even the rent boys who stalked the streets at night in search of business? It was known that his wife had suffered physically at his hands. If her story was to be believed, she'd suffered to the extent that she had wanted him dead.

Of course Wael Al Hussain hadn't been the only Syrian in Tarlabaşı. There were lots of them – some legal, some illegal. Ömer had seen some of their women plying their trade on several notorious street corners, and he didn't know any of them. But he did know a couple of the Turkish girls, and he saw one of them now coming out of a half-demolished house with a man wearing a remarkably expensive suit. Italian by the look of it. He knew this because his boss wore Italian suits, although he looked a damn sight better in his than this flabby example of what Ömer surmised was some sort of local government official. Some men liked the danger and degradation of places like this.

Ömer waited until the girl had reattached her stockings to her garter belt and then went over to her.

'Lagun,' he said. 'How's it going?'

She hadn't known he was there, and was shocked.

'Oh, Ömer Bey!' she said. 'You frightened me! Oh no, you're not going to . . .'

'I'm not going to arrest you today,' Ömer said.

She visibly relaxed. Lagun, though pretty, was one of the girls who usually serviced clients at the bottom end of the financial scale: the disabled, the insane, the poor, the exceptionally depraved, and sometimes refugees. This was because in spite of her pretty face and body, she was epileptic. Uncontrolled, she would fit much of the time. Even when she had enough money to buy her medication, she would sometimes fit.

Ömer took her arm and went with her back into the half-demolished house.

'This where you're working these days?' he asked as he surveyed a rudimentary bed made of stained blankets on the floor, a scattering of used condoms and a lot of fallen masonry.

'Sometimes,' she said. 'Do you wanna sit down?'

They both sat on the bed, which, Ömer noticed, was damp. He turned his mind away from it.

'I want to talk to you about Syrians,' he said.

Gonca kissed him.

'You know, baby, you didn't have to give Rambo money,' she said.

She was moving up and down on top of him while his hands caressed her breasts.

'Don't talk about that now . . .'

'But you didn't.'

'Shh!'

Later, as they lay in each other's arms, she said, 'I will pay you back.'

Süleyman shook his head. 'It's worth it to be alone with you,' he said.

'Two hundred US dollars is a lot.' She put her hand around his penis and then bent down to lick it. 'I'd better be worth it.'

'You're always worth it.'

But as she made to go down on him, she had a sudden twinge in the side of her neck. She sat up.

'Ow!'

'What is it?' he asked as he put a hand out to her.

'Old age,' she said. 'Sometimes I get this sort of shooting pain in my neck.'

'Do you have any massage oil?'

'No,' she said as she rubbed at it. 'It'll be all right in a minute. Sorry, baby.'

'No problem.'

But it was, and they both knew it. He reached out to his jacket, which was on the end of the bed, and took a small bottle out of its pocket.

'I've got this,' he said. 'It's just cologne.'

He poured some into his hand and began to rub it into the side of her neck, which she stretched out the better to get the full benefit of his massage. After a few seconds he said, 'Helping?'

'Getting there.'

He rubbed some into her back and then, predictably, her breasts.

'Naughty baby!' But she was aroused.

He laughed. 'Couldn't resist,' he said, and then, in an effort to get the residue off his hands as quickly as possible, he stroked the cologne into her hair. As he moved his fingers through her great black and grey mane, he noticed that little golden highlights appeared. It made him sad to think that he'd never noticed those before.

Lagun looked at the photograph. 'I dunno, Ömer Bey, they all look the same to me.'

'Syrians specifically, or men?'

She sighed. 'Both, really. As you know, things go on here that most people out in ordinary life wouldn't believe.'

'This man was murdered two nights ago,' Ömer said. He knew she wouldn't have read the papers and clearly didn't have a TV. 'In Sarıyer.'

Lagun laughed. 'Bit out of my league,' she said. She pointed to the photograph. 'If he's Syrian and he was in Sarıyer, he's obviously done well for himself.'

'But he lived here.'

She didn't say anything and so Ömer attempted to jog any memories she might have in another way.

'His wife was put in prison last year,' he said. 'For attempted murder.'

'Somebody on television, wasn't it?' she asked.

'Yeah.'

She thought about it for a moment. 'I dunno. There's something rattling around about that in my head. Last year, you said?'

He nodded.

'Let me ask around. I don't know whether it means anything, but . . . Leave it with me, will you?'

'OK. Do you have a phone at the moment, Lagun? It is urgent.'

'No,' she said. 'Some bastard robbed it off me a few weeks ago. I was fitting and . . . You know how it is.'

He did and had suspected she didn't have her old phone any more, because every time he called it, it just rang out. He took an iPhone out of his pocket and gave it to her.

'Here.'

'For me?'

'For you to call me and nothing else,' he said. 'Find out whether any of the other girls knew him. We're trying to discover as much as we can about him.'

'Why?'

'Because he's been murdered!' Ömer said.

'Oh, yes.'

'And we want to know why.' He stood up. 'Because at the moment we've just got two corpses, loosely connected by circumstance, but with no reason we can yet find for one to kill the other.'

'You think that's what happened?'

'It's possible,' he said. He pointed to the phone. 'My number is in there. Call me. Oh, and are you managing to afford your meds at the moment?'

She shrugged. 'I'm eking out my supplies.'

He opened his wallet and took out a hundred lira.

'Consider this a payment on account,' he told her.

It was dark by the time Çetin İkmen made his series of phone calls. All the kids were in bed and Samsun had probably decided to make a wild night of it over in Tarlabaşı. It was a full schedule, even if he discounted Gonca Şekeroğlu. Not that he actually could do that . . .

In the normal course of events, and given the nature of his call, it wouldn't matter what time he called her. But it was past midnight and he felt very strongly that she wasn't alone.

He shrugged, lit a cigarette and made the call anyway. It took her a long time to answer, and when she did, she didn't sound best pleased.

'İkmen?' She coughed. 'What the fuck do you want?'

'Did I wake you up? I'm sorry,' he said.

'Yes, you did!'

He heard her shuffle about, possibly in bed. Another voice groaned. She was with a man. He heard what he thought was a kiss and then the sound of her bare feet slapping against the floor as she went somewhere else.

She yawned and said, 'So where's the emergency then? You know if I don't get my beauty sleep people get visited by curses.'

He laughed. He loved her spirit. She might be sleeping with his daughter's boyfriend, but he still couldn't help but love her a little bit.

'I need to find someone who has disappeared,' he said.

'Then look on your computer. There's some register of missing people, isn't there?'

'There is. But when I say disappeared, I mean that in the sense of . . .'

'Oh, I see.' He heard the interest pique in her voice. 'That's another matter.'

'I have very mundane reasons for asking,' he said.

'Magic without the mundane would be nothing but normality, İkmen.'

'Trust you to get to the nub of the matter, hanım.'

'Ha!'

'So can I encroach upon your time?' İkmen asked. 'In the morning?'

'Afternoon will be better,' she said.

His other contacts had said he could visit them whenever he wanted. But then Gonca was always more focused upon time – when she had a man in her bed.

'All right then, I will see you tomorrow, and thank you.'

She put the phone down on him. Now all he had to do was get Patrick Süleyman back to his father by lunchtime, or else take him over to Kemal's apartment for the afternoon.

Chapter 8

The son of the imam, because he was so clever, set himself up as a scribe. With his box of pens and his fine sheaf of parchment, he offered to write for those who couldn't, for those who didn't have time and for those who thought writing beneath them. And as he explained to his father, because he was such a clever boy, he put a sign up in front of his stall that said, 'The Wisdom of a Man is worth twice the Wisdom of a Woman.' His father, the imam, frowned.

Eylul Yavaş hadn't been able to interview Mrs Kiyamet Yavuz the previous day. Time not spent with her boss, Kerim Gürsel, had been occupied with interviewing the two other women Betül Gencer had been with at the Ulus 29 nightclub the night her husband was killed.

Asked to take a seat in an almost entirely empty reception area, Eylul found herself looking out of the floor-to-ceiling window that took up the whole of one long wall. A fifth-floor apartment, the Yavuz place overlooked the shopping mall known as the Zorlu Centre in Ulus. Not the most fashionable district in which to live, Ulus was not, however, somewhere most people could afford to purchase an apartment.

When she arrived, Kiyamet Yavuz said, 'Sergeant Yavaş?'

'Yes.'

She smiled. 'Come into the drawing room. We can see the Bosphorus from there.'

Eylul followed her into a vast living room sparsely furnished with cool, expensive Scandinavian furniture. They both sat down on chairs that looked as if they defied the laws of physics. The policewoman knew that Kiyamet Yavuz was sixty-three years old, but she looked much younger. Not, however, in a Botox/plastic surgery way. Though clearly immaculately groomed, she was a far more socially acceptable middle-class Turkish version of the woman a lot of people said was Inspector Süleyman's mistress, Gonca Şekeroğlu.

The maid who had answered the door brought tea and then left the women alone.

'You want to know whether Betül Hanım's story checks out?' Kiyamet Hanım said without preamble.

Eylul hadn't even taken her notebook out. 'Er, yes.'

'I was with her all evening at the Ulus club. All four of us had dinner first, and then it was drinks and dancing.' She smiled, but not in a friendly way. 'I know we may seem a bit old to be clubbing, and I know you may think we were just there to pick up men half our age . . .'

'I don't think that,' Eylul said. 'I have no opinion. My only concern is to find out why two men have died.'

'Of course it is.'

It wasn't said unpleasantly, but it did make Eylul wonder whether this woman was one of those secular types who believed all covered women were sexless. Women like her own mother.

'Betül and Erol were very happy together,' Kiyamet continued. 'I know some people will gossip about them because they have no children, but Betül never wanted any and Erol, of course, had a daughter from his previous marriage.'

Eylul had never heard of any such gossip and wondered why Kiyamet had mentioned it.

'So you danced . . .'

'Yes,' Kiyamet said. 'And I'm not going to lie and tell you

that we didn't dance with men. We did, Betül included. But it was just fun – well, it was for Betül, Elif and Emine.'

'And you?'

She smiled. 'Unlike my friends, I am not married.'

'Oh, I thought . . .'

'You thought wrong, Sergeant,' she said. 'I have never been nor ever want to be married. I work in publishing. I enjoy my job, I make good money and I have lots of friends. Men, for me, are by way of being a hobby. I pick them up and put them down as and when I please. I brought a man back here that night, I won't lie.'

'So you weren't with Mrs Gencer all evening?'

'I left the club at the same time as my friends,' she said. 'I believe Elif went back to Betül's apartment for a nightcap, and Emine went home.'

This reflected the other women's statements. Although none of them had spoken about Kiyamet and a man.

'I'm afraid I can't give you any further details about the man I brought back here,' Kiyamet said. 'He was Mehmet something or other and he worked in IT. Don't they all? He was about thirty, I imagine. Very nice body.'

If she was expecting Eylul to blush because she wore a headscarf, she was going to be disappointed. Eylul Yavaş had become what she called a born-again Muslim when she was twenty-one. She'd just left university and had come to her conclusion about her future all by herself. She'd had sex and she'd enjoyed it. But living without it had been a choice. She was no prude.

'And so this gentleman left here . . .'

'He stayed the night,' Kiyamet said. 'I'm a feminist, but I'm not rude. When I bring a man home, I let him stay. I even give him breakfast if he's been particularly gallant.'

Eylul smiled and then Kiyamet Hanım joined her. 'Look,' she

said, 'everything I've told you is true, but I admit I was trying to shock you, because . . .'

'I cover,' Eylul said. 'That's OK. I'm used to it.'

'But what's important is that Betül Hanım was nowhere near her husband when he died,' Kiyamet Hanım said. 'She loved him and that's the truth.'

Kerim had heard shouting, but he was used to that. Police headquarters was always a tense place in which to work, and sometimes suppressed emotions simply boiled over. What he hadn't been expecting was the sudden appearance of a sweating Ömer Mungun in his office. As soon as he was in, the younger man closed the door behind him and put his back against it.

'Ömer?'

'Just, please, a moment, Kerim Bey!'

He had a good idea about what had just happened. Mehmet Süleyman was due in to see him, even though he was on leave, and had probably gone to his own office first. Finding that Ömer had used his desk, because his own was too untidy, to lay out scene-of-crime photographs had probably driven Süleyman insane. He was a man who liked order, particularly when it came to his own work space.

Once he'd allowed Ömer to catch his breath, Kerim said, 'What's wrong?'

Ömer sat down behind Eylul Yavaş's desk.

'I'd forgotten the boss was in today,' he said. 'I'm sorry, Kerim Bey, you know I have the greatest respect for him, and I wouldn't say this to anyone else . . .'

'I did ask you to take all those things off his desk.'

'I know. But I didn't expect him to scream,' Ömer said. 'It was as if I'd murdered his family or something.'

'You know what Mehmet Bey is like.'

'Yes, but even by his standards . . .' He shook his head. When they'd been sergeants together, Ömer and Kerim had become good friends, and although things had changed, and in spite of the fact that Ömer still didn't know Kerim was gay, they remained close.

Ever practical, Kerim said, 'Have you had coffee this morning?'

'Yes. At home.'

'Do—'

'No,' he said. Ömer leaned in towards his friend. 'Kerim, you know we don't talk about such things . . .'

Kerim Gürsel frowned, wondering what things Ömer might mean.

'The boss's personal life.'

'Ah.' That was a relief. Kerim had no doubt that even if Ömer knew he was homosexual, it wouldn't change anything, but still . . .

'I don't often say anything, as you know, but he looks terrible. As if he's not slept for weeks.'

Kerim held up a hand. 'Best not to speculate.'

But Ömer couldn't help himself. 'He's still seeing Çiçek Hanım, but he hasn't given Gonca Hanım up, he never will, and—'

The door opened and Süleyman walked in. Smiling, he said, 'Good morning, gentlemen, shall we make a start?'

He'd never been in a room like it. If Patrick Süleyman had been obliged to describe where he was, he would probably have said it was like something out of a fairy tale crossed with the science labs at his school. Presided over by a man who looked like an old goth, there were swords hanging from the walls and something that might be a guillotine. Çetin İkmen had told him they were going to see a magician, but he hadn't been expecting this. Magicians were tired middle-aged men who came to your birthday party and then fell over drunk. But Sami Nasi wasn't one of those. Çetin bey had informed him that Sami was the great-grandson of the most famous magician at the Ottoman Court, Professor Josef Vaneck. Perhaps that was why Sami Nasi made the hairs on the back of Patrick's neck stand up, even though he couldn't understand a word the man was saying. And then it got worse . . .

'Oh, you are Inspector Süleyman's son? I can see that so clearly!'

The voice, which came from behind, was female and light. Patrick turned and saw the head of a beautiful young woman looking at him from on top of a silver salver. He glanced away quickly and everyone except Patrick laughed.

Ruya, Sami Nasi's wife, could speak English, and so once she had put her head back on her shoulders, she came to show him around while her husband and Çetin İkmen talked. Just how such massive chemistry vessels had been got up five flights of stairs to sit on the floor and bubble away filled with who knew what, Patrick couldn't imagine. Ruya told him they were called alembics and that they were used by her husband in his practice of alchemy. Patrick had enjoyed a wonderful evening at the İkmens' apartment and had been looking forward to seeing a mad old magician fall over due to the drink, but this was doing his head in.

Mehmet Süleyman had always imagined himself in the role of Çetin İkmen's successor, but now he saw that man was actually Kerim Gürsel. Not only did Kerim put his feet up on his desk as İkmen had done, he also kept a very scruffy office, had been seen smoking occasionally, and asked the sort of questions İkmen would have asked, the ones that sat behind the crime.

'What were your impressions of Erol Gencer as a person?'

Kerim had never met the man, but Süleyman and Ömer had. Süleyman looked at his sergeant, who was seemingly lost in thought. Now, after the fact, he wished he'd not bawled him out quite so fiercely about the state of his desk. It had just caught him off guard, and after a night of so little sleep, he'd been ready to erupt. All that ridiculous business with Gonca's son had put him in a bad mood, only some of which the gypsy herself had been able to dispel. What really hurt was the knowledge that he'd been so intoxicated by her until that boy interrupted. It had been as if they were hormonal kids again, losing themselves in passionate kisses and caresses and bites . . .

'He'd not long had heart surgery when we saw him,' Ömer Mungun said. 'So he was a bit frail. Shaken up, of course, but he was not unduly frightened. The woman, Samira Al Hussain, had been trying to get to him for some months.'

'He'd not reported it?'

'No, although his wife said she'd tried to persuade him.'

'Why didn't *she* report it?'

'Don't know.'

'Her husband had experienced fanatical fans before,' Süleyman said. 'Given the position of the woman, an impoverished Syrian refugee, Erol Gencer didn't want to make trouble for her. Perhaps he thought she'd get deported. Anyway, that was the story. Gencer said he didn't know Samira Al Hussain, and when questioned, she changed her story about sleeping with him and said she didn't know him. She stuck to her story about meeting Betül at the storytelling event. Then finally, as you know, she confessed.'

'Mmm. What about her husband?'

'He claimed to know nothing about Gencer. We could identify no points of contact. Seeing Wael Al Hussain in Gencer's garden was a shock.'

'Al Hussain was at his wife's trial, sir,' Ömer said.

'Yes, but he and the Gencers were not together.'

'No.'

Kerim Gürsel sighed. 'This story Samira Al Hussain told,' he said. 'Did you ever give it any credence?'

'What do you mean?'

'Well forgive me, Mehmet Bey, but it sounds to me as if her story was dismissed.'

There was a moment of icy silence. It wasn't usual for anyone to challenge Süleyman's opinions, not even his friends.

Eventually he said, 'There was no evidence for it. There was no coffee house, no storyteller. How could someone like Betül Gencer have known about such a place even had it existed? She doesn't speak Arabic.'

'You know that?'

'I know she had a very basic education,' he said. 'She didn't attend high school. She later attempted to make up for it by attending Erol Gencer's psychology classes at Boğaziçi, which is where they met. Kerim Bey, I accept you may have some issues with my previous investigation—'

'I don't,' Kerim said. 'You did exactly what was required, Mehmet Bey. But what worries me in the light of this new investigation is a nagging doubt I have about Betül Hanım's love for her husband. I've read through Samira Al Hussain's statement and she was very clear that Betül Gencer wanted her husband dead. Then there's Berat Tükek's testimony that Gencer verbally abused his wife. There are questions to be answered here.'

Ömer Mungun watched without breathing as the two men looked at each other. When Süleyman finally smiled, he found himself letting his breath go in relief. Especially when the boss said, 'And I will help you, Kerim Bey, in any way I can.'

Sami Nasi poured İkmen a very large glass of brandy.

'You're not driving, are you?' he asked him.

'No. Çiçek uses my car more than I do these days,' İkmen said. 'The roads send me crazy.'

Sami smiled, then continued their conversation. 'There are so many tales about storytellers,' he said. 'Magicians without the sleight of hand. In terms of performance, we've been competitors since the dawn of time. What else is weaving a story if not magic?'

'Your father had one to stay here, I remember my mother speaking about it,' İkmen said.

Sami smiled. 'Dad let anyone and everyone stay,' he said. 'Provided they paid the entrance fee.'

'Which was?'

'If the guest was a magician, he had to teach Dad one of his tricks; belly-dancers danced for him, sometimes shared his bed; and storytellers, well, they were obliged to tell stories to keep us kids amused.'

'So did you ever come across a storyteller called Ahmad Al Saidawi?' İkmen asked.

'Seriously?'

He lit a cigarette and took a gulp from his glass. 'Come on, Sami,' he said. 'You know as well as I do that it's useless to talk about life and death in this context.'

'Ah, you have me.' Sami shrugged. 'The answer is no. But that doesn't mean that the teller of tales about the great Sultan Bayburs has never been in the city. Three hundred and seventy-two nights he kept them entranced in Aleppo – until the Ottoman governor told him to wrap it up or he'd distance his head from his body. That must have been some story. I should like to be able to weave that much magic. But no, he never stayed with us. Why?'

'There is a tale that exists that he was in Fatih last year.'

'I didn't hear it,' Sami said. 'Have you spoken to İbrahim Dede?'

'No, but I will when I leave here,' İkmen said. 'Al Saidawi came to spin his magic to his Syrian brethren in our lovely city.'

'Do you know what tale he told?' Sami asked.

'No.'

'Try to find out. It may give you a clue about his movements, about why he was here. Do you want to know where he is now?'

'Yes. He may have been witness to a crime.'

'You know that the rational explanation for this, and therefore the most likely, is that you're looking for a charlatan?'

'I do. My mother used to talk about a holy man back in Albania who was two hundred and fifty years old. I never quite believed it.'

'Why?'

'When I was a child, I don't know,' he said. 'I believed most things she said. As an adult, I suppose I've seen too many dead people for me to accept that it's possible.'

'Has Samira Al Hussain been informed about her husband's death?' Kerim Gürsel asked.

Eylul Yavaş had now joined her superior, Süleyman and Ömer Mungun. She looked up. 'The prison authorities have been told,' she said. 'Whether that information has been passed to the prisoner I don't know.'

'We should find out.'

'Yes, sir.'

'I should like to talk to her.' He looked at Süleyman. 'I'm assuming her Turkish is up to it.'

'Quite good, actually,' Süleyman said. 'Maybe I should accompany you. To put what she may say into context.'

'You're on leave,' Kerim said.

'And you could be going on leave any time soon,' Süleyman countered.

It was true. Sinem Gürsel could theoretically go into labour at any moment, since she'd passed her eighth month of pregnancy.

Ömer began, 'I could . . .'

The boss stared him down and Ömer fell silent.

'My son is perfectly happy staying with our family in

Arnavautköy,' Süleyman continued. 'And so while I would like to spend as much time as I can with the boy, I am prepared to accompany you to Bakırköy in order to assist, Kerim Bey.'

He had run the original investigation into the Gencers and he wasn't prepared to let it go just because he had leave to look after his son. Everyone else in that office could understand, although none of them could sympathise. Ömer Mungun, at least, knew that the Süleymans' dark yalı in Arnavautköy was a grim place, and unless the boy's uncle and cousin were there too, it would be dull for the poor kid. The boy's grandmother, as far as Ömer knew, didn't speak English and was as old as time.

'That's very good of you . . .'

'It's nothing.'

Kerim's face, Ömer observed, was somewhat at odds with what he was saying. He looked undermined.

Eylul, who was becoming accustomed to the men with whom she worked, broke the silence that ensued. She looked at Kerim. 'Sir, do you want me to call the prison to make arrangements?'

'Thank you, Sergeant, yes,' he said with a smile. Then he looked at Süleyman. 'And in the meantime, perhaps, Mehmet Bey, you would like to tell us about your investigation. Specifically I'd like to know more about how Betül Gencer and Wael Al Hussain responded to Samira's allegations.'

'With derision,' Süleyman said. 'In the case of Betül Hanım. Of course she was horrified that a woman had been stalking her husband and had actually tried to kill him, but the story behind that attempt I think amused her.'

'The one it was believed Samira had made up?'

'Yes. Apart from anything else, I couldn't find anyone who thought the Gencers' marriage was in trouble.'

'And yet there have been rumours,' Eylul said.

'What rumours?'

'Nothing serious. But when I went to visit her friend Kiyamet

Hanım this morning, she told me that some people in their circle gossiped about the fact the Gencers had never had children.'

'In what way?'

'I don't know exactly,' she said. 'I think maybe along the lines of although Erol had a child, why didn't he want one with Betül? Kiyamet Hanım was of the opinion that Betül didn't want any.'

Süleyman shrugged. 'That's her choice. Doesn't mean her marriage was in trouble.'

'No, but . . .' She frowned. 'Kiyamet Hanım said nothing out of place. It's just that I got the feeling from her that Betül wasn't necessarily an easy woman to be with. I don't really know why, I just did.'

Chapter 9

It was going to become unbearably hot later, and so Gonca Şekeroğlu had brought her latest work-in-progress out into the garden. She'd made a start on a piece of commissioned artwork for a Romanian collector. Roma like her, he wanted something that captured the spirit of the Hıdırellez spring festival so beloved by all travelling peoples in the Balkans. Gonca had something in mind around fire and flowers and the ribbons and slips of paper people tied to trees and rose bushes representing their wishes for the year to come. As a collage artist she used a wide range of materials, from paint to fabric, preserved flowers and even some human bodily fluids.

She'd made a start as soon as Mehmet Süleyman had left. Whenever he was around, she didn't have much time for anything or anyone else. Her work had suffered because of it over the years. She could have made much more money had he not been in her life. But then if he wasn't, she'd be sad and broken hearted and she might even have ended it all . . .

'He gone?'

She looked up and saw her son Rambo.

'What did you mean by yelling your head off at me last night?' she said. 'You knew Mehmet Bey was here. That discussion was for when you and I were alone.'

He sat down beside her.

'We can share his money.'

'It's not about his money and you know it! Anyway, you'll need that to go back.'

'I got all I could,' he said.

'Which would be fine if Harun Bey wasn't such a fucking bastard.'

They both sat in silence for a moment, and then she said, 'Anyway, I thought you said you were in love with the girl.'

He shrugged, and in spite of herself, Gonca sympathised. When she was twenty, she hadn't known what love was. Back then she'd been married to her first husband and already had four kids. She'd known she loved them, but men were another matter. She'd not really loved a man until she'd met Mehmet Süleyman.

'Well whatever's going on in your love life, the fact remains that you have to go back,' she continued. 'Harun Bey has delusions of grandeur that he's prepared to pay for, and I owe him. We just have to thank fate that his bride is a tiny thing.'

'She's fifteen.' Rambo smirked.

She hit him round the head.

'Ow!'

'It's no joke being a child bride!' she said. 'Why do you think I fought so hard to keep your sisters at home for so long?

'I was laughing at Harun Bey, not Elmas!' he said. 'How old is he now?'

Gonca lit a cigarette. 'I don't know. Seventy-five? He's had five wives so far. The only reason he wants Elmas is because he's addicted to Viagra. Sitting in that house in Tarlabaşı with a huge erection he can't control, and an even bigger ego. Poor little bitch! I never thought I'd say it, but I wish Hasan Bey was still alive . . .'

'He was a monster!'

'Yes . . .'

Before Harun Sesler, a thug called Hasan Dum had been the most powerful godfather amongst the Roma people of Tarlabaşı. When Dum had been murdered some years before, Harun, his cousin, had moved in to take his place. Old, fat and vicious, he was due to marry pretty local virgin Elmas in the autumn. The girl's father, long ago separated from her prostitute mother, had as good as sold the child.

'I don't know why you don't tell *him* about Harun Bey,' Rambo said.

She hit him on the head again, and although he didn't say anything this time, he rubbed the place with his hand.

'Stupid kid!' she said. 'What do you think Mehmet Bey could do about it?'

'Arrest him?'

'Don't be ridiculous!'

'He'd do anything for you,' Rambo said. 'Beat him up then?'

Gonca shook her head. 'I don't want him to,' she said. 'I don't want him to get hurt. Mehmet Bey is kept out of all this, do you hear me?'

'Yes.'

'I hate it when you throw the fact at him that he's not one of us. That's what the gaco do to us. But in this case he must be kept out of it. It's my own fault for getting into Harun's debt, and so I must pay.'

'And me,' Rambo said.

This time she stroked his head and smiled. 'You, my poor little boy, were just in the right place at the wrong time,' she said.

İbrahim Dede the Dervish lived in a tall Ottoman house that clung to one of the outer walls of the Topkapı Palace.

'This area is called Cankurtaran,' İkmen explained to Patrick Süleyman as they walked down the middle of the road because the pavement was too narrow for them to walk two abreast. 'Your father and I worked on a case years ago on this street.' He pointed at a dilapidated house on their left. 'The Sacking

House as was. A man killed his brother in there. Your father was my sergeant back then.'

'Before I was born.'

'Oh yes,' İkmen said. 'But it was on that case that your father and mother met. Your father faced down an armed man, as I recall. He was very brave.'

The boy said nothing. İkmen was becoming accustomed to his comments about Mehmet Süleyman's many virtues being ignored. Patrick might love his father, who knew? But he certainly didn't like him.

'Çetin Bey!'

He saw the old man sitting on the step outside his house. Tiny and brown as tree bark, İbrahim Dede wore a white shirt over baggy şalvar trousers, a crocheted taqiya cap on his head.

İkmen and the boy walked over to the man, who smiled. İkmen took the old dervish's right hand in his, kissed it, and then held it to his forehead in a gesture of love and respect.

'İbrahim Dede.'

The old man got to his feet. 'Come and take tea in the garden,' he said. 'It's far too hot to be inside.'

Patrick looked at the house. 'So is the back wall of the house the palace wall?' he asked.

'Yes,' İkmen said.

'Oh.'

'And now we must follow İbrahim Dede to his garden.'

'His garden?'

'Around the side of the house,' İkmen said. 'You will see.'

Although he didn't believe in any sort of overarching deity, Kerim Gürsel thanked God that Mehmet Süleyman and Ömer Mungun had left his office. Usefully, they were going to Süleyman's office to review their case notes on the attempted murder of Erol Gencer back in 2018. That might help a lot.

What was also helping was being alone with Eylul. Her calmly methodical approach to her work was a soothing relief after being with the two men, who had both, in their own ways, been in confrontational moods.

When Kerim had still been İkmen's sergeant, Süleyman had apparently 'stolen' a woman Ömer had been seeing from him. It had hit the younger man hard, and Kerim wondered whether he still harboured some personal resentment. And of course Mehmet Bey had been in a foul mood today, shouting and screaming because things had not been done his way in his absence. Kerim strongly suspected that Süleyman's love life was at the bottom of it. Dating İkmen's daughter while simultaneously bedding Gonca Hanım wasn't a good idea – if indeed that was what was happening.

His phone rang.

'Gürsel.'

'Oh, hello, Inspector,' Dr Sarkissian said. 'If you're free, I'd like to talk about Erol Gencer, or rather the poison that killed him. Have you got time now?'

'Absolutely.'

Kerim put his feet up on his desk and silently mouthed for Eylul to shut and lock his office door. She smiled. She knew he wanted a cigarette.

He lit up and said, 'Doctor.'

'As I think I told you before, Inspector, the substance that killed Gencer, Compound 1080, is very difficult for its victims to detect. Used in general on vermin, it has been designed not to imbue any food rats or mice may eat with any clues as to its lethal nature. Results of the final tranche of tests on Gencer's stomach contents, liver and kidneys show beyond doubt that he was exposed to a lethal dose of 1080.'

'Do you know how it was administered?'

'Not definitively,' he said. 'But going by the contents of

Gencer's stomach compared with that of Al Hussain, I would venture it was probably something they didn't share.'

'They ate together?'

'It seems so.'

The thought of Al Hussain and Gencer eating together was an odd one. Why would they?

'Forensic evidence would seem to suggest that Gencer killed Al Hussain,' the doctor continued. 'I can tell you that the murder weapon, cleaned of blood, was on the table beside the pool at which the men dined.'

'Where?'

'Stuck into a slab of tulum cheese. It is my contention that Gencer stabbed and, effectively, filleted Al Hussain at the dining table and then dragged him, dying, to the other side of the pool, maybe so that he could finish his meal in peace.'

'Doesn't really chime with the idea of Gencer as a caring doctor of the mind, does it?'

'Not really, no. So, to review, Gencer and Al Hussain enjoyed part of a meal together. Analysis of their stomach contents has revealed they ate bread, tulum cheese, tomatoes and cucumber, and drank approximately one glass each of a pinot noir wine called Kalecik Karası. Comes from Denizli, courtesy of an Irish vintner, I understand. Anyway, there was also a half-empty water carafe on the table, which I assume they also availed themselves of.'

'They shared everything?'

'Yes. It seems they consumed what can loosely be described as the starter before Gencer attacked Al Hussain. There was an untouched tray of İskender kebab in the kitchen, which was probably the main course. However, Gencer also had Scotch whisky in his system. There was none present on the table, but there was an empty bottle of Vichy water . . .'

'What?'

'French sparkling water. It was beside Gencer's place setting.'

'Is Compound 1080 always lethal?' Kerim asked.

'Yes, and as I mentioned, there's no antidote,' the doctor replied. 'Further, in the concentration I have observed, it would have acted upon Gencer within thirty to sixty minutes after ingestion. The question for me is: how was it administered and in what; and the question for you is: could it be possible that Gencer administered it to himself.'

'You mean suicide?'

'I do. I mean, after having murdered Al Hussain, had he lived he would now be looking at life imprisonment, wouldn't he?'

İbrahim Dede didn't speak English, so İkmen had to translate Patrick's words for him.

'He says that all this tea drinking reminds him of Ireland,' İkmen told the old man. 'Apparently they drink it all day long there too.'

İbrahim smiled at the boy. 'Tell him we all live in very sensible countries.'

İkmen translated, then said to the boy, 'I need to speak to İbrahim Dede for a little while. I am sorry if it will be boring for you.'

'Does he want to watch television inside?' the old man asked.

'Do you want to watch TV?'

Patrick shook his head and then put his hand in his pocket and took out a deck of cards. 'Ruya taught me some tricks,' he said. 'I'll practise.'

İkmen smiled. Ruya Nasi had given the boy a lesson in basic card magic when they'd gone to Sami's place, and Patrick had been enthralled. 'Good.' He patted the boy's back. 'Just let us know if you need anything, OK?'

'OK.'

İkmen turned to the old man. 'İbrahim Dede, I've come to you because—'

'You want to know whether I have provided shelter to a travelling meddah – or should I say hakawati,' İbrahim said. Then, seeing the look on İkmen's face, he added, 'Sami Nasi telephoned me. You know the rule about seeking the most likely, rational explanation, Çetin Bey.'

İkmen bowed.

'And while I can say with some certainty that all of my guests have given me their names,' the old man continued, 'whether they were lying or not, I don't know. Certainly no one has ever been here calling himself Ahmad Al Saidawi. Not that I am ruling out that he may have visited me in disguise . . .'

'This was in April and May last year,' İkmen said.

'Sadly I don't keep records, but . . .' İbrahim nodded his head. 'Syria is not a place for people who see beyond the ordinary, those from fragile communities . . . A lot have availed themselves of my hospitality; none have abused it. I am an old man, my children have left home and my wife is dead. I relish the company. All the better if such company is intelligent and interesting. Nothing comes to mind, but that doesn't mean that it won't, Çetin Bey.'

'I will leave it with you, İbrahim Dede,' İkmen said. 'I'm going to see Gonca Şekeroğlu.'

'Not with the boy.'

'No,' he said. 'Patrick will go back to his father soon.'

'So where is Mehmet Efendi?' the old man asked, using Süleyman's now defunct Ottoman title.

İkmen sighed. 'Working,' he said. 'Like I used to do when my children were young. I told him years ago that he should try not to follow my example in that respect, but he didn't listen, and here we are. As addicted to the job as I used to be.'

They sat in silence for a few moments while they watched Patrick produce the Queen of Hearts out of thin air, his face alive with wonder.

İkmen clapped. 'Bravo, Patrick! Brilliant!'

But then he felt the old man's hand on his arm and he looked around to find him looking very grave.

'A thought,' İbrahim said.

'Which is?'

'This Ahmad Al Saidawi, spinner of tales about the Egyptian Sultan Bayburs . . . you know that unlike so many of the hakawati, he doesn't have a grave?'

'I didn't know that, no,' İkmen said.

'He doesn't have a grave, and when I was young, I did once meet a man who claimed to have met him. This was in Damascus, and the man was a friend of my father. He also said, if my mind is not playing tricks on me, that he had once seen the Frenchman Napoleon Bonaparte when he conquered Egypt. But that is very far away in my mind now, Çetin Bey. I will have to meditate upon it to arrive at the truth.' He smiled. 'Now go and see the Gypsy Queen, Mehmet Efendi's Queen of Hearts, and see what tales she is willing to sell to you.'

Standing outside police headquarters wasn't comfortable for Pembe Hanım. Although she was dressed down for the occasion, she knew that at nearly two metres tall, she stood out in spite of her headscarf and stifling raincoat. Did she have the courage to go in?

Her lover was in there somewhere, a man she had hardly seen since his wife had become pregnant. Sinem's baby was due any day now and Pembe really wanted to see the woman she had cared for before her mother had decided to move in with the couple. But then how would Sinem Gürsel respond if she did see her?

Everything had gone wrong. When Kerim had married Sinem, it had been on the understanding that they'd become a couple in order to cover their real sexual preferences. But Sinem had not been entirely honest. Not only had she loved Kerim as a friend, she had also desired him, and now they were about to become parents. And in spite of the fact that Pembe knew Kerim was still in love with her, she also knew that anything they had together was ultimately doomed. And she was back on the streets. Kerim knew, but he didn't know to what extent. He didn't know about the Smack . . .

If she told him absolutely everything, what would he think of her? He'd find out what a user, what a manipulator, she was. He'd be horrified she was back on the gear. But she had something to tell him!

She saw Kerim's colleague, Inspector Süleyman, leave the building. Did this mean that Kerim would be leaving soon too? Pembe bit her lip. What Lagun had told her had made her think. Lover or no lover, she had information for Kerim Bey that she had to get to him somehow.

She shook her head and pulled her spine straight. Whatever she might face in there, she had to get on with it. There was no choice.

'Have you seen Mehmet's son?' Çetin İkmen asked. He'd met Süleyman in Sultanahmet Square and handed a reluctant Patrick back to him. The boy'd had a good morning among the magicians and esoterica of İstanbul, and had looked crushed when he'd got into his father's car. Mehmet would have to make things right between them before Patrick flew back to Dublin, or he'd lose him.

Gonca puffed on her cigar. 'Yes. You know me, I waited outside Mehmet's apartment block and saw them both leave together soon after the kid arrived. He's beautiful.'

'Like his father.'

'And his mother,' she said. 'Those emerald-green eyes . . . Maybe I'm projecting the little I know about Ireland, but they look pure Irish to me.'

İkmen laughed. 'He'd be so pleased to hear you say that!'

'Not that he ever will,' she said.

'No.'

They were sitting in her garden, looking at her latest work-in-progress, her interpretation of the Hıdırellez festival. So far İkmen could make out one dancing figure, all in red, and what looked like a celebratory bonfire.

'I like it,' he said as he pointed his cigarette at the canvas.

'I don't,' she said.

'Why not?'

'My heart's not in it.'

'You don't usually do anything your heart isn't in,' İkmen said. 'What's wrong?'

She shrugged. He'd come to talk to her about storytellers, but she very clearly had other things on her mind. She wasn't happy, and that concerned Çetin İkmen. Although she was sleeping with his daughter's boyfriend, she was still someone he cared about.

She looked up at him, but still she said nothing. It would take more than words to get her to open up, he felt. She was truly down, and although he thought he might know what was wrong, he knew he had to break down that sturdy carapace she wore to deflect attention.

He put his hand underneath her chin and pulled her face up towards his own. Then he kissed her, very gently, very lovingly, on the lips. It was a tender kiss, which she responded to in kind. But when it was over, she began to cry.

'Gonca.'

He put his arm round her shoulders and she laid her head on his chest.

'What's the matter?'

Once she'd calmed her sobs, she said, 'You know that is the kindest, sweetest kiss anyone has given me for a long time.'

He thought about her lover, his friend, and said, 'Mehmet . . .'

'Everything is passion and fire with him,' she said. 'I love him, but . . .' She shrugged again, then looked up at İkmen. 'Come to bed.'

He smiled. Now that was a temptation he'd not had put in his way for a very long time.

'Do you know when I last had sex, Gonca Hanım?' he said.

'When Fatma was alive?'

'Which was three years ago.' He shook his head. 'Apart from the fact that I would never betray Mehmet Bey, I have a strong suspicion that after all this time, it might kill me.'

'You won't know until you try,' she said.

'And betray my daughter as well as my friend? You know that's not my style,' he said. 'Anyway, I'm not your type, Gonca.'

'What is my type?'

'Tall, handsome, dangerous. I've never known you do short, ugly and a bit like a comfortable old slipper.'

She laughed, then said, 'You know, İkmen, I didn't say what I did because I wanted to get back at either Mehmet or your daughter. I do truly love you. I know you; we are alike. I should be with you.'

'But you're not,' he said. 'And you are in love with Mehmet.'

'So is your daughter.'

'No.' He hugged her. 'Çiçek is in love with a sweet young man she remembers from her childhood. A lovely twenty-six-year-old boy who used to take her and her younger siblings to Gülhane Park from time to time. He'd carry Kemal on his back and buy them all ice cream. They'd come home covered in the stuff. But that boy grew up and became the handsome, arrogant prince he was destined to be. And that is the man *you* love.'

'So you think . . .'

'My daughter has suffered a lot in the last ten years,' he said. 'Losing her marriage, her mother, her career. Sometimes I think about what my old friend Max Esterhazy said about her years ago.'

'He was a crazy man!' Gonca said.

'But he had something. He had magic, and he said that Çiçek had it too. Maybe that is her destiny.'

He hugged Gonca close and kissed her hair. She wiped her face with her sleeve and appeared to pull herself back together again. 'So why *are* you here, İkmen, if not for sex?'

Apparently a woman wanted to see him. When Kerim Gürsel heard a knock at his office door, he called out, 'Come.'

When he looked up, she was there, Pembe Hanım. He felt his eyes widen, his skin burn red, and he was grateful that Eylul had gone out to get coffee. He jumped out of his chair and pulled her into his office, closing the door behind her.

'What are you doing here?' he asked. 'We always said never at my place of work. Never!'

Pembe sat down. She could see he was furious and scared, but also, underneath that, just so joyful to see her.

'I have some information for you, Kerim Bey,' she said.

She was being very formal, in case anyone might be listening, and Kerim, once he'd managed to calm himself, took his cue from her. These walls, as he knew, could have ears.

'So, Miss . . .'

'My name is Hüseyin Kılıç,' she said, using the name she had been born with. 'But now my name is Pembe Hanım. As you can see, Inspector Bey, I am a transgender woman.'

Aghast, Kerim sat down again. Caught between wanting to kiss his lover and bawl her out, he said nothing.

'Last night, I met a friend. A woman of the streets, like me, in Tarlabaşı.'

'A trans—'

'No. But I'd rather not use her name, Inspector Bey. Well, she was asking about a man.'

'What man?'

'An Arab.'

He looked up at her, but she glanced away.

'He died recently,' Pembe said. 'Wael Al Hussain.' Then she did look into her lover's eyes as she added, 'He was a customer.'

'Mehmet Bey worked on the original attempt on Erol Gencer's life,' Gonca said.

'He did.'

'And now you think he got it wrong?'

'I'm not saying that,' İkmen said. 'I am simply working for Samira Al Hussain's sister, who does.'

He still had his arms around her. She was disturbed and needy and he didn't know why.

'What about Kerim Bey?' she asked.

'I've not spoken to him.'

'Have you spoken to Mehmet?'

'Yes,' he said. 'Although only in very general terms. He doesn't know what I'm doing.'

'Trying to find this storyteller?'

'No.'

She twisted around and looked into his eyes. 'So you're here to find out what I know about this man?'

He nodded. 'I know that when such people come through the city—'

'What people?'

'People like magicians, the mad, the bad, the spinners of tales – people like us,' he said. 'I know they sometimes lodge with the Roma. Especially a certain type of Roma.'

She smiled.

'His name is Ahmad Al Saidawi,' İkmen said. 'He came or comes from Aleppo. And although we don't know his exact age, it would seem he is somewhere in the region of three hundred years old.'

She didn't turn a hair, as he'd known she wouldn't.

'I know of him,' she said after a pause. 'A dead man who isn't, or is. In his time he would have travelled the Silk Road.'

'There is not just one Silk Road.'

'The route from Aleppo to Constantinople,' she said.

'Even if he did and does use that route, how does that help me?' İkmen asked. 'He could be anywhere now. He could be in the city. I know the Syrian refugees are vulnerable, I know they will and in fact probably should close themselves off from us. That is what minorities do when they feel threatened. And that is why I've come to you, Gonca, because you understand that.'

'I am not Syrian.'

'No, but you are an outsider.'

'After five hundred years here in the city.' She smiled.

'You keep some things just to yourselves,' he said. 'In fact I think you're keeping something significant from me now.'

'Let's just stick to Syrians, shall we?'

He paused, and then said, 'My point is made. Tell me what to do, Gonca. How do I get one of them to speak to me? I don't even know any Arabic.'

'A lot is at stake, Çetin Bey.' She kissed his cheek. 'And so I think it is a question of offering something.'

'Money?'

'Maybe. But I would go back to the sister if I were you. She will know something or someone.'

'I don't think so; that's why she came to me.'

'Oh, she does.' She kissed him again, and then she said, 'One thing I do know is that there is one Syrian who is very much wanted in this country.'

'Who?'

'One of my daughters has a man she sees sometimes who is Syrian,' Gonca said. 'Not a refugee. He works here in a . . .' She changed tack. 'Someone has stolen from the regime.'

'Stolen what?'

She shrugged. 'This person is sought, that's all I know. Oh, except it was some sort of personal theft. It wasn't arms or state funds.'

'And so?'

'It was from Assad himself,' she said.

Chapter 10

Mehmet Süleyman finished the call and put his phone back in his pocket. Kerim Gürsel had told him two things: firstly that they had an appointment to see Samira Al Hussain at Bakırköy women's prison in the morning at ten; and secondly that Wael Al Hussain had apparently had a transsexual lover. Although he hadn't said anything to Kerim, Süleyman wondered whether his colleague knew this unnamed person. But then just because Kerim was gay didn't necessarily mean he knew everyone in the LGBT community. Süleyman had to remind himself about generalising sometimes, because people did it to him too. He certainly didn't know every member of the former royal family – far from it. But that didn't stop people making assumptions.

He walked back into the kitchen, where his son was playing a game on his smartphone. The boy would either be devastated or he wouldn't care. Either way Süleyman knew he wouldn't be able to tell the difference. He was not good at being a parent to a teenager and he knew it.

'Patrick . . .'

The boy looked up.

'Yes.'

Süleyman sat down opposite him. He was such a beautiful boy. Dark, tall, with the most wonderful green eyes and cheekbones worthy of a supermodel. People said he looked like his father, but Süleyman could never remember himself being so beautiful.

'We have a trip tomorrow,' he said. 'On the Bosphorus.'

As well as being beautiful, Patrick Süleyman was also, like his mother, no one's fool. He said, 'And you have to work.'

'I am afraid I do.'

Mehmet Süleyman was no coward, but he couldn't meet his son's eyes. How could he, after the laissez-faire fathering he himself had experienced, be so careless about his own child? But then he knew exactly why in this instance. He had to see Samira Al Hussain; he had to know whether she was going to stick to her story about meeting Betül Gencer and making a pact with her, and whether Kerim Gürsel was going to believe her.

Patrick looked down at his phone.

'However,' his father continued, 'I have spoken to your cousin Edibe . . .'

'I wanted to go with you.'

Those green eyes were as sharp and accusatory as his mother's. How Mehmet had hurt and let her down! Inwardly he cringed.

'It would have been nice, I agree,' he continued. 'But Edibe is your cousin and she knows as much, probably more than I do, about the palaces of our family beside the Bosphorus. She will certainly take you somewhere very nice to eat when you reach Anadolu Kavağı.'

Bosphorus cruises aboard municipal Şehir Hatları ferries started from the Eminönü docks in the middle of the city and concluded just before the entrance to the Black Sea at a village called Anadolu Kavağı.

Still looking at his game, Patrick said, 'All right.'

His mother had told him his father was a busy man, just like she was a busy woman. Since his mother's father, his dede, had died, there had been no one just for Patrick, or so it seemed to him. Now he was being palmed off on his cousin – who he liked, but that wasn't the point. It was clear that his father didn't know what else to say, and so Patrick said, 'Mind if I go to my room?'

'No. I'll . . . Would you like to have dinner out tonight? In Nevizade Sokak?'

That was a lively enough part of Beyoğlu, but on his own with his father it wasn't a lot of fun. Patrick shrugged, went to his room and closed the door.

Madam Edith had first arrived in Tarlabaşı back in the late 1960s. Originally from Konya in central Anatolia, she'd been called Serkan Memişoğlu back then and had come to İstanbul to seek her fortune. Serkan, as was, had a head full of wild ambitions about becoming a film star or a singer, but like a lot of teenagers seeking their fortunes in big cities across the world, he had ended up turning to sex work.

Reflecting back on that time, Madam Edith would always say that the first ten years in the city were the worst, because it had taken her that long to get settled into her persona of French chanteuse Edith Piaf. Drag turned Serkan and his back-street blow-jobs into Madam Edith, a Piaf impersonator who made up for her lack of musical talent with raw, broken passion and a mouth like a sewer when it came to hecklers.

Although she'd lived in Tarlabaşı since the sixties, Madam Edith had moved around within the district and had shacked up with numerous people, both men and women, during that time. She'd been sharing with Pembe Hanım, on and off, for the last four years. And although until recently Pembe had also lived part of that time with her lover Kerim Gürsel and his wife Sinem, Edith's small apartment on Şahin Ağacı Caddesi was her home.

Knowing that Pembe was due to take on a shift at Kurdish Madonna's trans brothel later that evening, Edith had been shopping for a good dinner to sustain the girl through who knew how many inept and guilty straight men, and so when she arrived at her building she was laden down with bags full of food. Aubergine, onions, garlic, rice and lamb.

Four flights of splintering stairs almost did her in, but she finally arrived in one piece and put her key in the door just as old Neşe who lived opposite came out and yelled down the stairs for someone to come and rescue her from her wicked mother. Mad old woman needed to be in a home.

Edith walked in and let the bags of food slip out of her hands onto the floor. She kicked her shoes off her swollen feet and then called out, 'Pembe!'

There was no answer. The girl was probably out and about getting drunk somewhere. Or high. Edith just hoped she remembered that she'd promised to work for Kurdish Madonna. Poor Pembe spent a lot of time off her face these days. She missed Kerim Bey, poor bitch. And who could blame her? He was a lovely man, even if he was a copper. Kind, gentle, good looking too. What more could a girl want?

Edith walked into the kitchen, and it was then that her world exploded.

Difficult conversations were things Çetin İkmen never got used to. He'd had them all his life – indeed, he had made a career out of them – but they got no easier.

'Did you go to people you know in the Syrian diaspora and try to persuade them to tell you about this coffee house?' he asked Rima Al Numan.

They were sitting beside the fountain in Sultanahmet Square. She'd just finished work for the day.

'Of course!' she said. 'I know people who were there. But they don't speak.'

'Because they fear interaction with the Turkish authorities?'

'Yes! I don't know how many are here with papers . . .'

'Legally.'

'. . . how many not. I cannot ask for people to do something that mean they get sent back.'

'So you didn't push it?'

'What?'

'You were not, er, strong with them?'

'No!' She shook her head. 'How I do that? We are at war in my country.'

İkmen nodded. She was right, of course. But what if, as Gonca had suggested, there was another reason why Syrians were not talking? What if whoever had stolen from Assad had been there? What if the thief and the hakawati were one and the same? Was that what all the claims about immortality were disguising? The Assad regime was terrifying, and being sent back to Syria had to be a nightmarish thought. But if Gonca's story was true, surely there was a price on the head of whoever had stolen from Bashar Al Assad? And why did only marginalised people like the Roma know these things?

'Rima Hanım,' he said. 'Do you know anything about a theft – I don't know what of – from President Assad?'

'From Assad? No,' she said. 'Nobody get close to Assad. You mean taking things from his palace?'

'Not sure.'

'No.'

'Would your sister know?'

'I never hear such a thing,' she said. 'Assad, he like people to think is impossible to be close to him. If this even happen, no one will know.'

'OK.' He lit a cigarette. 'So these fellow Syrians who attended this coffee house, did the police interview any of them?'

'Police don't believe it,' she said. 'My sister tell them to go and find them, but nothing. I don't know. Samira's story they say is stupid. There is nothing. They don't listen! Only to Gencer's wife. Do you find hakawati, Çetin Bey?'

She looked so hopeful. He dashed those hopes.

'No. And I don't think I will,' he said.

'So it is hopeless.'

'Oh no,' he said. 'It's not hopeless. I'll just need you to help me, because I am not Syrian and I don't speak your language.'

'Help how?'

'I need to speak to Syrians,' he said. 'I need to persuade, seduce, maybe even frighten the truth out of them, and I need to start by identifying the most prominent person in that group in the coffee house the day your sister met Betül Gencer. I also need to speak to my colleagues in the police.'

'Why?'

'Because if we can find someone who will tell us the truth, then we will need to make sure that person doesn't get sent back to Syria.'

The screaming just went on. The drag queen who called herself Madam Edith and some crazy old Kurdish woman vying for screaming supremacy in a tiny part of Tarlabaşı seemingly gone insane. And then there was Inspector Gürsel. Eylul Yavaş had seen him work a few homicide scenes now, but she'd never seen him like this. His face was white and suddenly lined, his great black eyes staring, glazed with an unnatural stillness.

Eylul squatted down beside the pathologist, Dr Sarkissian. As usual a patch of still water in a boiling ocean, he said, 'Castrated.'

'What?'

The victim was a trans girl known, according to Madam Edith, as Pembe Hanım.

'Castrated today, Sergeant,' the doctor continued. 'That's why there's so much blood.'

'I thought . . .'

'The wound to the neck was, I think, administered as the victim was dying. The major sanguinous area emanates from the groin. Wonder where the penis and testicles are?' He looked around.

'Sir, it will take a while to search the scene.'

'Oh I know,' he said. 'Just be nice if they were close by. My profession is of necessity obsessive-compulsive about these things. I know in an ideal world that . . .' He looked at where she was looking, which was into Gürsel's face. 'Inspector?'

Scene-of-crime officers milled around him, but Gürsel didn't make a move.

The doctor looked at Eylul and said, 'Excuse me.'

It wasn't easy for an elderly man of some girth to get up from the floor, but somehow he managed it and walked over to Kerim Gürsel. The whole apartment stank of rakı and, the grotesque body aside, that alone was enough to make most people gag.

'Inspector?'

This time Kerim moved his eyes and then said, 'Doctor . . .'

Arto Sarkissian took one of his wrists between his fingers and looked at his watch.

'Forgive me, you don't look well.'

Eylul watched them – or rather, she watched her boss sway slightly. The doctor said, 'Good strong pulse, but really rather fast at the moment. Tell me how you feel.'

'I . . . ah . . .'

'Mmm. Well there's no point wondering what might be wrong,' the doctor said. 'Castration has a particular resonance for most men. Go into the other room and sit down.'

Kerim didn't move, and so the doctor took his arm and guided him out of the room.

Eylul had noticed a change in her boss as soon as they had arrived at the building. Usually a very businesslike officer, he had been visibly shaking by the time they'd got to the apartment. Now she looked down at the body on the kitchen floor. Like a lot of trans girls in the area, Pembe Hanım had both female breasts and male reproductive organs. Most of the girls worked the streets, and it was well known that a lot of men liked to have sex with them. Eylul knew better than to ask why. In places like Tarlabaşı, all sorts of tastes were catered for; 'chicks with dicks', as some people disparagingly called them, were just one example. Did Kerim Gürsel find it particularly stomach wrenching? she wondered.

Two phone calls from women. Both very different. The first was Çiçek, who had cut straight to the chase with 'How's Patrick?'

Mehmet Süleyman lay down on his bed and said, 'Asleep, I think.'

'It's not late. Aren't you taking him out to dinner?'

'He didn't want to go,' he'd said.

'But you've got tomorrow together, right?'

He'd told her he couldn't go because of work and there had been a silence. Eventually she'd said, 'You do know he's going back to Dublin in just over a week, don't you?'

'Yes . . .'

'So make the most of the time you have.' It had been by way of an order, and it had caused him to sigh.

She'd added, 'And don't get angry with me, Mehmet. I grew up like this, remember. My dad always promising to be places he never turned up to.'

'I'll make it up to him.'

'Will you?' she'd said, just before she slammed the phone down on him. 'Will you really?'

Less than a minute later, it had been Gonca.

'Baby, I have to go over to Tarlabaşı to see my brother,' she'd said. 'Can I come and visit?'

As well as having a son called Rambo, Gonca also had a brother of the same name who ran a very low-rent nightclub.

'Patrick is here.'

'He's sixteen,' she'd replied. 'I was married with a baby by that age.'

Mehmet had heard himself groan. The last thing he needed was for his son to see him with the woman who had, in part, broken up his parents' marriage. He'd also be disgusted that his father was cheating on Çiçek.

'He goes to a strict Catholic school run by Jesuits.'

'I don't know what that is! Do you want me to come and see you or not?'

'We agreed not until Patrick goes home . . .'

'Fine!'

And then she'd put the phone down on him too. Of course she had wanted sex, to which he wasn't averse, but she wasn't the most discreet or quiet individual, and if she woke Patrick with her screams, Mehmet knew he would die of shame. There was of course a wicked side of him that wanted her to ignore what he'd said and come over anyway . . .

Madam Edith put a hand up to Kerim Gürsel's face. 'What are you doing here, Kerim Bey?'

He was crying, silently. 'There was no one else . . .'

She reached into her black lace handbag and took out a packet of cigarettes.

'Who would hurt her?' Kerim asked as he lit up. 'Who?'

'I don't know. Some punter.'

'They cut her—'

'I know what they cut off!' she said, squeezing her eyes shut at the thought of it. 'I will never be able to unsee that.'

'You know we were not seeing one another,' he said.

'She was in love with you.'

He closed his eyes.

'But she understood,' Edith continued. 'She loved Sinem too, in a different way.'

'If only Sinem's bloody mother hadn't come to stay! Left alone, the three of us would have been fine.'

Edith shrugged. 'She's a Turkish mother, what else would she do?' she said.

'I wish I'd never—'

Edith put a hand up to his mouth and shook her head. 'Don't say it,' she said. 'Your baby is a fact, Kerim Bey, and he or she will love you.'

'Yes, but Sinem . . .'

'She loves you too. You love her. You got her pregnant, Kerim Bey, you owe her.'

'I know. It's not Sinem's fault.'

'So keep reminding yourself of that,' Edith said. 'Pembe was, I know, your lover. You adored each other. But the only thing you can do now, Kerim Bey, is to find her killer. And luckily, my dear boy, finding killers is your job.'

Rima sat on her bed and stared at the wall. The Turk, İkmen, was either mad or someone was having a laugh at his expense. Nobody stole from the Al Assads, nobody. But then who would have thought that the uprising against them back in 2011 would still be raging eight years later. That family had always behaved with utter ruthlessness, and previous breaks for freedom had been put down with staggering brutality.

Rima remembered her cousin İman, who had joined the older Assad's all-female regiment back in the 1990s. One of the tests of loyalty she was obliged to perform in his presence was to bite the head off a snake. Poor İman had literally lost her mind. But she did it, and for years she told no one and made no complaint. Because people didn't say, do or even think anything against the Assads. And although the people had eventually risen up to fight their brutality in 2011, the regime was now gaining ground again. Bashar, with help from his Russian allies, was set to win.

So who on earth would take anything from him now that he was almost completely all-powerful once again?

*

Gonca hadn't been to see her brother and they both knew it. Süleyman made a pretence of being casual about the whole thing by making her a gin and tonic, and they both spoke in hushed tones, but as soon as he took her into his bedroom, everything changed.

'You must be quiet,' he said as he pulled down the zip at the back of her dress. 'And don't talk dirty or—'

She laughed.

'Shh!'

He threw her dress onto the floor and laid her on his bed.

'Baby, I've been thinking about you all day,' she whispered. 'I know this is my fault.'

'It's mine too,' he said, as he took his clothes off and lay down beside her. 'I could've said no.'

She began to run her hand along his erect penis.

'You know one way to silence me,' she said.

'Yes, but when you do that, I am very noisy,' he said. Then he kissed her. 'Not that I'm saying no . . .'

And then his phone rang. He reached for it, but Gonca got there first and switched it off.

'Gonca! That might be important!'

She shrugged. 'You're on leave.'

'Yes, but—'

'You should relax more and have some fun,' she said.

Suddenly he looked grave. She put a hand up to his face, and he kissed it. 'What is it?'

'I was thinking that was how we got into this,' he said. 'You and me. All those years ago, when you took me back to your house and I ended up staying for two days. You told me I needed some fun back then.'

'You did.' She laughed. 'I showed you every trick in my book.'

'And then we lived together for a while.'

'Until you decided you needed to fuck around.'

He looked into her eyes. 'Where are we going, Gonca?'

Chapter 11

It was the straw that broke the camel's back. Not only had Pınar Hanım been there when he had finally got home at two in the morning, now she was in his kitchen and underneath his feet, talking.

At first Kerim simply ignored her. He'd already put the samovar on and so he knew that tea was on its way, but apparently he hadn't done this in the right way. He continued to ignore her.

When he had finally managed to leave the crime scene at around 1 a.m., he'd spent a little time talking to Eylul and Dr Sarkissian before they had all gone their separate ways. 'Better' was how he had described himself to them as they had parted, although whether they believed him or not, he didn't know. Or care. Pembe was dead and it felt as if the pain would kill him. Every muscle, bone and organ ached. He'd arrived home to a furious reception courtesy of Pınar Hanım, and had gone to bed and cried with his head in Sinem's arms. She'd cried too, because she had loved Pembe. Then, triggered by something he couldn't begin to understand, he'd made love to his eight-months-pregnant wife, and she'd held him, rocking him like a baby.

Now he had to go with Mehmet Bey to Bakırköy women's prison to speak to Samira Al Hussain. And in addition to what they were going to ask her anyway, now they had to do this in the light of Pembe's death. Because prior to her death, less than a day before, Pembe had told him something.

'Wael Al Hussain was a customer,' she'd said.

'Of yours?'

She had nodded. Kerim knew she had other men in her life; it was how she made her living now that she was no longer Sinem's carer.

Almost the last thing she'd said to him had been, 'Wael was very into me. I'm sorry.'

He'd said it was OK, but he should have kissed her to make her feel secure. He hadn't because he'd been in his office. He regretted it bitterly.

'. . . home at a reasonable hour tonight,' Pınar Hanım was wittering. 'Leaving my daughter in her condition! You're the man, you've got the car! No point asking me . . .'

'Get out!' As he stood, Kerim upset the chair behind him.

'I beg your—'

'Get out of my apartment, Pınar Hanım!' he yelled. 'Get out and don't come back!'

It was clear from the expression on her face that she was outraged, but she wasn't going to back down.

'How dare you speak to me like that, you disgusting little pervert!'

Kerim felt as if he'd been smacked in the face. Did she know? How?

'Oh yes!' She nodded her head. 'You think I don't know? Unnatural and disgusting you are, you—'

'Mum!'

Sinem, her hair tangled around her shoulders, thin hands clutching her crutches, had risen from her bed and shuffled into the kitchen.

'Get back to bed, Sinem!' her mother ordered. 'Although why I'm bothering with you . . . It's that unborn child I fear for! The two of you, having sex . . .'

She'd heard them. Sinem walked over to Kerim and he put an arm round her.

'I don't know what this is about,' Sinem said, 'but I want you to go too, Mum.'

'What, and leave you with him?'

Sinem leaned on Kerim. 'He is my husband and I love him.'

'He's a—'

'I know what he is, Mum!'

The two women looked at each other, and then Sinem said, 'I always have. He is also the father of our child and the love of my life. Now please get your things and go. We will pay for a taxi to take you home.'

'If you tell me to go now, I will never come back and neither will anyone else in our family!' Pınar threatened.

But Sinem had reached a place – between her own tiredness and pain and the love she felt for her husband and her child – where she really didn't care.

'Just go,' she said. 'And let there be an end to it if that is what is written.'

'Patrick?'

It was 6.30 a.m. and the boy was standing in the street outside his father's building.

He looked at her and smiled. 'Çiçek,' he said. 'Hello. I'm waiting for my cousin Edibe.'

Çiçek remembered that Mehmet had palmed his son off on his niece.

'What time is she due?' she asked.

'Seven thirty.'

'You're way too early!'

'I know, but . . .'

Had his father pushed him out the door, or had he left because he wanted to get away from him? Çiçek put an arm around his shoulder. 'Come with me. It's my turn to open up the café. I'll make you some coffee and breakfast. Anyway, Edibe will be late.'

'How do you know?' he asked.

'Because she's a Turk, and Turks are always late.' She laughed. 'Haven't you noticed?'

'Er . . .'

'Of course you have! You're just too polite to say. Send her a text and tell her you'll be in the Yemenli Café. She knows where we are.'

He smiled.

'I will cook you my special menemen for breakfast,' she said.

'What's that?'

She looked at him aghast. 'You don't know? Well let me educate you. It is delicious.'

'Did you watch the Erol Gencer show, Rima Hanım?'

Niyazi, Güven Bey's 'boy', who helped customers try on jackets, made tea and basically did everything else while his boss charmed foreign tourists, wasn't very smart. But he did, on his one day off per week, watch a lot of TV. Like Güven Bey, he had no idea that Rima was the sister of the woman who had tried to kill Gencer back in 2018.

'No,' she said. 'I do not have television.'

'Oh, that's sad.'

Rima switched on the vacuum cleaner and began to pick up crumbs, bits of leather and fluff from the carpet. The boy was nice enough, but he seemed to want to talk about Erol Gencer, which Rima did not.

İkmen had told her that what he needed was some sort of 'in' with the Syrian community. But Rima didn't have that. Samira had been the one who had got involved with them. Rima had concentrated on trying to get to know the Turks, mainly because she believed that this was it now and they would never go home.

Trusting fellow Syrians, unless one already knew them, was difficult. Everyone knew that the regime had spies outside the country, and because Rima was an Alawite, like the ruling caste, she was always in danger. Also she had no idea where İkmen had picked up this idea that someone, possibly in Turkey, possibly not, had stolen something from Assad. Whoever had done that had to be insane! The things the Assad family did to people were indescribable.

But what if it were true? Although how that affected her sister's dilemma, Rima couldn't imagine. However, while she was vacuuming, pondering these things, she did come up with a name that could be useful to İkmen. A Syrian, powerful in the local community, someone she occasionally went to see – and her drug dealer.

'Gonca?'

She lifted her head off the pillow and looked at her watch. 'Seriously?'

'Patrick has gone to meet his cousin and I need to meet Kerim Bey.' Mehmet Süleyman, washed and dressed, sat on the side of the bed. 'I let you sleep for as long as possible. If you don't mind my not driving you home, you can take a shower; if not, I'll take you now.'

She sat up, pushing the duvet back to expose her nakedness.

'Do I have time for a smoke?'

'One,' he said. He gave her a cigarette and lit it for her.

'Well that was an unusual night,' she said. 'I hadn't expected all that talking.'

He smiled. He hadn't meant to talk to her almost all night. But when she'd spoken about how they had met, he'd felt compelled to do so. Whoever either of them became involved with, they always went back to each other in the end. Their relationship was fiery; she'd even threatened to kill him once. But they were in love, and not just because they continued to fulfil each other's sexual fantasies.

'We need to do more,' he said.

'Why?' She took one of his hands and pressed it against her breast. Reflexively, he massaged it. 'We're fine as we are, baby.'

'With me seeing Çiçek İkmen and you doing who knows what? No,' he said. 'We either need to be together—'

'I'm not getting married!'

'I'm not asking you to.'

'I did that twice, never again!'

'But we should be together – or not,' he said. 'I spend large parts of my life wanting you, and I suspect you spend a lot of time wanting me too.'

'All the time!' She leaned forward and licked his mouth. 'Baby, what if I don't have a shower and you don't take me home and we have sex instead?'

'It's scrambled eggs with . . . stuff,' Patrick said. He looked up at Çiçek, 'It's lovely.'

'Scrambled eggs, you call it?'

'Yes, beaten-up egg in a pan,' the boy said. 'Mammy does it sometimes but not with the onions and peppers and stuff. Scrambled eggs just come with butter. Everything in Ireland comes with butter.'

She laughed. 'That sounds wonderful!'

'It can be a bit boring,' he said.

He carried on eating and she made him a cappuccino.

'Çiçek?'

'Yes, darling?'

'You know you're going out with my father?'

'Yes . . .'

'Do you think you'll marry him?'

Well that was a question!

'I don't know,' she said. 'We have to see how things work out.'

'Oh.' He went back to his food, a little crushed, she felt.

She sat down beside him. 'You know, I remember when your parents got married. Have you seen the photographs?'

'No.'

Çiçek had always liked Süleyman's wife, Dr Zelfa Halman, but from what she could gather, it seemed she had all but cut her ex out of her life. Which was all well and good unless you had children. Patrick had been born in İstanbul and had spent the first four years of his life in Turkey. But he apparently knew or remembered nothing.

'It was at the Pera Palas Hotel,' she said. 'I met your grandfather, a very nice man. It was a big party and a man even came from the Irish consulate. And then of course there was also your father's parents and your Uncle Murad and Edibe.'

'Scary Granny.'

She looked at him and saw that he was red in the face from trying to hold in a laugh. She smiled. 'Nur Hanım, yes,' she said. 'She can be a little bit frightening.'

'That house she lives in . . .' The boy shook his head.

Çiçek patted him on the back. 'It is very dark,' she agreed.

'She doesn't like us using the pool.'

'Yes, but I do not think even your grandmother could stop your cousin from going swimming. Anyway, I have to go outside for a while to put out the flowers. Will you be all right here on your own?'

'Yeah.'

She walked to the front door of the café, picked up some plant pots containing small conifers and went outside. It was still early, and so the heat of the day hadn't yet swung in. After she'd put the pots down on the ground, Çiçek looked around. Cihangir was a nice place to work. Full of little cafés and bars as well as some really interesting shops.

As she looked up towards Sıraselviler Caddesi, she found that her eyes lingered on Mehmet Süleyman's apartment building. How could he have just allowed Patrick to wander out of his apartment on his own? The boy didn't know the city; anything could have happened. Mehmet should know better. But then should he? As the spoilt younger son and the handsome prince, probably not.

She was just about to go back inside the café when she saw a tall, brightly coloured figure leave the building. Gonca Şekeroğlu.

The guard who escorted her wasn't someone Samira Al Hussain had seen before. A young man with an expression of pure hatred on his face. Perhaps he was new. What he wasn't was outside the usual mould. A grunt in a uniform. But then even when these law enforcement people dressed in suits, it didn't mean anything. That Inspector Süleyman she was seeing again today had just ignored everything she'd said, which had resulted in her being in this place and Betül Gencer walking free. But now, she understood, things had changed. Now Erol Gencer was dead, and Wael also. Samira wondered whether she should feign grief, but decided she wouldn't. She had admitted during her trial that she'd wanted her husband dead; there was no point lying about it now.

Süleyman had someone else with him this time, so maybe he or she would listen. But Samira didn't hold out much hope. Although her Turkish hadn't been bad before her arrest, during her initial detention and interrogation what they said had not made sense to her. They'd had to bring in an Arabic translator. She didn't need one now. What was there to be frightened of once the worst had happened?

Rima, according to her letters, was still trying to get her out somehow. Poor Rima, she didn't understand. Samira didn't necessarily want to get out. She had been quite rightly convicted of attempted murder. What she resented was that the other party involved had walked free. And who knew, maybe she had finished off her poor husband after all. Although why Wael had died too was a mystery. Samira still needed her day in court to tell her truth. Because that needed telling; because that in a sense, in part, did help her cause.

Kerim Gürsel had sent a text to ask Süleyman whether he minded driving out to Bakırköy. He hadn't, and when he had arrived at headquarters, he'd found Kerim waiting in the car park for him. He looked alarmingly unwell. Pale and haunted. When he got into the car, he just said, 'Good morning,' and then descended into silence. It wasn't like him.

Once they were on the road, and stuck in an inevitable traffic jam, Süleyman said, 'You're quiet, Kerim Bey. Is there anything wrong?'

Kerim turned to look at him and said, 'Didn't you get Dr Sarkissian's message?'

And then he remembered that Gonca had switched off his phone when someone had tried to call him the previous night.

'No. Patrick is staying and—'

'We attended a scene in Tarlabaşı,' Kerim said. 'One of the trans girls. Must've been killed sometime yesterday afternoon.'

'Oh. Well that happens sometimes,' Süleyman said. 'They're vulnerable.' And then, realising he might have been too flippant, considering who he was talking to, he added, 'It's terrible.'

Çetin İkmen had told him a long time ago that Kerim was homosexual. Back then, he had been involved with a trans girl. But Süleyman had never spoken to him about it himself. All his information had come from İkmen.

'Whoever did it castrated her,' Kerim said.

'Oh, that's—'

'It was awful!' He turned away. 'I've never seen anything . . .'

The only way forward was to treat this in exactly the same way as he would any homicide.

He didn't know whether this girl was the one Kerim had been involved with or not. Although given his colleague's appearance, he surmised that he probably knew her. 'Any witnesses?' he asked.

'No,' Kerim said. 'Only some demented woman who lives opposite who seemed to think her mother had done it.'

'How was she discovered?'

'She lives . . . lived with a drag queen. She came home yesterday and . . . there she was. And there's something else . . .'

What was this? Was Kerim going to come out to him? In a way, Mehmet hoped he was. The awkwardness of this conversation was making him sweat.

'My wife and I once employed this Pembe Hanım,' Kerim said. 'As you know, Sinem is disabled, and because I couldn't be with her during the day, we hired Pembe.'

'Yes, ah, that makes sense . . .'

But it didn't. Why had he employed a trans girl as opposed to a nurse? He wasn't poor, he could afford professional help. Mehmet snatched a glance at his passenger and saw that he was looking at him intently.

Kerim said, 'You know, don't you?'

'Know what?' Now he was obfuscating, and it irritated him. 'That you're homosexual? Yes,' he said.

There was a pause, then Kerim said, 'How did you know?'

It was pointless to lie. Kerim was no fool.

'Çetin Bey,' Süleyman said. 'But he had your best interests at heart. He only told me because he wanted me to look out for you. I know I may come across as the sort of man who might disapprove, but I don't. My own romantic life is far from exemplary, as you know. And I do care for you, Kerim Bey. You are a good officer and a friend and I value you on both counts.'

There was a slight sound that could have been a sniffle from his passenger, and then Kerim said, 'That means so much to me.'

'Then we will talk of this again later,' Süleyman said. 'After we have interviewed Samira Al Hussain. We will decide how to move forward.'

'Good morning, Doctor.'

'Ah, good morning, Sergeant Yavaş,' Arto Sarkissian said. 'I've been trying to get hold of Inspector Gürsel.'

'He's at Bakırköy interviewing Samira Al Hussain, sir,' she said. 'Can I help you?'

'An interesting development,' he said. 'If you could pass it on to the inspector I would be grateful.'

'Of course.'

She brought up the notepad on her tablet and prepared to make a record of this conversation.

'On preliminary examination, the cause of death of Pembe Hanım, otherwise known as Hüseyin Kılıç, was exsanguination due to full castration of both the testes and the penis. Quite a feat, it must be said, although it was not achieved without assistance.'

'The killer had an accomplice?'

'No, or rather I don't think so,' he said. 'The assistance I refer to was chemical. If you recall, when we entered the apartment the whole place stank of rakı.'

'Yes.'

'Forensics tell me they found two ceramic cups from which they believe the liquor was drunk, but no bottle.'

'OK.'

'Whoever visited must have taken it with him,' the doctor said. 'Assuming it was a man, which I think is fair given Pembe Hanım's profession.'

Most of the trans girls made their living on the streets, Pembe Hanım being no exception.

'In addition,' he said, 'and here is where it becomes interesting, my toxicology analysis request has come back positive for not just alcohol but also diazepam. A considerable dose, which if combined with alcohol could result in confusion, inertia, loss of consciousness. Of course, we don't know who administered this. It may be that Pembe Hanım had a diazepam habit anyway, or perhaps she had been prescribed the drug. But due to the paucity of defence wounds on the cadaver, I think it is safe to say that when the penis and testes were removed the victim was in a state of torpor at the very least. Pain would have to some extent counteracted the hypnotic effects of the drug, but not enough I think to cause the assailant too many problems. Also, Pembe Hanım was taking hormone therapy, which meant that her physical strength was somewhat diminished when pitted against a testosterone-filled man in particular.'

'Could the murderer have administered the drug to her?' Eylul asked.

'It's possible,' he said. 'Diazepam comes in tablet form. Ground down and mixed with the spirit, it's possible. So far forensics have not identified any benzodiazepines on site, although that doesn't mean they won't. Oh, I should add that the victim hadn't eaten for some while.'

'Thank you, I'll pass that on.'

'Good. You can also pass on some information I have received from forensic examination of the apartment used by Wael Al Hussain,' he said.

'Oh?'

'Not a lot of interest, with the exception of a small box that was found underneath the sink. I do recall it being bagged up at the time, because one of the scene-of-crime officers commented that the lettering on it was not Roman. I assumed wrongly that it was Arabic.'

'So what was it?' Eylul asked.

'Hebrew.'

'Oh.'

'Yes. I am reliably informed that it tells any reader that the substance inside is hazardous, to wit Compound 1080.'

'The stuff that killed Erol Gencer?'

'It seems so. I have also learned that this substance is used in Israel to kill rodents. So, Sergeant, the question has to be: how did a Syrian national get hold of it, and what did he do with it when he did?'

Chapter 12

One day the imam's son was visited by the principal wife of one of the sultan's most powerful paşas. And although her face was covered, as her religion required, the scarf she used was of very fine, almost transparent silk. When he saw her, the imam's son was captivated. She was so beautiful!

Gonca slashed the canvas and all the embellishments on it to pieces. Crying and screaming, her hair dragging across wet blobs of acrylic she'd squeezed onto her palette in an effort to distract herself. But it had done no good. She'd returned home smelling of her lover, something that usually made her happy, but she was also confused.

If he wanted to be with her, why didn't he want to get married? Oh, she had said she didn't want that, but she had been lying and surely he would know that? But then he had been lying too. Or had he? Had he said he wouldn't marry her because she wouldn't want that? She couldn't remember and it wasn't important. She knew why he wouldn't marry her and so did he.

Her fame, which was diminishing, made no difference. All her wealth had gone to her children – their useless fathers having no interest in them beyond boasting about how many of them there were. But even if she was still Turkey's foremost Roma artist, it would make no difference. She was Roma and her lover was not. He had a respectable job and came from a family of quality. He couldn't marry her even if he wanted to. That mother of his would probably disinherit him, and the police . . . What would they do? Probably snigger behind his back, make sure his career never progressed.

She couldn't do that to him. She threw a pot of blue paint across the studio at a finished canvas that was due for delivery to a customer. She didn't care. She slumped down onto the floor in a puddle of red oil paint she'd thrown around earlier, and cried.

'Mum?'

She looked up and saw her son, Rambo. She quickly pulled herself together and wiped her arm across her face. Unfortunately she smeared red paint across her nose.

'I thought you'd gone,' she said.

'Tonight.' He sat down beside her, carefully avoiding the paint. 'What's happening?' If she hadn't been crying, he would have been tempted to think that maybe she had been experimenting with a new technique.

'Nothing.'

He looked at her. 'Is it him?' he said. 'Has he been fucking other women again?'

She didn't reply.

'I could have him sorted,' the boy said. 'If you'd let me.'

'Well, I won't!' She put her head in her hands. 'You've got to come back as quick as you can.'

'I told you I would.'

'Well you must,' she said. 'You know what a fucking lunatic Harun Bey is. I've not done nearly enough and he's coming over tomorrow. The only way I'll be able to stall him is if I can tell him we've more on the way.'

'There will be more,' Rambo said.

'Well you'd better be sure,' she said. 'He's getting married in two weeks' time, and if I don't deliver, you know what will happen.'

*

It had been just possible to see the inmates' exercise yard from the admin block, but because the glass was tinted, they couldn't see you. The guard who took them to the interview room explained.

'Some of them have been here for so long, if they see a man who isn't one of us, it agitates them,' he said.

Süleyman looked at Kerim Gürsel, who shook his head. It was clear that he was thinking, *poor things . . .*

The guard unlocked the door and let them into a room. A second guard stood over by the far wall, which was, if the officers were not mistaken, a two-way mirror. A woman, small and very dark, sat behind a table fiddling with an unlit cigarette. Probably late thirties or early forties. Samira Al Hussain.

The two men sat down and she looked at them. She pointed to Süleyman, 'I know you.'

'Yes.'

'What you want this time?' she asked. 'I know Wael is dead, by the way. And Erol Gencer.'

'I'm sorry . . .'

She shrugged.

Kerim cleared his throat. 'My name is Inspector Gürsel,' he said. 'It is my job to investigate the unlawful killing of your husband and Mr Gencer.'

'So you think of me,' she said. 'Because it's easy? I think so. But you know I am here all the time. I cannot walk through the walls.'

'We understand that.'

'You are not a suspect, Samira,' Süleyman said.

'So? Why you come here?'

'We'd like to go over what happened when you met Betül Gencer in the coffee house in Fatih,' Kerim said.

'I tell you this.'

'We need to hear it again,' Süleyman said. 'And before you tell us we won't believe you, maybe we will.'

She looked at Kerim. 'Because you disagree with him?' she asked.

'No . . .'

She laughed. 'You do,' she said. 'You fucking disagree with the big boss man!'

Çetin İkmen had always had a way of getting what he wanted from people. Sometimes he made this obvious and sometimes he didn't. Falling into the latter category were instances where people just arrived at his apartment unbidden. Ömer Mungun, on a rare day of leave, was thinking about this as he sat on İkmen's balcony waiting for İkmen to bring him tea.

What was he doing here? And why? He didn't know, even though he was fairly sure that İkmen did.

When İkmen returned with the tea, he said, 'So, Ömer Bey, Syrians . . .'

'Syrians?'

'You were brought up around a lot of them. Before the war, that border between Turkey and Syria at Nusaybin was almost walking distance for you.'

'Çetin Bey,' Ömer said, 'can you please just ask me what you want to know?'

İkmen laughed.

Ömer said, 'In spite of coming from Mardin, I don't always understand how these things work. You've summoned me here by some method . . .'

'No!'

Ömer looked at him.

'And yes,' İkmen said as he lit a cigarette. 'Look, I know Mehmet Bey is working in spite of his son being in the city, and I know what he and Kerim Bey are working on.'

'Çetin Bey . . .'

'Nothing to do with Erol Gencer, I swear,' İkmen said. 'But that woman who tried to kill Gencer last year, she interests me.'

Strictly Ömer should say nothing, but this was Çetin Bey and so . . .

'The boss and Kerim Bey have gone to see her in Bakırköy,' he said. 'Kerim Bey wants to reconsider her story about a Syrian café in Fatih.'

'Do they suspect Betül Gencer then?'

'I don't know,' Ömer said. 'To be honest, they're not really telling us, me and Sergeant Yavaş, very much.'

'Why not?'

'I don't know.' Then he thought for a moment and said, 'They both seem distracted.'

'Distracted? How?'

He shrugged. 'Apparently Kerim Bey was called to an incident last night and wasn't very well, but that's all I know.'

'Mmm.' İkmen frowned. 'Ömer, I know you have a Suriani contact in the city, a drug dealer.'

'From Urfa.'

Like a lot of Syrian Christians, this man, Wahid Saatçi, had actually been born and raised in Turkey. But he had relatives across the border.

'I need to ask a Syrian about—'

'The hakawati?' Now Ömer knew why he had come. 'Yes, we know of this Ahmad Al Saidawi,' he said. 'The dead-but-alive storyteller. The boss couldn't believe it.'

'Did you try to persuade him?' İkmen asked.

Ömer smiled. 'Little Ömer who sees a snake goddess on the Mesopotamian plain? No.'

The Mungun family, like a select but influential few in Mardin, worshipped a Mesopotamian snake goddess called the Şahmeran.

İkmen frowned. 'Do you think he's getting narrow minded in

his old age? He always made time for magic back in the day, even though I know he has no belief.'

'Ah, that was you, Çetin Bey,' Ömer said. 'And don't refer to him as old, whatever you do!'

'He's fifty.'

'Yes, but look at him! Anyway, I'll see what I can do,' Ömer said. 'The hakawati have been known to come through Mardin on the old route to Aleppo. I grew up on their stories. Oh, and we had a djinn in our kitchen too, just like yours but bigger.'

İkmen had never even thought about whether Ömer Mungun could see the djinn that lived beside the oven, but of course for a man who talked to a goddess, a lot of things were possible.

Samira Al Hussain had coarsened during her time in prison. When Süleyman had first interviewed her, she'd been so timid she had barely been able to speak. Now her Turkish had improved, and that included her mastery of cuss words.

She said to Kerim, 'Did you read my fucking statement? He show it you?'

'Yes,' Kerim said.

'Is still the same.' She lit her cigarette. 'No change.' She turned her head away.

'But we have questions . . .'

She turned back and looked into Süleyman's eyes.

'Questions you don't ask before?'

'Yes.'

She shrugged.

Süleyman cleared his throat. Smoke from her cigarette went up his nose and almost made him gag. Whatever she was smoking smelt as if it included burning tyres.

'In your original statement, you said that you went to hear this hakawati, Ahmad Al Saidawi, at what you described as a coffee house.' He looked up at her. 'If you recall, I took you to the apartment in the Şekerci Han part of the Malta Çarşısı that you had indicated, where we found an empty unit that we subsequently discovered had been used for warehousing for the previous year.'

'Yeah, well for one day it wasn't,' she said.

'Not only did no one in that building underwrite your story, no one recognised you. And although you claimed to recognise some faces, you couldn't put names to them. Only Betül Gencer.'

'I talk to her.'

'Why was she there?'

'To see hakawati.'

'You said in your original statement that Betül Hanım didn't speak Arabic. You conversed in Turkish.'

'Yes.'

'So I reiterate, why was she there?'

'She says she was not.'

'I know. But you say she was, so why?'

'Because she was there! I tell you, I admit I want my husband dead. I am not sorry he is dead now. I speak my truth, but you don't believe me.'

'But what if we did?' Kerim asked.

'Would not change anything,' she said. 'Not for me.'

'Maybe not, but if we can prove your story . . .'

'You did not before.'

'But if we did now . . .'

There was a moment of silence, and then Süleyman said, 'Samira Hanım, you said in your statement that the idea for swapping murders, as it were, came from Betül Gencer.'

'It did.'

'So if – *if* – we can prove somehow that the meeting you describe in your statement actually happened, if we can find some tangible evidence that what you told us was true, then there may be a way to review your case. What I am not saying is that you will get out of here, but there may be grounds for a reduction of sentence if it can be proven that Betül Gencer actively influenced your thinking.'

'She did,' she said. 'But you don't believe me.'

'Well, now that this has happened, I have had cause to think again,' Süleyman said.

'Now Erol Gencer is dead.'

He didn't reply. Had he taken the easy way out to a result last year? Or had he, worse, been too involved in his own issues at the time?

He said, 'Let's go back to the beginning. How did you find out about this hakawati performance at the Şekerci Han?'

'I tell you, I don't know.'

'You must know,' Süleyman said. 'This was not an event that was advertised, and yet according to you, it was attended by approximately thirty people. How did they find out about it, and where?'

She shrugged. Then she frowned and put her chin in her hands. 'I was working . . .'

'People who worked with you denied all knowledge of the event,' Kerim said. 'As did your husband, with whom you agreed.'

'I would,' she said.

'What does that mean?'

'I am afraid of him.'

'You were in custody,' Süleyman said.

She looked at him with contempt. 'You are not a woman beaten up by your husband,' she said. Her eyes filled with tears. 'Wael, he was in my head, you know? Why you think I wanted him dead, eh? Why you think I only speak to that woman for minutes and I am convinced? Betül Hanım had a plan to get me free!'

'So Wael . . .'

'He told me hakawati was coming,' she said.

'Did he attend too?' Kerim asked.

'No,' she said.

'Why not?'

'I don't know.'

'So why didn't you tell us that it was your husband who told you about the event?'

'Do you not listen?' she said. 'While my husband lives, how can I say anything?'

'And now that he is dead?'

'Now he is dead, I can say that,' she said. 'But there is no more to tell. Wael told me about hakawati and he say I can go. So I go. To hear stories, to be away from him.'

Arto Sarkissian had never smoked. He always maintained that it was Çetin İkmen's incessant smoking that had put him off. But now, in a way, he wished he did. It would give him something to do while dealing with hysteria.

'She needs to come home, Bey Efendi!'

Arto, unused to having a tiny person dressed in black lace clawing at his feet, said, 'Oh please do get up! Get up!'

'Her soul is in torment!' Madam Edith cried.

Despite having known İkmen's cousin Samsun for most of his life, Arto Sarkissian wasn't accustomed to other trans people, or drag queens like Edith. Of course, as Pembe Hanım's flatmate, she'd come to see whether she could have her body prepared for the grave. Edith, like Pembe, was a Muslim, albeit in the loosest sense, and Muslims believed that an unburied body equalled a soul in torment.

And this on top of Erol Gencer's wife asking that morning – somewhat more quietly – when her husband's body might be released.

Arto put a hand down and gripped Edith's fingers. 'Please get up, madam,' he said. 'I'm sorry, there's no amount of pleading that can change things. Pembe's body has to stay here for the time being.'

'Why?'

'Because we've yet to complete our forensic tests on it,' he said.

'What, cutting her open and that?'

'If you want to be blunt about it . . .'

She cried.

'But, my dear, standing outside my laboratory will not change anything.'

And then she said something that chilled Arto's blood. It was something he had suspected for a while but for which he'd had no evidence, except perhaps what had happened when they'd found Pembe's body.

Edith said, 'What about if I speak to Kerim Bey?'

'What about it? What's he . . . Madam, this body is under my care whatever Inspector Gürsel may . . .'

She scuttled away, fearing maybe that she'd said too much. Did she know that he'd listened in to part of her conversation with Kerim Gürsel the previous evening? Was she aware he had seen the policeman cry?

'You still have nine days' leave remaining.'

Without asking, Süleyman sat down opposite his superior. Although Commissioner Selahattin Ozer had undeniably been foisted on the department, and remained unpopular, his subordinates now at least had some regard for him. This was because, in spite of being recruited to his post for what everyone suspected were political reasons, he had proved to be rather more on his officers' side than had been anticipated. On the face of it a humourless, rigidly religious man, he was nevertheless more open to suggestion, and more knowing, than he looked.

'Sir, Inspector Gürsel has a conflict of interest with regard to the Tarlabaşı victim,' Süleyman said.

'Which is?'

'The victim, er, Hüseyin Kılıç, was employed as a carer for the inspector's disabled wife.'

'Mmm.' The commissioner looked down at something on his desk. 'Strange choice . . .'

Süleyman had discussed this with Kerim Gürsel, and so he said, without missing a beat, 'Mrs Gürsel used to work in the art world, sir, before her marriage.'

'Art world?'

'A gallery, sir.'

Apparently for a short time after high school Sinem had been the curator of a small gallery in Galata dedicated to work by women – including those from the trans community. Kerim's friend Kurdish Madonna had apparently got her the gig.

'Oh?'

'Experimental work,' Süleyman continued. 'Attractive, I am told, to people in the entertainment world.'

'Kılıç was a prostitute,' Ozer said.

'Not when he worked as a carer for Mrs Gürsel.'

Ozer stared at him with his cold, pale eyes and Süleyman felt himself inwardly shudder. Ozer knew that something here was amiss, even though he probably couldn't articulate it. But he also knew – and Süleyman was relying on this to a large extent – that his predecessors, by giving their subordinates rather more slack than he would have liked, had gained their trust and loyalty. Ozer currently had very little of either.

'Well, I assume not,' he said. 'And I will of course take Inspector Gürsel's previous association with the victim into account. Although I have to say that he was only put on the Kılıç case because he took that call. He will of course revert to his previous investigation.'

'Which is where the plot, as it were, sir, deepens.'

'Oh.' Again those eyes.

'Yes.' He smiled. Of everyone in the department, it was probably Süleyman who caught Ozer most easily off guard. A man of humble beginnings, the commissioner was both intimidated by and in awe of the inspector's education and pedigree. It made him both obsequious and resentful, and Süleyman knew it.

'In response to requests made to the public for information regarding the Gencer case, Kılıç came to see Inspector Gürsel yesterday afternoon.'

'Why was I not told?'

'Late yesterday afternoon,' Süleyman said. 'Of course he knew Inspector Gürsel and was, it seems, content to give him details about his association with the other victim at the Gencer property, Wael Al Hussain.'

'What information?'

'Al Hussain had been a customer of Kılıç's. For sexual favours . . .'

'Really.'

'And so Inspector Gürsel was preparing a report for you when events overtook—'

'So why isn't he here now?'

It was a good question. The truth of it was that Kerim had been unable to face Ozer given his current state of mind. He was truly afraid of what he might say.

'Sir, I should like to return to duty and take over from Inspector Gürsel in the case of Pembe/Kılıç.'

'We do have other investigative teams.'

'I know, but given my superior knowledge, via my association with Inspector Gürsel, and knowing as we do that these two incidents may be connected . . .'

'Even though you are on leave?'

Süleyman smiled again. 'I feel it is my duty to my colleague to support him and his wife, who is extremely upset. As I have heard you yourself say on many an occasion, sir, our work is not merely a job, it is a vocation. It is our sacred duty to protect the public and our way of life. Homicide breaks the contract we as citizens have with each other and so it is incumbent upon us to heal that wound as quickly and efficiently as possible. My son, who is a young man, albeit of foreign nationality, understands this.'

Patrick didn't know, but Süleyman was aware of ways in which he could have the boy entertained in his absence. Not that his son actually seemed to like him. Maybe it was better that his first experience of İstanbul as an adult should be curated by others. Or was Süleyman just telling himself that in order to assuage his addiction to his work? Or rather, his need to find out whether he had been wrong about Samira Al Hussain and her ridiculous story. And if he had been, to somehow control the situation.

It was said that Suriani Christian Wahid Saatçi had not so much lost his left eye as given it away. Desperate to get out of his home city in south-eastern Turkey, he'd traded it for a bus ticket to İstanbul and enough money to set himself up as a very niche drug dealer. Or so it was said.

As his fellow Syrian, Ahmad Al Saidawi the hakawati, was said to live between worlds, so Wahid lived between the İstanbul districts of Cihangir and Fındıklı, in an apartment overlooking the eighty-five-metre-long Rainbow Stairs. Brightly coloured and reminiscent of the LGBT rainbow flag, the stairs had originally been painted at the time of the Gezi Park protests back in 2013.

Rima Al Numan had never touched drugs until she'd fled her homeland. The occasional glass of wine had been her only vice back home. But the journey from Aleppo to İstanbul had been a hard one. Hiding from the Turkish military and the police, getting by on little food as well as enduring her brother-in-law Wael's often volcanic temper tantrums. Even when they arrived in İstanbul, things had got no better. Wael had pushed her sister out on the streets, while Rima eked a sort of existence collecting plastic bottles. Wael himself had sat on his backside. Things had only changed when Rima had met Wahid Saatçi.

She'd been sitting in the gutter somewhere near the old city walls when he'd approached her, surrounded by bags full of plastic bottles, exhausted and unable to get up. At first he'd spoken to her in Turkish and she had pretended not to understand. Men propositioned her all the time. But then he'd switched to Arabic. He'd taken her to a tea garden for a drink, they'd talked, and he'd asked her to take a package for him to some house in one of the Bosphorus villages. He'd paid her handsomely to do it.

She'd known what Wahid was from the start. She'd seen enough of life to recognise a drug dealer when she met one. She'd worked for him again after that, and again, and then she'd sampled his wares. Pure opium. Oh, but that could put a shine on the dullest day. Rima could see why the rich people loved it so much. She could also see how easily she could become addicted. And so she practised discipline. She saved up to go and see Wahid and she hadn't worked for him in the last year. And now here he was, sitting on the Rainbow Stairs, cigarette in hand, talking to a smart young man in a suit.

Rima began to move towards him, but then he looked at her and she backed away into the shadows. It was then that she recognised the smart young man. He was that police officer she'd seen at headquarters, the one who had run after her.

Chapter 13

'Where are you?'

'On the sofa,' Sinem Gürsel called out to her husband.

Kerim walked through the kitchen, which smelt of garlic and spices. And was that freshly baked bread too? If he hadn't been feeling so tired and bereft, he would have been cheered by such odours. But he just worried that Sinem had worn herself out.

'Have you been cooking?' he asked as he walked into the lounge and bent down to kiss her.

'No,' she said.

'Good.' He looked around, his eyes wide with anticipation. 'Your mother . . .'

'No, Mum went, like you told her to,' Sinem said.

Kerim flopped down onto the floor beside the sofa and his wife ran her fingers through his hair.

'I'm sorry . . .'

'You did the right thing,' Sinem said.

He shook his head. 'It's all a mess.'

'What is?'

'Life.' He took a packet of cigarettes out of his pocket and lit up.

Sinem, shocked, said, 'When did you start again?'

He shrugged. He couldn't remember. Sometime after Pembe left . . .

'So who did the cooking?' he asked.

'Kurdish Madonna. She came round to offer her condolences.'

He nodded.

'She saw Mum go and I told her what had happened, and she stayed and cooked for us. Pembe was meant to be working for her last night.'

He wanted to say 'I wish she wouldn't', but stopped himself. What was the use? Pembe was dead.

'How are you?'

Kerim looked up at her.

'Oh darling . . .'

She kissed him. As he drew away from her, he said, 'Mehmet Bey knows.'

'About . . .'

'About me,' he said. 'Known for a long time, apparently. Çetin Bey told him to look after me when he retired. I know you think he's an arrogant bastard, but he really does have my back.'

'Are you sure?' she asked.

'As I can be.'

They descended into silence for a few moments, then he said, 'What about your mother?'

'What about her? She's gone.'

'She knows . . .'

Sinem put an arm around his shoulders. 'Derviş phoned.'

Derviş was Sinem's eldest brother and current head of the family. Kerim had always got on with him.

'We talked,' she continued.

'And?'

'And he has told Mum that if she does anything to damage us or your career, he will cut her off. He has always—'

'Known about me, yes,' he said, 'I'm beginning to realise that the entire world knows about me.'

Patrick was thrilled, or rather, as close to being enthusiastic as he got. When they arrived at the İkmen apartment, he left his father and went off with Çiçek to show her the magic tricks he'd been practising on his cousin Edibe during their Bosphorus ferry trip.

Before the two of them got settled down, Çiçek cast Mehmet an infuriated glance, which caused her father to suggest he and his friend leave the building and go down to the Mozaik for a drink. The hasty relocation of his son had been done by phone, and so Süleyman at the very least owed the older man an explanation.

Once they'd settled down at a table, with drinks in front of them and cigarettes lit, he said, 'I'm sorry, Çetin, I didn't know what else to do. I can't leave him with my mother, she'll kill him, and Murad and Edibe have to go to work. It was fortunate my niece had today off to be honest. Don't know what I would have done.'

'Oh, I'm happy to have the boy, Mehmet,' İkmen said. 'He's a little shy, but he's an absolute delight. He's interested in things, he's got conversation.'

'Has he?'

İkmen shook his head. 'Talk to him,' he said. 'All this silent, moody stuff is just what they do. I had it with all of my boys. It's an act to get your attention, and men like you and I need to give our children our attention.'

'What do you mean?'

'I mean, Mehmet,' İkmen said, 'that there are times when the job comes second. Took me forever to learn that, which is why I'm telling you, hoping you won't make my mistakes.'

'Too late.'

'No it isn't.' He shook his head. 'Anyway, look, it's done for now. The İkmen family will entertain Patrick, although quite where all this will leave you and Çiçek . . .'

Süleyman waved the problem away. But İkmen said, 'I know you care for her and she cares for you, and I will not interfere, but I know Çiçek and she's angry with you.'

'I know.'

'Well . . .'

Marlboro the cat appeared from nowhere and sat on his master's lap waiting for food. İkmen duly ordered him a plate of sardines.

Stroking the cat's greasy, ragged fur, he said, 'So tell me about Kerim Bey.'

It was because of Kerim, in part at least, that Süleyman was back at work. A pair of eyes to watch Kerim's back now his lover had been killed was no bad idea. Süleyman told İkmen how Pembe's death could be connected to that of Wael Al Hussain.

After a moment's silence, İkmen said, 'I am working, although not successfully so far, for Samira Al Hussain's sister, Rima.'

Süleyman frowned.

'She wants me to look into this story Samira told about a nebulous Syrian coffee house in Fatih and a mythical storyteller.'

'Ahmad Al Saidawi,' Süleyman said. 'Kerim Bey is reopening that.'

'How do you feel about it, Mehmet?' İkmen asked. 'Given that you dismissed her story?'

'I still find it fantastical,' Süleyman said. 'But I feel it will do no harm to look.'

It was as close as he was ever going to come to saying he had made a mistake, and İkmen knew it.

'Now that I know you are involved, that makes me think . . .' Süleyman shook his head. 'You feel . . .'

'Oh, there's something there,' İkmen said. 'Although whether it will be what Rima Al Numan wants to hear or not, I don't know. It won't get her sister out of Bakırköy.'

'No.'

'And in the spirit of intelligence sharing . . . do you know anything about a theft from President Assad's palace in Damascus?'

'No,' Süleyman said. 'Why?'

'There is a rumour, which could be nonsense, that someone close to Assad has stolen something from him. What I don't know, who I don't know. But there is a notion that those within the Syrian diaspora may be shielding this person.'

'Maybe in the guise of a mythical storyteller?'

'Maybe,' İkmen said, 'but then again maybe not. Maybe it's rubbish, but I think you ought to bear it in mind.'

'Helping me at your own expense?' Süleyman smiled. That was very İkmen.

But then the older man said, 'Oh no, Mehmet. Not in this case. No, I will find whatever magic there is behind this, and you and Kerim will get the bad guys.'

Addiction was just part of human nature as far as Wahid Saatçi was concerned. Although always straight when doing business, Wahid was as addicted to his product as any of his customers. And so it was with some ill humour that he went and brought Rima Al Numan out of the shadows once Sergeant Mungun had gone on his way. Odd that those two were sort of connected.

He said, 'What do you want? I'm desperate for a pipe.'

Because they were speaking Arabic, no one could understand what they were saying, and so Rima just came out with it. 'Do you know anything about someone stealing from Assad?'

For a moment he said nothing. Then he sighed. 'You're Syrian,' he said. 'You know how many rumours surround that family. I might be an Arab, but I've never lived in Syria. Why are you asking me?'

'Because I know you have been in and out over the years,' she said. 'You told me.'

He'd probably been high.

'Well, yes,' he said. 'I had family in Damascus. Not now. Stealing from Assad seems particularly hazardous to me. Stealing what?'

'I don't know.'

He shook his head. 'I thought when I saw you that maybe you needed something.'

'Obviously I'd like to . . . but I'm not going to,' she said. 'Was that man you were talking to a police officer?'

'Why?'

'Was he?'

'Look, he comes from the east, like me,' he said.

'But a police—'

'Yeah, all right. We have a . . .' His voice trailed away. 'He came to see me on behalf of someone not in the police. Something about do I know any hakawatis . . .'

'Oh?'

'To do with some old conviction,' he said.

Wahid didn't know much about Rima apart from her occasional need for money and opium. He certainly didn't know she was Samira Al Hussain's sister.

'So what now?' Rima asked.

'I'll have a pipe and think on it,' Wahid said.

'Think on what?'

'Whether I want to meet this man the sergeant says needs the information, and whether I can remember anything.'

Mobile phones were marvellous. Gonca Şekeroğlu had been an early adopter. She used her iPhone for everything – to call, to email, to take photographs, and best of all, to text. Mehmet Süleyman had sent her a text not ten minutes before telling her he was coming over, and she was thrilled. With Rambo on his way back to Sardinia, they had the place to themselves. Even though her mind was still buzzing with fear at the idea of her meeting the following day with Harun Bey, she knew that a night with her lover would at least make her feel good for now. Even if that lover was a man who had told her, in so many words, that they could never really be together.

But luckily Gonca's visceral need for Mehmet Süleyman made her temporarily forget that, or rather shelve it. She put on her deepest red balcony bra and slipped her tight ruffled dress over her head. That ensemble made her breasts look big and precarious, as if they were about to fall out of her clothing. He liked that.

She sprayed her favourite rose perfume all over her hair and body and then slipped her feet into a pair of black stilettos. Make-up was easy. She used broad strokes, strong colours, bold eyeliner. Did it make her look older than she was? No, it was amazing, he always said so, and anyway, it wouldn't stay on for long.

When he knocked on her front door, she had just put all her gold chains around her neck and heavy platinum earrings threaded with peacock feathers in her ears. As she walked lazily towards the front of the house, she rattled. She opened the door, and there he was.

She smiled and stood aside to let him in. 'A nice surprise,' she murmured.

He let her shut the door, then he threw his jacket onto a chair and took her in his arms.

'Young woman!'

Eylul Yavaş knew she was young, but she was rarely called that by other people.

The sun had just started to set on the clothes-line-decorated skyline of Tarlabaşı as the air filled with the smell of grilling lamb, olive oil, rakı and cannabis. She recognised the old woman who barrelled towards her.

'Hello, Neşe Hanım,' she said.

'You know there has been a murder?' the old woman said.

'Yes, Neşe Hanım,' Eylul said. 'I interviewed you about it. Don't you remember? I am Sergeant Yavaş. We talked about your mother.'

'Because she did it!' the woman said. She pulled Eylul into the shadow of a crumbling and forbidding building that the sergeant knew was an unofficial male brothel. From the window above came the sound of men very loudly gaining sexual relief.

'Neşe Hanım,' Eylul said, 'don't you remember that we decided your mother was dead? She died a long time ago.'

'No, no, no, no, no!' The woman shook her head. 'She killed the man who is a woman. Not on purpose, although she is evil and I curse her!' She spat on the ground. 'She was curing him, by operation!'

The woman was deranged, but had she seen something? Obviously her mother, who Madam Edith had told Eylul had been dead for decades, hadn't done it. But had it been maybe someone who had looked like her mother? A woman?

Inspector Gürsel wasn't the sort of officer who simply dismissed people just because they were mad, but he had been very clearly elsewhere in his mind when dealing with this case. In fact he'd looked really unwell. It had been a relief to Eylul that they were going back to concentrating on the Gencer/Al Hussain investigation. Inspector Süleyman had taken over the castration of Pembe Hanım, and so any new evidence that came to light should be referred to him.

Eylul took her phone out.

'Hanım,' she said, 'can you describe your mother to me, please?'

The old woman beamed. 'Ah, now you listen, eh?' she said. 'Those men you were with, they don't listen, but you're a good girl.'

'I hope so!' Eylul smiled. 'So your mother . . .'

'Very lovely,' Neşe said. 'Tall, not like me.' Her face clouded. 'That's why she wants me dead. She says a djinn raped her one night and that I am its child. So no good for working, none, no good!'

Working at what Eylul didn't know, but she could guess.

'I make the tea,' Neşe said. 'I make the tea . . .' She gazed off into the distance. Made the tea for whom? For the men her mother serviced?

'Hanım . . .'

She looked up. 'Oh, Mother, yes. Yes, she killed that woman. She doesn't like pretty girls. They get above themselves, they do! I say, that's just like you, that is, lady! With all your tits and your flaming red hair and all made up! But she just laughs. Says I'm jealous. When she came yesterday to kill that girl, I thought she'd come for me! I sat at the top of the stairs and I watched her as she did it, because she left the door open. Or maybe I opened it? I watched and then I was scared and so I wet myself. I went back in my room then.'

'Why?'

'If she sees I've wet myself, my mother will slap me until my bottom is raw.'

'I looked it up, it's called a lamassu,' the doctor said.

Kerim, who had just helped Sinem into bed, shut their bedroom door and walked back into the living room, his phone tucked underneath his chin.

'An Assyrian creature said to protect portals and doorways,' Arto Sarkissian continued. 'Clearly it meant something to Mr Al Hussain, otherwise why have one tattooed on his bicep?'

'He was Syrian.'

'This image is more prevalent in Iraq than in Syria.'

Kerim said, 'The two countries were always close, weren't they?'

He was finding it hard to concentrate. It had been blisteringly hot all day, and now that night had come, the heat had settled into a thick, muggy blanket across the city. If only it would rain.

'Both Baa'thist regimes at one time,' the doctor said. 'Although Saddam Hussein and Hafez Al Assad didn't really like each other. Anyway, I thought I'd let you know that is what the tattoo is, even though I can't decipher what it means.'

'Thank you, Doctor.'

'So are you, er . . . are you feeling better?'

'Yes. Thank you. I . . . The victim used to be a carer for my wife.'

'I understand so . . .'

'It was a shock, and, well, now that Mehmet Bey is taking that case over from me, I feel as if a weight has been lifted.'

'Ah, so I will need to liaise with him regarding the Tarlabaşı case.'

'Yes.'

'I'll send him an email,' the doctor said. 'Post-mortem nine o'clock sharp tomorrow morning.'

Kerim Gürsel felt his stomach turn over and ended the call.

Yet again Ömer Mungun found himself at Çetin İkmen's door. The rest of the family had long since gone to bed, but Çetin was still up, reading, talking to his wife, smoking, stroking his cat.

He gave the younger man a beer and the two of them walked out onto his balcony. There was a storm on its way from the Sea of Marmara and they watched as bolts of pink forked lightning began to flash in the distance, moving slowly ever closer.

They both sat down and Ömer noticed that much of the space around his feet was crowded with old olive oil cans filled with plants.

'Oh that's Çiçek's doing,' İkmen said. 'When she moved back in, she started growing these plants. I've no idea what they are. The only green plant I think I'd recognise now is cannabis.'

Ömer smiled. 'I went to see Wahid,' he said. 'He's a man who moves at his own pace. He's also a man who only talks to people if it suits him. So I don't think he'll speak to you, but I do have some expectation that he will look into what I told him.'

'Thank you.'

'But if he doesn't, I may have some leverage.'

İkmen frowned.

'I left Wahid on the Rainbow Stairs,' Ömer said. 'I ran down to get the tram. But when I looked back, he was with someone. I'm almost certain it was Rima Al Numan.'

'Samira Al Hussain's sister?'

'Yes. Unless she has a pure opium habit, I find them an odd pairing.'

'Kerim Bey needs to speak to her, I imagine.'

'He does. I've sent him a text. It's up to him. The boss and I are on that Tarlabaşı case now.'

'I know, I have his son here.'

Ömer shook his head. 'This visit's not worked out well, has it?'

'No.' İkmen smiled. 'But we're entertaining the boy. I took him to see Sami Nasi yesterday and he seems to have caught the stage magic bug. Been producing pencils from thin air all evening.' He frowned. 'What I really need is for someone to talk to me,' he said. 'Ever since this whisper – and that's all it is at the moment – about a theft from Assad came my way, I've been obsessed by the possibility that it is, in part, involved somehow in the circumstances surrounding the attempt on Gencer's life last year.'

'Assuming that's why the Syrian population won't own up to this coffee house event?'

'Mmm. Something else besides the meeting of Betül Gencer and Samira Al Hussain happened at that coffee house. Something we're not seeing. Who told Samira that the event was taking place?'

'The husband, Wael,' Ömer said. 'Then he denied all knowledge. The boss and Kerim Bey went to see Samira this morning.'

'Have you found any connections between Betül Gencer and Wael Al Hussain?' İkmen asked.

'No.'

'Mmm.'

And then a huge crack of thunder broke into their conversation, followed by a scattering of heavy, fat raindrops.

'Gonca?'

Mehmet Süleyman had been woken up by his phone telling him he had an email from Arto Sarkissian. Only then had he noticed that he was alone, and that a thunderstorm was raging outside.

She was standing naked in front of the open French doors, which led out to a small balcony, her long hair whipping around her in the wind. She looked like a pagan sorceress.

He got out of bed and walked up behind her.

'Sweetheart . . .'

Her face was pale and she'd been crying. He put his arms around her, which made her jump.

'Baby . . .'

'Fantastic storm,' he said as he pulled her against him.

She leaned her head on his shoulder. 'I love you so much, baby.'

Her words were laced with sobs. He turned her around and kissed her, holding her tightly.

'Gonca, what's the matter?' he asked.

'I want to be with you,' she said.

'You are with me.'

'You know what I mean!'

He kissed her lips and then leaned down to kiss both her breasts.

'You are a remarkable woman,' he said. 'The most extraordinary woman I've ever met.'

'But do you love me?'

'Of course I do. I've told you I love you many times.'

The tears came again. 'So why do you go to Çiçek İkmen?'

It was a fair question and was in fact something he had occasionally asked himself. The trite answer he usually gave was that one woman wasn't enough for him. And maybe that was true, but it shouldn't be, and he knew it. He also knew that the very socially unsuitable woman in his arms was the love of his life.

'Well . . .'

'No, don't answer that,' she said. 'I don't want to know,'

Çiçek was almost twenty years Gonca's junior. Of course her body was firmer, her skin smoother, and she was probably still fertile . . .

Lightning screamed across the sky in jagged pink arcs.

Mehmet Süleyman kissed Gonca's mouth and then her breasts, then he made his way down her belly, kissing her skin as he went.

'Baby . . .'

He put his head against her pubis and breathed in her scent. Why didn't he just stay with her and let himself be bewitched for the rest of his life?

Chapter 14

It was a new day, and although he'd slept very little the previous night – due to his own dark thoughts and the incredible thunderstorm that had taken place – Kerim Gürsel was determined to make progress with the Erol Gencer case.

This new determination had started early. After reviewing notes he'd made overnight in his phone, he'd made tea, gone down to the bakkal for fresh bread and cheese and presented Sinem with not only a drink but a substantial breakfast. As he'd kissed her goodbye, she'd said, 'Be careful, Kerim.'

Now that she was so close to giving birth, her anxiety was increasing. Kerim wasn't happy about her being alone in the apartment, but he couldn't think about that now.

Eylul Yavaş came into the office bearing two enormous paper cups full of Starbucks coffee. The woman was addicted and drank the stuff all day long, but when she arrived in the morning, she also brought Kerim a massive cup too. More of a Turkish coffee man himself, he didn't have the heart to tell her he didn't really like cappuccino.

She put his cup down on his desk and he smiled.

'Did you hear the thunder last night, sir?' she said.

'Oh yes. Kept me awake. The lightning was amazing. Then when it was over, I couldn't get back to sleep and so I made some notes.' He picked up his phone.

Eylul sat down. 'Sir, I was in Tarlabaşı yesterday evening,' she said. She didn't say why and she knew he wouldn't ask.

'Oh?' His eyes were on his phone.

'I was pulled aside by our victim's neighbour, Neşe Hanım.'

He looked up.

'Still going on about her mother having murdered Pembe Hanım,' she said.

'Her mother is dead, and she's mad.'

'Yes, I know, but what if she did see someone and it was a woman? She described a tall woman with red hair. I know she didn't see her mother, but what if she saw someone like her?'

He frowned.

Eylul said, 'I mean, aren't we to some extent looking at what may be unsafe testimony in relation to the killings of Erol Gencer and Wael Al Hussain?'

'Yes,' he said. 'And that is what we need to talk about now. Oh, did you make a note of your encounter with Neşe Hanım for Mehmet Bey?'

'I sent him an email.'

'Good. He is at, er, Hüseyin Kılıç's post-mortem this morning, but he may wish to speak to you about it later.'

'Yes, sir.'

'And so to our own case.' He smiled. 'I have decided we need to proceed allowing for the possibility that the story told by Samira Al Hussain last year might be true. Betül Gencer, as wife to Erol Gencer and heir to half his fortune – the other half reverting to his daughter – is already a person of interest, even though we cannot place her at the scene. So further questioning of Mrs Gencer and her associates will not appear unusual. But I want us to keep in mind what she might have done in the past. What have you discovered about her so far?'

Eylul activated her computer and accessed the notes she'd made.

'Born 1963 in a village called Gazimurat, twenty-five kilometres outside Adana. She always maintains she left her village when she was sixteen, but it would seem she was actually fourteen. So that was in 1977. She claims her modelling career started the following year, in 1978, and she does begin to appear in magazines in 1979, but what she did in the intervening time isn't clear.'

Kerim leaned back in his chair and put his feet up on his desk. 'Young girl from the countryside, alone – your mind instantly turns to sex work, or am I being too cynical?'

'Probably not,' she said. 'She has been recorded saying her father was a sheep farmer, but whether that meant he owned land or was just a farm worker, I don't know. But I think it's safe to assume she didn't come from money. So when she came to the city, she either got some sort of menial work or she sold her body. And the modelling route would suggest . . .'

'Prostitution,' he said. 'Then modelling, then she worked at Harem Medya on *Büyük Risk* as a TV show hostess, then on some awful Bridezilla show . . .'

They both laughed. He said, 'I don't know why I find that so funny. Those shows are awful.' He shook his head. 'So then she gets sacked from her Bridezilla show by her new boss, Filiz Tepe, who used to work with her on *Büyük Risk*. A slap in the face, especially for a woman who had tried to educate herself.'

'At Boğaziçi University, where she met Erol Gencer in 1988, married him in 1990 . . .'

'And then he became a star, while she did not,' Kerim said. 'She must have been ambitious to even come to the city in the first place. I wonder how she felt about that?'

'Yes, but sir, if we look seriously at Betül, surely that implies that we believe Samira Al Hussain's story?'

'Maybe we do and maybe we don't,' he said. 'But it does no harm to consider her as a possible suspect. Forensic evidence strongly suggests that Gencer killed Al Hussain. Why? We don't know, but before Al Hussain died, the two men shared a meal and wine. What had they come together to do or discuss? Al Hussain we know had a liking for hardcore old-fashioned porn and transsexuals.' He frowned. 'Maybe Betül did a bit of that in her youth?'

'And Wael was blackmailing her?'

'It's possible,' he said. 'We have anecdotal evidence that Erol was not always the gentleman he liked people to think he was. He verbally abused his wife. Did he also hit her? What indeed was their relationship?' He paused for a moment. 'And what was Wael Al Hussain doing with a box of Compound 1080?'

Eylul said, 'Wael had the poison?'

'In his apartment, yes,' Kerim said.

'So he killed Gencer, or rather he could have done.'

'He could have done, but did he? We know that Wael didn't ingest it. Dr Sarkissian thinks that Erol drank it either in some mineral water or in whisky.'

'Did forensic find traces of it on glasses?'

'Not as far as I know,' he said. 'The doctor's performing a PM on the Tarlabaşı victim this morning. I'll ask him this afternoon. Apparently Mrs Gencer contacted him yesterday to request the release of her husband's body for burial. Whether she asked him how Erol died, I don't know; he didn't say. But I think I should do this formally and I think you should come with me. Let us shake the tree and see what falls to the ground. Gently, of course.'

She smiled. 'Yes, sir.'

'And now,' he said, 'I must go and brief the team I've got going out to Fatih amongst the Syrians. I've managed to find two Arabic speakers. Let's see whether anyone remembers Samira Al Hussain's coffee house now. Oh, and I'm also curious as to why the Al Hussains lived so far away from the main Syrian refugee contingent.'

'There are other Syrians in Tarlabaşı apart from the Al Hussains,' Eylul said.

'Yes, but what type of Syrians are they? Are they, as could be assumed knowing what we do of Tarlabaşı, of the poorer, less well-educated variety? Because the Al Hussains did not fit that demographic.'

After twenty-five years' experience attending post-mortem examinations, there weren't many sights that could make Inspector Mehmet Süleyman's stomach turn. But smells were another matter. The underlying stench of formaldehyde was one thing, but what emanated from dead bodies was quite another. The remains of Pembe Hanım, aka Hüseyin Kılıç, lay spread eagled on Dr Sarkissian's dissecting table like one of the brutalised and bloodied women one saw on the worst imaginable Internet sites. Bereft of her long blonde wig, her short black hair coupled with her long Roman nose made her look unrecognisable.

The doctor removed the two breast implants in her chest and weighed them. Outside of her body they were ghastly, and Süleyman wondered how Kerim Gürsel was feeling knowing this was going on.

When Ömer Mungun had seen Süleyman that morning, he'd recoiled a little. Then he'd asked him whether the thunderstorm had kept him awake, and Süleyman said it had. Which wasn't strictly true.

One of the great attractions Gonca Şekeroğlu had always held for him had been her dignity. She might joke about how much she wanted him, but she never begged. Last night had been different. Not that she had begged, but he had found himself soothing and placating her because she'd been so upset. He'd made love to her twice, and had got almost zero sleep, which was why he now looked so pale and dark around the eyes. When he'd left her to drive to work, she'd made him promise he'd be back that night. Was he beginning to feel hemmed in? He adored her – she made him laugh, made him cry, talked about things he barely understood and made the maddest, most wonderful art. She was also beautiful and spectacular in bed. Just thinking about her made him horny.

'She had cancer.'

Ripped from his reverie, Süleyman said, 'Pardon?'

'Pembe Hanım,' the doctor said. 'Lung cancer.' He shook his head. 'The street girls all smoke so much, it's not surprising. But this appears to have been quite advanced. I imagine she must have started to have breathing problems at the very least.'

'Treatment?'

'I can see no signs of radiotherapy, and bloods as yet do not indicate that she was on any sort of chemotherapy regimen.'

'She was dying.'

'Yes. But as we know, it wasn't the cancer that killed her.'

'Where did you say you discovered the penis and testes, Doctor?'

He saw Ömer look up at him.

'I'm sorry, I'm a little vague . . .'

Arto Sarkissian smiled. 'Ah, watching the storm last night. I did too. Got very little sleep, but I have to say I feel energised by it.'

'I wish I did.'

'Yes, the organs of generation,' the doctor said. 'In the oven.'

Suddenly Süleyman was fully and horrifically awake. 'Was it on?'

In spite of his protestations of well-being, the doctor appeared to slump slightly. 'Yes,' he said. 'I was actually getting to that.'

Ömer took a deep breath. 'Were they . . .'

'Cooked? Yes,' Sarkissian said.

'Do you think . . .'

'Psychology isn't in my purview,' he continued. 'Thank God. But it shocked me, and as you know, gentlemen, I've seen everything. Whether the intention was simply to defile, or there was an intention of eating, I don't know. There is no sign that any consumption took place. I'll show you when we have finished here. Let us continue . . .'

'Good morning, Patrick.'

İkmen had just put the phone down when the boy walked into the living room.

He looked at İkmen and said, 'You have a landline.'

'Yes.'

'Nobody has a landline.'

'I do,' İkmen said. 'But then I am a very old bastard.'

Patrick sat down. 'And you swear,' he said. 'My father doesn't.'

Figuring that Mehmet Süleyman was in quite enough trouble with his son, İkmen lied. 'No. He's a good man.' Then he changed the subject. 'Now, Patrick, do you remember Sami and Ruya who we went to see in Çukurcuma?'

The boy's face lit up. 'The magicians!'

'Yes.'

'Cool! Are we going to see them today?'

'Tonight,' İkmen said. 'They are performing at a small theatre in Karaköy.'

'Will Sami do the head trick?'

'I imagine so,' İkmen said. 'But then, after the show, there is going to be a performance of meddah that I would like to see.'

'What's that?'

'Storytelling. It will be in Turkish and so you may wish to not stay. But I need to. Çiçek will come, and so if you want to leave, she will bring you back here.'

'I'd like to stay,' he said.

'It will be late.'

'Good.'

Samsun came in from the kitchen and, seeing the boy, said in very halting English, 'Is the breakfast ready.'

Patrick, not knowing whether she was asking a question or not, looked at İkmen, who said, 'It seems that breakfast is served in the kitchen.'

The boy left. Alone again, İkmen lit up a cigarette and thought. Although not much more than a child, someone who had escaped from Syria was actually right underneath his nose.

Betül Gencer walked up and down in front of the officers like a caged animal. Eventually she stopped and repeated what Kerim Gürsel had told her.

'Poison.'

'Something called Compound 1080,' he said. 'It's a pesticide.'

'So how did that happen?' She sat down.

Eylul Yavaş said, 'Mrs Gencer, was your husband particularly distressed about anything in recent weeks?'

She lit a cigarette and then got up and began walking again. 'No more than usual,' she said.

'What does that mean?'

'It means that my husband had been a very vibrant and fit man until his heart attack,' she said. 'After his illness, he wasn't the same man. Nor would I have expected him to be.'

'In what way?'

'It mainly manifested as tiredness,' she said. 'His work wasn't significantly affected, but he wasn't going out socially as much as he had. And of course his visits to the gym were less frequent.'

'Did it make him angry?' Kerim asked.

'Not angry, just . . .' She shook her head.

'Did he abuse you?' Eylul asked.

Betül Gencer widened her eyes. In a distant part of the city the midday call to prayer wound its way around the hot, stifling populace. She said, 'Not physically. Erol wasn't like that.'

'Verbally?'

'Sometimes. Frustration . . .'

This bore out what Berat Tükek, the boy who had found the bodies, had said.

Betül Gencer sat down again. 'This poison . . .' she began.

'We're not yet sure whether your husband administered it to himself, whether Wael Al Hussain gave it to him, or whether he was poisoned by someone else,' Kerim said.

Eylul looked at him. Was he going to tell the woman that a packet of Compound 1080 had been found in Wael Al Hussain's apartment?

Betül said, 'Someone else? No one else was there, were they?'

'Not as far as we know,' he answered. 'Mrs Gencer, do you have any idea why Wael Al Hussain might have been eating with your husband that night?'

'I've told you before! No!'

'What did your husband say to you about his intentions for that evening?'

'Nothing.'

'Did you cook for him before you left home?' Eylul said.

'Yes, I always do if I go out without him.'

'We found an awful lot of food for one person,' Kerim said.

'I always cook large amounts,' she replied. 'We freeze what isn't used.'

'Which I imagine you usually take control of,' Eylul said. 'Given your husband's heart condition, I imagine that his food intake is limited to some extent, especially when it comes to high fat content.'

'Yes.'

'But if you weren't going to be at home, weren't you worried in case he ate too much?'

'He wasn't a child!' she said.

'No, but he was, by your own admission, really quite an unhappy man,' Kerim said.

*

There was a small tea garden two streets away from the pathology laboratories to which Süleyman took Ömer Mungun after Dr Sarkissian had finished Pembe Hanım's post-mortem.

They took a table underneath a tree and Süleyman ordered glasses of tea and bottles of water for both of them. When his water arrived, Ömer drank it straight down in one go.

Süleyman said, 'Thirsty?'

Ömer wiped his mouth on the sleeve of his shirt. 'I wish I could unsee what we saw in there,' he said. 'Dr Sarkissian was right. And I speak as a man who has eaten lamb's testicles.'

Pembe Hanım's partially cooked penis and testicles had been a horrific sight, especially for men to contemplate. What was more disturbing, however, was the state of mind that lay behind that act.

'The woman Pembe shared the apartment with has given a statement?' Süleyman said.

'Yes, boss. Madam Edith. Doctor says she's requested the body for burial. Sergeant Yavaş has handed over a list of Pembe's contacts she got from the old girl. Mostly transsexuals. According to Madam Edith, they're all ready and willing to talk to us.'

'Good.'

'Although the impression Sergeant Yavaş got was that Pembe didn't have any enemies.'

No one ever did, in Süleyman's experience. But Pembe must have had at least one, and one, furthermore, who had really hated her guts.

'Any whispers about Wael Al Hussain?'

'No. Genç of the mucky movies and hard-core fuck books claimed not to know him, or any other Syrians come to that. But he admitted he had made books for the Arab market in the past. The example we took from Al Hussain's flat was one of his, from the nineties.'

'Recognise any faces?'

'Couldn't see many faces, boss,' Ömer said.

'Doubtless.' Süleyman lit a cigarette. He'd have to talk to Kerim about Pembe when they were alone. He might know more about Pembe's enemies than he realised. And of course there was also Pembe's rival for Kerim Gürsel's affections, Sinem Gürsel. That had been festering in his mind for a while . . .

'So do you want me to get out amongst the trans girls of Tarlabaşı this afternoon, boss?' Ömer asked. 'It'll mean getting them out of bed.'

Süleyman smiled. 'It was ever the way with those who work at night, Ömer. Yes.' He leaned back and stretched, rolling what had become tight shoulders. 'I'll come with you, then we will look into Pembe's background. She's got form for soliciting, but not recently.'

Ömer looked around to make sure no one was listening to their conversation, then said, 'I've heard she worked for Kerim Bey's wife.'

'As a carer, hence the lack of recent convictions.'

'Strange person to have as a carer . . .'

'A friend of Mrs Gürsel's, I believe,' Süleyman said. He finished his tea and stood up. 'Come on. To work.'

For someone Çetin Bey had described as 'a little bit transparent, as in not of this world', magic-shop owner Fahrettin Bey seemed very corporeal to Patrick Süleyman. Corpulent was, in fact, the word his mammy would have used to describe him. And he spoke English, if not well, with lots of complicated words.

'Prestidigitation,' Fahrettin Bey exclaimed as he laid out a selection of magic trick sets in front of the boy, 'is an art form like painting, like thespians.'

Patrick couldn't read what it said on the lids of the boxes, although it was clear from the illustrations that most of them contained decks of cards, cups and balls, dice and magic wands.

The shop itself, which didn't seem to have a name – or not one that Patrick could identify – was tiny, packed to the rafters with books, and had a glass display case right in the middle that was full of scarves, cards, coins and many, many plastic fingers.

Fahrettin Bey said, 'All trick boxes have instructional material in Turkish and in English. But not Irish. No.'

In Patrick's experience it was refreshing to find someone who wasn't Irish who knew that Eire had its own native language, and so he smiled. Even if his own Irish language skills were dire.

'Çetin Bey can assist,' his host said.

Then another young man came into the shop and Fahrettin Bey rattled off a lot of Turkish words that made no sense. The youth smiled at Patrick, who smiled back, and then busied himself looking at one of the bookcases.

Çetin İkmen had deposited Patrick in this shop, down a tiny, almost invisible alleyway towards the end of Ticarethane Sokak, while he went to talk to someone at the Mozaik bar. He'd given the boy a heap of banknotes with the instruction to 'buy whatever you want and meet me at the bar'. Çetin Bey was a mysterious man, to Patrick's way of thinking. He had been a very successful police inspector, he spoke several languages really well, and he had *loads* of children, all of whom seemed to be really clever. He had no money, but also no regard for money, which he seemed to just hand out at will. And he knew cool people. Patrick had never known anything like the disappearing pencil trick that Ruya Nasi had taught him. It was like a drug. Which was why he was in this shop, to get more magic.

He had never known what he wanted to do with his life until now.

Hafiz Barakat's Turkish had come on in such leaps and bounds in recent months that İkmen felt confident speaking to him in it. A word in waitress Yasmin's ear had allowed him to take the boy to one side for half an hour. He'd also bought him a drink and a plate of cheese pide.

Hafiz had entered Turkey illegally from Syria with his grandmother the previous year. The old lady, called Kelebek, had become the victim of an organ-trafficking ring that İkmen, Süleyman and their colleagues had helped to break up. Now working as a waiter at the Mozaik, seventeen-year-old Hafiz was one of Çetin İkmen's most grateful fans.

'I will ask around,' the boy said when İkmen told him about the disappeared coffee shop in Fatih and the mythical hakawati. 'Everyone in Syria knows about Ahmad Al Saidawi. I can remember going to the coffee house with my dad and listening to hakawatis. But Al Saidawi is a legend. I think he means something to the people, like he managed to tell his stories in spite of, excuse me, the Ottoman paşas.'

'Oh don't apologise,' İkmen said. 'I've no great love for that period of our history myself.' He frowned. 'So would you say that Al Saidawi is a sort of a symbol of resistance for the Syrian people?'

'Some of them.'

'Mmm.' İkmen lit a cigarette. Hafiz had been a voracious smoker when İkmen had first met him as a hungry refugee sleeping in a graveyard, but he had given up, which was heartening. 'I imagine that resistance these days is to Assad.'

'Of course.'

'So if a person did something to Assad and got away with it . . .'

'That wouldn't happen,' Hafiz said. 'No, no, it could, just that you would never hear about it.'

'If someone stole from him . . .'

Hafiz looked as if he almost didn't understand the question, then he said, 'That would be suicide. Bashar has the army, the

Mukhabarat – secret police – ordinary police and now the Russians. All the power.'

'Yes, but aren't there maybe rumours, stories . . .'

'Oh yes, but they're all just made up. In Aleppo there are people selling gold they say has been stolen from Asma Al Assad, Bashar's wife. But it's just some old rubbish jewellery taken from a bombed-out jeweller's. If anyone had stolen from Bashar, they would be dead.'

'No exceptions?'

Hafiz narrowed his eyes. 'Sometimes you hear something that could just be true.'

'Example?'

'Just before I left Syria, so not recent,' he said, 'my cousin Ali – a lot older than me, I think he's dead now – said he'd met a man who claimed to have been one of Asma's bodyguards. He said he'd been dismissed when he robbed clothes, but nobody believed him because that doesn't happen. You don't leave Bashar; you stay with him or you die. But Ali said this man had a suit made in London that only someone like Bashar would have. Some people thought he was a spy. Then he disappeared.'

'What do you think?' İkmen asked.

'I don't know. Then there are stories about Bashar and porn stars.'

İkmen frowned.

'You know, girls who do sex on film . . .'

'I know what porn stars are, Hafiz. I just had the impression that Assad was clean living. It was always said that his father, for all his cruelty, was a family man.'

Hafiz smiled. 'Yes, they like that image,' he said. 'But there are rumours about Bashar. That he takes young women and then has them killed, that Asma pays them to go away, that the women are spies, and on and on. But no proof.'

'Can you ask around anyway?' İkmen said.

'Of course.' Hafiz thought for a moment. 'I will speak to some Sunnis I know.'

İkmen had always assumed that Hafiz was, unlike the Assads, a Sunni Muslim. 'You're . . .'

'An Alawi.' The boy smiled. 'Like Assad. I should like him. But I hate him. He is too cruel. Syrian Sunnis sometimes won't speak very much to us because of him. But I know some and they may speak. They know the worst of Assad and his regime. They also keep things to themselves. I will do my best.'

Chapter 15

A lifetime ago, when Gonca had been a child, her mother had placed small packets behind the walls of their old house in Sulukule. In those days the gypsies had worked dancing, selling, telling fortunes and, like her father and older brother, with the bears. Then in 2008, the municipality had razed Sulukule to the ground. The Roma population had scattered across the city, although many had regrouped in Tarlabaşı. When they had left that old house for the final time, her father had taken all her mother's spells and votives out of the walls and carried them with him to their new home. Such things could not fall into the wrong hands.

Now, as she scraped away at the plaster in her bedroom, Gonca Şekeroğlu wondered whether what she was putting into her wall would stay there, or whether she would one day have to remove it as she fled her past yet again.

She looked at the small parcel on her bed. What was inside was self-explanatory, which was why no one must ever find it. Soon Harun Bey would be arriving and so she had to work fast. There was no way he would be coming into her bedroom, the great fat pig! But when Mehmet returned she didn't want him to see it, and, depending upon how long she had to put up with Harun Bey, that might not give her much time.

'Darling, I am merely taking precautions.'

Having let her guest into her living room, Betül Gencer sat down primly on one of her many sofas and crossed her legs.

The guest, a tall, smartly dressed young man with perfectly chiselled features and a very sensuous mouth, sat down opposite.

'Betül Hanım . . .'

'To say that they were actively implying anything is stating the case too strongly,' she continued. 'But I fear they may well move in that direction and so I felt it just made sense to call you, dear Eyüp.'

Eyüp Çelik, otherwise known as Lawyer to the Stars, had only just hit thirty, but already, it was said, he had most of Turkey's media glitterati on speed-dial. Ragingly ambitious, charming and handsome, it was rumoured that he had once appeared in porn movies and that he had mistresses in İstanbul, Ankara and İzmir. He was also very wealthy.

'Of course.' Even his voice dripped charm.

Betül Gencer said, 'I have no idea what that Al Hussain was doing here the night he and Erol died, but I think the police inspector believes I do. I worry in case he's got some sort of fabricated evidence. I mean, you know what some people can be like with celebrities. They make things up in order to raise their own profile. And as for the police, well, we all know about them . . .'

Çelik took a notebook and pen out of his jacket pocket. 'So who is this officer, hanım?'

The notebook was a Moleskine, the pen a Mont Blanc. Early exposure to celebrities had taught Çelik that image was everything. The thrusting young lawyer with comforting habits.

'He's called Gürsel,' she said.

'Kerim Gürsel?'

'Yes.'

He wrote it down. 'Very good. Betül Hanım, do you have any reason to believe that someone might want to point the finger of blame at you for your husband's death?'

'What, you mean apart from Filiz Tepe?' she said. 'I know this Gürsel went to see her at Harem Medya. My old make-up girl called to warn me.'

'Filiz Tepe?'

'Oh I must've told you the story, darling,' she said. 'How she got rid of me as soon as she took control of the company after screwing her way to the top.'

'Not that one can allude to—'

'Oh, I'd never say it publicly!' she said. 'But we all know it.' She shook her head. 'I was Erol's wife, and so however improbable my involvement might be, I'm a suspect.'

'In a way, that's perfectly normal,' the lawyer said. 'Those nearest to a suspicious death are always under suspicion themselves until the matter is resolved.'

He leaned forward, took her hands and looked into her eyes. 'But in spite of that, Betül Hanım, I will make sure that this Gürsel man behaves himself in the future. He has obviously caused you distress and he won't be allowed to get away with it. I actually know this man, and believe me, if anyone has the measure of Kerim Gürsel, it is myself.'

It was 3 p.m. and they were eating their breakfast. For some this consisted of bread, cheese, jam, yogurt and fruit, while others shared menemen and others still opted for just tea or coffee and cigarettes. One of the ladies was already on the rakı.

The madam of what was, but was never called, a transsexual genelev, or brothel, called them to order.

'Ladies! Ladies!' Kurdish Madonna clapped her leather-covered hands. 'We all know about the terrible, vicious death of our sister Pembe Hanım.'

The girls stopped what they were doing and looked up at her. Madonna, once a shepherd in a Kurdish village near the city of Van, was a tall, imposing trans girl with platinum-blonde hair just like her namesake. She was, in addition, a very shrewd businesswoman.

'And I know that you all have offered to help the police with their enquiries. In normal times this would be a problem . . .'

One of the girls began to cry.

'. . . but as you know, we're doing it for Pembe. And also we're doing it for ourselves. Because if there's someone out there killing us, we want him caught.'

'We want him fucking dead!' said a girl with long curly black hair.

'Yeah, but we ain't going to do that ourselves, Sucuk Hanım,' Madonna said. 'Now, two officers have just arrived and I'm going to show them in. I want all of us to behave with dignity and play nice. No inappropriate comments and no talk about what we all know but mustn't say about our Pembe.'

A large girl wearing bright green glittery eyeshadow asked, 'Will Kerim—'

'Don't use that name! What did I just say, Gigi?' Madonna said.

'Yes, but her body'll need to be buried and we can't have her thrown into some hole in the graveyard for the anonymous. We need to know what he – her man – what he's doing about it.'

'Yes, but not now,' Madonna said. 'Are we clear?'

Nobody said anything.

Then a rather older chestnut-haired girl said, 'Are they good looking? The coppers?'

Madonna looked down at the girl in question. 'Honey, they're police. It doesn't matter.'

All this waiting around for others to get back to him was driving İkmen mad. And so, after depositing Patrick and his box of tricks with Çiçek at home, he set off for the Malta Çarşısı with its large Syrian population.

Proximity to the great imperial mosque of Fatih made the Malta Çarşısı a popular destination for local Turks, tourists and the Sunni Syrians who had made this part of the city their own. Many of the shop signs were in Arabic, İkmen noticed and, ominously, the household equipment displayed outside hardware shops included orange life jackets. Some people were still trying to get to Europe across the sea by any means possible.

Although he had been told that many of the Syrian inhabitants of the area didn't speak Turkish, he wandered up to a sweet shop, his eye caught by a display of little pastry cones he didn't recognise as part of Turkish cuisine. He asked the owner what they were, and after the elderly Arab behind the counter had managed to process what he had said, he replied, 'They are called ma'amoul, sir. Is very good.'

They were only small, and so İkmen asked for five, which the man put into a paper bag. As he was handing over his money, İkmen asked, 'Do you know whether there is a bookshop round here?'

Some Syrians were said to have set up a small bookshop for their fellow countrymen in the area, which İkmen hoped might provide him with access to some perhaps more intellectual types who might just talk to him. There was an argument that Sunni Muslims like those in this part of Fatih had more to fear from the long arm of Bashar Al Assad than Alawites like Hafiz. It was then that he wondered why he hadn't found out what branch of the religion Rima Al Numan belonged to.

'There is bookshop on Fatih Türbesi Caddesi,' the old Arab said. 'But no for Turk books.'

'Thank you.'

And he wasn't wrong. The bookshop, which had no name that İkmen could decipher, was housed in a tall, thin late-nineteenth-century building that had most definitely seen better days. Characterised by crumbling, jaundice-coloured stucco, it had a set of hazardous-looking steps up to its open front door, which İkmen approached with caution. Another burning hot day was making him sweat heavily, which in turn made him a little dizzy. Not for the first time, he wondered why he still wore the same suits every day he had used for work. Other old bastards wandered around in casual clothes; why not him?

Once inside, he was struck by the crazily angled bookshelves that lined the walls. Other books sat on the floor in precarious piles, and in the middle of the large space was a young man at a desk, who looked up when İkmen came in and said something unintelligible.

İkmen said, 'I'm sorry, I don't speak . . .'

But he stopped when he saw something just behind the young man's chair.

Gonca Şekeroğlu was not a woman who scared easily, but Harun Sesler made her skin crawl. There had been other Roma godfathers before him, but Sesler was particularly odious. A poorly preserved and wheezing seventy-five-year-old, he always travelled with two bodyguards, young men who were basically little more than sheets of muscle and gristle, armed with guns.

Gonca showed him the work she'd done for him so far, which consisted of ten small squares of glittering woven material. When he saw them, Sesler said, 'What's this?'

He picked up one of the squares and threw it to the ground. 'This is nothing!'

Gonca picked it up. 'You just threw ten thousand dollars on the ground,' she said. 'I told you right from the start that all I could do was use the sea silk to embellish the dress.'

'You won't be able to see these when they're stitched onto it! I promised Elmas . . .'

She threw her arms in the air. 'You promised her something that isn't possible!'

The two bodyguards moved closer to their boss.

'And let me tell you that when these are stitched onto the dress, everyone will see them,' Gonca said. She picked up two of the squares and walked over to the window of her studio. 'Come with me.'

Reluctantly he followed her. She held the squares in her outstretched hand so that they caught the sunlight, dazzling pure gold.

'There,' she said. 'If that isn't impressive . . .'

'I wanted the whole dress covered in it!'

'Well if you would like to try another source of sea silk, Harun Bey, that is up to you.'

He narrowed his already small, pig-like eyes. 'You know of another source?'

'No. But there might be one,' she said. 'I really do not know. What you must understand is that the mussel *Pinna nobilis* is dying out in the Mediterranean. Human beings are killing it with our pollution.'

'You said—'

'I am in your debt, Harun Bey,' she said. She drew close to him, fronting him out. 'I am giving you tens of thousands of dollars' worth of a material that is the rarest thing in this world. I will, as I've said before, interweave this miraculous material, worn by emperors and pharaohs, with spells that will protect both you and Elmas and bring you prosperity and love. All this I do in gratitude for your kindness in helping to pay for my daughter to go to university and enabling my brother to buy premises for his meyhane . . .'

He grabbed her by the throat. 'He's very lucky to have you as his sister,' he said.

Carefully and with shaking hands she removed his fingers from her throat.

'Not lucky, Harun Bey,' she said. 'I love him and my love has power. *I* have power. Don't cross me.'

'Or what?' he said. 'You'll curse me?' He laughed. 'I don't believe in your magic, Gonca Hanım. That is my special power. I'm not some stupid gypsy who cannot read or write or think.'

She moved away from him. 'And you, Harun Bey,' she said, 'do not believe a word of what you've just said.'

The young man was called Nabil Nassar, and he was a Syrian Christian. A precise and well-spoken master of the Turkish language, he was also a man who saw the world in much the same way as İkmen.

'Yes,' he said when İkmen a little reluctantly finally admitted he could see a djinn behind Nabil's shoulder, 'we inherited it when we moved into this property. I could sense that you saw it immediately. But you're the first Turk to do so.'

İkmen bowed. After seeing the djinn and then realising that the young man was fully aware of its presence, he had not even tried to prevaricate, and had got straight to the point, which was Samira Al Hussain's mythical coffee house.

The young man leaned back in his chair. The djinn, small now, crouched at his feet.

'I remember that incident,' Nabil said. 'There were police all over Fatih talking to people at that time. Just like today really.'

İkmen frowned.

'I've had two uniformed officers here today,' Nabil said. 'Asking about that precise matter.'

'What did you tell them?'

İkmen had seen more uniforms on the streets than usual, but then Süleyman had told him that Kerim Gürsel was intending to look again at Samira Al Hussain's story, because of course it also included Betül Gencer.

'What I will tell you,' the young man said, 'is that any such phenomenon is unknown to me. What other Syrian communities do is their affair.'

'You're saying this was an exclusively Muslim coffee house?'

He shrugged. 'I don't know. I know nothing of it. What I do know, and what I told the police officers, is that the majority of Syrians in Fatih are Sunni Muslims. You need to ask them. But if Samira Al Hussain was at such an event, I cannot imagine that her husband would not have been with her. I believe he claimed at the time that he wasn't.'

'He did,' İkmen said. 'But why would she not have gone to a hakawati event on her own?'

'Because she is an Alawite,' he said. 'The Al Hussains were a mixed marriage, Çetin Bey – Samira an Alawite, like the ruling family, and Wael a Sunni.'

'Did you know them?' İkmen asked.

'Slightly. They came to the shop from time to time. He looked at art books mainly. They lived in Tarlabaşı, although Samira worked over here. I think in a way it is almost harder in my country for a Sunni to marry an Alawite than it is to marry a Christian. The ruling party is Alawi, and people hate the Al Assads. Every Alawi is suspected of being connected to them in some way. Sunni people want to hit back, even from exile.'

'And Christians?'

He smiled. 'We are somewhat conflicted on the matter,' he said. 'Bashar gave and still gives us a lot of autonomy in Syria. However, those of us who retain a sense of justice – and it's hard, believe me – we have to leave too. A dictator may turn at any moment, and that is hard to live with.'

'Do you know anything about someone stealing from President Assad?' İkmen asked.

'There are all sorts of stories about people who have done things to hurt Bashar or hurt his pride,' Nabil said. 'Some may be true.'

A man walked into the shop, greeted Nabil and then began scanning the shelves.

İkmen said, 'Do you want to . . .'

'Mr Maalouf,' Nabil said. 'He doesn't speak Turkish. Why don't you sit, Çetin Bey?'

İkmen took the chair that stood in front of Nabil's desk.

'As well as for my own curiosity, I am also working for Samira Al Hussain's sister,' he said.

'I know nothing of her. As I say—'

'Alawis, yes. And yet Samira and her sister left Syria. Not all Alawis like Bashar, do they?'

'No. My country is a very mysterious place, Çetin Bey. Together with Iraq, we are part of ancient Mesopotamia, heirs to the Assyrian Empire. Annexed by the Ottomans, taken over by the French, which was of course when our borders were set, borders that we did not make and which mean very little. Only the oldest symbols mean anything now; only something from the dawn of time can unite us.'

'Like your traditional hakawati stories?'

Nabil smiled. 'And so back to your mythical coffee house, Çetin Bey,' he said. 'You know that if the great Ahmad Al Saidawi had been here in Fatih, I would have known and I would tell you, because such a person would have united us. But he has not been here. Although I do suggest that you listen to some of our stories if you can; they are always instructive. They also feature a lot of instances where women make very great fools of men.'

'Some of our Turkish stories are like that,' İkmen said. 'Nabil Bey, thank you, I will not take up any more of your time.'

'My pleasure.'

He went to get up, but then stopped and said, 'These symbols you say that people might unite around, apart from the stories, what sort of things do you mean?'

'I mean the artefacts of our past that have been stolen by the Al Assads, Saddam Hussein, Daesh, and which now are sometimes sold to rich people on the Dark Web. You know this?'

'The Dark Web?' İkmen said. 'I know of it, of course.'

'We have lost so much in that way,' Nabil said. 'You know that I did once talk to Wael Al Hussain about it. As an art historian, he was most concerned. These artefacts are similar to your treasures in the Topkapı Museum. Giant winged bulls with men's heads, called lamassu, that once guarded the palaces of Babylon.

Some, it was said, were made of gold. And winged djinn, which represented purity.'

At the mention of its name, the djinn underneath Nabil Bey's table stuck its head out and pulled a hideous face at İkmen.

Both men recognised some of the girls, and some of the girls recognised them. Süleyman sat down first, on the far side of the table, which was cluttered with bread, dirty plates, bowls of olives, packets of cigarettes, overflowing ashtrays and brightly coloured lighters. The place stank of rakı. As he sat down next to his boss, Ömer Mungun noticed that the chintz curtains were filthy, and the sofa creaked ominously beneath him. Trans brothels were hard places, where money was short and need abundant.

Kurdish Madonna introduced her girls, anticlockwise around the table.

'Now, gentlemen,' she said, 'here we have Virjin Maryam, then Matmazel Gigi, that's Bear Trap Hanım, our dear Sucuk Hanım with the stunning black hair, and then last but not least, Zenne Kleopatra, our token man. Girls, these officers are . . .'

The Virjin Maryam murmured, 'We know who they are.'

'. . . Inspector Süleyman and Sergeant Mungun,' Madonna said before turning to the Virjin and adding, 'yes, we know you know everyone, honey. Comes of being around since the dawn of time.'

She sat down between Sucuk Hanım and Zenne Kleopatra, who was a very young, fawn-like dancer with a beautiful face covered in a sprinkling of glitter.

Süleyman said, 'Good afternoon, ladies . . . gentleman. I don't have to explain why we are here today. Pembe Hanım, otherwise known as Hüseyin Kılıç, has been murdered, and so we all need to help each other in order that I may bring a very dangerous person to justice. Anything you tell us will be, at this stage, confidential. And if any of you wish to speak to us alone, then we can accommodate that. We are on your side, ladies, sir . . .'

'It's all right,' Zenne Kleopatra said, 'You can include me with the girls, it'll save time.'

Süleyman nodded. 'Madonna Hanım tells me,' he continued, 'that Pembe only worked here sometimes. Obviously the home she shared with Madam Edith has been searched and is in the process of being forensically examined. But do any of you know what else Pembe did?'

They all sat in silence for a while. This was nothing new. People frequently hounded by the police often found opening up to them hard. Then Sucuk Hanım, all raging chestnut hair and Botox, said, 'She had a job until a few months ago . . .'

It hung in the air like a bad smell. Süleyman saw Madonna glare at Sucuk Hanım and knew he had to close this down. Ömer Mungun knew that Pembe had cared for Sinem Gürsel for several years, but that was all he knew and Süleyman wanted it to stay that way – unless that position became unsupportable.

He said, 'Yes, hanım, we know. Caring for the wife of one of our colleagues.'

'Don't you think that was a bit strange?'

Everyone looked at her, and so Sucuk Hanım said, 'I'm only saying . . .'

'I believe the lady, Sinem Gürsel, worked at an art gallery here in Beyoğlu before her illness took her out of employment.'

'The Feminista,' Madonna said. 'Years ago, but you'll remember it, Sucuk Hanım. All female artists. Sinem Hanım was the curator.'

Sucuk Hanım shrugged.

'Pembe told me she sometimes did street work,' Zenne Kleopatra said.

'Recently?' Süleyman asked.

'Yeah. She was hard up for money. Madam Edith paid her rent sometimes, but of course she couldn't do that forever. Losing her job—'

'When Sinem Gürsel's fucking mother turned up,' Sucuk Hanım cut in.

'I want to know how Pembe has been supporting herself since she left Sinem Gürsel's service,' Süleyman said firmly.

The biggest of the girls, Matmazel Gigi, put her hand up.

Underneath all that make-up, she was very young.

'She had some private clients,' she said.

'Know anything about them?'

'Not names or anything.'

'Any foreigners, as far as you know?'

'She picked foreigners up sometimes,' Gigi said.

'Where?'

'The Sailors' Bar.'

Otherwise known as the Bahriyeli pub, it was a trans bar where İkmen's cousin Samsun sometimes worked.

'What kind of foreigners?' Süleyman asked.

She shrugged. 'Any sort. Tourists out to get cheap thrills, mainly.'

'Arabs?'

'Dunno, sir.'

'Why'd you ask about Arabs?'

They all turned to look at Sucuk Hanım again.

She said, 'There's a lot of them round here.'

'Customers?'

'We do get Arab customers, yes,' Madonna said. 'Inspector, do you have someone in mind?'

But before he could answer, a small voice said, 'She did have a stalker.'

Chapter 16

All the girls, and Süleyman, lit cigarettes.

'That's what Pembe called him,' Bear Trap Hanım said. 'Her stalker. But she used to laugh about it, said she could take him in a fight, easily. I think she thought he was a bit pathetic.'

She was tiny and looked very young, with naturally blonde hair. It was easy to see how she had acquired her nickname. Someone like her would appeal to the rough, hairy gay men known as 'bears'.

'Do you know his name, hanım?' Süleyman asked. He couldn't call her Bear Trap, he just couldn't.

'No,' she said. 'But I did see him, once.'

Süleyman took out a photograph of Wael Al Hussain and handed it over to her. The other girls crowded around to look.

Once they'd all frowned at the picture, Bear Trap said, 'I don't know. I only saw him for a moment. He was quite tall, like this man, moustache . . .'

'All the Arabs have them,' the Virjin Maryam said.

'Not all.'

'I can remember a time when all Turkish men had them too,' Sucuk Hanım said. 'My father had a great big moustache. Not like these little things they have now.'

'Is that the man who died with Dr Erol?'

This time the whole room's attention was on Zenne Kleopatra, who was still looking at the photograph.

He said, 'It's been all over the Internet. That's the man, I'm sure. And he was an Arab. But he couldn't've killed Pembe, because he was already dead, wasn't he?'

'Yes,' Ömer Mungan said.

'And anyway,' Zenne Kleopatra said, looking at Bear Trap Hanım, 'he wasn't the one Pembe was worried about.'

'What do you mean?' Süleyman said.

'Oh, Pembe had a lot of men,' Zenne Kleopatra said. 'The Arab, couple of guilty magandas. I know they got a bit rough sometimes, because of the guilt.'

'Was she in love with anyone?' Süleyman asked.

The room went very quiet. Ömer Mungun looked confused and Süleyman said, 'I'll take that as a no.'

Then the Virjin Maryam said, 'There was that man who wanted to marry her.'

'What man?'

'I've no idea, honey. It was sometime last year.'

She knew him so well. As soon as Sinem Gürsel picked up the phone and heard her husband's voice, she knew that something was wrong.

'What is it?' she asked.

'I need to speak to Mehmet Bey, so I've asked him to dinner tonight,' he said.

'That's fine,' she replied. 'I've been much better today and I've been cooking. What's really the matter?'

He sounded as if he was outside somewhere; she could hear traffic in the background. Maybe he'd left his office for a cigarette.

He said, 'Oh, I've just found out that someone involved in the Gencer case has engaged a lawyer.'

'So?'

'So, we haven't even charged this person! But then I guess that is what rich people do. They get lawyers involved before anything happens, just in case.'

'If they have the money, why not?' she said.

'Wouldn't be so bad if the lawyer concerned wasn't Eyüp Çelik.'

'Eyüp Çelik? Who's he?'

'He's an arrogant bastard,' Kerim said. 'Basically he phoned to tell me that I had to be a good boy from now on and know my place or he'd accuse me of harassing his client. I am in no way harassing his client!'

'Kerim, darling, calm down,' she soothed. 'Look, everything is fine here for tonight. We have food, we have beer in the fridge, and if you and Mehmet Bey want to be alone, then I will happily go to bed.'

'I'm sorry, I'm sorry!'

'No, it's fine,' she said. 'I've had a good day but now I am tired. We will all eat together and then I'll go to bed.'

'Of course.'

Then she asked, 'Any news about Pembe?'

She heard him sigh. 'Ömer Mungun spoke to her father. The family don't want the body.'

'So what will happen?'

'I don't know,' he said. 'When I get the chance, I will speak to Madam Edith. I can't have her just flung into an unmarked grave. I can't.'

He'd agreed to meet her on one of the benches around the fountain in Sultanahmet Park. They spoke in English, as was their custom.

İkmen said, 'I didn't know you and your sister were Alawis.'

'We do not talk of it,' Rima Al Numan said. 'There are many things of which we do not talk.'

'Which makes my job all the harder,' İkmen said.

'Well you do not have to think about it any more, Çetin Bey,' she said. 'The police are investigating what my sister told them last year now. All over Fatih they are talking to Syrian people.'

'Yes,' he said. 'You should go and see Inspector Gürsel. I know him and am happy to come with you.'

'That I would appreciate,' she said.

'Consider it done.'

They sat in silence for a few moments, watching a man with a huge black moustache trying to sell cheap-looking fezzes to tourists. As evening approached, the air was beginning to smell spicy from the many restaurants and büfes on Divan Yolu that were cooking for the evening trade.

'We left Syria because of Wael,' Rima continued. 'He is Sunni.'

'I know.'

'He criticised the regime. He said they were stealing our art, allowing foreigners to buy Syrian treasures. He was passionate about it. I have no other family but Samira, so I came too.'

'So how do you feel about Assad?'

'He is a monster,' she said. 'But I know I am poor here and I would not be poor in Syria. All I had to do was keep my mouth shut.'

'You regret coming to Turkey?'

She sighed. 'No. There is no future in my country for anyone, even Alawi people. Wael, he becomes very angry here, though. Samira was happy with him until he come here.'

'Why was he angry?'

'No person will listen to him,' she said. 'He tell the police that our art is coming here in Turkey. It is illegal. But they do not listen. At the time it made me very sad. Wael I think lost the desire to carry on and became lazy. He did nothing, he shouted at my sister. This was why I left them to live alone. I wish I had not now.'

An old man selling small bracelets made from blue beads hobbled over, and wordlessly İkmen gave him a twenty-lira note. Aware that his own pension was a good one, he always tried to support those with little or no pension to rely upon. He didn't take a bracelet, and the old man went away smiling.

'I will help you as much as I can,' he told Rima. 'And please, no money. It is my pleasure.'

'You are not rich . . .'

'Compared to the majority in this country, I am,' he said. 'I own my apartment, I have a pension, I have a car, there is food on my table and clothes on my back. What else is there?'

She looked down at the ground. 'Wael was not a bad man,' she said. 'My sister loved him. But when he lost hope and began to act badly, they fought and she hated him. Çetin Bey, when his body is released for burial, I would like to do that properly for him. Could you help me with that?'

'Of course,' he said. 'The pathologist who has been examining his body is also my friend. I know everyone, Rima Hanım, which is why you will continue to need my help.'

They hadn't had much time to talk before they headed over to Kerim Gürsel's apartment in Tarlabaşı. They went in separate cars because Süleyman had promised to go and spend the night over in Balat with Gonca afterwards. Before he turned up at the Gürsels' apartment, he stopped off at one of the flower stalls in Taksim to purchase bunches of lavender and valerian for Sinem Hanım. Not only would they perfume her home, but they might also help her to sleep during these hot nights. His Armenian nanny had tried to teach Mehmet and his brother Murad as much as she could about the natural world, a great fascination for her, but very little had stuck. The only exceptions seemed to be her sleep remedies.

When he arrived at the apartment, Kerim was already there. He presented Sinem Hanım with the fragrant herbs and kissed her hand, which almost brought her to tears. A very pretty little woman, hugely pregnant, she walked with difficulty due to the cruel twisting of her limbs by arthritis. Upon whatever basis their relationship rested, they obviously loved one another and were looking forward to the birth of their child. Conspicuous by her absence was Sinem's mother, Pınar Hanım, who had replaced Pembe Hanım as Sinem's carer some months before.

When dinner was over and they were alone, Kerim explained.

'I lost my temper with her,' he said as he handed Süleyman a small glass of rakı and then poured a large measure for himself. They both topped their glasses up with iced water. 'She wouldn't leave us in peace,' he continued. 'I know that is how mothers are, but . . .' He shrugged. 'I resented her because of Pembe, I know. Before she left, she told me I was "unnatural", giving me more than just a hint that she had known my secret all along. But I think I am all right on that front. Sinem's eldest brother has been head of the family since their father died and he has told Pınar Hanım that he will cut her off if she flaps her mouth.'

Süleyman lit a cigarette. What he was about to tell Kerim was not going to reassure him. But then that was not its purpose. Much as he liked Kerim Gürsel, his first loyalty had to be towards the victim whose death he was investigating, Pembe Hanım.

He said, 'Ömer and I went to see the girls who worked with Pembe at Madonna's brothel this afternoon.'

'Yes, I know.'

'You probably don't know how difficult it was,' Süleyman said. 'Mainly because of Ömer.'

'He doesn't know.'

'Precisely. And of course it is up to you, but my feeling is that the fewer people who know, the better. But it does leave me with a problem.'

'Which is?'

He took a sip from his glass. 'Pembe's friends are very loyal. But because you were once her lover, and because you have told me that you had strong feelings for her, you have to be a suspect, Kerim Bey.'

'I would never hurt her!'

'Hear me out,' Süleyman said. 'Look at it from my point of

view. Pembe knew something about you that could have ruined your career. Theoretically, if she loved you as much as you loved her, she could have wanted you for herself. One way she could have done that was to make sure you would not be able to support your wife, so that then you would have had to go and live with Pembe.'

'She would never have done that!'

'Maybe not, but she could have done,' Süleyman said. 'Now on the day she died, you interviewed her about her connection to Wael Al Hussain. According to you, she then left headquarters and went home. It was there that she was killed some hours later. What did you do after Pembe left, before you got the call to go out to the crime scene in Tarlabaşı?'

Kerim lit a cigarette. 'I was . . . I was in my office.'

'Can anyone verify that? Sergeant Yavaş?'

'No, she was out,' he said.

'What were you working on?' Süleyman asked. 'Did you write a report, send emails?'

Kerim breathed deeply in order to calm himself.

'Kerim, I'm not saying I don't believe you. I do,' Süleyman said. 'But you have to be able to account for that time in case your name comes up. And you have to give that account to me in order to cover both of us. You must see that.'

Kerim just looked straight ahead.

On the basis that it was better to get everything out in the open now, Süleyman said, 'And the same applies to Sinem Hanım.'

'Sinem?'

'It is clear even to a cynic like myself that Sinem Hanım is deeply in love with you,' Süleyman said. 'She is also having your child. I have no idea about the dynamic that existed between you, your wife and Pembe—'

'Sinem loved Pembe!'

'I am not in a position to judge either way. But think about how your . . . arrangements might look to people with no regard for or sympathy with those who pursue same-sex relationships, to wit, our superiors. I will need to know where Sinem Hanım was that evening, and where her mother was. If, as you say, Pınar Hanım knew about you, she might well have had reason to want Pembe dead. And remember, the only eyewitness account of what happened in Madam Edith's apartment that evening, albeit emanating from a woman who is probably dementing, cites a female assailant.'

'You know, Mehmet,' Kerim said, 'one thing I have learned from this nightmare is that if you love someone, you need to be with them, whatever the cost. You will know when you meet someone who is the love of your life. I did, and I let her go. Pembe slipped through my fingers like mist and now I don't know where to go with my pain. Don't do what I've done.'

'Hello, Patrick!'

İkmen held the silver salver on which Ruya Nasi's head sat in a puddle of its own blood.

The boy screamed and then threw himself at Çiçek, who put her arms around him. But he was also laughing. İkmen, to whom Sami Nasi had given the salver, said to the magician's wife, 'Sorry about that, Ruya.'

She smiled while Sami took her back up on stage. The audience clapped and yelled and called out for more. It was always a packed house whenever Sami played the Castle of Magic Club in Karaköy. Housed in a venue created from the ballroom of an old Armenian house, the Castle of Magic was attended by a lot of young middle-class leftists as well as their older counterparts, who included established magicians, artists, writers and a smattering of famous actors.

On the stage, Sami held Ruya's head aloft on its platter, then, with a flick of a wrist, smoke sprang out of the stage and Sami, Ruya and the platter disappeared. By this time Patrick had left Çiçek's arms so that he could stand up and clap too.

The audience began to file out into the street, prior to the storytelling event afterwards, and İkmen, Çiçek and Patrick followed them. Once in the open air, İkmen and Çiçek lit cigarettes.

'That was *so* good!' Patrick said. 'Jesus, seeing Sami actually swiping Ruya's head off . . .'

'Well then it's good that Ruya has invited you and Çiçek for dinner, isn't it?' İkmen said.

'For real?'

'Yes.'

Although Sami could be a moody character on occasion, Ruya was a very hospitable woman and had been only too happy to invite the magic-besotted Patrick and Çiçek to eat with her. Sami would join İkmen in the auditorium for the meddah performances.

'She's taking us to a really beautiful restaurant called Lokanta Maya,' Çiçek said. 'I have been wanting to try their food for a long time, but it's very expensive.'

'Thank God Ruya is paying,' İkmen said.

'Is my father coming?' Patrick asked.

There was a moment of silence before İkmen said, 'The reason you are here, my boy, is because your father cannot be. If what he is doing was not so serious, he would be. But it is.'

Çiçek shared a look with her father that told him she was not happy either. Mehmet Süleyman was probably working, but there was an equal probability he was doing something else.

When he'd finished his cigarette, İkmen said, 'I had best go back in for the meddah.'

He kissed his daughter and embraced Patrick before disappearing back into the small theatre.

*

Gonca Şekeroğlu took Mehmet Süleyman's suit off the bed and hung it up on the outside of her wardrobe. He'd arrived exhausted, but apparently fed, and was now having a shower. It was hot, and so she was wearing just a very thin silver chiffon nightdress, which, she always felt, clung more than it should and not to good effect. But she was really too tired and stressed to care.

Harun Bey, the Roma godfather of Tarlabaşı, had upset her. She had never once told him she could cover his child-bride's wedding dress in sea silk. He'd just chosen to believe that. Now her son was on his way to Sardinia to get more of the stuff if he could. On one of his rootless forays outside Turkey, he'd met the daughter of one of the last divers who collected byssus. Whether he was in love with the girl or not, she didn't know. But she was clearly besotted by him, otherwise why would she steal the stuff from her mother? Gonca felt bad about it. True, sea silk was a magical fabric that should belong to the world, but this family it seemed always treated it with respect, only ever giving small pieces away to worthy recipients. Gonca blamed only herself. Her son had shown her the fabric and she had seen a way in which she could repay her debt to Harun Bey. But it was unworthy of her and she knew it.

She lay on top of her bed and waited for her lover to emerge from the bathroom. When he did, he had a towel around his waist, his thick black and grey hair slicked back from a face that now looked rather more refreshed than when she had let him into her house.

'I've put water by the bed for you,' she said as he lay down beside her.

'Thank you.'

She snuggled into his side and he put an arm around her.

'Do you want to tell me about it, baby?' she asked.

'I can't,' he said.

'You know I would tell no one.'

He didn't reply. Should she tell him about Harun Bey? If she did, she could be fairly certain he'd do something about it. He was the kind of alpha male who would seek to protect her. And Harun was breaking the law by marrying a fifteen-year-old. But how would that resolve, if not badly? Harun was a gangster who claimed to have killed. She didn't want her man to die. She moved her body closer to his, aware that his breathing had changed and he was now asleep.

She kissed him and told him she loved and adored him even though she knew he couldn't hear her. Then she lay down in the crook of his arm again and went to sleep.

There were two meddahs on the bill, a man and a woman.

The man, who was probably in his twenties, told two stories straight out of the *Arabian Nights*. He was good, but İkmen found his appearance – heavily tattooed, dreadlocked – distracting. There were a lot of young middle-class men like him in Beyoğlu, and although İkmen personally felt that their generally left-wing agenda was well meant, he also realised how privileged they were and how scathing they could sometimes be about the working class. Patrick described them as 'hipsters', and had told İkmen that in Dublin they spoke with an accent everyone called 'D4', reflecting their origins in a very affluent part of the city. He admitted that his own accent was D4 and was a little bit ashamed.

The other meddah was a young woman, who called herself Hakikat – 'truth'. Smartly dressed in a tailored trouser suit, she told two stories – one a traditional Turkish tale about a woman making fools of two men, and the other a story she had written herself about the mother of the nineteenth-century sultan Abdul Aziz. Called Pertevniyal Sultan, this woman's origins were shrouded in mystery. Some said she was Romanian, others that she came from Georgia, but the more potent story, and the one

Hakikat told, was an obscure one that had her portrayed as a gypsy.

As he listened, İkmen thought of Gonca Şekeroğlu. Pertevniyal had been a buxom, beautiful woman, just like Gonca. It was said she had worked in a bathhouse, where she had been spotted by Sultan Mahmud II. She bewitched him and became his only female companion until the end of his life. And when her son, the fat and power-crazed Sultan Abdul Aziz, came to the throne, the stories about his mother became ever more lurid. It was rumoured that when he committed suicide in Dolmabahçe Palace, she refused to believe it and accused the Minister of War of murder, kicking him in the stomach. Towards the end of her life, she spent a lot of time with her nephew, Sultan Abdul Hamid, teaching him spells, telling fortunes and chanting incantations.

'Do you really believe Pertevniyal was a gypsy?' Sami Nasi asked Hakikat, whose actual name was Sibel Akşener.

She smiled. 'It's a good story,' she said.

İkmen and Sami had asked Sibel to join them for a drink after the performance at a small bar on Necatibey Caddesi. It was plain to see that she was flattered to be asked to join the famous 'Professor Vaneck', as Sami was known. Sitting outside in the stifling evening air, they were all drinking cold Efes beer, and İkmen and Sibel were both smoking.

'The women of the harem had their own power,' Sibel continued. 'And that went beyond sex.'

'Some of the harem women as good as ruled the empire,' İkmen added.

'And yet in spite of that, they remain a footnote, like most women.' She drank some of her beer, straight from the bottle. 'In fact a lot of the harem women were well educated, they had almost complete control over life in the harem and they maintained good connections with women outside, especially with the gypsy fortune-tellers and seamstresses they allowed into their presence. If you believe in such things, you might be tempted to say that Pertevniyal bewitched Sultan Mahmud.'

'It would seem from your story that she did,' İkmen said.

She laughed. 'Being a gypsy is not enough to make you a powerful woman, Çetin Bey,' she said. 'You have to be a temptress and a witch as well. Can't have nice Muslim girls doing sexy things to keep their imperial lovers, can we?'

He smiled.

'That's why I tell stories that feature women getting the better of men, particularly Muslim women,' she said. 'That's what my first tale, the story of the imam's son and the paşa's wife, is about. In their arrogance, both those men underestimate her.'

İkmen said, 'I feel, hanım, that you may have a personal agenda . . .'

'Mmm, you have me,' she said.

'Çetin Bey is the actual magician as opposed to myself, a mere performer,' Sami put in. 'He can read your mind.'

'I grew up in Ayvansaray, went to an Imam Hatip school and was betrothed to be married at sixteen,' she said. 'My young life was entirely governed by religion and tradition. I knew nothing else, but I felt the marriage was wrong. So when my sister took me to the Kapalı Çarşı to be fitted for a wedding dress, I asked to use the toilet and jumped out of the window. I have never been home since and my family have never, as far as I know, looked for me.'

The two men stared at her aghast.

'I have done every menial job you can imagine,' she said. She looked at İkmen. 'And as an ex-policeman, I think you can imagine some of the other things I had to do to survive.'

As a sixteen-year-old runaway, she'd almost inevitably had to sell her body.

'But all the time I educated myself, made sure I met the right people, and now I'm a performer,' she said. 'On a mission to tell the world not to underestimate Muslim girls.' She laughed. 'Women like Pertevniyal, wicked though she could be, and the seductive paşa's wife prove that we're both clever and can kick ass.'

'And yet,' Sami said, 'these stories would originally have been told by men.'

'Of course. But you know we've always had allies.'

He frowned.

'It's my belief,' she said, 'that men who don't have what some would call a problem with women – who aren't threatened by us – would appreciate the fact that a mighty sultan could be bewitched by a clever gypsy or gulled by an educated paşa's wife. But of course these things mean more to women than to men.'

'Do you know where the story of the paşa's wife comes from?' İkmen asked.

'In the form in which I tell it, from the nineteenth century,' Sibel said. 'But that trope is much older. I mean, that is the essence of the Scheherazade story, isn't it? Powerful man and clever woman.'

İkmen said, 'Have you heard of the Syrian meddah Ahmad Al Saidawi?'

'Who hasn't!' she said.

'Have you heard the story about his never having died?'

She laughed. 'Oh, that's an old myth. But then if you count those who impersonate him . . .'

'Impersonate him?'

'Yes,' she said. 'Never seen one myself, as they're only popular with the Arabs and I don't speak their language. But yes, I've heard there are several. Oh, and Al Saidawi used to tell a version of the paşa's wife story. I imagine that, like a lot of the old meddahs, he was probably a bit of a feminist at heart.'

Chapter 17

The imam's son saw the paşa's wife looking at his humorous new sign and imagined how impressed she had to be with it. Then he asked her, 'Can I help you with anything, hanım efendi?'

'Gonca?'

She was still asleep, but when he kissed her, she woke up. If anything, he wanted her more and more with each passing day. He sometimes felt that he hardly knew himself. He pulled her towards him and caressed her thighs.

She reached for him. 'You feel ready to go, my prince.'

He ran his hands over her breasts. 'You're so beautiful.'

He made love to her slowly, delighting in the feel of her hard nipples between his fingers and groaning with pleasure as he came inside her.

As he lay in her arms, he heard her say, 'Must you go to work?'

Conflicting images arrived in his mind. Making love to Çiçek, imagining she was Gonca, which he did all the time now. His father talking about how his grandfather had been besotted with a gypsy woman, who, it was said, had bewitched him. An ancient idea, involving pointing the finger at someone else in order to excuse one's own weaknesses. And then there was Gonca herself, endlessly fascinating, passionately in love with him.

After all this time of paying lip service to the words 'I love you', he was falling for her all over again. A kind of magic, but she hadn't bewitched him. He'd just realised how much she meant to him.

Hürrem Gencer was the image of her father. Tall, slim, with rather regal features dominated by a large Roman nose. Dressed from head to foot in Gucci, not a bead of sweat on her despite the extreme heat, she looked every centimetre the career diplomat she was. Kerim Gürsel, by contrast, felt like a complete mess. After his conversation with Mehmet Süleyman the previous evening, he'd hardly slept, and when he'd got up that morning, there had been no water and so he'd had to come to work dirty.

'I wasn't happy when Dad and Mum split up,' Hürrem Gencer said in answer to Kerim's question about her parents' divorce. 'But I wasn't surprised. My father became distant right from the very moment he met Betül.'

'What was your mother's response to that?'

'At first we both thought he was just quiet,' she said. 'But then when her name began to creep into his conversations, we, or rather I, realised that he was seeing one of his students.'

'Your mother didn't realise?'

'No, anything she doesn't like she ignores. Even if it's destructive.'

'Like your father's fancy for a new woman?'

'It wasn't a fancy, it was an obsession,' she said. 'Not that I personally have any reason to complain. Betül was always nice to me, and still is. And to be honest, last time I saw her together with Dad, last year, it was clear to me that he was beginning to tire of her.'

This was new. From what Kerim had heard so far, if one discounted allegations of verbal abuse, the Gencers had still been very much in love.

'Can you elaborate?' he asked her.

'He was bored,' she said. 'It was like a replay of what had

happened with my mother. Don't get me wrong, Inspector, he was perfectly civil and respectful. But I could see the signs.'

'Was he, do you think, paying attention to other women?' Kerim asked.

'No,' she said. 'Of course he soaked up a lot of concern from women after his heart attack, but . . .' She paused. 'I thought at the time that he had someone new.'

'Did he talk about someone?'

'No,' she said. 'And of course I can't be sure about that, I have no proof. It's possible he was simply tetchy because he couldn't do as much as he did before his illness. But there was a dark side to my father. Don't misunderstand me. I loved him and I am hurt beyond reason now that he is dead. But I am a diplomat and so every hour of training I have had prevents me from letting my emotions cloud my vision.'

Kerim instantly wondered whether she was playing him.

'Erol Gencer was a loving father, an intelligent and articulate man, but he was also vain,' she said. 'It was that vanity that led him to Betül and the television, and to be brutally honest with you, Inspector, I think it was probably his vanity that got him killed.'

'In what sense?'

'In the sense that he hurt someone,' she said. 'Be that Betül or someone I don't know. But I would lay money on a theory that involves my father doing something to someone, something unwanted or cruel, in order to get what his vanity demanded.'

'Did you get the feeling that Madonna's girls were holding back about something yesterday, boss?' Ömer Mungun asked.

Süleyman looked up. Ömer was no fool. Süleyman knew he'd noticed something.

'Like what?' he asked.

'I don't know.'

Süleyman had sent Pembe's phone to Technical Officer Türgüt Zana for analysis and was waiting for an email. It couldn't come quickly enough, if only to make sure that Kerim Gürsel's name and number didn't feature.

He changed the subject and picked up a piece of paper from his desk. 'House-to-house has yielded nothing.'

'Never does in Tarlabaşı,' Ömer said. 'What did you make of what that Virjin Maryam said about some man wanting to marry Pembe?'

The Virjin Maryam had asked to speak to Süleyman alone after their meeting. She'd told him she wanted to make it clear that she didn't mean Kerim Gürsel when she referred to a man who had wanted to marry her dead friend.

'I don't know who he was,' she'd said. 'Try asking Madam Edith . . .'

Now Süleyman put his phone in his pocket. 'We should get over to Tarlabaşı,' he said. 'Catch Madam Edith before she hits the streets. Speak to her neighbour.'

'She's mad,' Ömer said.

'Maybe, but I doubt she's blind. A very long time ago, a wise man we both know well told me never to discount what anyone says in relation to a crime scene. People detect the most unlikely things, which may well be just the details we need.'

Ömer put his jacket on.

'Çetin Bey,' he said.

Süleyman shrugged. 'Of course.'

Then his phone beeped to tell him he had an email.

Even just a scan read of the incident report log on Erol Gencer from Harem Medya was enough to convince Kerim Gürsel that complaints by or about Dr Erol had increased over the past eighteen months. Apart from the incident around the polygamy episode Filiz Hanım had told him about, there were also instances of unreasonable behaviour, plus evidence of a possible pay-off to a guest on *The Dr Erol Hour* back in June. Filiz Hanım had been rather too keen, he felt, to save Dr Erol's reputation post mortem, if that was what was happening.

He checked his phone to see whether Betül Gencer's brother, Levent Özcan, had got back to him. He hadn't. Kerim had been trying to contact him for some time, mainly in order to discover whether Mr Özcan could add anything to his knowledge about the Gencers' marriage. He knew he had to see Samira Al Hussain's sister, finally, as soon as he could. She and İkmen were apparently waiting downstairs ready to be sent up to his office.

He looked across at Eylul Yavaş. 'I keep trying to get hold of Betül Gencers' brother, but he doesn't pick up. He lives in Kadıköy. I want you to drive over there and see what you can find out. I've emailed you the address.'

Eylul looked at her screen and entered the address into her phone. 'Yes, sir.'

'Oh, and can you tell Çetin Bey and Rima Al Numan to come up when you leave?'

'Is that Samira's sister?' Eylul asked.

'Yes, tried to see me the day after her brother-in-law's death but got frightened away by some caveman downstairs. Thank God she had the presence of mind, or good luck, to contact Çetin Bey.'

Eylul left and İkmen and Rima arrived in Kerim's office. The two men shook hands and embraced and then all three sat down.

Kerim said, 'I feel I must first apologise to you, Rima Hanım, for the behaviour of our officer when you first came to see me. It was inexcusable.'

She smiled.

Çetin İkmen turned to Rima and said in English, 'Are you confident to speak Turkish? The inspector can speak English if you prefer.'

'That would be good,' she said.

'No problem.'

Kerim cleared his throat. His English was good but he didn't use it often. It was a question of fitting his brain back into the right slot.

'Can I have my brother-in-law's body for burial?' Rima said. 'He has no family as far as I know. All are dead. I did not like Wael, but he was my sister's husband and she cannot help where she is.'

'I am sorry, that is not possible,' Kerim said. 'The body is still to be used for . . . ah . . .'

'Evidence,' İkmen put in.

'Exactly.

And maybe you can help us,' Kerim said.

'In what way?'

'Did you know your brother-in-law had a tattoo?' he asked.

'Yes, a lamassu,' she said. 'Wael was an art historian. He felt very strongly about our history, especially history before Islam. He think it was not valued. Lamassu guarded the doors of Assyrian temples and palaces. Many have been taken from our country.'

'Who by?'

She shrugged. 'Everyone. Assad, Saddam, many rich people too. Now is a time when if you have money, you can have everything.'

The men agreed, and then İkmen said, 'Inspector Gürsel, there are things that Rima Hanım wants you to know and things that I have to tell you.'

'Good.'

İkmen looked at Rima, who said, 'I am an Alawi Muslim, sir, like my sister. We come to Turkey partly because my brother-in-law, a Sunni, was one who resisted President Assad. We have only very few relatives left in Syria. We come for a better life. But here Wael became unhappy. He grow away from my sister.'

'Do you think there was anyone else in his life?' Kerim asked. 'A woman?'

'I do not know,' she said. 'Samira work all the time, but Wael, he just do nothing.'

'How did Wael know about the meddah performance?' Kerim asked.

İkmen translated. 'Hakawati.'

She said. 'I do not know, sir. I had no knowledge of it myself.'

'There is a rumour among the Syrians,' İkmen said, 'that someone stole something from President Assad, and yet everyone I have spoken to about it seems to think that is impossible.' He looked at Kerim. 'This may well be a dead end, Inspector, but it has occurred to me that perhaps the community is hiding this person.'

'And this is related to meddah how?'

'I don't know that it is,' İkmen said. 'I simply feel that the notion of secret movements and meetings amongst the community lend weight to Samira's story regarding a meddah performance that was not widely known about. Also I have discovered that this mythical storyteller, Ahmad Al Saidawi, is widely impersonated within the Syrian tradition.'

'This I do not know,' Rima said. 'But I do not see hakawati since I was a child.'

'Your sister did not tell you she was going to see the meddah?' Kerim asked.

'No. And afterwards, she said nothing about hakawati. She just say she goes, then . . .'

'Can you remember whether she told you about the stories the hakawati told?' İkmen asked.

'No,' she said, but then she frowned. 'Old stories is all she say. Maybe you will ask her?'

*

'You do know she's mad, don't you?' Madam Edith whispered to Süleyman as she gave him a glass of tea.

He smiled.

Neşe Alan was, according to her Identity Card, a woman of seventy-five, originally from Diyarbakir. Thin and short, she talked to someone almost incessantly. Most of the time it was her dead mother, whom she berated; sometimes another woman, whom she called a 'whore'. No one, according to Edith, knew anything about the background to her delusions. Whatever living she had was made from begging, and cheap hand-jobs for the truly desperate.

Edith went over to the woman and sat down beside her.

'Neşe Hanım,' she said, 'these two gentlemen have come about Pembe. You know Pembe . . .'

'Your daughter?'

'Yes.' Edith glanced at Süleyman. 'Sometimes she thinks Pembe is my son, just to let you know.'

'It was my mother,' Neşe said as she looked violently into Süleyman's eyes. 'Başak Hanım. She follows me here. Does terrible things, and then she blames me. Are you police?'

'Yes.'

For a moment Neşe Hanım's mood looked as if it could go either way. She was either going to continue to confide in Süleyman and Ömer Mungun or she was going to bite them. Fortunately, she continued talking.

'She beats us children all the time,' she said. 'Me and my sister, she says we put things up ourselves because we don't have men.'

Madam Edith visibly cringed.

'She killed her daughter!' Neşe said, pointing to Edith.

Süleyman said, 'What does she look like?'

'My mother?'

'The woman who killed Pembe.'

'Tall,' Neşe said. 'She was always tall.'

'Your mother?'

'No, not my mother. She was tiny!' She looked confused. 'My mother never wore a suit.'

'A suit?'

Neşe leaned towards him and shouted, 'You're wearing one, you stupid bastard!'

Knowing Süleyman's reputation for arrogance and a quick temper, Madam Edith looked away.

But all he did was smile and apologise. 'How stupid of me,' he said. 'Please go on, Hanım.'

'She had a stick,' she said. 'Although more like a tree it was. She could hardly lift it sometimes. She broke Meral's arm. Her feet were swollen, always swollen feet . . .'

'This is your mother?'

'Yeah.' She pulled her headscarf tight underneath her chin.

'The person who hurt Pembe . . .'

'Başak Hanım!'

'She was like your mother?' Ömer asked.

'Who was?'

Levent Özcan lived in an apartment overlooking the Kadıköy Bull. A popular meeting place for İstanbullus of all ages, the statue represented a large charging bull and stood at the intersection of six roads in the middle of Kadıköy. Stories about its origins were blurred by competing opinions amongst the populace, as one would expect in a nebulous city like İstanbul. Some said it had been cast by the French sculptor Isidore Bonheur in 1864 for Sultan Abdul Mecid, others that it had been given by the German Kaiser to his Ottoman allies in 1917. Either way it had become an İstanbul character, and featured in probably millions of selfies. Local kids liked to tell tourists that if they rubbed its testicles it would bring them good luck.

The entrance to Levent Özcan's apartment block was down a small, dark alleyway scented with smart coffee and sour rubbish. Kadıköy, though generally regarded as one of İstanbul's upscale Asian neighbourhoods, still had areas of deprivation only faintly below the surface. Officially the Enver Bey apartments were on Kuşdili Caddesi, but actually the entrance to the building was in this conveniently dead-ended mugger's gift of an alleyway, choked with litter.

Eylul Yavaş pressed the buzzer on a filthy keypad she had deduced related to apartment number 9. Luckily she rarely went anywhere without gloves, and so she leaned on the buzzer hard to make sure that it worked and then took her gloves off and put them in her handbag for later washing.

But no one came, even when she retrieved her gloves and buzzed again. After a few minutes, she pressed the buzzer for the kapıcı's apartment. An elderly woolly-hatted individual appeared at the glass front door and mouthed, 'What do you want?'

Eylul held her badge up to his eye level and he let her in.

Once in his tiny, sweaty little office, he asked Eylul for the third time whether she was really a police officer, but this time she ignored him.

'I need to speak to Levent Özcan,' she said. 'But he isn't answering his buzzer. Do you know where he might be?'

The kapıcı, Müslüm Bey, shrugged. 'Never see him,' he said.

'You never see him?'

'Nobody does.'

'So he doesn't live here?'

'No.'

'Who lives in apartment nine, then?'

'No one.'

'But someone pays the rent?'

'Yes.'

'Who?'

'Don't know, you'd have to ask Mevlüt Bey.'

'The landlord?'

'Yes.'

Müslüm Bey wasn't the most forthcoming individual, but when Eylul asked to see inside apartment number 9, he agreed to show her without argument.

Çetin İkmen didn't know lawyer Eyüp Çelik, but he saw the effect his arrival at headquarters had on Kerim Gürsel. İkmen had stayed on to speak to Kerim while Rima Al Numan went back to work. Kerim had just arranged another interview with Samira Al Hussain at Bakırköy for the following morning when his phone rang. When he put it down, he said, 'Mrs Gencer's lawyer wants to see me.'

'Oh?'

'He's called Eyüp Çelik,' he said. 'Not yet thirty, educated abroad, lots of money and handsome. Mehmet Bey had a falling-out with him when Çelik acted for that charlatan Professor Tolon.'

Professor Aşık Tolon was a well-known pseudo historian who had his own television show.

Kerim leaned across his desk. 'To be honest with you, Çetin Bey, Çelik is a problem for me.'

'In what way?'

'In the way that . . . Can you lock the door, please?'

'Cigarette?'

Kerim nodded. İkmen locked the door and the two men sat by the open office window and lit up.

'I don't know how, but Çelik knows about me,' Kerim said.

'Knows or has guessed?'

He shrugged. 'I don't know. He may have guessed. It seems a lot of people have.' He put his head in his hands. 'Why do I have to deny who I am? Why is what I am a problem?'

İkmen put a hand on his shoulder. 'Because people like you – and me to a lesser extent – have been weaponised. Not just here; look at America. We always thought of America as a beacon of gay rights, a place where a man like me could openly declare his lack of religion. But not now. So has this Çelik threatened you with exposure?'

'Yes,' Kerim said. 'At the end of the Tolon investigation.'

'Not this time?'

'No.'

'Does Mehmet Bey know?'

'No.'

It wasn't Edith's fault. She'd done what she thought was right, but Ömer Mungun was getting more and more suspicious about the trans girls and his boss.

Once Süleyman had finished his private conversation with Madam Edith and joined him back in the car, Ömer said, 'Boss, all these women know we work together, so why—'

'They've known me for years,' Süleyman said. 'They have problems trusting anyone, least of all the police. And I will be honest with you, Ömer, I am merely standing on the shoulders of giants round here. Çetin Bey always had a huge sympathy with the trans community. His cousin Samsun is one of their number. I can do what I do here because of that.'

Ömer still felt aggrieved, as well as slightly suspicious.

Süleyman took his phone out of his pocket. 'Now,' he said, 'I have some texts to answer as well as this report from Türgüt Zana about Pembe Hanım's phone, so I'd like you to drive.'

Ömer liked driving Süleyman's white BMW. It was the sort of vehicle he could show off with. They swapped seats, and while Ömer enjoyed looking like a young executive behind the wheel, Süleyman perused his phone.

One text was from Çiçek, who told him that if he didn't come to dinner at the İkmen apartment that evening, his son would forget who he was. He accepted her invitation. Whenever he thought about Patrick, he felt guilty. Which was why he put the boy out of his mind as often as he could.

The second text was from Gonca, who told him she was going to be busy that evening and would he mind coming around later. That was fortuitous, even though he wondered what she was doing. He texted back to say that was fine and that he looked forward to seeing her.

The report from Technical Officer Zana listed Pembe's phone directory, which didn't seem to include Kerim Gürsel's number. Maybe she had him listed under another name? A lot of the names in the list were clearly nicknames. Recent calls were also recorded, and Zana said he was working through those now. It seemed Pembe had been on the phone a lot to one particular number prior to her death.

His phone beeped to indicate he had another text. It was from Gonca and it said, *I will be wearing that bra you love.*

He smiled. It was black and red, and held, rather than covered, her nipples. He tried not to think about it, or her. But then that was easier than it usually was, given the conversation he'd just had with Madam Edith, who'd told him something she thought Kerim didn't know.

Pembe, she'd said, had been depressed for a long time. She took pills to alleviate her symptoms whenever she could afford them. Maybe she had medicated herself with diazepam on the day she died? But there had been no empty packets in evidence. 'She'd lost hope,' Edith had said. 'She knew that Sinem Hanım was in love with Kerim Bey. She said nothing, but then when Sinem got pregnant, she knew it was over. This was before Sinem's mother moved in. Poor Pembe, she began to do mad stuff.'

Süleyman had asked her what she meant.

'She had clients who were besotted with her,' Edith had said. Süleyman had asked her whether there was anyone in particular.

'No. I don't know who they were. She never brought men home unless she could help it. I do know that one of them had money.'

'How do you know that?' Pembe had possessed very little, if her room in Edith's apartment was anything to go by.

Edith had smiled. 'He was getting her smack,' she'd said.

Süleyman had told Edith there hadn't been any heroin in Pembe's system when she died.

Her answer both did and did not surprise him.

'Oh, she told me he'd left her a couple of days before her death.' And then she had cried, 'If only she could have been with Kerim Bey, none of this would have happened!'

Chapter 18

'Oh,' said the paşa's wife. 'I see, young man, that you write for your living. My writing is poor and so maybe I could use your services?' The imam's son was flattered and delighted and said, 'Yes, hanım efendi, of course!' Then she said, 'But I do not have time to do that now. Please come to my yalı this afternoon. My husband, the paşa, will be out.' The imam's son said that he could come at three, bowing low to his beautiful conquest.

Eylul Yavaş hadn't even been born when apartment number 9 had last been decorated. Like a time capsule from the 1970s, the bare plaster walls were covered with faded posters of music and film stars from that era. People like long-haired Anatolian rock exponent Baris Manco, classical singer and gay icon Zeki Müren, beautiful blonde Sezen Aksu, and the greatest Turkish transgender pop icon of them all, Bülent Ersoy. And although the posters were faded, it was still possible to see that the costumes the performers wore were glitzy, glamorous and just a little bit ridiculous. These posters, together with a bathroom that still featured a squat toilet and desiccating clothes-washing bowls, placed the apartment firmly in a past that was now well and truly dead. Whoever had lived there hadn't even had a proper bed, but had used a bedroll hidden behind cushions on the floor.

Müslüm Bey, the kapıcı, had been joined by the only resident of the Enver Bey apartments who claimed to have actually seen Levent Özcan, eighty-year-old Belkis Hanım.

Eylul said to the old woman, 'When did you last see him?'

'Many years ago,' she said. She pointed to one of the posters of Zeki Müren. 'He was still alive back then. Probably at his most famous. We all loved Zeki Bey.'

'Do you remember what Levent Özcan looked like?' Eylul asked.

Belkis Hanım shrugged. 'Just a kid,' she said. 'Tall and skinny. Black hair.'

'There's no point you asking us about him, hanım,' the kapıcı said. 'You'll have to speak to Mevlüt Bey.'

The kapıcı had given Eylul a number for Mevlüt Aktürk, the landlord, but he hadn't picked up. She'd left a message.

'Do you know whether he lived here with anyone?' she asked Belkis Hanım.

'He had a sister . . .'

'Yes, I know.'

'How?'

'Never mind. What was she like?'

Belkis Hanım crossed her arms underneath her considerable bosom. 'Like him. Skinny thing. Black hair, both of them. Can't've seen him for thirty years. Or her.'

Eylul looked at the kapıcı. 'Didn't it strike you as strange that someone would rent an apartment and not use it?'

'Up to them,' he said. 'Although to be honest, as the years went on, I forgot about it. Anyway, by the time I came along, the place had been empty for at least fifteen years. I've never known anyone to live in it.'

'So no one comes here?'

'No,' he said.

'And yet whoever pays the rent presumably has a key . . .'

'Just come home,' Gonca said into her phone.

Her son, apparently waiting for a boat to take him from Sardinia back to mainland Italy, said, 'But what about Harun Bey?'

'What about him?'

'He'll kill you, or take the house or something, if we don't do what he wants!'

Maybe he would, but Gonca just had to push on, and so did Rambo. Apparently the little Italian girl who had fallen for him and given him access to her mother's dive sites for sea silk had thrown him over for a Tunisian. And her mother had found out what Rambo had been doing, which was why he was now on his way back to İstanbul.

'Just get home, baby boy,' his mother said, and then cut the connection.

She'd been weaving the little that remained of the sea silk for much of the afternoon. She still had to wash what she'd done in lemon juice and try to work in some non-sea-silk embellishments to make more of what she'd already created. She was giving Harun a fortune as it was. It had to be more than she owed him. Probably.

As her fingers moved swiftly to pull thin fibres through even thinner ones, she wished she'd asked Mehmet to come earlier. Maybe she could call him and see if he would. But then she thought better of it. Boring though the work was, working with sea silk required her full concentration, as well as her respect. This was the material that had been worn by pharaohs, emperors, magicians. It was powerful, which was why she'd used it in her spells of late.

Why had Mehmet agreed so readily to visit her later? He couldn't get enough of her. Waking her up to fuck her really passionately that morning. Just thinking about it made her need him.

'Do you think Neşe Hanım's description is anything other than just madness, boss?'

Mehmet Süleyman leaned back in his chair.

'She saw something,' he said. 'She saw blood and she heard screams.'

'No one else did,' Ömer said.

'Everyone else in that house was either out or high.'

'True.'

'What we seem to have,' Süleyman said, 'is an assailant who is tall, with red hair, and wears a suit.'

'And carries a stick?'

'Not sure about that,' he said. 'I think that related to her mother. Then there's Edith's testimony that Neşe was sometimes confused as to whether Pembe was her daughter or her son. I wonder whether Pembe sometimes went out as a man?'

He remembered seeing her dead body in Dr Sarkissian's laboratory. Without her wig and make-up, it was probable she could have passed for a man.

'I'm saying,' he continued, 'that I think we need to keep an open mind as to the gender of the assailant.' His thoughts turned to Ömer's sister Peri, who was a very tall, very slim woman. She could easily pass for a young man, although he didn't share this thought with Ömer.

'Boss, what do you make of the cooking of the, er, the . . .'

'Testes? This to me indicates a level of personal malice,' he said. 'Why do that if all you wanted to achieve was death? I've left a message for our new psychiatric expert. I'd like to discuss it with him. My opinions are not informed as his will be. To me this appears to be an act of unusual spite, but what may lie behind it, he is more qualified to say than I.'

'Right.'

'Now,' he said, 'I've sent you a copy of the email from Technical Officer Zana regarding calls made and received by Pembe Hanım on the day of her death. Your job is to contact these people, find out who they are, where they live and why they spoke to her.'

*

'Eylul?'

Was she mistaken, or did Kerim Gürsel sound a little shaky?

She pressed her mobile phone to her ear. 'Sir, I'm on my way to see the landlord of the Enver Bey apartments. He's called Mevlüt Aktürk and he lives in Üsküdar.'

She told him about Levent Özcan's apartment and how it appeared to be unoccupied.

'I've spoken to Mr Aktürk briefly,' she said. 'He says that Levent Özcan is still paying his rent by standing order.'

'Through which bank?'

'We didn't get around to that,' she said. 'But presumably Levent would have to have provided ID to open an account. Aktürk claims to have met him on several occasions, which is why I'm going to see him. Although I'm not really sure what I'm hoping to find out.'

'Betül Gencer spoke about her brother on the night her husband was killed,' Kerim said. 'The landlord's perspective on their relationship could be useful in light of the competing accounts we have so far. See whether the name Wael Al Hussain means anything to him; apart from the obvious connection with the Gencers via Samira Al Hussain, I feel there might be something more, something we're not seeing.'

'Like what?'

'I don't know,' he said. 'But Wael Al Hussain had a box of Compound 1080 in his possession when he died.'

'From Israel. How—'

'Eylul, in the mess that is the Middle East these days, things pass through borders all the time. I don't know how he got it, but I do know it is possible he used it to poison Gencer, though I don't know why.'

'Maybe he was seeing Mrs Gencer?' she said.

'We have no evidence for that, but it is possible. Or maybe,' he said, 'there was another reason we're just not seeing. But the fact remains that the more we know about the Gencers and Wael, the better.'

'Yes, sir.'

Kerim Gürsel's account of his movements on the afternoon Pembe died were helpfully supported by evidence in the form of emails he had sent and phone calls he'd made. Reading all of this from his phone in the car park at headquarters wasn't ideal, but it was necessary for Kerim's security. Süleyman would have to check his colleague's references later.

As he looked up from his phone, he felt his blood pressure rocket. Eyüp Çelik, the lawyer he'd had a disagreement with regarding one of his clients some months before, was approaching. Young and arrogant, the preening advocate had made him furious. Horribly, he'd taken out his fury on poor Çiçek shortly afterwards. He still felt ashamed of what he'd done to her that night, which had been tantamount to rape.

On seeing Süleyman, Çelik smiled. Süleyman lit a cigarette and didn't smile.

'Muhammed Süleyman Efendi.' The lawyer bowed. Had he deliberately used Süleyman's late father's name?

'It is Mehmet Süleyman Efendi,' Süleyman corrected, bowing graciously in his turn. 'Şahzade Muhammed was my father, Mr Çelik.'

He rarely used his father's long-defunct princely title, but there was something about Çelik's arrogance that made his blood boil.

'Can I help you with anything, Mr Çelik?' he asked.

Çelik smiled. His teeth were blindingly white. 'I doubt it,' he said.

Süleyman began to walk away. But then Çelik called after him, 'Oh, Mehmet Efendi?'

He turned. 'Yes?'

'If it will not be any trouble, I would be grateful if you could let Inspector Gürsel know that I am here to see him.'

'Do you have an appointment?'

'No. I don't need one.' The lawyer laughed. 'This is the second time I've been obliged to see him today.'

Samsun had just about given up with the cooking when her phone rang. How Fatma had cooked for twelve people, back when the İkmen children had been little and her father-in-law was still alive, she didn't know. Even cooking for five was making her sweat.

Strangely, the person on the phone was Mehmet Bey's sergeant, Ömer Mungun.

'I honestly don't remember calling her,' she told him when Ömer asked her about the call she'd made to Pembe Hanım on the day of her death. 'It can't have been about much.'

'It would be really useful if you could remember, Samsun Hanım,' Ömer said.

'I'm sure it would, but . . . Honestly, Sergeant, I have no memory of it. Pembe and me, we weren't close, but—'

'Samsun Hanım,' he said, 'you're not being accused of anything. I just want to be able to eliminate you.'

'Mmm.'

Every trans girl who died represented a tragedy, but of course Samsun knew some better than others. Pembe had been on the edge of her circle; she'd known her mainly via Madam Edith. A nice enough girl, but according to Edith, she had very poor taste in men, inasmuch as she seemed to be addicted to unsuitable ones.

Then she remembered.

'Oh yes!' she said. 'It was about Kerim Bey. With my usual cynicism, I was giving her my speech about all men basically being trash, and anyway, with the baby coming, she should just forget him . . .'

She felt herself go white.

There was a pause on the other end of the line, then Ömer said, 'Kerim Bey?'

'You have an admirer,' Sami said.

İkmen, who was enjoying a nargile with his old friend and one-time informant, Vedat Bey, in the graveyard in front of the tomb of Sultan Mahmud II, had been having a meditative moment when his phone rang.

'Sami?'

'That lovely meddah Sibel Hanım wants to see you,' Sami said. 'I told her you'd meet her at the Imperial Tombs on Divan Yolu at four.'

İkmen looked at his watch, which showed him it was 3.55.

'I don't suppose you're going to tell me how you knew I was here?' he asked.

'No, not really,' Sami said. 'Anyway, look out for her, and give my regards to Vedat Bey. It's been a long time since you shared a nargile with him.'

When he hung up, İkmen looked at Vedat for an explanation, but didn't get one.

Sibel arrived on the dot of four, smart and untainted by sweat in a crisp white trouser suit. İkmen, by contrast, looked as if he'd just got out of bed and then poured a bucket of water over his head. Vedat Bey sloped off to tend the graves.

Sibel sat down beside İkmen, who offered her a clean nargile mouthpiece.

'What are you smoking?' she asked as she took it from him.

'Tömbeki, I fear,' he said. It was the powerful leaf tobacco only really hardened smokers used.

'Good.' She fitted her mouthpiece to the pipe and began smoking.

He smiled. 'You're a remarkable young woman, Sibel Hanım,'

he said. 'What can you possibly want with a terrible old bastard like me?'

'I've come to give you some information.'

'Oh?'

While she puffed on the nargile, he lit a cigarette.

'Last night you asked about Ahmad Al Saidawi,' she said.

'You told me there are impersonators, yes?'

'There are,' she said. 'And it seems there's one in town tonight.'

'Where?'

'Fatih. At a restaurant called Bab. It's on Sari Nasuh Sokak, near the Belediye.'

'How do you know this?' he asked.

She took another puff. 'I asked around. A friend of a friend knows a couple of the Syrian hakawati. This one is definitely an Al Saidawi impersonator. Word is he's doing a version of the paşa's wife story, in Arabic, of course.'

'Is it a closed event? What time?'

'You don't have to have a ticket or anything,' she said. 'You'll probably be the only Turk in the place, and it starts at nine.'

Inwardly İkmen cringed. Samsun had been cooking all day and wanted no doubt to give them all a leisurely meal.

'I'd come with you if I wasn't working,' Sibel said.

He laughed.

'No, really!' she said. 'I'd love to see a Syrian hakawati. You're cool, you know, Çetin Bey.'

'Cool? I'm a scruffy old man with nine children, some of whom are in their forties!'

'Yes, but you're still cool,' she said. 'Sami told me all about you and I think you're great.'

He patted her hand. He'd have to tell Kerim Gürsel and get him to come along. This was the first time there had been so much as a whisper about something like the event Samira Al Hussain had attended. But he'd have to speak to Süleyman first.

Unusually, Ömer Mungun was standing up when Süleyman entered his office.

Before his superior could even close the door he said, 'When were you going to tell me?'

Süleyman sat. Genuinely confused, he said, 'Tell you about what?'

'Kerim Bey.'

He felt himself go cold. Then he pulled himself together. This could be anything. 'What about him?'

Ömer dashed his hopes.

'About the fact that he had an affair with our victim.'

Süleyman stood up, walked across the room and locked the office door. Then he turned and looked at the sergeant, whose eyes were hard, the flesh around his mouth taut.

'One of the people who called Pembe on the day she died was Samsun Bajraktar,' Ömer said. 'I phoned her to find out what it had been about. She told me they spoke about Kerim Bey. Samsun Hanım advised Pembe to forget about him, especially now that he and Sinem Hanım had a baby on the way. I repeat, boss, when were you going to tell me?'

Süleyman sighed. 'Do you want the truth, or—'

'Truth!'

'Never,' Süleyman said.

'So let me get this straight – sir – you were going to conceal from me the fact that our colleague and friend Kerim Bey had been conducting an affair with a transsexual prostitute, our victim!' He put a hand to his head. 'How could you? How could *he*? If this were to come out, we would all be implicated in concealing evidence!'

'Which is why I concealed it from you, so that you could say, if questioned, that you didn't know.'

'He could've killed her,' Ömer said.

'Don't be ridiculous.'

'He could have, even though I believe he didn't.'

'It was up to Inspector Gürsel to tell you. I left it to him.'

'That's shit, boss!' Ömer said. 'We're a team. We have each other's backs. That neither you nor Kerim Bey trusted me is what hurts. What kind of man do you think I am? Do you think I'm some sort of maganda who will get Kerim Bey beaten up by his ignorant friends? Do you? Or is it that I'm from the east, so you don't think I'll understand anything as sophisticated as homosexuality? I am shocked, I will be honest, and I am sorry for Sinem Hanım—'

'She knows,' Süleyman said.

'She knows?' Ömer sat down.

Süleyman returned to his desk.

'So Kerim Bey leads a . . . a double life?'

'It's his business.' Süleyman shrugged.

Ömer, emboldened in a way he'd never been before, said, 'Oh don't come on all Ottoman walled private lives—'

Süleyman was up and had him by the throat in less than a second. Ömer's frightened eyes showed how much he realised he had miscalculated.

'Boss!'

'Don't you dare use the standards of my ancestors against me!' Süleyman roared. 'This is not about you, Ömer! This is about Kerim Bey and his family and how we, as his colleagues and friends, have a duty to support and protect him. Believe me, if he murdered Pembe Hanım, I will find out!'

Ömer, red in the face, said, 'Sir . . .'

'I didn't tell you because firstly I didn't know how you would react, and secondly because the fewer people who know about Kerim Bey, the safer it is for him!'

He let go of his deputy's throat and stood back. 'Understand, Ömer, that I have only a very basic knowledge of your faith. I do not know how your people view things like homosexuality . . .'

Ömer Mungun and his family came from the ancient city of Mardin and were one of a very small group of people who worshipped an ancient Mesopotamian snake goddess called the Sharmeran. For official purposes he was a Muslim, but his close colleagues and friends knew otherwise.

'As badly as anyone else,' he said. 'But not me. You should know that, Mehmet Efendi. You should know that I can keep people's sex lives separate. I've never said a word to anyone about Barçın . . .'

Süleyman visibly flinched. Barçın Demirtaş had been a young traffic cop with whom both men had been romantically involved. Ömer had genuinely liked her, but Süleyman had stolen her from him for his own amusement. Barçın Demirtaş herself had wanted the older man and had been let down, by which time Ömer had decided that he preferred being single.

'That subject is closed,' Süleyman said.

The two men fell quiet. Invoking the spectre of Constable Demirtaş had taken both of them to a place they didn't want to be. Ömer had hated Süleyman at the time, and his boss in his turn had resented what he perceived as his inferior's attempt to take on his alpha male mantle.

But it was Ömer who proved himself the bigger man. He said, 'I respect you, boss, you know that. I'd like it if you respected me too.'

Süleyman said nothing.

'Nothing about Kerim Bey's personal life will fall from my lips. And further to that, I want to help. I can see that this is going to be really hard for him.'

Süleyman nodded. 'I have a statement from Kerim Bey regarding his activities on the day Pembe Hanım died,' he said. 'If you could check it out for me, that would be very useful.'

'Of course.'

'I will send it to you.' He sighed. 'It may also be better if you go and see Sinem Hanım and ask her about her movements and those of her mother.'

'You can't possibly—'

'We have to cover every angle,' Süleyman said. 'And with Sinem Hanım we must be careful, given that she is pregnant. I am, I feel, sometimes too authoritarian in my approach. You are . . . gentler.'

'Kerim Bey will have to know that I know.'

'I will tell him,' Süleyman said. 'He's with someone at the moment. Oh, did Dr Doksanaltı, the psychiatrist, call?'

And with that the subject was closed, and Ömer knew it.

As a child and young man, Kerim Gürsel had led a charmed life. Not only had he been one of the cleverest boys at his school, he'd also been popular. However tough and humourless other boys might be, they always appreciated Kerim, who helped everyone and anyone and who always managed to make people laugh. He'd also, as now, had Sinem by his side. For a gay man in a conservative country, he had done well. He'd even managed to do the job he had always wanted to do.

Except that now he could see that changing – mainly in the slightly amused face of lawyer Eyüp Çelik.

'Do you honestly believe I would tell you how I know you have been attempting to drag my client's brother into this so-called investigation you are running, Inspector Gürsel?' the lawyer said. 'Find who killed Erol Gencer and we'll all be happy.'

'That's what I'm trying to do,' Kerim said.

'By targeting his wife?'

'I am not targeting anyone. At this stage of the investigation everyone who knew Erol Gencer is a potential suspect, and that includes his wife.'

'What forensic evidence do you have?' Çelik asked.

'I am not at liberty to say.'

'Being police-officer-speak for you won't.'

The room went quiet for a moment, then Çelik said, 'Inspector, why were you taken off the case of the Tarlabaşı transsexual murder? You were first on the scene . . .'

'Not by design,' Kerim said. 'I was available that night. But as you know, I had already been assigned to this case.'

'Not a conflict of interest, then?'

Kerim began to feel his face sweat.

Çelik leaned across the desk towards him. 'As I told you when I represented the Tolon family, Inspector, I know precisely who and what you are and I won't hesitate to allow others to share my knowledge.'

'Really?' Kerim's heart was pounding now.

'Really.'

'So, Mr Çelik, do I understand that you are attempting to subvert my investigation? I do hope not.' He heard his own voice waver, but he ignored it.

'Oh course not!' Çelik said. 'No, you look at whomsoever you wish, Inspector Gürsel. All I ask is that you don't persecute my client, Mrs Gencer.'

'I am not.'

'Oh, I think you are.'

Kerim felt his chest tighten. 'I will do my job, Mr Çelik,' he said. 'You will not stop me.'

Çelik's face coloured. He stood up.

'Your choice,' he said.

'It is.'

He walked towards the office door. Just as he was about to leave, he said, 'I imagine it must be hard for you at the moment, what with your heart being broken . . .'

Chapter 19

He saw Çiçek spot him and noted that she called one of the waiters over and spoke to him.

'What are you doing here?' Süleyman asked when he got to her table, which was the same one her father always used when he drank at the Mozaik.

'I've ordered you a gin and tonic,' she said.

'Thank you.'

He went to kiss her, but she turned her head away. He lit a cigarette.

She said, 'Samsun and Patrick are creating a cake and it's taken over the apartment. They can't understand each other, but they both seem to think that the more Guinness is used in it, the better. Dad's sitting out on the balcony.'

The waiter brought his drink.

'And you?' he said.

'Just having a drink while I waited for you.'

'And now I am here.' He smiled, but she didn't.

'Mehmet,' she said, 'I want us to go back to just being friends.'

'Oh.' He sat back in his chair as if he'd just been hit.

'I'm sure this doesn't come as a shock.'

'Well . . .'

It did. He was generally the one who broke up with women, not the other way around. And on top of Ömer Mungun's outburst, he was beginning to feel as if he'd been knocked out in an emotional boxing bout.

'I know you've been seeing Gonca Hanım,' Çiçek said. 'I also know she loves you.'

He went to speak, but she silenced him.

'You and I are too different,' she said. 'I'm not going to ask you anything about Gonca Hanım; I don't know and I don't want to know. But I can't be part of it any more. I had hoped to do this once Patrick had left, but I felt I owed you the courtesy of telling you now. I don't know why. You've used me.'

He sipped his drink. 'Çiçek, I'm sorry about—'

'Mehmet, it's not about the sex!' She lowered her voice. 'I told you I didn't like the risky encounters you seem to favour, but I could live with that. It's the deceit and the lies. It's Gonca Hanım sashaying out of your apartment first thing in the morning. It's not ever really knowing where you are. And the final straw has to be Patrick.'

'Patrick? What about him?'

'He's a nice boy, Mehmet,' she said. 'He wants to get to know you.'

'I had to work.'

'No you didn't, you volunteered,' she said.

'You don't understand.'

'You wanted to protect Kerim Bey,' she said. 'That I do understand. Dad told me. But you could have taken Patrick back to your apartment at night. You could have put the effort in.'

'He likes being with you and your family,' he said. 'He's bored to death with me.'

'Because you don't talk to him!'

'I do, but he just grunts.'

Çiçek shook her head. 'And have you slept at your own apartment yourself since Patrick came to us?' she asked.

As she had anticipated, he was completely unapologetic. 'No.'

'No – and you expect me to still let you into my bed?'

He looked down and then up, then sighed. 'No.'

'It's about self-respect, Mehmet,' she said. 'I can't let you do this to me. I will always, always love you, but as a brother, as you were when we were young. This man you've become is not one I can tolerate. You know I deliberately chose to speak to you like this, in public, because I don't want to scream and shout like a woman with no dignity. Even though I feel sometimes as if you have stripped that from me . . .'

He took one of her hands. 'You're so beautiful and sexy . . .'

Çiçek shook her head. 'You just can't help yourself, can you?' she said. 'For God's sake, Mehmet, look after Gonca Hanım, be faithful to her, but be my friend.' Reflexively, she stroked his hair and then, infuriated with herself, pulled her hand away. 'And be a friend to Patrick too. He's a really lovely boy and you should be proud of him.'

'I sometimes wonder,' he said, 'whether Gonca has bewitched me.'

'Don't change the subject!'

'But I do.'

She shook her head. 'And if she has? What does it matter?' she said. 'Have you ever seen a photograph of my mother when she was young?'

'No.'

'Well let me tell you, she was beautiful,' Çiçek said. 'Dainty and curvy and just exquisite. And look who she fell for. Skinny, hook nosed, strange. Did Dad bewitch her? Who knows or cares. But they were married for over forty years and they adored each other. It doesn't matter, Mehmet. What you have with her is priceless.'

It felt very strange being in the Gürsels' apartment knowing what he knew. Hearing Kerim Bey explain to his wife why Ömer was at their apartment was even stranger. Ömer Mungun was just grateful that, although initially stilted, things between himself and Kerim appeared to be normal. Except of course that Kerim had cried with relief when Süleyman had told him that Ömer knew.

When the couple came back into the living room, Sinem sat down on the sofa opposite Ömer.

'I'll make tea,' Kerim said, and left the room.

For a while it seemed as if Sinem Gürsel didn't know where to look. Eventually Ömer said, 'Sinem Hanım . . .'

She said, 'What must you think of me, Ömer Bey?'

'In what way, hanım?'

'That I live this life . . . with Kerim . . .'

'He is your husband, you're having his baby.'

'And I love him.' She looked him straight in the eye now. 'I've always known.'

Ömer was finding it impossible to suppress his discomfort. He said, 'Sinem Hanım, I have to ask you what you did on the day of Pembe Hanım's death.'

Kerim returned with glasses of tea and put them on the coffee table. Then he sat down and laid a hand on his wife's arm. 'Just tell Ömer Bey everything, Sinem,' he said.

She looked down at the floor. 'I was not well that day,' she said. 'Being pregnant when you have arthritis is a hard thing. I get a lot of pain in my joints and so I usually take painkillers. Sometimes I take morphine, but at the moment I can take very little because of the baby. I didn't get up until midday.'

'Were you here on your own?'

'No. With my mother,' she said. 'She was cleaning and cooking all morning. Then in the afternoon we sat on the balcony. I read a book while my mother mended her clothes.'

'What did you read?'

'Elif Şafak,' she said. '*The Bastard of İstanbul*.'

Ömer didn't know it, but he knew that its author was famous and contentious. Sinem Gürsel was a clever woman.

'And then?'

'Then I went back to bed,' she said. 'Oh, and Kerim called to say he would be late.'

'I had some emails to send,' Kerim put in.

Ömer nodded.

'And what did your mother do?' he asked.

'She stayed on the balcony.'

'What time was this?'

'When I went back to bed? About five,' she said. 'I called out to Mum to let her know that Kerim would be late, and she said she didn't care.' She looked down at the floor. 'We'd argued, Mum and me.'

'What about?'

'Kerim.' She looked up at her husband and then squeezed his hand. 'She'd been on about how she thought you were ignoring her, especially concerning the baby.'

Kerim looked at Ömer. 'My mother-in-law is old fashioned,' he said. 'She's obsessed with the notion that the slightest draught will kill a small child. The thought of her sealing this apartment up after the birth, in this heat, was making me anxious.'

Ömer said, 'So you went to bed, and what happened next?'

'I slept,' Sinem said. 'Oh, and—'

Kerim's phone rang. He looked at the screen and then swiped to receive. He stood up and said, 'I'll take this in the kitchen.'

Once he had gone, Sinem, frowning, said, 'Yes, I slept until Kerim came home, which was late, but . . .'

'But?'

She shook her head as if trying to remember something.

'I think Mum went out,' she said.

'When?'

'Sometime after I went back to bed. She was home by the time Kerim came in. She'd cooked.'

'Do you know where she went?' Ömer asked.

'No. I don't think I asked her,' she said.

Samsun Bajraktar wasn't amused.

When Patrick placed the strange black cake they'd baked together on the dining table, she said, 'I don't know what the fuck it is, but we spent all afternoon on it and the boy's really pleased with it.'

Although it had been presented with a bowl of kaymak on the side, there was no getting away from the fact that the dessert bore a startling resemblance to a large nugget of coal.

By way of explanation, Patrick said, 'It's Guinness cake.' He looked at his father. 'You've had it.'

'Yes,' Süleyman said. 'In Dublin.' He looked at İkmen, Çiçek and Samsun. 'It's very nice.'

Unusually, İkmen served everyone. Also unusually, he ate his portion with apparent relish. When he'd finished, he looked at the boy and said, 'Very good, Patrick. Plenty of Guinness. I approve.'

Samsun chimed in in Turkish. 'It tastes metallic if you ask me.'

Çiçek put a hand on her arm. 'No one did.'

İkmen stood up. 'As you know, I have an appointment . . .'

Samsun said to Çiçek, 'What did he say?'

'He's going out.'

'. . . for which I apologise.' He looked at Patrick. 'But before I go, I need to speak to Mehmet Bey.'

The two men went out onto the balcony and lit cigarettes. Süleyman knew that İkmen was going to see a hakawati performance in Fatih.

'Kerim Bey is coming with me,' İkmen said as they both sat

down. 'And it's him I want to speak to you about before I leave. I should say first of all that I am sorry my cousin flapping her mouth without thought caused you trouble with Ömer.'

Süleyman shrugged. 'Probably it's best he knows,' he said. 'Keeping it from him was becoming a full-time job. I think we can trust him. He likes Kerim.'

'Unlike attorney Eyüp Çelik,' İkmen said.

Süleyman visibly bridled.

'Yes, I know there's no love lost between you and Çelik either.'

'He was waiting to see Kerim Bey earlier today,' Süleyman said.

'Yes, representing Erol Gencer's widow apparently. More to the point, he knows about Kerim.'

'How?'

'I've no idea. But you need to know that. If Çelik has what he considers to be dirt on Kerim, then his investigation could be compromised. My own opinion, for what it's worth, is that you gentlemen need to work very closely with one another.'

She hadn't wanted to come back to the house in Sarıyer. Even with the police tape removed and everything cleaned, it still felt alien. But being in the city had become oppressive. The press wanted to speak to her, as well as the hordes of social media bloggers and vloggers who had followed Erol's every move. It made Betül smile when they behaved as if they knew him. They didn't.

It was said that in spite of the often sexual content on display in Erol's show, conservative people liked him. Betül imagined the headscarfed teyzes sitting on sofas all over the country being horrified and outraged and giggling. And then when their husbands came home, they would scold the women for watching rubbish and make them go into the kitchen. Then the men would watch too and be horrified, outraged and giggle.

She lit a cigarette. In retrospect, it had been a good thing she'd told Eyüp Bey about Levent and his apartment in Kadıköy, because Inspector Gürsel's team had already been to check it out. She was confident that enough space existed between herself and Levent. But even if it didn't, Eyüp Çelik had told her something about Gürsel that, should it ever get out, could finish his career. So she had options. The fact that she didn't like that particular option very much was neither here nor there.

The restaurant Bab was a dismal, slightly dirty-looking place. Fronted by a smeary plate-glass window, it was lit by flickering neon strip lights that did nothing to build any sort of ambience. This was not helped by the floor-to-ceiling tiles, which were dingy, cracked and yellowing.

Once inside, İkmen and Kerim Gürsel were confronted by a sea of dark male faces. Seated at small wooden tables on slightly rickety plastic chairs, the diners ate and drank in silence, except for a small group in one corner who appeared to be arguing in rapid-fire Arabic.

A waiter in a stained white jacket came over to them and said something in Arabic.

İkmen said, 'Apologies, I only speak Turkish.'

'Oh.'

The waiter showed them to a table very near the door and pushed two laminated menus in front of them.

As he sat down, Kerim said, 'Basic.'

İkmen laughed, 'Says the White Turk from Beyoğlu. You've been spoilt.'

'Well!'

It was then that they noticed that everyone was looking at them.

'This,' İkmen said, 'could be challenging.'

*

He was desperate to see her. He let himself in with the key she'd given him and found her in her studio. When he walked in, she looked up.

'Mehmet Bey. You're early.'

She had some material in her hand through which she appeared to be weaving silver thread.

'I hope it's not inconvenient,' he said.

She put down what she was doing and walked over to him. 'No.'

They kissed and he held her close.

She said, 'Do you want a drink, baby?'

'No.'

'Then what do you want?'

'You,' he said.

She smiled. Then she began to loosen his tie. 'What, here?'

'Why not?'

She laughed, a deep, dark, throaty sound. 'On the floor?' she said. 'How wild! But we can't mess up your lovely Italian suit . . .'

The tie gone, she began to unbutton his shirt. He stopped her.

'Before that,' he said, 'I've something to ask you.'

'Oh?' She leaned against him, pressing her breasts to his naked chest. 'What's that, Şahzade Mehmet?'

He took a breath and then he said it. 'I want you to be my wife.'

There was a huge silence and a stillness, and then he added, 'I know you said you don't want to get married again, but . . .' He took her hands and led her over to the big old leather sofa in the middle of her studio. 'A man much younger and in so many ways much more sensible than myself recently lost the love of his life. He said that if anything positive could come out of that tragedy, it would come from his telling others not to make the mistakes he had made. In other words, if you love someone, you should be with them. He, you see, he never was . . .' He put a hand up to his head. 'I'm doing this really badly.'

'Mehmet, who—'

'It doesn't matter!' he said. 'What does matter is that it made me think. We love each other. We always come back to each other. Not a minute passes when I don't think about you. We need to be together. I need to come home to you every night.'

'Baby, you can—'

'No. No! I want us to be together as man and wife,' he said. 'I want to make love to you as your husband, I want you to walk out with me as my wife. I'm so proud of you. You're an extraordinary woman.'

'Baby, you're a police officer . . .'

'Yes.'

Her right hand, which had a tattoo of a tiny viper curled around the middle finger, unzipped his trousers. Watching her do this was suddenly, strangely unnerving. He put a hand on her wrist.

'I need an answer from you, Gonca,' he said.

She took her hand away and sat back on her haunches. 'Really?' she said. 'And what about Çiçek İkmen? You got her lined up if I turn you down, or has she already told you to fuck off?'

'Yes, she did,' he said.

'Ah.'

'No!' This time it was his turn to attempt to bring matters back to the pleasures of the flesh. He stroked the tops of her nipples, held high by the very sexy bra he liked so much.

In spite of herself, Gonca became quiet.

He said, 'It was a relief when she . . . well . . .'

'When she dumped you.'

'Yes. She said that she wanted me to treat you with the respect you deserve.'

She had started to take her clothes off.

'Gonca, are you listening?'

She held his hands in place in front of her until she was naked, and then she dragged him to his feet. While he continued to massage her breasts, she took his remaining clothes off and then she pulled him to the floor. On top of him now, she put one of his hands between her thighs and said, 'That's for you, baby.'

They made love several times on the paint- and chalk-stained studio floor. Only when Gonca felt she was satisfied did she give Süleyman her answer, which was that yes, she would marry him. She'd never been legally married before; it would be novel.

'What's this called again?' İkmen asked Kerim Gürsel.

'Kibbeh,' he said. 'Sort of Syrian köfte, but with bulgur.'

İkmen put one of the golden fried parcels into his mouth. 'And pine nuts.'

They'd ordered what seemed to be popular with the other diners, together with a salad called a fattoush, which incorporated bread, and also a dish of cacık.

While they waited for their food – which, unaccountably, had taken nearly an hour to appear – they'd noticed that the focus of the Bab seemed to centre around the men who were arguing in the corner. It was hot, and İkmen and Kerim Gürsel drank a lot of water and a considerable amount of diet cola. Some of the other men were passing around a bottle of arak, an Arabian version of rakı, although it seemed they had brought it themselves rather than buying it from the restaurant.

İkmen said, 'This may sound stupid, but I was expecting somewhere with a bit more ambience. The performance I saw last night was held in what had once been a ballroom.'

'Yes, but that was Turkish, Çetin Bey,' Kerim said. 'These people are refugees, they pursue their culture wherever they can.'

'True. But I suppose I'm thinking props, costumes . . .'

'There's something that looks like a pastav propped up behind those loud men,' Kerim said.

İkmen looked round and saw a long silver-topped cane balanced against the back wall of the restaurant. Then he noticed a cheap red fez on the men's table. The pastav was used in the meddah or hakawati's performance in order to command attention and also provide some sound effects. The fez was used to denote character, usually of a rather snooty variety.

'Mmm.'

'So,' Kerim said. 'Is the hakawati here yet, do you think, Çetin Bey?'

İkmen turned again to look at the raucous table. 'What do I know? What I do have to say, however, is that whatever is happening doesn't to my mind look entirely benign.'

'Agreed.'

Their food had arrived at this point and they'd begun to eat. It was a fair way into what they were trying to portray as a relaxed meal that the gunshot rang out from the back of the restaurant.

'Police!'

Kerim Gürsel had called for backup, which had come from the local station and arrived in less than a minute. Kerim, pistol drawn, stood in the middle of the restaurant while İkmen restrained one of the loud men up against a wall with his hands behind his back. The man who had been shot in the leg was still groaning in pain on the floor.

As four constables piled in, Kerim said, 'What's going on here?'

İkmen, whose vantage point allowed him to see underneath the loud group's table, said, 'There are at least three semi-automatics on the floor.'

The lone waiter, who earlier had given İkmen and Gürsel the

impression he couldn't speak much Turkish, said, 'It's not what you think . . .'

'Which is what, exactly?' Kerim said.

'It was an accident,' a voice said. A man who had been sitting opposite the wounded diner stood up, holding a pistol above his head.

'Stay where you are and do not move!' Kerim yelled. He walked over to the man. 'Give me the gun.'

'It was—'

'Put it down on the table or I'll shoot!'

The officers behind him moved slightly forwards. The man put the gun on the table. Kerim picked it up and disabled it.

'OK—'

But he was cut off by the man apparently rolling around in agony on the floor, who produced a gun from his jacket and shot himself through the mouth.

Chapter 20

Çetin İkmen drove Kerim Gürsel's Renault Megane to the younger man's apartment in Tarlabaşı. Although not taking any active part in the interrogations of the Syrians from the Bab restaurant, İkmen had stayed at headquarters with the man who had once been his sergeant. In the early hours of the morning, they had been joined by Ömer Mungun, who, as an Arabic speaker, assisted the translator, a nervous woman from Iraq.

All the men, including the waiter, had remained silent, although they had managed to identify the hakawati, who had turned out to be a thin, nondescript-looking man carrying a book that Ömer told them was a collection of the stories of Ahmad Al Saidawi in Arabic. Predictably the man who had shot himself had died. Unfortunately Kerim Gürsel had taken the full force of the blood, bone and brains that had resulted from the shot. In part, the state of his suit was the reason why İkmen was accompanying him to his apartment now. Sinem Gürsel was pregnant, and something like this could be very shocking.

As he entered the hallway of his apartment, Kerim took off his shoes and called to his wife.

'Sinem! Are you up, darling?'

A small figure dressed in an over-large dressing gown came out of the kitchen and just stared.

'I have brought Çetin Bey—'

'What's that?' Sinem Gürsel pointed to her husband. 'On your jacket, shirt . . .'

'It's all right, Sinem Hanım,' İkmen said. 'Kerim isn't hurt.'

'Oh my . . .'

Kerim went up to her and touched her face. 'A suspect shot himself, Sinem,' he said. 'But we're all fine, I promise you. I just need a shower and a change of clothes.'

She began to cry. İkmen remembered how emotional Fatma had become every time she was pregnant, especially towards the end, when she'd always been enormous.

Kerim, wanting to comfort his wife while at the same time not wanting to get a dead man's blood on her, just stood until he could bear it no longer and put his arms around her.

İkmen, who had been in the Gürsels' apartment before, said, 'I'll make coffee for us all.'

'Why do you speak Arabic?'

'Why is that relevant?' Ömer asked.

'Because not many Turks do.'

The hawakati, whose name was still unknown, had asked to speak to Ömer, in private. As ever, this had turned out to be a compromise. Ömer was with him in a cell with a constable guarding the door on the inside.

'What do you want? Who are you?' Ömer asked. 'I know you're not Ahmad al Saidawi, but beyond that . . .'

The man was physically unremarkable except for his glittering blue eyes. They were, Ömer felt, a little unnerving, especially now that he was looking at him closely.

'You will never understand what was going on last night,' he said.

'Oh, well thank you for that information,' Ömer said. 'Is that what you wanted me to know? That my efforts are doomed? It won't endear you to the public prosecutor.'

'I can help you,' the man said.

'Can you? Then tell me where the guns came from.'

'I'll tell you about the money,' he said.

'What money?'

He smiled. 'If your people haven't already found it, it's at the bottom of the chest freezer in the kitchen.'

Mehmet Süleyman looked at the text Ömer Mungun had sent him an hour ago and frowned. Gonca, who had brought him a glass of tea, sat down underneath the ancient gnarled olive tree in her garden.

'Problem?' she asked.

He looked at her sitting cross legged on the ground and smiled. 'What's this?' he asked.

'Oh, I like sitting on the ground,' she said.

'I've never seen you do it before.'

'No,' she said. 'I don't do it when you're around. But if we're to be married . . .'

'I know you walk in the street barefoot,' he said.

'I do.' She paused. 'Why the frown, baby?'

'Oh, it's Ömer,' he said. 'Been out all night, working. Can't say I understand. Something to do with Kerim Bey. Now he's interviewing a suspect.'

She shrugged.

Süleyman put his phone back in his pocket. 'Problem is,' he said, 'I have an appointment with Dr Doksanaltı, the psychiatrist, this morning. I wanted Ömer to accompany me.'

He was drinking his tea when Harun Sesler appeared. Not a little taken aback to see one of the Tarlabaşı Roma godfathers in his fiancée's garden, he said, 'Mr Sesler?'

Harun Bey scowled. 'Inspector Süleyman,' he said. 'What are you doing here?'

Süleyman's reply was instantaneous. 'Visiting my friend Gonca Hanım.'

Sesler's small, lizard-like eyes did not smile like the rest of his face. He knew. He looked at Gonca. 'I come on business, Gonca Hanım. My commission.'

'Of course.' She stood up and turned to Süleyman. 'I hope you have a successful day, Inspector.'

'Thank you.' He bowed and left. But he had questions for later – and concerns.

Kerim Gürsel was very pale. But then he hadn't slept, and so it was understandable. Waiting for Samira Al Hussain to be brought to them seemed to be taking forever. The little room they had been allocated in the prison administration block was hot and stuffy, and Eylul Yavaş felt faintly sick. After a silence, her boss said to her, 'Did you manage to trace that bank account for Levent Özcan?'

'Yes,' she said. 'Akbank. Long-standing account from 1979.'

'Wow.'

'But when I finally did get to see the landlord, Mr Aktürk, he told me he hasn't actually seen him or even spoken to him for years.'

'So how do increases in rent work? Repairs?'

'The kapıcı deals with repairs,' Eylul said. 'Although the place looks as if nothing has been done to it since 1979. Correspondence is via email, which is under Betül Gencer's domain name.'

He sighed. 'Then it seems we will have to speak to Mrs Gencer again whether her lawyer likes it or not.'

The door opened and two guards brought Samira Al Hussain into the room. As before, she looked defiant and pissed off. They all sat down and Kerim said, 'Samira Hanım, I know we've been over this before, but I need you to think back to that hakawati performance where you first met Betül Gencer.'

She slumped in her chair. 'You believe me now?' she snorted.

'As I told you before, I have an open mind.'

'Unlike Süleyman.'

'I have an open mind,' he repeated. 'Samira, we need you to tell us everything you remember about that incident. And I mean *everything*. What you drank and ate, whether you recognised anyone . . .'

'I didn't.'

'. . . what you wore, what Betül Hanım was wearing, what story the hakawati told, what he looked like, what other people were doing . . .'

She sighed. 'I tried to tell Süleyman.'

'Well, now tell me,' Kerim said.

She leaned forward. 'So you're saying you believe me? Have you got new evidence?'

Eylul said, 'We can't discuss anything with you, Samira Hanım. But if you will help us, maybe we can help you.'

'Roasting balls.' Dr Emir Doksanaltı, a slim, attractive man in his fifties, propped his chin up on his hand and shook his head. 'In this profession, you sometimes think you've seen everything, but this is a new one on me. Even the Italian Cosa Nostra only stick the balls of their victims in their mouths, which is nothing compared to this.'

He pushed the crime-scene photographs back across the desk.

'So – circumstances surrounding the incident?'

'It seems the victim was partially sedated,' Süleyman said. 'A transsexual.'

'On the game?'

'Sometimes, yes,' Süleyman said. 'I've asked for your help, Doctor, because I feel I need some assistance understanding how anyone could do this.'

Doksanaltı smiled. 'You're not alone there, Inspector.' He crossed his legs, and Süleyman wondered whether this was an unconscious response to the photographs he'd just seen.

'Our pathologist has told me that this – castration – would

have resulted in considerable blood loss. And yet we found no bloody footprints, no discarded clothes.' He shrugged. 'This says to me that the attack was planned.'

'Yes.' Doksanaltı nodded. 'And I would also say deeply personal. I can't tell from the photograph, but the penis, was it large?'

'Er . . .' Süleyman looked at the notes Dr Sarkissian had attached to the photos. 'Oh, er, nine-point-two-five centimetres,' he said. 'Of course, not . . .'

'Erect? No,' Doksanaltı said. 'Average . . . not spectacular.'

'Penis, er, envy?'

The psychiatrist laughed. 'Not in the Freudian sense, unless the assailant was a woman. No, I'm thinking ordinary envy that might exist between men who are normal – whatever that is – and those who are, as it were, over endowed.'

Süleyman tried to remember whether a discussion of penis size had ever happened in his life. Maybe at school? With his brother? He couldn't remember. He'd never had any complaints from women.

The doctor continued. 'Some men, while swearing on the lives of their mothers that they do not have feelings for other men, do allow themselves to have sexual relations with transsexuals. In our country, for better or worse, it is only the passive partner who is considered to be truly homosexual. So there could be huge guilt at play here. Maybe castration was a way of expunging that guilt? By which I mean that the removal of the penis may in some light be viewed as a way of saying "this penis never existed, therefore I am straight".'

'Really?'

Süleyman's thoughts turned to Kerim Gürsel, and he wondered what he might make of that theory.

'If you put the cooking to one side, the possibilities are endless. Maybe your killer was under endowed and the sight of your victim's penis enraged him? Generalised self-loathing? Maybe the killer let the victim have anal sex with him and then regretted the act?'

'What about the, er, the cooking?'

'Ah.' The doctor sighed and paused for a moment to think. 'This is where you may have to work with me a little, Inspector.'

'Meaning?'

'I like to consider myself a liberal,' he said. 'I am married, I have children, I really do my best to live my life as an enlightened man, particularly when it comes to women. My wife works, she is a lecturer in medical ethics, and my two daughters are at university – one with the ambition of becoming a biologist, the other headed for a career in the law. Discussions at home often centre around the negative connotations of linguistic and societal norms that may promote the view that women are lesser in some way than men. In my practice I always try to challenge such assumptions.'

Süleyman nodded.

'However, in this instance, I find myself wrestling with stereotypes.'

'In what sense?'

'In the sense that whenever I think about the cooking of the testes, I see a woman. Please don't judge me, but . . . I just do. And if it was a woman, I feel she's saying something.'

'Like what?' Süleyman asked.

'Of course I don't know,' the doctor said. 'But I feel that by cooking the organs of regeneration, she is asserting herself above her victim, as a woman.'

'It wasn't a story I recognised, and so I switched off,' Samira Al Hussain said.

'You've no idea? At all?'

'As soon as I sat down, Betül Gencer join me,' she said. 'She spoke to me in Turkish. I reply in Arabic, to see whether she could speak; when she didn't, I go back again. I asked her why she was at performance if she couldn't understand the language. She said she wanted to see what traditional storytelling event was like. She said you don't have them in Turkey now.'

They did, but Kerim said nothing.

She carried on. 'We were both alone, Betül and me. We sat in corner, as women do.' Did she unconsciously look at Eylul when she spoke? She shook her head. 'So I order coffee from a man who was acting as waiter. I had Syrian coffee. It is better than Turkish, it has cardamom.'

'And Mrs Gencer?'

'Water, I think,' she said. 'Betül, she is very slim. She don't eat, I think.'

'How did you get into conversation about your husbands?' Eylul asked.

She said, 'You know hakawati performances, they take a lot of time. Is not just one story, you know? And then there are pauses. This day there is much business being done.'

'Business?'

She shrugged. 'Men talking, people coming, going.'

'And you recognised none of them?'

'Wael tell me about this hakawati.'

'Why?'

'I like such things,' she said. 'Old things from my country.'

'But you recognised no one?'

'They are like Wael, I think,' she said. 'Sunni. I do not know them. Betül Gencer say she come to be away from her husband.'

'Did you know who he was?' Eylul said.

'No. Later. We talk. Then hakawati begins.'

'What did he look like?'

'Tall is all I can remember now,' she said. 'But the voice I would know. Was very deep. But at this time I am thinking so much of Betül, I do not pay attention too much. This stranger, you see, she had told me that she wished her husband was dead. It was shocking. Also at that time Wael was very violent to me and I felt a lot of sympathy.'

'Did she say that her husband beat her?'

'No. More like abuse. And he had other women. When hakawati begins his story, I cannot concentrate.'

'Because . . .'

'Because Betül, she says she has idea how both her and me can be free.'

There was a lot of money. Eight hundred and fifty thousand Turkish lira. It had been spread out in small bags across the floor of the restaurant's chest freezer.

Ömer Mungun held a bag up in front of the hakawati. 'So we've found the money. What does it mean?'

The man turned his bright blue eyes on Ömer. 'The money is aid.'

'For whom and where from?'

'For Syrian diaspora,' he said. 'It comes from Syria. This money is not taken from Turks.'

'I don't care,' Ömer said. 'I want to know where it comes from. Have you ever heard of money laundering? And by the way, since you have no passport or other documentation, I would be obliged if you would give me your name, even if you have to make one up.'

The man smiled. 'You are very fair, Sergeant, and so I will give you my name. It is Abbas. As for where the money originates . . .' He shrugged. 'It was to be distributed at my performance.'

'Does that happen a lot?' Ömer asked. 'Money being distributed to people at hakawati performances?'

'Sometimes.'

'That tells me nothing. What about the guns?'

'That I cannot tell you about.'

'You can't or you won't?'

Abbas remained silent.

Eventually Ömer said, 'I'll take that as won't. Tell me where the money comes from.'

'Syria. It's aid for our people.'

'Where from?'

Once again he said nothing.

Ömer breathed deeply to calm his nerves. None of the other men who had been in the Bab the previous night had yet said a word. So far, they only knew the full names of three participants. However, there was one thing they all had in common, and so, with absolutely nothing else to go on, Ömer said, 'Tell me about the tattoos you all have.'

He saw Abbas pale.

Süleyman entered the office. For just a moment it was as if time had gone backwards. Sitting if not in his old chair, in the one Kerim Gürsel had replaced it with, İkmen looked up at him in exactly the way he had always done when the younger man had come to his office without knocking.

'Çetin.' He closed the door behind him. 'What are you doing here?'

İkmen rose to his feet and the two men embraced.

'Waiting for Kerim Bey,' he said.

Süleyman sat down. 'I heard about arrests of Syrians . . .'

'I was there,' İkmen said.

'Of course!' Now he remembered. 'Open the window, Çetin,' he said. 'The door is closed. Tell me all about it and let us smoke.'

İkmen went over the incidents of the previous night. At the end he added, 'Of course the one who could have suffered from all this is your son.'

'Patrick?'

'I'd booked to take him on a culinary tour of Beyoğlu this

afternoon,' İkmen said. 'But it's all right, Kemal isn't working, so he's agreed to take him.'

'I should really—'

'Yes, we know,' İkmen said. 'But . . .' He changed the subject. 'What of Pembe Hanım?'

Süleyman shook his head. 'A familiar Tarlabaşı story.'

'No one's seen anything, heard anything . . .'

'Only a madwoman apparently confused about Pembe's gender and whether or not the assailant was her mother.'

In spite of his friend's obvious frustration, İkmen smiled. As he knew only too well, one didn't have to be at the margins of society to be confused about the nature of reality.

'I spoke to our new psychiatric consultant,' Süleyman continued. 'Dr Emir Doksanaltı.'

'What's he like?'

'In his fifties, very open. He sees the murderer as a woman.'

'Why?'

'The cooking of the testes clinches it for him,' Süleyman said. 'He sees it as a particularly feminine form of revenge.'

'Revenge for what?'

'Pembe had several lovers apart from . . .' He left a gap where Kerim Gürsel's name might have been. 'Anecdotally, one who was obsessed, and one who was rich.'

'Wael Al Hussain?'

'Not rich as far as I know,' Süleyman said.

'Wasn't he? You know that Kerim's team found what is rumoured to be a lot of money in that Syrian restaurant we were in last night.'

'I thought that was about guns?'

'And money and who knows what else,' İkmen said. 'Kerim is with Samira Al Hussain this morning, trying to make sense of things.'

*

Kerim Gürsel took the call from Ömer Mungun. When he had finished, he put his phone down and looked at Samira Al Hussain.

'Tell me about your husband's tattoo?' he asked. 'The one of the lamassu.'

'I think he have it because he can't do anything about the art he loves,' she said.

'What do you mean?'

'In Syria, Wael had a real profession. Then he come here and he is nothing. He maybe tried to hold to his life by having this tattoo. When he have it, I do not say nothing.'

'So he had it done here, in İstanbul?'

'Yes.'

'Do you know of any other Syrian men who have a lamassu tattoo?'

'No.'

And then suddenly she said, 'I remember one hakawati story from that day now. It is called "Philopena".'

'I will not name anyone,' Abbas said. 'I will not give details. I would rather die, and I mean that.'

Ömer Mungun could see that he did. Then he had an idea. Leaning back in his chair, he said, 'You're a professional storyteller, Abbas Bey.'

Abbas frowned, suspicious already. 'Yes.

'So tell me a story.'

Abbas said nothing.

Ömer said, 'OK, let me tell you one. Some years ago, I had a colleague, an older man, an unusual person who believed very strongly in the power of stories. When he found himself in a situation like this, he would ask whoever he was questioning to tell him a story. Not one to be repeated to anyone else, you understand. Just a story between friends, from which certain connections could be, but not necessarily would be, inferred.'

Still there was no reaction, and so he continued. 'Not that the one telling the story would be referenced, maybe because that person is in our country illegally . . .'

Abbas took a breath. 'I see.'

'I hope so,' Ömer said.

There was a long pause before the Syrian spoke again. 'Once upon a time there was a terrible king. He killed anyone who opposed him, but especially people who did not belong to the same religion as he. That he was part of a minority himself in his country did not stop him, and in fact he consciously recruited people who were outsiders like himself to make sure some of those groups were faithful to his cause, even though he killed so many of them.

'He kept them close, these people that he chose to serve him. He gave them money and fine houses and cars, but in return they had to do terrible things for him and live all the time in dread. One such person was an idol worshipper. The king had elevated many of their kind, and those in the majority hated them. This made this person sad, because they didn't like the terrible king. In fact they wanted to kill him. But they didn't, mainly because they knew that if they did, the king's people would find and kill their family. And so instead they stole from him.'

Ömer leaned forward and attended closely.

'They stole something gold, of great value both to the king and the country. An object full of magic, a protector of gateways in this world and the next. This person ran and ran, and once they were as far away as they could get – many, many, many kilometres away – they sold the thing of great value to a rich man.'

'So this person became rich?' Ömer said.

'No,' Abbas replied. 'No, they became a great supporter of the poor. Wherever people from their country were in need, anywhere in the world, this person sent them money. Wherever people of good heart plotted to overthrow the evil king and make his country a better place, this person distributed cash. And whenever they gave this aid, the people they gave it to made a sign.'

'What sign?'

Abbas said nothing, waiting for Ömer to catch up.

'Ah . . .'

'This person is out there still, distributing money to the people that, by the way, the people actually own. And people love them for this and wish nothing but death to the evil king who now looks for this person with ferocity. Not realising, in his arrogance, that people are prepared to die for them.'

Ömer said, 'And this person – have they been here in Turkey?'

Abbas turned his face to the wall.

Chapter 21

Gonca Şekeroğlu sometimes regretted giving one of her sons the same name as her baby brother, much as she loved him. So when the latter came calling, hammering on her door and shouting out, 'It's Rambo!' she thought it was her son.

'Oh,' she said when she opened the door to him. 'It's you.'

He pushed past her, out of breath and sweating heavily. 'Can I stay here for a few days?'

She shut the door behind him. 'What have you done?'

Rambo Şekeroğlu senior, who was only in fact twelve years older than his nephew, ran an unofficial nightclub out of his house in Tarlabaşı. It was a popular haunt of not just other Roma İstanbullus, but anyone who didn't fit in, including trans girls, immigrants – both legal and illegal – and anyone who earned a lira or two in the city's black economy.

Once he'd caught his breath, he said, 'What do you mean, what've I done?'

'I've only ever known you to stay here either when you owe someone money or you've got some girl pregnant,' his sister said. She shook her head. 'Come into the garden and tell me about it. Of course you can stay.'

Rambo breathed a sigh of relief.

Later, in the garden over tea and cigarettes, he told her.

'Harun Sesler . . .' he began.

'He was here this morning,' she said. 'About that fucking wedding dress.'

Her brother knew about it and so she had no need to explain.

'What have you done to upset him?'

'Nothing,' Rambo said. 'That's down to you.'

She slumped in her chair. Of course Sesler wasn't going to buy into the idea that the sea silk she'd already obtained for him more than paid off her four-hundred-thousand-lira loan. She'd not wanted to take money from him, but at the time, only Sesler had that kind of cash and she'd needed to pay for her daughter Asana's last year at Boğaziçi University. Not many Roma girls were university educated, and Asana was clever and deserved it. Some of the money had also gone to Rambo for his bar.

'I told Sesler this morning that I would pay him what he felt was the balance of my debt,' Gonca said.

'Well, his men have moved into my house and shut me down,' her brother said. 'I've nowhere to go and I can't even earn a living.'

Furious, Gonca said, 'Tarlabaşı won't put up with your place being closed!'

'It will if Sesler opens up using my stock,' Rambo said.

'Bastard! I'll fucking kill him!'

'Gonca, he is far more likely to kill you,' Rambo said. 'Which will then mean that I'll have to kill him.'

Gonca stood up. 'No,' she said. 'You stay here. I will go and talk to him. How dare he treat you like this! I won't have it!'

'Sister . . .'

She sat again. 'Rambo,' she said, 'now that our brother Şükrü is dead, I am the head of our family.'

'You are not a man.'

'No, I am a witch, and if I put my mark on Sesler, he will be as good as dead and he knows it,' she said. She lit a cigarette. 'I am not having that pig dishonour our family. He will pay for this, my brother.'

*

The dead man had been called Ittack Halabi, a Syrian Christian originally from Damascus. He was a legal migrant and now he was dead by his own hand. The man who had originally and apparently accidentally shot him was also a registered migrant, called Farid Al Azm. None of the other men brought in after the shooting at the Bab restaurant had ID or would speak. Al Azm would only confirm his name and his status as a Sunni Muslim.

The four men and one woman had locked themselves into Süleyman's office to consider how they could best support each other's investigations.

'I looked up this "Philopena" story Samira Al Hussain said she remembered from when she met Betül Gencer at the meddah event,' Kerim Gürsel said. 'And I don't really understand it.'

'It's about a forfeit,' İkmen said. 'A man and a woman agree upon a situation that, if it arises, can provoke the calling of "Philopena", which means that the caller may demand a sacrifice from his or her opponent.'

Kerim said, 'But that's ridiculous! I mean, if that were me, as soon as I saw that person I'd call it just in case my opponent did.'

'Ah, but it's about the battle of the sexes and it originates in the past,' İkmen said. 'When women had even less power than they do today, this was a way in which they could even up the score in a legitimate fashion. It's a game. A man and a woman find a nut with two kernels. They hold one kernel each, and in the event of a previously discussed situation, the woman may call "Philopena", demanding a sacrifice from the man. It's actually a very dangerous game.'

'So what does it mean in the context of the deaths of Erol Gencer and Wael Al Hussain?' Kerim asked.

'I don't know, maybe nothing,' İkmen said. 'That was just one of the stories told at that hakawati performance.'

'What if Betül Gencer approached Wael Al Hussain to kill her husband?' Eylul said.

They all thought for a moment, and then Ömer Mungun said, 'Wouldn't that be dangerous? Given the history between Samira and Betül?'

'Yes. But wouldn't it also be the last place we would look?'

'But why would Wael do it?' Ömer said. 'What's his motive? I know he didn't live in luxury, but if his lamassu tattoo is anything to go by, he had been given money by this person who was once in Assad's inner circle.'

'Which could just be a story,' Süleyman said.

Kerim nodded. 'I agree. At this stage, much as we may be tempted to explore the fascinating possibility of a former loyalist stealing from Assad, we don't have time. The fact remains that as things stand, it seems most likely that Gencer killed Al Hussain and then either killed himself or imbibed the poison unwittingly.'

'But where's the motive?' İkmen asked. 'Just being Samira Al Hussain's husband can't be enough, surely? Wael wasn't involved in his wife's attempt upon Erol's life.'

Kerim said, 'If you believe Samira Al Hussain, he was an intended victim.'

'Do you believe her?'

He thought for a moment. 'Part of me does. No disrespect to Mehmet Bey, but in retrospect there may be something there.'

'I understand that,' Süleyman said. 'Personally I need to find someone who remembers or has at least seen these two lovers alleged to have been in Pembe Hanım's life.'

He saw Kerim Gürsel shrink away slightly and didn't look at him.

'One man with money, apparently, and another who was obsessed with Pembe. Not one and the same, I am told,' Süleyman said. 'But even the trans woman she lived with doesn't know, while our psychiatrist, Dr Doksanaltı, is of the opinion that the killer is female.'

'Female?'

He looked at Eylul Yavaş. 'The doctor believes the cooking of the testes is a particularly feminine act of spite.'

He saw her face colour. 'Oh,' she said, 'because all women cook, of course!'

'Dr Doksanaltı freely admitted he was stereotyping, Sergeant,' he said. 'But as a psychiatrist, that is how he sees it. A woman asserting her dominance over a transsexual.'

'Why?'

'Revenge, he said.'

'Revenge for what?'

'We don't know,' Süleyman said. 'And because we don't know, we have to accept that Dr Doksanaltı may be wrong. My own opinion leans towards a male assailant. I mean—'

His phone rang. He looked at the screen. 'Sorry. It's Dr Sarkissian. I must take it.'

The others continued their discussion around him, but Süleyman was completely absorbed in what the pathologist was telling him. So much so that eventually the others stopped talking and just looked at his pale, frowning face.

'Do you like it?'

Patrick Süleyman smiled. 'I've always liked pancakes.'

'We call it gözleme,' Kemal İkmen said. 'This one with the cheese and potato is my favourite. If you're still hungry, we can get another one later.'

'I don't think I will be,' Patrick said.

Their street-food tour of Beyoğlu had involved many different types of food, including stuffed mussels (midye), kokoreç (grilled lamb's intestines), şerbet in various flavours, köfte, şiş kebab and finally gözleme or savoury pancakes.

'You might be,' Kemal said. 'After I have taken you over into bad İstanbul.'

'Bad İstanbul?'

Kemal laughed. 'Tarlabaşı,' he said, pointing across the noisy and choked Tarlabaşı Bulvarı that separated Beyoğlu from its more raucous neighbour. 'Where all the naughty people go. Where Auntie Samsun works.'

Patrick knew that Samsun Bajraktar worked in a bar, but he didn't know where.

Kemal and Patrick crossed the Bulvarı and disappeared into the vast honeycomb that was Tarlabaşı. It was a strange place, characterised by small unmade streets lined with tall, ornate nineteenth-century buildings, many of which seemed to be crumbling into the ground. Some of the roofs had long since caved in, replaced by sheets of blue plastic. There was a smell in the air that was a cross between fermenting fruit and faeces, and kids ran about in gangs, pushing past old grannies in headscarves, tall, heavily made-up trans girls, and young men striking drug deals in dark alleyways.

'This is where, a long time ago, a lot of Greek and Armenian people lived,' Kemal explained. 'They were bourgeois, shopkeepers and artisans. Your dad had a nanny who came from here when he was young, I think.'

Patrick looked up and saw washing slung across on lines above his head. When he looked down again, he saw an extraordinary figure walking up a steep incline towards them. It was a woman, extravagantly dressed in red and black, and she appeared to have hair down to her feet.

Kerim Gürsel rang the doorbell and then stepped back to be on the same level as Arto Sarkissian. After what seemed like a lifetime, but was really only a few seconds, the door opened and Betül Gencer said, 'Hello?'

Kerim smiled. 'I am really sorry to disturb you, Mrs Gencer,' he said.

She looked at the doctor.

'This is our pathologist, Dr Sarkissian,' Kerim continued. 'May we come in?'

'Of course.'

Last time he'd seen this house, it had been in the wake of Erol Gencer and Wael Al Hussain's deaths. Now cleaned and tidied, it almost looked like a different place.

Betül Gencer led them into the large living room, where Kerim remembered talking to Süleyman when'd he arrived in the middle of that awful night.

'Do sit down, please,' Betül said, and once the men were settled, she seated herself. 'So how can I help you?' She smiled.

The doctor took the lead, which was fitting.

'Mrs Gencer,' he said, 'you may remember that on the night of your husband's unfortunate death, we took a cheek swab from you in order to compare your DNA with that which must of necessity be all over this house.'

'Yes?'

He looked grave now. 'Well, I fear your sample has been contaminated. This does happen from time to time and I can only offer you my most sincere apologies.'

'Contaminated? How?'

'I'm afraid that even in laboratories accidents happen,' he said. 'However, what this means is that we will have to ask you for another sample.'

'Oh.'

'This is purely for the sake of elimination,' Kerim said. 'Quite standard practice, as we explained to you the first time.'

She paused for a moment, and then said, 'I don't need to contact my lawyer?'

'Not unless you want to,' Kerim replied. 'Inform him by all means, but this is routine. The only reason the doctor has attended personally is to ensure that this sample is taken correctly.'

'I will perform the re-test myself,' Sarkissian said.

She acquiesced, and the cheek swab was duly taken. However, once out of the house and back in Kerim Gürsel's car, the doctor said, 'Thank God she didn't insist on having Eyüp Çelik in attendance.'

'We would have stuck to the same story,' Kerim said as he drove to the end of the road.

'Yes,' Arto Sarkissian said, 'but depending upon how much he knows, he might well have made trouble.'

'You think?'

'He is educated. She, for all her latter-day learning, isn't.'

Kemal bowed to her. Gonca Şekeroğlu wasn't just a friend of his father's, she was also the lover of Patrick Süleyman's father. His sister Çiçek had told Kemal that she had finished her liaison with Mehmet Süleyman because of this woman. But in spite of himself, Kemal liked Gonca and knew that his father would be angry were he to ignore her. If only he wasn't with Patrick . . .

'Gonca Hanım,' he said.

But her eyes were fixed on the boy. Kemal didn't know whether she'd seen him before or not.

'This is . . .'

'Yes,' Kemal said. 'Patrick.'

The boy looked right at her and, to his surprise, Kemal saw Gonca flinch.

Summoning the sum total of her English skills, she said, 'Hello.'

'Hello,' Patrick said.

Gonca moved her head so that she could look at Patrick from several different angles.

Kemal eventually said, 'Can we help you with something, Gonca Hanım?'

'No,' she said, still looking at the boy. 'Is your father well, Kemal Bey?'

'No, but it's kind of you to ask,' he said.

Suddenly all her attention was on him.

'İkmen is ill?'

He laughed. 'No,' he said. 'It's just that being well and being my dad are things that are mutually exclusive, hanım.'

'Ah!' She smiled. 'So what are you doing in Tarlabaşı? This isn't the sort of place you should be bringing foreigners.'

'Patrick is a Turk,' Kemal said. 'And he should see all aspects of life in his father's city. I'm sure he's seen some rough places in his own city.' He switched to English. 'Patrick, are there places like this in Dublin?'

'Yeah. Not exactly like this. More, like, sort of old blocks of flats. Ballymun, in the north of the city, is rough. People do drugs – skag and that – and there's a lot of drinking.'

'Here too,' Kemal said. He turned back to Gonca and switched to Turkish. 'He says he's been to rough places in Ireland.'

'Oh.' She pulled the black spider's web shawl she wore up to her shoulders. 'I must be on my way.'

'Of course.'

She waved a hand and then she was gone.

Once she had disappeared down the hill into a tiny blackened alley, Patrick turned to Kemal. 'I do know who she is.'

'Gonca Hanım . . .'

'She's my father's lover,' he said. Then, seeing Kemal struggle to respond, he put a hand on his shoulder. 'It's all right, I know. Mammy told me about her when I asked her why they'd got divorced.'

Kemal looked down at the ground. 'Sometimes people don't do the things we want them to do.'

'Like Çiçek?'

He looked up.

'I know that too,' Patrick said. 'She told me last night that she'd finished with him. I thought it was too good to be true that she'd want someone like him.'

Kemal put his arm around the boy.

'Your dad is great,' he said.

'Your sister's better.'

'Maybe.' He shrugged. 'I think so, but then she's my sister.'

They began to walk.

Kemal said, 'You know, Patrick, Gonca Hanım is not a bad person. She's very clever and creative and she really loves your dad.'

'Mammy said she's amazing looking.'

'She is!' He laughed. 'But what is important is that your dad loves her. We can't choose who we love, Patrick.'

'Will he marry her, do you think?'

Kemal shrugged. 'I don't know.' He took the boy's arm. 'Come, I want to introduce you to someone,' he said. 'You know, many years ago, we had a mayor in the city who used to call Tarlabaşı "the Poisoned Princess" because of all the drug addicts that live here. What he didn't know is that there has been a real princess here for a very long time . . .'

When Kerim Gürsel had left, the three remaining police officers, plus İkmen, sat in tense silence for a while. Eventually it was Süleyman who spoke.

'Of course, it could be a mistake.'

'It could,' Eylul said. 'But . . . No, it's pointless speculating.'

'What about all these Syrians you have in custody?' Süleyman asked Ömer Mungun.

Eylul answered for him. 'Charged with possession of firearms.'

'Impossible to get any more out of them at this stage,' Ömer said. 'The man who shot the man who then committed suicide won't explain why he shot him. Just stays silent, occasionally mumbling his name and religion.'

'What about the meddah?'

He shook his head. 'Can't work out whether he's an enigma or is simply playing at it.'

'You don't think he's three hundred years old?' İkmen asked.

Ömer smiled, but then almost immediately frowned. 'Of course not, but . . . If he's not lying, he's involved in something that could mean members of Assad's security forces may be in this country. People like Assad don't just let things go. Theft from him personally will be taken seriously. You and Kerim Bey, Çetin Bey, watched a man take his own life for some reason: either fear, or an ideal, or both.'

Süleyman's phone rang and he picked it up. He said, 'I'll put you on speaker so we can all hear.'

It was Kerim Gürsel. He said, 'I've just dropped Dr Sarkissian off at the lab.'

'Did everything go to plan?'

'Yes,' he said. 'Although at one point Betül Gencer did consider calling her lawyer.'

'But you managed to dissuade her.'

'We told her the re-test was to make up for incompetence on our part, which she bought. But she may well call Çelik now. That could be problematic.'

'It could be,' Süleyman said. 'Provided he understands what DNA testing can reveal.'

'He's a criminal lawyer . . .'

'Who uses scientific experts to inform his arguments,' Süleyman said. 'What he personally knows may be very little. When did the doctor say he would have a definitive result, provided the sample proves viable?'

'Tomorrow lunchtime,' Kerim said.

'And so we sit on this until then.'

'Seems so. I need to speak to this meddah Ömer Bey interviewed.'

Ömer said, 'I'm here, Kerim Bey.'

'Good. Let's speak when I get back.'

İkmen, who had been frowning, said, 'Kerim Bey, do you mind if I sit in on that?'

The serving officers all looked at each other.

İkmen continued, 'I promised Rima Hanım, Samira Al Hussain's sister, that I'd find any hocus-pocus if I could, if it existed.'

There was another pause, then Kerim said, 'All right, Çetin Bey. But just as an observer.'

'Agreed.'

'Not a word.'

'No.'

Kerim Gürsel ended the call. Once again the group looked from one to another and then Süleyman stood up. 'And so until tomorrow, everyone . . .'

Ömer shrugged. 'Boss, do you really think—'

'I know we need to wait,' Süleyman said. 'Because if this is real. If the DNA sample Betül Gencer gave us the first time was in fact male . . .'

İkmen held up a hand. 'Do not tempt fate.'

Eylul and Ömer left Kerim Gürsel's office. When they had gone, Süleyman turned to İkmen. 'You're staying here?'

'Yes. Can't resist the opportunity of seeing this meddah for myself. I told you I'd find the magic, and if anyone has it, I feel it may be this man. You know that if the doctor is right, you may have some explaining to do about Samira Al Hussain?'

'I do. I'm not infallible.'

İkmen laughed.

'What?'

'Oh Mehmet,' İkmen said. 'If I have to explain . . .'

Süleyman sniffed and then changed the subject. 'Is Kemal taking Patrick back to your apartment this afternoon?' he asked.

'He is,' İkmen said. 'Do I take it you'd like to see the boy?'

'If I may.'

'Well, Samsun will be in even if no one else is. Don't know how long I'll be, but you're always welcome.' He put a hand on his friend's shoulder. 'Even if my daughter has decided she no longer wants to be your girlfriend.'

Süleyman offered İkmen a cigarette, which he took, and they both lit up.

'She was right to dump me,' he said.

Although he wanted to say *I know*, İkmen managed to restrain himself. 'Your heart belongs to Gonca Hanım.'

Süleyman sat on the edge of Kerim's desk. 'Even if she's bewitched me?'

İkmen pushed the question away with a wave of his hand. 'So what if she has?'

'That's what Çiçek said.'

'I know. Gonca is a wonderful, half-mad, gloriously fabulous and sexy woman, and she has magic. You're lucky to have her and she's lucky to have you. I've never seen a woman so besotted.'

'I've asked her to marry me and she's said yes.'

'Good.' İkmen smiled. 'It's about time. But cheat on her and what happened to poor Pembe Hanım will also be your fate.'

'I know. Çetin, did you know that Gonca had never been officially married?'

'I guessed as much,' İkmen said. 'The Roma do their own version of marriage. I'm assuming you want to have a formal ceremony.'

'I've little choice. And of course, I find it preferable. Gonca, however, would like a traditional Roma wedding too.'

'Expect to be very poor afterwards,' İkmen said. 'You know how their weddings are. Free food and drink for thousands, a wedding cake like a skyscraper, a ring that can be seen from the bottom of the street, and don't get me started on the dress.'

Süleyman smiled. 'I love her,' he said.

İkmen kissed him on both cheeks.

'I hope you will both be blissfully happy.'

*

Gonca Şekeroğlu found her brother pacing back and forth across her garden.

'What did he say?' Rambo asked.

'I've dealt with it,' she said. But her face was white and she was sweating.

'What happened?'

'You can go back tomorrow. He wants some party for his troops tonight.'

'Using my liquor!'

She grabbed him by the throat. 'Let him do it,' she said. 'Don't argue with me, Rambo.'

He pulled away from her.

'I'm telling you, I have sorted this out. I'm selling my soul to the Devil, but everything will be as we want it, and that is all that matters.'

He knew that like all the women in his family, she practised witchcraft, but did she really mean she was actually selling her soul? And for what?

'Gonca . . .'

'You will have your bar and I will . . .' She stopped, as if she'd just remembered something, then took her brother's hand and led him indoors. Once inside her kitchen, she said, 'I'm getting married, Rambo, and I want you to be all right about it.'

Stunned, he sat down. 'Married?'

'To Mehmet Bey. He asked me last night. I said yes.'

Was this what she meant by selling her soul to the Devil? Marrying a gaco? Who was also a policeman? Was she going to get *him* to go and deal with Harun Sesler?

He shook his head. 'How?'

'How what?'

'After all this time?' he said. 'Why now does he want to marry you? And what'll his family think? What will ours think?'

'Well, as the most senior member of the family now that Dad

and Şükrü have gone, it's down to me,' Gonca said. 'And I want him and so I'll do it.'

'Don't know what the rest of the family'll make of it.'

'No, and I really don't care. Apart from you, that is, little brother.'

What did he think of it? He'd always quite liked Mehmet Süleyman, even if he had found his position as 'the law' sometimes problematic. Eventually he said, 'What sort of wedding you having?'

'I'm having two,' she said. 'Traditional, and a legal one for Mehmet's family.'

'Do you think they'll . . .'

'Oh, his mother hates me,' she said.

Rambo looked down at the floor, bemused. Then he said, 'So what about Harun Bey?'

'You leave him to me,' she said. 'Stay here tonight, go back tomorrow and things'll be all right.'

As simple as that? Harun Sesler was a gangster who killed people. Rambo couldn't see any world in which that would just suddenly be 'all right'.

Chapter 22

'Who did this person sell it to?' Ömer Mungun asked Abbas.

Either the Syrian didn't hear, or he was too intent upon İkmen, who sat by the door saying nothing, holding his gaze. Either way, he didn't answer.

'People are dying because of this,' Ömer continued. 'I fear that a man whose death I have been investigating may be one of them. Does the name Wael Al Hussain mean anything to you?'

Again nothing.

Kerim Gürsel tapped his colleague's arm. 'Ask him about the guns.'

This time the Syrian spoke, in Turkish.

'I have told you I know nothing about the guns,' he said. 'The money that is distributed may be used by the diaspora in any way they see fit.'

Now that they'd finally got him talking in Turkish, Kerim addressed him directly.

'If, as you say, this person is only interested in supporting Syrians forced to flee your country, don't you think it is irresponsible to enable them to purchase arms?' he said. 'Especially in a country like Turkey that has its own problems with terrorism. From my point of view, how do I know those arms we found at the Bab were not destined for Kurdish separatist fighters?'

'They are not,' Abbas said.

'And I'm supposed to take your word for that?'

'We have no problem with Turks or Kurds, only Assad.'

'Explain to me how these arms might be used against President Assad.'

Abbas became silent again. It was then that İkmen spoke. 'Prior to this interview with you, Abbas Bey, Inspector Gürsel, Sergeant Mungun and myself talked for a while about what this treasure you spoke of might be. We know it's made of gold, and in order to make a difference to the lives of Syrian nationals abroad, it must be both large and historically significant. You also referenced gateways. Is it a gold lamassu?'

Abbas just looked at him, then he said, 'Who are you?'

'Me?' İkmen smiled. 'Don't worry about who I am, Abbas Bey.'

'But I do.'

'And why would that be?'

The Syrian lowered his strange blue eyes momentarily. When he raised them again, they looked silver.

'Because,' he said, 'you are not like these other men.'

'Oh? In what way?'

Abbas turned his head away.

Betül Gencer picked up her phone and then put it down again. Eyüp was a friend as well as her lawyer. But then he *was* a lawyer . . .

He had also been her lover. In a sense.

She took off her make-up, layer by layer. First the lipstick. Deep red had always been her colour, but it wasn't until she'd discovered lip liner that it had really worked for her. Then fillers. Thin lips looked bad whatever colour they were painted – and if they were not.

Foundation next, topped with contouring powder, brightener, blemish concealer. Glided on over Botox, enhancing that smoothness, that lack of movement. Taking it all off revealed the nasties – broken veins, uneven skin tone, a pimple, a chalk spot, a stray facial hair. Only the eyes remained now.

Looking deep into her own face in the mirror, she murmured, 'It wasn't me. I wasn't there.'

Only then did she peel off the false eyelashes, revealing just how small her eyes really were. That bitch Filiz Tepe had been right about them. 'Piggy', she'd called them – and they were. And without the carefully layered eyeshadow, the expertly applied liner and the mascara, her eyes all but disappeared.

İkmen sat in silence, as did Ömer Mungun and Kerim Gürsel. Only Abbas's eyes moved, as if he was struggling with the hiatus.

Eventually he cracked.

'What are you waiting for?' he asked them. 'What do you want of me?'

'Are you Ahmad Al Saidawi, or an impersonator of him?' İkmen asked.

Abbas laughed. 'He's been dead for three hundred years!'

But no one else was laughing and so he stopped.

'Is money always distributed at an Al Saidawi story reading?' İkmen asked. 'Is that how people know what's going to happen? Or is it the stories on the programme that give it away? Or is it both?'

Abbas turned to Ömer and said, in Arabic, 'Who is this man? Is he secret police?'

'What man?'

'Don't play games with me!'

Kerim Gürsel said, 'What did he say?'

'He said not to play games with him, sir.'

Kerim shrugged.

İkmen said, 'Was the story "Philopena"? Was that the signal? You know, the old Ottoman tale about the paşa's wife and how she fooled both her husband and that smart-arse imam's son?'

'That is not in Al Saidawi's canon; that is Turkish!'

'Exactly,' İkmen said. 'And so maybe that is how people

know it is you and not the real Al Saidawi or one of his impersonators.'

This time Abbas said it in Turkish. 'Who is this man?'

İkmen said, 'Unless, sir, you are the real Al Saidawi, who surely if he can live for three hundred years can do anything, I would start to answer some questions. One man shot another one, who later killed himself in front of you. You were in the Bab restaurant in the presence of firearms and a considerable amount of money from who knows where. This scenario involving Syrian refugees and a stolen pre-Islamic artefact is just too fantastical.'

'It is my fate.'

'You're not going to get out of here,' İkmen said. 'Maybe not ever.' He stood up. 'Think about it. Rotting in one of our prisons will not get the money to the right people. After all this person had to do to get to this point. These policemen here, they could send you back to Syria . . .'

The boy was completely absorbed by a small box. He just about managed to whisper a hello to his father when he arrived with Kemal at the İkmen apartment, then he sat looking at the box, turning it over, mesmerised.

Watching him, Mehmet Süleyman said, 'What is that?'

'It's a puzzle box,' Kemal İkmen said.

'Where did he get it? Did you buy it for him?'

'No, it was a gift from Princess Brigitte.' Kemal sat down. 'Where's Auntie Samsun?'

'On the balcony,' Süleyman said. 'Who is Princess Brigitte?'

'She lives in Tarlabaşı. Dad knows her.'

İkmen knew most people, in Süleyman's experience. He said, 'Yes, but who is she, Kemal? And why is she a princess?'

Kemal said, 'Oh, she was in films years ago. Yeşilcam.'

Yeşilcam was the dominant film production company in

Turkey from the 1950s to the 1970s. Based in İstanbul, it produced low-budget comedies, romances and family sagas using a large stable of talented comedians, lead and character actors, and beautiful superstars like Türkan Şoray.

'What films?'

'I don't know,' Kemal said. 'Ask Dad.'

A voice spoke from the corner of the room, in English. 'One about a girl who leaves her village to become a film star.' Patrick looked up from his box, which now appeared to be in pieces. 'She becomes a maid in a big house and the master of the house fancies her and so she runs away and gets into films. I did it, Kemal, I got it open.'

Kemal went over to the boy and watched as he put the box back together again. 'Bravo!'

Süleyman, infuriated that no one appeared to be listening to him, said, 'But who is Princess Brigitte? And why did she give you that box?'

'She liked me,' the boy said. And then, with an edge of defiance in his voice, he added, 'I think I want to be a stage magician.'

Feeling the cold chill of his ex-wife's disapproval run down his spine, Süleyman said, 'We will see.'

The boy was, he knew, meant to follow his mother into medicine. But Mehmet had been concerned about that for a while. Patrick was a very intelligent and capable boy, but from his school reports it didn't seem that he was particularly enthusiastic about science. He excelled in English, drama and history.

Kemal sat back down opposite Süleyman. He said, 'Princess Brigitte reckons her mother was the daughter of one of the women in the imperial harem. Abdulhamid II was said to have had this Frenchwoman in his harem. She went in there because she loved him or some stupidity. Anyway, Brigitte reckons she's the granddaughter of that woman. Had blonde hair in her youth. Dad said it was out of a bottle.'

Princess Brigitte sounded typical of the sort of people İkmen sought out, especially in Tarlabaşı.

'So why did you and Patrick go to see her?' Süleyman asked.

'Oh, she used to be a magician's assistant,' Kemal said. 'Don't know whether that was before or after Yeşilcam. Anyway, she's got lots of magical stuff in her house and so I thought I'd take Patrick to see her. He had a great time.'

'Thank you,' Süleyman said.

'That's OK.'

Although looking at the boy engrossed in that box didn't make Mehmet Süleyman happy. If he went back to Ireland with a fully fledged magic obsession, Zelfa wouldn't be pleased. What was more, it would also reveal just how much time her son had spent not with his father but with family friends.

'Where were you on the afternoon of Wednesday April the fourth 2018?' Kerim Gürsel asked.

Abbas looked confused. 'How should I know?'

'Were you in Fatih?'

'I don't know!'

'Were you in Turkey?' Ömer Mungun asked.

'I don't know!'

'I can check,' Ömer said. 'Unless you were here illegally.'

'Who are you?' Kerim said. 'You have no documents about you. I can have you deported from this country.'

'Which means that if you are the person you speak of, President Assad will be waiting for you!'

But after an initial apparent foray into panic, Abbas appeared to calm down again and shrugged.

'What is written,' he said, 'is written . . .'

Kerim sat down opposite the man. 'Look,' he said, 'I am in

no way interested in what you may have done in Syria. There are ways, rather time-consuming ones, in which I may track down the guns you were found with in the Bab. Also the money. I can do this, I can find where those things came from. What I cannot do, as yet, it seems, is find out whether you were performing at a hakawati event in a coffee house in the Malta Çarşısı in Fatih on the fourth of April 2018. The money and the guns are irrelevant to me. All I need to know is whether you were there.'

'Why?'

'Because as I think I've said already, one of your fellow Syrians claims she was in this coffee house on that day. I will take you to her, in time, but she is in prison at the moment, so that may take a little while to arrange.'

'So she would recognise me?'

'Possibly. I don't know. But if, as you seem to be implying, you love your own people, you should know that this Syrian woman is currently in prison for attempted murder.' He paused. 'The details are not important, but there is a possibility that this woman met another woman, a Turk, at this hakawati performance, who persuaded and encouraged her to make an attempt upon an innocent man's life. This is nothing to do with hakawati, or Syria. It's to do with a case I am trying to solve about two unexplained deaths. Now . . .'

'So take me to this woman,' Abbas said. 'Let us see.'

İkmen, who had been observing the two younger men as they tried to break Abbas, couldn't make up his mind whether the Syrian was bluffing or not. What he was certain of, however, was that Abbas was unlike anyone Ömer and Kerim had come across before, even if he himself had.

Nothing was happening in Sarıyer. The officers watching Betül Gencer's house said that no one had come in or gone out, and the only people they'd seen on the street had been various workmen and a couple of maids putting rubbish into bins. Süleyman put his phone back in his pocket and let himself in to Gonca's house.

It was early evening, so she was probably still in her studio. He walked into the garden, where to his surprise he found her brother Rambo sitting underneath the olive tree, smoking and swigging from a bottle of rakı.

'Rambo?'

'Mehmet Bey!' He tried to stand up and failed.

Mehmet walked over to him. 'Aren't you meant to be working?'

'Oh, I'm closed for the evening. Thought I'd come and see my sister.'

It was odd for any member of Gonca's family to just turn up to see her. Usually, these days, they only appeared when they wanted something from her.

'My sister tells me you're going to be married,' Rambo said.

'Yes . . .' Of course she'd told him. She'd probably told everyone.

'Well I'll drink to that!' Rambo said as he held out the bottle of rakı.

Mehmet pushed it away. 'Of course, I'm delighted, but I'm on call at the moment. Thank you, though.'

Pity,' Rambo said. 'She's in her studio if you want her.'

Under the circumstances, it was probably better to be with Gonca than with her excessively intoxicated brother, good natured though he was.

He'd begun walking back towards the house when he heard Rambo say, 'It'll take us months to get the family together, you know.'

He did. The Şekeroğlu family was vast, and scattered across not just Turkey, but in at least two eastern European countries to Süleyman's knowledge.

Gonca was in her studio, but she wasn't working. When he entered, she looked up from her computer and said, 'Hello, baby! I've been looking at wedding dresses.'

He smiled. İkmen had warned him. He walked over to her and kissed her neck. On the computer screen was something glittery in red.

'Have whatever you like, sweetheart,' he said. 'Just don't show me. I want it to be a surprise.'

'They're all very expensive,' she said as she stood up and walked into his arms.

'So send me the bill. But when it comes to rings, we must go and choose together.'

'I know.'

He kissed her. 'Çetin Bey's son-in-law Berekiah will make whatever we want.'

She was so excited, child-like in a way, but he had work to do, albeit of a remote variety. He said, 'I'm on call tonight, Gonca.'

'Oh? Why?'

'That I can't tell you. But I'm warning you that's how it is. I'm sorry.'

'Mmm.'

She fiddled with his tie, then said, 'I've cooked sarma, like a real little wife.' These were the filled vine leaves he knew as dolma.

'I'm sure they'll be delicious,' he said.

'Rambo's here, but he won't bother us.'

This sudden leap into matrimonial subjects and wifely cooking wasn't her, and he didn't really like it that much. When he'd first asked her to marry him, she had acted almost with disdain. She hadn't given him an answer until they'd made love several times. A tamed Gonca was not what he really wanted.

But then she unknotted his tie and began unbuttoning his shirt.

He said, 'I may have to go, as I'm on call . . .'

She kissed his chest. 'Not before you've pleasured me, Mehmet Bey.'

The relief he felt as she stroked his crotch was indescribable.

Eylul Yavaş returned to the two men in the corridor with Abbas behind her.

'She doesn't recognise him,' she told them.

Kerim Gürsel sighed. It was getting late and he was keen to be home with his pregnant wife, even if he was on call.

'Did you recognise her?' he asked Abbas.

'I've never seen her before,' he said. 'To my knowledge.'

Kerim shook his head. 'So back to headquarters . . .'

'How about we get Betül Hanım in to take a look at him, Kerim Bey?' Ömer said.

'She won't recognise him, or rather she won't say she does. She says she wasn't there.'

'But what if he recognises her?'

All three of them looked at the man, who said, 'I really cannot say whether I was at this performance last year or not.'

'Yes. We know that.'

As they began to make their way back along the corridor towards the prison administration offices, Abbas, older and slower than the others, lagged behind. And although Kerim Gürsel didn't get any sort of feeling that he was about to try and bolt – which would have been very stupid in a prison – he did want him to keep up. He turned and said, 'Come along!'

The old man stopped.

'Kerim Bey,' he said, 'that man who was with you earlier, I should like to see him again.'

He meant İkmen.

'What for?'

'Because I feel I can talk to him,' he said.

'Talk? About what?'

A look came into Abbas's eyes that made Kerim feel uncomfortable.

'Well?' he asked.

'Oh, the world,' Abbas said. 'Many things. He is a most unusual man and so, I think you may realise, am I. We should have much in common that may be to your benefit, Inspector Bey.'

And though he knew, or thought he knew, he was being manipulated, Kerim Gürsel said that he would try to contact İkmen when they returned to headquarters.

Once outside the prison and back in his car, he put a call through to Betül Gencer, but she didn't pick up.

It was still so hot. Even with all the windows open, Sinem Gürsel felt sticky and uncomfortable. Her baby was due in three days' time and she was exhausted.

'You know that posh woman I used to clean for sometimes over in Cihangir?' Madam Edith said as she staggered into the Gürsels' living room carrying a bowl of water and a jar of something black and moving. 'She had her baby in the hospital, like you, and they called her in before her time. Have you spoken to your doctor, honey?'

'Yes.' Sinem sat down. Edith put the bowl on the floor and then lifted Sinem's feet into the water.

'Let's get those ankles down,' she said. 'And then I can have a go at your veins.'

Sinem was grateful for the cold water, which, though rather a shock to the system, did feel good. The leeches Edith had brought to get her swollen veins down were another matter. Sinem's mother used them and she herself had always hated them, but Madam Edith was being so kind and attentive, she didn't have the heart to refuse her.

The only person Sinem really wanted was her husband, but Kerim hadn't been able to give her any idea of when he might be home. All he had said when he'd phoned her was that he had something big on that he couldn't leave. Poor Kerim, she knew he was still broken up about Pembe. Sometimes she felt as if the prospect of their baby was the only thing that was keeping him sane. She also knew that Madam Edith was hurting too, and that her coming round to help Sinem was as much about distracting herself as it was caring for a pregnant woman.

'How are you doing with your pain today, lovey?' Edith asked.

'Oh it's not too bad,' Sinem said. 'Just my legs really. But then they'd be bad by this time anyway.'

'You've got a big baby in there,' Edith said, pointing to her belly. 'You a tiny little thing and Kerim Bey not exactly a giant.'

'Kerim's father is tall,' Sinem said. 'Anyway, just because this is a big baby doesn't mean it will be a big adult.'

'I s'pose not.'

Edith sat down.

'Did Kerim Bey say anything to you about the investigation into Pembe's murder?' she asked.

'We had Süleyman round. He's taken over from Kerim.'

'Mmm.'

'Edith,' Sinem said, 'it's affected us all. Kerim told me that my mother will be questioned.'

'Süleyman's been to see your mum?'

'I don't know,' she said. 'We don't talk any more. I don't think so. It all seems to move so fast. Kerim has hardly been home.'

'Why do they want to talk to your mum?'

'She was out that afternoon,' Sinem said. 'I was in bed.'

'I thought she didn't know about . . .'

'Apparently she did. That last row Kerim had with her, she brought it up.'

'Oh.' Edith thought for a moment. 'You know that mad old Kurd who lives opposite me, Neşe?'

'I don't know her, but I've seen her.'

'She told Süleyman she thought the killer was a woman. Mind you, she's mad. Thought it was her dead mother.' She looked up at Sinem. 'Do you think your mum would've killed Pembe?'

'I don't know,' Sinem said. 'But maybe I should ring her and tell her she'll need to provide Mehmet Bey with a statement. She lives with my brother, so maybe I'll speak to him first.'

'Does he know? About you and Kerim?'

'Oh yes,' she said. 'He's fine. He just wants me to be happy.'

'And are you?' Edith asked.

'At the moment? I don't know,' Sinem replied. 'I've never had a baby before and I'm frightened. And then there's Kerim . . .'

'What about him?'

'He's so sad and yet he's trying so hard not to express it. I think he feels he mustn't for my sake. But I wish he would. I know I'm not what he really needs, that I've selfishly made him make this baby, but I do love him so much. I can't bear to think of him in pain.'

Down in the street below, one of the local meyhanes began its evening programme of deafening live music. There were also fireworks. Even if Sinem or Madam Edith wanted to speak, it had become a pointless enterprise.

Chapter 23

And so the imam's son arrived to do the bidding of the beautiful paşa's wife. She greeted him with chilled rose water and lokum. Then she began to dictate a letter. Minutes later there was a commotion outside the yalı. Alarmed, the lady said, 'Oh no! It is the paşa, my husband! He cannot find you here!' And so she hid the imam's son in a chest underneath a window.

Rima Al Numan had left him a message to the effect that she didn't know what the police were thinking and did he? Well, İkmen thought, he did, but with some forensic evidence in doubt now, there was nothing he could say or do that would reassure her either way. Besides, even if it were proven somehow that Betül Gencer had indeed encouraged Samira to kill Erol Gencer, she was still guilty of attempted murder.

It was unsettling to be visiting a prisoner in the cells at night. He'd had to do it from time to time when he was a serving police officer. But as the duty guard led him down the corridor towards the Syrian's cell, he wondered why he had acquiesced so quickly to Abbas's request. But then he knew the answer to that. He knew the type.

Neither three hundred years old, nor really rooted in the twenty-first century, the Syrian was one of those people who enabled important things to happen. This was why İkmen, unlike Kerim Gürsel, didn't think that Abbas and the elusive one-time intimate of President Assad were one and the same. But Abbas was part of that person's world and he knew to whom the golden artefact had been sold. It was why, in a sense, he could be so casual about it. A Syrian patriot, a man prepared to die for his country – he knew he was going to get the lamassu back.

And that wasn't strictly İkmen's business. What was his business was to find whatever lay behind these overt phenomena. He was there for the magic.

Kerim Gürsel couldn't remember when he'd last had a proper night's sleep. When Betül Gencer answered neither her mobile nor her landline for the third time, he called the officers watching her house.

'Cover both the entrances, knock on the door and . . .' He stopped. 'No, wait. I'll come. Fuck this!'

'Sir?'

He yelled into his phone. 'Stay where you are! I'm on my way!'

As he stood up, he knocked his chair over. Eylul went to pick it up, but he stopped her.

'Leave it!'

She moved back. 'Sir, do you want me to drive?'

On the basis that he didn't need to translate for the Syrian prisoners any more, Ömer Mungun had gone home, and so it was only the two of them in the office.

Kerim lit a cigarette and said, 'No.' Then he changed his mind. 'Yes. Yes, it's probably better if you do. Sarıyer. You know the way.'

'Yes, sir.'

'Mum?'

Now that Edith had gone, Sinem had taken herself to her bedroom in order to phone her brother, who had handed his mobile to their mother.

'What do you want?' she snapped.

'Mum, I'm phoning to warn you about something.'

'What? That husband of yours who—'

She heard her brother shout at her mother to keep her opinions to herself. Which she did.

Sinem said, 'Mum, Kerim's colleague Inspector Mehmet Süleyman will need to come and talk to you about what you were doing when Pembe Hanım died. I went to bed, if you remember, and then—'

'I will tell Inspector Süleyman about your husband!' her mother hissed.

Sinem closed her eyes. 'Mum, Kerim and Inspector Süleyman are trying to find people who have killed. Please listen. I know you went out late that afternoon, I don't know where. But you will have to account for that time.'

'Why?'

'Because if you can't account for it, Inspector Süleyman may think that maybe you killed Pembe.'

'And what if I did?' She was getting more and more aggressive by the second. Emir must have left her alone with his phone.

'Mum, I know you didn't,' Sinem said. 'Apart from anything else, you're always saying you're so tired and ill.'

'Well that's where you're wrong,' her mother hissed. 'I killed that abomination your husband loved so much. Tell him! Tell this Süleyman that your mother killed your husband's unnatural odalisque and see what he says!'

She ended the call, leaving Sinem lying shaking on her bed while the bright multicoloured lights from the meyhane across the road made her face look by turns red and devilish, yellow and jaundiced, green and long dead. And when she tried to get off her bed to fetch herself a drink, she vomited over her duvet.

*

Süleyman couldn't sleep, even though he was tired. His phone could ring at any moment and he knew what might be at stake if it did. Or he thought he knew. There were so many unknowns, so many questions . . .

He knew that Gonca was awake. He could feel the tension in her body as she lay in his arms. And so he asked her the question he had been wanting to ask all day.

'What was Harun Sesler doing here this morning?'

'I told you,' she said. 'I'm making something for him. He's a customer.'

'What?'

'Some ornaments for his bride's dress.'

'Do you know who he's marrying?'

Harun Sesler wasn't just getting on in years; he was also fat, sweaty and ignorant. Not to mention brutal.

'No,' she said. She looked up at him. 'I don't care.'

'I'd rather you had nothing to do with him,' he said. 'You know what he is.'

'Mehmet, I needed the money,' she said.

He stroked her hair. 'And Rambo?' he asked.

'My brother? What about him?'

'Why's he here?'

She hauled herself up so that her head was level with his.

'He's not opening the meyhane tonight,' she said.

'Why not?'

She shrugged. 'I don't know.'

'I mean, I'm assuming that like most people who run businesses in that part of Tarlabaşı, he pays Harun Bey his dues . . .'

'I don't know.' She kissed him. 'Your phone still hasn't rung, baby.'

She was offering him sex. But there was a tension and it was over Harun Sesler.

'Gonca,' he said, 'I don't want you going to Sesler any more.'

'I have to finish what I've started!'

'Yes, but when that is done, never again. If you want money, you come to me. From now on, I will take care of you.'

Even though it was dark, he could see the incredulous expression on her face.

She said, 'Baby, you don't have any money.'

'Gonca . . .'

'You're a policeman,' she said. 'You don't have money. Anyway that's not why I'm marrying you.'

'So why *are* you marrying me?' he asked.

'For your body.' She laughed. 'For your beautiful body and your beautiful face and because you're really good in bed. And you love me. You know all this!'

He smiled. He knew she was playing him, but he wanted her. Later, he'd get to the truth. He leaned over and kissed her, felt her hand on his penis and heard her gasp. She always claimed that as soon as she touched him, she began to come.

His phone rang.

Although it was the middle of the night, it was hot. Çetin İkmen caught multiple rivulets of sweat running down his face. He was painfully aware that brewing up, as it were, in this stuffy little cell made him stink. Not so, apparently, Abbas the hakawati. He, irritatingly, looked as if he'd just spent the day in a perfumed air-conditioned environment. Apart from that, the two men had a lot in common.

İkmen said, 'What do you say, Abbas Bey, to the notion that the telling of stories is a form of hypnotism?'

This was something he remembered having discussed many years before with İbrahim Dede the dervish. The venerable gentleman had given it as his opinion that any art form, be it painting, dance, music, storytelling, involved both the artist and the spectator in a joint shift in consciousness. Some people, the dervish had said, called that union with God.

'Of course,' Abbas said. 'Or rather that is what I think differentiates a true artist from someone who simply goes through the motions. Look at all the really great artists; look at the fame, the devotion and outpouring of love that was given to Umm Kulthum.' Umm Kulthum was an Egyptian singer who, back in the twentieth century, had achieved superstar status across the Arab world. 'And of course your own architect Sinan,' he continued. 'Anyone who can look at the Süleymaniye Mosque and not be moved has no soul.'

İkmen smiled. 'Sinan was Albanian,' he said. 'I know you mean to flatter "the Turk", Abbas Bey, but my mother was Albanian and so I always feel that I have to support Albania's achievements. The actor John Belushi was Albanian too, you know.'

'I don't know who that is.'

'Never mind.'

There was a moment of silence, and then Abbas said, 'Everything we call magic is merely a shift in consciousness.'

'In stage magic,' İkmen said, 'it's misdirection, it's sleight of hand. I have very good friends who are stage magicians.'

'I know.'

İkmen frowned.

Abbas said, 'Has it never occurred to you that the misdirection they speak of is actually a misdirection in itself?'

Betül Gencer had gone. Her bedroom was littered with clothes, and three large wardrobes stood open, dresses, suits and blouses hanging out at crazy angles. Drawers had been pulled out, apparently emptied and left open. In the en suite bathroom there were soap stains all over the shower tiles and the floor was covered in dark red hair.

Kerim Gürsel looked at the four-man stakeout team in front of him. 'Did none of you see anything?'

The older constable, a thin individual nearing retirement, said, 'Some workmen, couple of maids . . . No one came out of this house, front or back.'

'Well clearly someone did!' Kerim yelled. 'Unless she walked through the fucking walls!'

Eylul said, 'Sir, could she not still be in the house?'

'Why?'

'I don't know. But if we search the place, we might at least find some sort of clue as to where she might have gone.'

'Probably in fucking Bulgaria by this time,' he said. Then he put a hand up to his head and lowered his voice, 'But I take what you mean, Sergeant.' He told the officers to search the premises.

Once he was alone with Eylul, he said, 'I'm sorry, I didn't mean to swear.'

'I understand, sir,' she said.

'But I told those meat-heads to look hard and photograph everyone they saw on this street, male or female. I particularly stressed they should pay close attention to males . . .'

'They probably did.'

He sighed. 'Maybe.'

In truth, he was still recovering from the phone call he'd received from Sinem just before they'd left headquarters. She'd called her mother to let her know that Süleyman would need to interview her about her movements on the day of Pembe's death. Pınar Hanım, it seemed, had flown into a rage and confessed to the murder. His brother-in-law had been unable to handle a situation in which his mother was demanding to be taken to police headquarters. And so Kerim had called Mehmet Süleyman to go over to Emir's apartment and try to disentangle fact from fiction.

Ever practical, Eylul said, 'Can we think of anywhere she might have gone?'

Kerim sighed. 'I would say the so-called brother's apartment in Kadıköy.'

'She knows we've been there. Wouldn't that be a bit obvious?'

'Possibly.' He knew he wasn't thinking straight. How could he? If Pınar Hanım's confession was taken seriously, if indeed she had killed Pembe, his career and therefore his ability to look after Sinem and the baby could be over.

'I suppose,' Eylul said, 'it depends upon why Betül killed Pembe Hanım. If she killed her . . . Sir, do you think Dr Sarkissian will have any results yet?'

'No,' he said. 'He's pushing to get it done by midday. Believe me, Eylul, I wish we were living in an episode of *CSI*, but we're not.'

Suddenly exhausted, he sat down on the chair beside the Gencers' bed. Sounds coming from downstairs indicated that the team were being far from sympathetic in their search.

Eylul said, 'If we assume that Betül Gencer killed Pembe Hanım, we have to ask ourselves why . . .'

Going back to sleep was impossible. Not because of the noise and the crazy multicoloured flashing lights outside – she was used to all that – but because Sinem couldn't believe her mother.

How could Pınar Hanım, fat, ill and forever pleading weakness, have managed to kill anyone, let alone Pembe Hanım. Pembe had been a tough girl who had lived a hard life and was street-wise. Slightly taller than Kerim, she'd been an imposing sight in her sky-high heels. But then Pınar Hanım had the kind of temper that could possibly imbue her with extra strength . . .

Kerim had asked Mehmet Bey to go out and see her, and so he would hopefully find out if there was any truth in her story. Sinem could understand why Mehmet Bey had questioned her about Pembe's murder. The transsexual had been her rival for years and there had always been part of Sinem that had envied her. Kerim had loved Pembe in a way he had never, and probably could never, love Sinem. Before she'd bought earplugs, she'd heard them making love and it had made her desperately sad. It had always sounded so passionate. Only once had Kerim ever made love to her with his whole soul, and that had been when he'd come home after being called out to the scene of Pembe's death. Had he felt that Sinem was now all he had left? Or had he just been seeking comfort anywhere he could find it?

It wasn't a noise down in the street that made Sinem go and look out of the window, but an absence of sound. That bar across the road had something to do with Gonca Şekeroğlu, the woman it was rumoured was Mehmet Bey's mistress, and generally it pumped out music, light and raised voices all night long. But now, while the lights were still in evidence, the music had stopped and she could see people standing about in the street looking, well, lost.

Then she heard the sirens.

The district of Zeytinburnu on the shores of the Sea of Marmara was home to a large section of the İstanbul city land walls. Back in the mid twentieth century, it had also been home to a thriving leather and garment industry staffed by migrants from Bulgaria, central Asia and central Anatolia. Two of the families who had settled in the area during the 1960s were the Gürsels and the Cebecis. And while the Gürsels had moved out to Üsküdar on the Asian side of the city in recent years, the Cebecis had remained in the dingy apartment where Sinem, wife of Kerim Gürsel, had been born.

To Mehmet Süleyman's eyes, it didn't look as if the place that Emir Cebeci shared with his wife and children and his mother had changed much in the last forty years. He could remember going to friends' homes when he was a schoolboy and seeing massive faux belle époque sofas dominating tiny living rooms beneath poorly hung cheap chandeliers. The only difference here was that everything was faded.

Emir Cebeci was a pleasant, easy-going man in his early fifties. According to Kerim Gürsel, Emir had always known about him and was just happy that his little sister had a man to treat her nicely. As the eldest in the family, he had ended up moving back in with his mother when his father died. But it was clear there was no love lost between the two.

As he took Mehmet Süleyman into the kitchen, where the old woman was sitting at the table, he said, 'I'll stay if you don't mind, Mehmet Bey.'

'Of course,' Süleyman said.

'Only she's really abusive at the moment,' Emir said. 'Saying anything. All the religious old lady stuff is still there, but it's overlaid with, well, spite, I suppose. Sabiha, that's my wife, she's just about at the end of her tether this time. Since Mum came home, she's been on Sabiha's back the whole time.'

They walked into a stuffy, clean but shabby kitchen, where Pınar Hanım, muffled up in numerous headscarves, sat at a table with wobbly legs. Süleyman bowed. 'Pınar Hanım,' he said. 'My name is Inspector Mehmet Süleyman—'

'I've heard of you!' she interrupted. 'You work with that creature my daughter chose to marry!'

Emir gestured for Süleyman to sit down.

'Would you like tea, Mehmet Bey?' he asked.

It was clear that Emir felt he needed to be doing something, and so Süleyman said he would. While Emir fired up the samovar, Süleyman said, 'Your daughter, Mrs Sinem Gürsel, has told me that you have confessed to the murder of Hüseyin Kılıç, otherwise known as Pembe Hanım, in Tarlabaşı on the seventh of August this year. Is that correct?'

'It is,' she said. 'Take me down the police station and I'll tell you all about it.'

Süleyman said, 'I thought we might talk about it here, hanım.' He smiled. 'That way we can make sure you do not have to make any unnecessary journeys.'

She frowned. She wasn't in the least charmed by him.

'I know what you're up to, may God forgive you,' she said. 'You're trying to protect that filthy pervert my daughter married.'

Ignoring her, he continued, 'Hanım, can you please tell me what happened on the day you killed Hüseyin Kılıç.'

Emir, who was intently watching the samovar come to the boil, cleared his throat.

Pınar Hanım said, 'My daughter Sinem is pregnant – somehow. But she's old, forty-two, and so she has to go to bed a lot. Then there's her arthritis. I don't know where she got that from. None of my other children have arthritis. It's an old person's disease. She's never been right, Sinem. But then he tricked her, made her marry him while he had filthy sex with that . . . creature.'

'Pembe Hanım.'

'That man!'

He ignored her. 'Tell me what happened, Pınar Hanım. Tell me how you killed Pembe Hanım.'

She shuffled in her seat.

'I know where she lives,' she said. 'So when my daughter was asleep, I went round there. I cut it off.'

'Cut what off?'

He wanted to hear her say it. In fact he *had* to hear her say it.

'His . . . you know . . . His . . .'

'What? His arm? His head?'

She looked at him with daggers in her eyes. Over at the samovar, he could see Emir cringing.

'Hanım?'

'His penis!' she said. 'There, you made me say the filthy word! I cut it off.'

'*How* did you cut it off?' Süleyman asked. 'You are a lady of a certain age, madam. Pembe was in her thirties, tall, strong . . .'

'She made tea,' she said. 'I said I wanted to talk. I put Valium in her glass. When I cut it off, the creature was insensible.'

Emir was unable to contain himself any longer. 'Mum!'

'And I'm proud of it,' she said. 'Teach him to be unfaithful to my daughter with that thing!'

Süleyman had been expecting a confession possessed of no veracity whatsoever, but here was a detail that made him wonder. He couldn't believe that Kerim had told his mother-in-law anything about the case. So how had she known? And if she hadn't known, was this just a lucky guess?

'Where did you get the tranquillisers?' he asked.

Emir brought their tea over. 'She's been taking them for years.'

'From the doctor?'

'No,' she said. 'He, stupid man, wouldn't give them to me. Recep gets them off the Internet.'

'Recep?'

'My uncle,' Emir said. 'I've told him not to, but he doesn't take any notice of me.'

Süleyman looked at the old woman, who he could quite imagine ripping into an enemy, and said, 'What did you do with the testes once you'd removed them?'

'Gonca!'

Suddenly she was awake. All the lights were on and her little brother was in her room.

'What . . .'

'Get up!' Rambo said.

'Why? What's going on? You look as if you've seen a ghost.'

He ran over to her and gripped her shoulders.

'We have to get to the meyhane,' he said. 'They'll fucking destroy the place.'

'Who?' She swung her legs out of bed and stood up. Thank goodness she'd put an old dress on after Mehmet left!

'Harun Bey's gang of thugs,' Rambo said. 'They're going mad.'

'Mad? Why?'

'Because he's dead,' Rambo said. 'He's dead, and everyone's losing their minds.'

Chapter 24

The paşa, seeing two drinks glasses on the table, said, 'You have had a man in here, madam!' His wife said, 'Oh no, my lord!' 'Indeed you have,' he thundered. 'And if I am not much mistaken, he is hidden in the chest underneath the window!'

Çetin İkmen said, 'But to give you an example, my friend who is a stage magician has taught me, and others, some of his tricks.'

'The ones he wants you to understand, yes,' Abbas said. 'That is, sir, by way of a perfect disguise. Your own profession is minutely examined in books and on television all the time. But I am sure that when producers of such things talk about accessing all areas of detection work, they are either inadvertently or maybe in full knowledge lying.'

This was true. There was and always had been an element of holding back information deemed too sensitive or too revealing. In the world of detection, as in the world of magic, secrecy could mean the difference between success and failure. İkmen thought about Sami Nasi's severed head trick. Other such illusions had been dissected and examined over the years, but not this one. Who was to say that when Sami appeared to sever his wife's head from her body, he wasn't really doing that?

'The story you told Sergeant Mungun,' İkmen said. 'How do I know that's not a lie?'

'You don't.'

'It could be a fiction, albeit I must say a plausible one, given the evidence we have so far. You could nevertheless have created it in order to distract us.'

'I could.'

'Abbas Bey,' İkmen said. 'My colleagues think that the murders of two men, both now sadly dead, may have been planned at a hakawati performance in Fatih last year.'

'If that was indeed so, and if, for the sake of argument, that hakawati was myself, then the concurrence of those two events is entirely circumstantial,' Abbas said.

İkmen couldn't help noticing how much more fluent in Turkish the man was becoming as time ticked by.

'Circumstantial or not,' he replied, 'something evil happened under cover of that performance, something my colleagues believe has persisted. It is my opinion that you know more than you are saying. You are doing this, I believe, both to protect this person you spoke of in your story, and also to obscure the distribution of their money amongst your countrymen. But when murder enters the equation, everything changes. In a way, it is a form of magic that transforms everything it touches. Unlike some, I have no interest in the no doubt very wealthy individual to whom Assad's golden lamassu was sold. I think it is tragic for Syria that such an artefact should pass into private hands, but the calculation of the person in your story that even art is not worth one human life is correct. If you are not this person and you were not at that performance in Fatih last year, I'd like you to tell me.'

Kiyamet Yavuz had been the only one of Betül's friends who had so much as hinted at any sort of problem in the Gencers' marriage. And that had only consisted of a bit of gossip about their childlessness.

Still half asleep after a rude awakening by Kerim Gürsel and Eylul Yavaş, she had closed the door on her latest squeeze to come and talk to them in her minimalist living room. Outside, the streets of İstanbul seemed to be choking on the sounds of multiple sirens. As she sat down, she said, 'Do you know what that's about?'

Kerim had received a text from Sinem to let him know that something was going on at the gypsy meyhane opposite their apartment. But he said, 'No. Hanım, we've come to ask whether you know the whereabouts of Betül Gencer.'

'She's not at her house?'

'No. Nor is she at her apartment,' he said.

She shook her head.

Eylul said, 'Kiyamet Hanım, when we spoke before, you mentioned that some people in the Gencers' circle were dismayed at their childlessness. Is that all you picked up?'

'Just about. Oh, and nothing serious,' she said. She lit a cigarette. 'I think it was just that certain people wondered what Betül might do with herself after Harem Medya dropped her show.'

'She'd studied psychology,' Kerim said.

'Oh yes, but she never actually practised. She liked people to believe she was always busy, but actually that wasn't the case.'

'So what does she do with herself all day?' Eylul asked.

'Apart from when we get together from time to time, I don't know,' Kiyamet said. 'She is patron of some charity for the poor, though I don't know anything about it. There was her husband, of course. When he was ill, she was always there for him. Then . . . holidays, trips abroad. I know she adores Italy. The life, I suppose you'd say, of the successful wife of a successful man.'

'Affairs?'

'No,' she said. 'She's not like me.'

Eylul, who was still contemplating Betül's career, said, 'The business with Harem Medya, did she take that badly, do you know?'

Kiyamet put her head on one side. 'Mmm, not really. Before it happened, she told me that in all likelihood when her original boss, Celal Bey, died – he'd had cancer for years – her friend Filiz Tepe would take over. She said this was because Filiz had been sleeping with Celal Bey. When Celal Bey died and Filiz was named as his successor, Betül was not exactly pleased, but she wasn't stressed about it either, as far as I could tell.'

'This was before she was actually dropped by the network?'

'Oh yes. She carried on with that bridal show for quite a few months before it was cancelled.'

Kerim said, 'I understood from Filiz Hanım that her friendship with Betül was destroyed when the network let Betül go.'

Kiyamet smiled. 'Oh, let me tell you, there was no genuine love lost between them before that.'

'So did Betül go quietly?' Eylul asked.

'Yes, she did.'

'Do you know why? Sounds as if they were rivals, and if so . . .'

'I don't know,' Kiyamet said. 'But then I never asked. I imagine Filiz Hanım might know. You should ask her.'

When they had finished talking to Kiyamet, Kerim and Eylul went back to the car. So far there was nothing at the Gencers' house or apartment that gave any sort of clue as to where Betül might have gone. Kerim switched on his tablet computer. 'I think Filiz Tepe lives in Yeniköy.'

'You think she might be there?' Eylul asked.

'I don't know,' he said. 'But the impression I got from Filiz Hanım when I spoke to her was of someone who might be open to rekindling this friendship. Just an impression, but . . .'

'Yes, but that sort of implies that Betül Gencer wasn't,' Eylul said.

'Mmm. You're right. But given Dr Sarkissian's suspicions about Betül, maybe there's more to that situation than we think.'

'You mean, you think Filiz Hanım might know about Betül's gender?'

Kerim turned the key in the car's ignition. Now feeling calmer, he had opted to drive.

'It would explain why Betül left the network without a fight,' he said.

'Although what does that say about Erol Gencer?' Eylul asked.

Kerim said he didn't know, even though he thought he might.

Some of the washing lines across the street had come down. There was a pair of massive pink bloomers hanging over the handlebars of a motorbike – the result of grieving men firing pistols into the air. Rambo, Gonca on his arm, elbowed his way through the crowds of onlookers and walked up to the tape that surrounded the tables outside his meyhane. Uniformed police officers were everywhere, securing the scene and trying to keep Harun Sesler's foot soldiers calm. In a corner over by the entrance to the meyhane, a middle-aged man was shouting at an old woman crouched down on the ground.

'Who are you?'

Rambo turned and found himself looking into the face of a tall uniformed man. He had a heavily lined, disappointed face.

'I own this place,' Rambo said.

'Where did you spring from?' the officer asked.

'I was in Balat with my sister,' he said. 'Harun Bey had a function here tonight.'

'Without you on the premises?'

'It was an arrangement,' Rambo said.

'Why are you here now?'

'My boy called me. He lives down the road.'

As if summoned, his sixteen-year-old son appeared. 'Dad . . .'

'It's all right, boy,' Rambo said. Then, addressing the officer, 'So Harun Bey is dead?'

The officer looked at the white nylon tent that had been erected in the street, but said nothing.

'What happened?'

The officer didn't answer immediately. Instead he nodded towards Gonca. 'Who's she?'

It took Rambo a moment to realise that the policeman had been indicating not so much Gonca as what she was looking at, which was the old woman on the ground and the middle-aged man who had been shouting at her but now wasn't. He too had been arrested by the sight of Gonca Şekeroğlu.

Rambo said, 'She's my sister.'

Other people nearby were now looking at Gonca too. In silence. It was weird.

Eventually the officer said to Rambo, 'Get her out of here, I would. Dunno what it's about, but some of this lot seem to be disturbed by her.'

'I've told you, I don't know!' Pınar Hanım told Süleyman. 'I left. The creature was dying, and so I left before that other unnatural he lived with returned.'

She meant Madam Edith.

Süleyman, who had just received a message from Kerim Gürsel to let him know that he and Eylul Yavaş plus a team of uniforms were on their way to an address in Yeniköy, said, 'What happened to the excised testes is important, madam.'

Pınar Hanım's son stood in front of the kitchen sink looking grey faced.

'Mum,' he said, 'if you did this, really, then you need to give the inspector details.'

She looked away.

Süleyman changed tack. 'Do you have any Valium at the moment, Pınar Hanım?'

'Yes, but you're not taking it away,' she said.

'I want to look at it,' he replied.

She dug into a vast tapestry bag at her feet and took out a packet, which she laid on the table. It looked genuine enough, although Süleyman knew there were some very convincing fake medical products on the market, especially via the Internet. On opening the box, he found two plastic strips, one with three tablets missing. He said, 'Is this the same brand of drugs you gave to Pembe Hanım prior to her death?'

'Yes,' she said.

'I'll need to take them for analysis.'

He took a plastic evidence bag out of his pocket and put the packet inside.

'You can't take those!' Pınar Hanım said. 'What will I do without them?'

'I imagine your brother will get you some more,' Süleyman said.

'Yes, but for now . . .' She began to weep.

Her son raised his arms helplessly from his sides. 'Inspector, I don't think she did it.'

'Maybe, maybe not,' Süleyman said. 'The make-up of these tablets should tell us something.' He stood.

The old woman looked up at him. 'So you going to arrest me?'

'No.'

'I've confessed,' she said.

He looked down at her. 'Madam, if you knew how frequently people confess to things they haven't done, you would know just how unsafe confessions can be.'

Pınar Hanım looked at her son, who said, 'Mum, I don't understand why you're doing this.'

'Because I did it!' she said. 'God will bless my actions!'

'But not, I fear, your daughter,' Süleyman said. 'Now, madam, I am going to take these tablets away for forensic testing. In the meantime, please do not leave the city, and if you remember where you left the victim's testes, let me know.'

He put one of his business cards on the kitchen table and left.

He wanted to go back to his bed, not to mention the woman he shared it with, but Gonca would be asleep and so he sent Kerim Gürsel a message to let him know he would be joining him in Yeniköy. After all, Betül Gencer was now of interest to both of them.

'Three days ago was the last time I saw one of Assad's thugs in this city. That's unusual inasmuch as I generally see at least one every day.'

'In Fatih?' İkmen asked.

'Or Tarlabaşı, Sulukule, Yedikule,' Abbas said.

'So there are many of these, what, Mukhabarat?'

'Whether they are actual members of Assad's secret police, I don't know,' Abbas said. 'But I recognise the type. Over the years I have developed a keen nose for the smell of evil.'

'What are you telling me here?' İkmen asked. Abbas was piling obfuscation onto obfuscation. He was somebody of great importance, whoever he was.

'You know,' he said, 'one of the problems about tolerating, or rather, being ground to powder by a dictator is that rising up against him is so very dangerous. I cannot even bring myself, a grown man, to tell you, also a grown man, what the regime will do to you if you cross them. In order to survive, our people have had to dredge up every bit of courage and intelligence, both now and in the past. People like the person in my story are precious. If they didn't exist, they would have to be invented.'

Kerim Gürsel didn't know the Bosphorus village of Yeniköy very well. Littered with the summer palaces of the Ottomans, it was as beautiful as it was wealthy. For years it had been the most expensive place on the İstanbul Monopoly board. Kerim knew it only from a visit he'd made to the Greek church of the Aya Panagia with his first ever boyfriend when he was a student. Guiltily, the two boys had come to see the bust of the poet and gay icon Konstantine Cavafy, who had lived in Yeniköy in the 1880s. They had kissed while reading the legend beneath the bust, which said, *If you find yourself lonely, stranger, know that you are in Yeniköy*.

Memories of that day came back to him as he approached the large Ottoman villa in a little alleyway off the main thoroughfare, Köybaşı Caddesi. Neither of the two cars had been able to actually get up close to the house on account of the narrowness of the alley. Kerim sent three of the uniformed officers around the back of the property. While they made their way into position, he said to Eylul, 'I imagined Filiz Hanım would live in one of those big modern apartments with lots of steel and glass.'

'I've not met her, sir,' Eylul said. 'I wouldn't know.'

The house, which was half stone, half wood, probably from the nineteenth century, was in darkness apart from one small light in an upstairs bay window. With any luck, Filiz Hanım would still be up. With even more luck, maybe Betül Gencer would be with her. Although knowing what he knew about Betül Hanım, Kerim did wonder whether her being here was a good thing.

The front entrance was one of those dark, heavily carved double doors that were generally extremely heavy. There was no bell that Kerim could see, but there was a beautiful knocker in the shape of a female hand. This would once, he knew, have denoted the entrance to the harem or women's quarters. He had two officers at his back, Eylul and a uniformed constable. He knocked on the door.

'Police! Open up!'

*

The police were saying nothing, and so Rambo Şekeroğlu spoke to a couple of men he knew as he dragged Gonca out of Tarlabaşı. Once they'd crossed the Bulvarı back into Beyoğlu, he pulled her into a dark alleyway and pushed her up against a wall.

Outraged, she tried to move her arms so she could slap him. But he held her wrists tight and said, 'What did you do?'

'What are you talking about?' she said. 'If you hurt me, I'll tell Mehmet Bey and he'll beat you into the ground!'

Rambo shoved her hard against the wall. 'I don't fucking care!' he said. 'That man who was screaming his head off was Elmas's father! And the woman he was shouting at? Well, you know who she is, don't you, sister?'

'She's deteriorated since I last saw her,' Gonca said. 'But I could tell it was Afife Hanım.'

'Afife Purcu, Elmas's whore of a mother,' Rambo said. 'What I also imagine you know already, Gonca, is that this evening she killed her daughter's fiancé, with a knife in his big fat gut. In my meyhane!'

'No,' she said. 'How would I know that?'

'Because,' he said, 'you were behind it.'

'Me? I don't—'

'Anybody who wants to can find Afife Purcu. Just look on any street corner in Tarlabaşı and eventually you'll come across her. You went to see her, didn't you, Gonca?'

'No!'

'She looked at you!'

'A lot of people looked at me.'

'Because they know what you are.'

'Which is?'

'You cursed Harun Bey, didn't you?' he said. 'You cursed him and then you helped that along by telling Afife Purcu how terrible it was that her greedy husband was selling their daughter to that fat pig!'

'Afife Purcu knew about Elmas,' Gonca said. 'She'd known ever since Harun Bey asked Hüsnü Purcu for her hand. Knowing her, all she'd be worried about would be how much money she might be able to steal from Hüsnü when Harun Bey paid up. She chose heroin over her daughter a long time ago.'

'I saw the way she looked at you,' Rambo said. 'Did you go and see her this afternoon when you told me you were going to see Harun Bey? Or did you see Afife and *then* Harun Bey? Or Harun first and then Afife? After he'd told you to fuck off with any more excuses about your fucking gold silk or whatever it is . . .'

'I went to see Harun Bey, as I told you,' Gonca said. 'He told me he wanted to hold a party for his men in your meyhane this evening and I told him on your behalf that he could. So he'd drink your liquor and break a few tables? You hadn't paid your dues, and I felt that was as good a deal as I could broker for you. As for me, he wouldn't move. I can't get any more sea silk, Rambo. The boy's fallen out with that girl in Italy, and anyway the bloody stuff is dying out.' She breathed hard. 'So I cursed him . . . so what? What else could I do?'

'You could have gone to Afife Purcu and persuaded her that it would be better for Elmas if her fiancé was dead. The woman's a junkie; if you'd told her there was some heroin in it for her, you could have got her to fuck a dead goat. You know this!'

Gonca, who had by this time wiggled her hands free, took her brother by the throat. 'So you think it's better that a revolting old man rapes and brutalises a child, do you? That her disgusting father gets money for her misery?'

He pulled away from her, rubbing his throat. 'Fuck, Gonca. What the fuck are we going to do if she blabs? What have you done? What are we to do if Harun Bey's boys find out?'

'They won't,' she said.

'Yeah, but Afife Purcu—'

'Will not talk,' Gonca said. 'Know that for a fact, brother. And anyway, why would she talk if there's nothing to talk about? Why would she talk if her life is over anyway?'

Rambo looked at his sister with hatred. 'If Mehmet Bey knew the real you . . .'

But Gonca had turned away. 'Don't bother to come back to the house,' she said. 'Your presence in my life is really not necessary.'

He watched her depart and then made his way back to Tarlabaşı.

Chapter 25

'My lord,' the paşa's wife implored, 'you are mistaken. There is no man in the chest under the window.' 'Oh yes there is!' her husband insisted. 'Now, madam, I insist that you open that chest immediately. I order you to do so!'

Some scraping noises came from inside the house, but no voices. Eylul Yavaş, seeing something moving behind the Venetian blinds in the dimly lit upper room, said, 'Something's happening, sir.'

But what? Kerim Gürsel didn't have authorisation to break into Filiz Tepe's home. He was following a lead in the wake of the disappearance of a possible suspect, but where that left him legally was uncertain.

He knocked again.

'Police! Open up!'

The scraping sounds from inside were getting louder. Kerim told Eylul and the uniform to draw their weapons. He had made the decision to first try the front door, then, if it didn't move, to shoot the lock off, when a terrible sound he would later describe as a splintering explosion happened above his head, and he threw himself away from the trajectory of whatever was hurtling through the upper window of the villa.

Thinking about whether Pınar Cebeci had actually murdered Pembe Hanım was making Mehmet Süleyman's head hurt. As if the spite she had directed towards her daughter and son-in-law were not enough, the fact that she'd alleged that she had used diazepam to drug Pembe was worryingly consistent with the facts. She hadn't answered his question about how she had disposed of Pembe's genitals, which could either mean she hadn't wanted to own up to such an outrage or she had been lying. In addition, she didn't fit Neşe Hanım's description of a tall woman with red hair.

Kerim Gürsel had been deeply concerned when he'd called. Not only had he been afraid that his wife's mother might indeed have murdered his lover, but he was also terrified about what she might reveal to the world about him. His life wasn't easy, and if what Dr Sarkissian had discovered about Betül Gencer proved to be correct, then the subsequent, no doubt hysterical, publicity that would follow would make it even harder.

Süleyman drove along Köybaşı Caddesi and checked his pockets for keys. If this trip out to the home of Filiz Tepe proved to be unproductive, he could go back and sleep at his mother's house in nearby Arnavautköy. But then if he did that, she would only question him about women, his son – of whom she did not approve – as well as his eating habits, the fact that he smoked too much and how much money he spent on clothes. He parked the car opposite the tiny alleyway Kerim had described to him and got out. He began to sweat straight away. Even in the upscale Bosphorus villages like Yeniköy, the air was still, sticky and wretched with heat.

Crossing the now almost silent road, he had begun to make his way down the alleyway towards the large villa at the end when the front upper storey of the house appeared to explode. He ran towards it.

The body, still strapped to the chair it was seated in, had landed on its head. As a consequence, it was impossible to see who it was, or had been. The only reason Kerim Gürsel had the notion it was a woman was because it had been naked and he'd had a fleeting glimpse of breasts. Everything else was just flung-out limbs, blood and brain tissue. Then silence.

Eylul Yavaş, pressed against the side of the building, her back to the bloody mess on the pavement, had her mouth open and looked as if she might be screaming. But was she? And then there was the young uniformed man. Bent double, soaked in what looked in the thin light from the street lamp like oil, he was vomiting onto the ground. Kerim tried to move, but he couldn't.

Only when a hand touched his shoulder did the wall of sound around him break through, and then his whole body began to shake.

'Is the door open?'

The man in front of him, his colleague, trembled.

Mehmet Süleyman repeated himself. 'Kerim Bey! The door, is it open?'

'Er . . .'

Süleyman turned the handle and put his shoulder to the door, which sprang open. He grabbed Kerim Gürsel by his collar. 'Who's in there?'

'I . . . I don't know . . .'

Avoiding looking directly at the corpse, he called out to Eylul Yavaş. 'Sergeant Yavaş! Are you hurt?'

There was a pause, then she said, 'No.'

'Call an ambulance,' he said.

'The head exploded.'

'Call an ambulance!' he yelled. 'That's an order! That's procedure!'

He knew that procedure was all they had to keep them sane.

'And call for backup!'

'Sir . . .'

He heard her put her weapon down and search for her phone.

'Constable?'

The young uniformed man was still being sick. Sometimes when the sickness reaction was evoked, it wouldn't stop.

Süleyman said, 'Stay here with Sergeant Yavaş. Do not leave the scene under any circumstances.'

Then he pulled Kerim along after him into the house.

Süleyman found himself standing in a large open-plan space characterised by smooth grey walls and angular furniture made from leather and steel. This Filiz Tepe woman must have had the place gutted.

Kerim Gürsel, at his back, had his pistol drawn, but it hung limply by his side. His demeanour, not surprisingly in view of what he'd just witnessed, was still one of shock. But he had to pull himself together if he was going to be of any use to Süleyman. Drawing the younger man towards him by his shoulder, he kept his voice low.

'Kerim,' he said, 'firstly who do you think is in this house?'

He shook his head. 'Betül Gencer, Filiz Tepe.'

'Do you know who that body out there was?'

'No.'

'But you'd recognise both women?'

'Yes.'

Süleyman himself would recognise Betül Gencer. She'd been on television for years, he remembered her from the attempted murder case the previous year and he'd seen her more recently with Kerim Gürsel.

'There are three officers in the back garden,' Kerim said.

He was starting to come back to himself. Süleyman knew he'd never really come back from what was outside that house, but he would function, as he himself had done for years.

Süleyman drew his weapon. He said, 'Room by room, Kerim Bey. You cover me; nobody goes anywhere on his own. Understand?'

*

It wasn't the first time Abbas had looked at the clock high up on the wall. İkmen said, 'Are you waiting for something?'

Abbas looked at him. 'No.'

'Then why do you keep checking the time?'

'Because it interests me.'

'In what way?'

'It's been said that time is an illusion,' he said. 'But it isn't. Time is a function of perception, and that is dependent upon individual perception. Time is therefore not an illusion at all. What it constitutes is an individually perceived system of order. It is that order that is the illusion, because it is something no man or woman can share.'

It was this last part of Abbas's speech that reminded İkmen of something he had said before.

'This person you described as someone who would have to be invented if they did not exist . . .'

'Yes.'

'You were very careful not to gender this . . . entity.'

'Entity?' Abbas laughed.

İkmen, against the regulations he knew his police colleagues would expect him to ignore, lit a cigarette.

'When one speaks of the concept of life being something that encompasses humanity, animals, plants, bacteria, djinn, the dead . . . One can only truly express these compartmentalised beings in terms of "entities", I think,' he said. 'And so, Abbas Bey, I do have to ask: is this person a man, a woman or something else?'

Abbas looked up at the clock again and smiled.

'What do you think, Çetin Bey?' he said. 'And how would it be if this person had twice, to my knowledge, been at your side?'

When it hit him, the idea made İkmen blanch. Since when – since *when* – had he allowed simple flattery to blind him?

He banged on the door for the night duty guard to come and

let him out while he brought up Sami Nasi's number on his phone.

Abbas the hakawati smiled.

She had her back to them. Long red hair flowed down to her waist. There was a knife in her right hand. It was dripping.

Süleyman looked at Kerim. Kerim nodded and raised his pistol.

'Betül Hanım.'

She was looking out into the garden. Armed men looked back at her through the glass. She didn't flinch.

'My name is Inspector Süleyman. I do not know what has happened here, but I do know that we need to talk. However, before that happens, I will need you to put the weapon in your right hand down. Put it on the floor now.'

She didn't move.

Seeing that this approach wasn't working, he said, 'I'd like you to turn around, please, Betül Hanım.'

She didn't move. Kerim, who had his gun lined up to her right shoulder, whispered, 'Try the other name.'

Süleyman glanced quickly at his colleague, who said, 'What do we have to lose?'

He took a breath. 'Levent Bey.'

And then, slowly, she turned. She was very beautiful; not breathlessly sexual like Gonca, not extraordinary. And yet Betül Gencer was magnificent. He wanted to use the word 'untouchable', because he wondered whether he had known all along.

'I should like you to give me the knife,' he said. 'I have no idea what has happened here, but I can tell you that if you attempt to use the weapon on myself or my colleagues, it will not go well for you. Let us talk. Put the knife down and we can go to headquarters, where you can tell me everything.'

She looked down at her hand, and an expression of shock came over her face. Then she said, 'I was waiting, you see.'

'Waiting for what?' This time Süleyman didn't call her anything.

She said, 'For her life to slide out, to drip through the floor-boards, onto the dining table, down the table legs onto one of the beautiful kilims, to end in the cellar, soaking into the earth. Like my own.' Then she smiled and added, 'Although not any more, eh?'

Neither of the officers knew what she was talking about, so Süleyman just said, 'Put the knife down on the floor, please.'

'Do you want me to place it or throw it down?'

Did it matter? All he wanted to do was disarm her. While he thought about this, she bent her knees to the left and very carefully placed the knife on the floor, its handle towards Süleyman. It was like seeing a very demure female film star from the fifties lay a present down in front of some dark, borderline-insane Yeşilcam villain. In different circumstances, it would have been amusing.

As she rose, Süleyman asked, 'Do you have a firearm?'

'No.'

'Arms out by your sides where I can see them.'

Kerim Gürsel went to step forward to search her, but Süleyman pushed him away.

'Cover me, Kerim Bey.'

And as he ran his hands over Betül Gencer's arms, down her body, between her legs, he felt his prisoner begin to laugh.

'Fucking hell, İkmen!' Sami Nasi said as he stood blearily in his doorway wearing only his boxers.

In spite of being out of breath after four flights of stairs, İkmen pushed his way into Sami's apartment. Staggering into the living room, he only just managed to avoid knocking over a huge alembic beside the sofa. He sat down.

'What is this?' Sami said, following him. 'I was asleep! Ruya still is asleep! If you wake her—'

'Oh shut up, Sami!' İkmen wheezed.

'This is my fucking home, İkmen! Don't tell me to shut up in my own fucking home!'

But he sat down beside his sweaty guest anyway. After a few seconds, realising that İkmen really couldn't do anything much more than wheeze, he said, 'Do you want water?'

'Yes.'

He went to the kitchen and filled a beer glass with water from the fridge. İkmen drank it down in one go. Then, after catching his breath for a further few seconds, he said, 'You know, Sami, the way you always carry on about your illustrious Hungarian ancestor often blinds me to the fact that you are actually an Arab.'

'I'm Turkish,' Sami said. 'Says so on my kimlik. What are you talking about and why is this important now?'

'All right, let me set it out for you, shall I? Firstly, your mother, as I recall, came originally from Aleppo. Ditto the Syrian working girl who lived with your illustrious ancestor, Professor Vaneck, when he came to perform in this city in the 1870s. Your entire pedigree hangs on that. Oh, and of course your paternal grandmother was an Arab too.'

Sami looked away. His professional life had been invested in his connection to a famous European magician. He didn't like to hear about his many Arabian relatives. Or at least that was the impression he had always given.

İkmen said, 'Tell me about the meddah. Or should I say the hakawati.'

'I don't know anything about that,' Sami said. 'I told you!'

'I don't mean Ahmad Al Saidawi,' İkmen said. 'I mean the girl.'

'What girl?'

'The one we met at the Castle of Magic. Sibel Akşener, Hakikat, whatever her name is.'

Hakikat, truth, the name under which the feisty young woman

plied her trade as a storyteller, was exactly the same in Arabic as it was in Turkish.

'She played me,' İkmen said. 'Even pandering to the last vestiges of my vanity.'

'I don't know what you're talking about.'

'And I am glad,' İkmen said. 'Without her I would never have been able to guide Kerim Gürsel to that restaurant in Fatih where the money and the arms were to be distributed. But then I was meant to do that, wasn't I? It was a pity that some sort of dispute broke out between the recipients, one of whom chose to die rather than face having to explain what had been going on.'

'This is madness!'

'Oh no,' İkmen said. 'Far from it. It makes much more sense for a woman to steal that golden lamassu from Assad rather than a man.'

Sami looked confused, but then he had always been a good actor.

'Everyone knows that the Assad regime is secretive. But to steal something from him, something so valuable . . .' İkmen shrugged. 'Something would have got out. However, a woman . . . a woman he was having an affair with . . . Not going to tolerate so much as a whisper about that, is he? She was very assertive, that young woman, very confident. And for your information, Sami, I believed and still believe her story about how she ran away from her family. How a Turkish girl ended up in Syria warming Assad's bed, I do not know. But this person who distributes money amongst the Syrians, this mortal who hides behind the identity of an immortal, she is a woman, and it is my belief that she is *that* woman.'

There was a pause, then Sami said, 'I'll get you a glass of brandy. Oh, and have a cigarette. Ruya's are on the table.'

While Sami prepared his drink, İkmen lit a cigarette. When he came back, İkmen raised his eyebrows. 'Well?'

'Well what?'

'Well are you going to tell me why and how you got involved with this?' İkmen said. 'I will be honest, when I first had my revelatory moment about this an hour ago, I did wonder why these people – Hakikat, Abbas, even that nice Syrian in the bookshop in Fatih – had done this, but then it became apparent to me that she had gone.'

'Gone? Who?'

'Sibel Akşener, Hakikat,' İkmen said. 'On to new places with her stories and her wads of cash. Eased from place to place by her grateful recipients, who probably call her a whore behind her back.'

Sami said nothing.

'Oh, I don't expect you to either confirm or deny any of this,' İkmen said. 'I can imagine, even if I don't know, how fucking dreadful it must be to be Syrian right now. I see them on the streets every day – begging, trying to get some shit job so they can feed their families. Something like this, some Robin Hood fantasy that in reality probably only affects a very few people, is the stuff of miracles and good dreams. And God knows they need that.'

Sami remained silent for a few moments, and then he said, 'My magic doesn't extend to knowing everything, you know, İkmen. I hope only to be on the right side of history, and to me that involves supporting resistance to people like Assad wherever I find it and whatever the cost.'

The two men looked at each other for a moment, then İkmen put a hand on Sami's shoulder.

Chapter 26

Süleyman got her booked in. The custody officer looked confused when he used both her names, but he didn't have time to explain. On the way to headquarters, she'd said she wanted to talk, and so he had to take advantage of that. Talking was something offenders did only sometimes; one had to try and catch those moments when one could.

After yet another body search, he moved her into an interview room and asked, even though he knew it by heart, for the name of her lawyer.

'You have the right to legal representation,' he said.

She just nodded. Had she clammed up already? Decided not to speak, fallen into shock?

'Do you want me to call Eyüp Bey for you?' he asked.

She nodded.

He left her with two officers, made the call and then caught up with Kerim Gürsel, his sergeant and the team who had attended the scene in Yeniköy. They'd all seen the body on the pavement outside Filiz Tepe's house; consequently none of them looked quite right in the head.

A veteran of such scenes, although not hardened to them, Süleyman had found his own way of dealing with them and with his own reactions. Basically he buried them, subsuming them beneath a thick layer of procedure, superiority and, later, some sort of personal risk-taking activity.

Taking the uniformed officers to one side, he instructed them to write their reports and get themselves home.

'If any of you want to see a doctor, let me know,' he said. The young constable who had been unable to stop vomiting was already in hospital.

Alone with Kerim and Eylul Yavaş, he said, 'In anticipation of Dr Sarkissian's DNA results, hopefully later on today, and because they pertain directly to the murder of Pembe Hanım, if, Kerim Bey, I may . . .'

'Take the lead,' he said. 'It's the only thing that makes sense.'

They moved to Süleyman's office. The front desk had instructions to call as soon as Eyüp Çelik arrived. Süleyman opened his window and the two men smoked; he had also called for someone to go and get Sergeant Yavaş the biggest cappuccino he or she could find.

Süleyman said, 'I didn't get a chance to speak to Dr Soylu. What did he say?'

Tuna Soylu was the pathologist on duty that night. A smaller, younger, though equally lugubrious version of Arto Sarkissian, Dr Soylu was also fond of grim humour.

'Not much,' Kerim said. 'Beyond "glad I didn't have a heavy meal".'

'It was definitely a woman,' Eylul said.

'So I understand.'

Süleyman had only glanced at the body. Later, during the course of the post-mortem, he wouldn't have that luxury.

'Now, Sergeant,' he continued, 'in light of the fact that you were outside the house when we detained Betül Gencer, I know you did not witness this lady apparently responding to the name "Levent". This pertains, we think, to Levent Özcan.'

'Her brother.'

'Or her,' he said. 'We all know that this is further evidence for Dr Sarkissian's contention that the DNA sample taken from

Betül Gencer is male in character. We also know that an identical DNA profile was found in a sample collected from the floor of Pembe Hanım's kitchen. What we don't know is why Gencer killed Pembe. I myself am unaware of any direct connection other than through Wael Al Hussain, who was one of Pembe's lovers.'

'Al Hussain wasn't really part of the case against his wife last year, was he?' Eylul said.

'No, but I imagine that Betül Gencer must have seen him at the very least. At Samira's trial.'

'And if he told Samira to go to that coffee house in Eyüp, then maybe he knew that she would meet Betül Gencer there. Perhaps he engineered it,' Kerim said.

Kerim's clothes were covered in dried blood spatter. There was even a smear on his face, which he had clearly tried to remove.

Süleyman's phone vibrated. It was Gonca. He switched it off.

Eylul said, 'Why would he engineer his own death?'

'Unless he wasn't ever meant to die?' Süleyman said. 'Unless Erol Gencer was intended to be, and always had been, the sole victim.'

Eylul's coffee arrived, brought in by a constable who, Süleyman observed to himself, looked about twelve.

Kerim Gürsel looked as if he was still shaking. Süleyman said, 'I suggest, Kerim Bey, that you go home and get some rest.'

He saw his colleague glance at his sergeant and knew what was passing through his mind. If Eylul Yavaş could hold up, so could he. Men and women, even of the most liberal kind, still fell very quickly into traditional gender roles.

The office phone rang and Süleyman picked it up. Eyüp Çelik had arrived. He said, 'Send him to my office.'

When he put the phone down, he said, 'Kerim Bey, I am going to insist you leave us.' He stood up. 'To be honest, I am asking you to leave more for Sinem Hanım's benefit than your own.'

'Why?'

'We heard on the radio that there was a disturbance in Tarlabaşı, and you commented on the location,' Süleyman said. 'Sinem hanım texted you, remember?'

'Oh . . .'

He was like a creature that had lost the will to live.

'Sergeant Yavaş,' Süleyman said. 'Could you please take Inspector Gürsel downstairs and drive him home. Then join me in interview room four.'

Gently Eylul took Kerim's arm and led him out of Süleyman's office.

She'd gone. Probably left the city by this time, İkmen thought. Abbas had been timing it, making sure he said nothing until she had disappeared. But he had said something; he'd told him this mythical person, this once and future hakawati had been at İkmen's side twice. So had Sibel Akşener – making sport out of him, taking the piss, but also showing him what was happening, because death was involved and because it was important.

A thick mist had come down overnight, and as İkmen crossed the Galata Bridge, he had been unable to see either the docks at Eminönü or the Topkapı Palace high up on Seraglio Point. When it all burned off as dawn broke, it was going to be another sweltering, humid, unbearable day in the city.

When he reached Eminönü, he walked towards the old Sirkeci railway station in order to catch his breath. He liked the Ottoman faux-Oriental station the Germans had built back in the 1890s. He remembered when the Orient Express still ran from Sirkeci to Paris – albeit a very run-down version of its glamorous 1930s incarnation. Now the station had been incorporated into the

Marmaray Metro system, which was very useful particularly if one wanted to go to the Asian side. But İkmen felt that compared to what the old station used to represent, it was all a bit tame.

'Çetin Bey?'

He couldn't see her. He took his time and lit a cigarette. And so she had one more surprise for him, did she?

'I thought you'd gone, Sibel Hanım,' he said.

He heard her laugh, a soft, pillow-like sound gently rippling through the mist.

'I meant to,' she said. 'But I had to see you one last time.'

'I'd quite like to see you too,' İkmen said.

'That's very flattering.'

He waited for her to show herself, but she didn't. As he stood in front of the shuttered entrance to the Marmaray, nothing moved. Everything was concealed by the all-encompassing mist.

'Tell me about Assad,' İkmen asked.

She said, 'My mother was Syrian, you know. When I ran away, I went there. It was stupid.'

'Why?'

A police officer walked past İkmen without so much as looking at him.

'Because it was terrible,' she said. 'Or rather it became so. I realised that life there was not much more than an exercise in fear. When I arrived, I was enchanted – by the architecture, the people, the old traditions like the hakawati. Then one day I disappeared. One moment I was walking on the street, the next I was in a beautiful prison. This is what happens there. If Assad sees you and wants you . . . I can't say that I saw much. I was kept in my own quarters most of the time, waiting for him.'

'How did you get away? And with that artefact?'

'I used someone,' she said. 'Like Assad used me. It took a long time and there were many false dawns. Like Ahmad Al Saidawi, I kept my enemy close and interested in what I would do next to delight him. When the protests began in 2011, everyone thought that was the end of Assad. But as we know, it wasn't. What he doesn't know, though, is that a door was opened during the Arab Spring. It's one that will never be shut. It's one that, one day, Ahmad Al Saidawi will walk through and completely destroy him.'

'Forgive me,' İkmen said. 'I take these things literally. Do you mean the actual Ahmad Al Saidawi?'

'I might.'

The air around İkmen was thick with concealment and he shuddered. Was this an ordinary mist?

He said, 'So why do you want to speak to me now?'

'Because I need to justify myself,' she said. 'After I told my stories in Fatih last year, I left the country. I didn't know anything about Samira Al Hussain and Betül Gencer. I had distributed funds to Wael Al Hussain some months before. I remembered him, but not his wife. I didn't know until now.'

'So you're trying to make up for that?'

'The men at the Bab will speak now,' she said.

'And Abbas?'

'If you can find him.'

'He's in a cell,' İkmen said. 'Where you put him. Indirectly, of course.'

'No he isn't.'

'I think you'll find he is,' İkmen said. 'I left him there three hours ago when I went to Sami's place and got part of the truth.'

He heard her laugh.

'I like the way you say "part of the truth",' she said. 'You are very careful to be accurate, aren't you? And you are, as I told you in the graveyard, very cool as well.'

'Seems no woman can resist either my accuracy or my cool at the moment,' İkmen said. He'd felt a definite frisson from this woman, just like he had detected a genuine desire to go to bed with him in Gonca.

'You shouldn't be alone, İkmen,' she said.

'I'm not. My family is so big it can be seen from space.'

'You know what I mean. You need a woman in your life,' she said. 'You need someone to warm your bed.'

Just the thought of it made him want to gag, but he kept his counsel. What would Fatma make of some stranger in their bed? What would the children say? Or Samsun?

He changed the subject. 'Who did you sell the gold lamassu to?'

There was a pause, and then he heard her say, 'I came back to Turkey to distribute money, and when I found out about what had happened last year, to put right what I could. I have done that.'

'A man shot himself, I think, to protect you, in the Bab,' İkmen said.

'No,' she said. 'He shot himself because he knew he was outnumbered. You know, Assad's people are everywhere. I owed him but I owe you nothing. The lamassu was sold, that's all you need to know.'

'But don't you think about the fact that it should be in Syria?' İkmen said. 'Where it belongs?'

'What makes you think it's not in Syria?' she said.

And he didn't know, apart from the fact that he'd never considered it.

'So is it . . .'

And then his voice trailed away, because suddenly he felt the absence of her. When he did finally move, he didn't even try to look for her, because he knew that she had gone, completely.

He couldn't hear what Eyüp Çelik was saying to his client, but Süleyman was aware of raised voices. Or rather one voice.

When Eylul Yavaş returned from taking Kerim Gürsel home, she said, 'What's happening?'

‘Çelik has five more minutes,’ Süleyman said. ‘How was Inspector Gürsel?’

‘His wife was up when we arrived,’ she said. ‘The street outside was full of squad cars, vans. Seems there’d been a fight at some meyhane across the road.’

There were several meyhanes in that area. One was owned by Gonca’s brother Rambo, who he knew had not been in Tarlabaşı because he was with his sister. But then Eylul said something that made him feel cold.

‘I spoke to a couple of constables I recognised down there,’ she said. ‘It seems Harun Sesler was stabbed.’

‘By whom?’ he asked.

‘A woman, apparently,’ she said. ‘I don’t know anything more than that.’

But that was enough to make Süleyman’s mind race. He’d told Gonca he didn’t want her associating with such people. Now Sesler was dead and Gonca had tried to phone him. But he’d switched his mobile off . . .

Later, or so it was said, some of the officers on duty down in the cells that night made up stories about where they were and what they did. Although quite whether whatever happened could have been made up was a good point. The interview rooms were a long way from the cells, and so Süleyman and Eylul Yavaş were not qualified to give their opinions. And down in those hot, airless spaces where men and women were detained, a more edgy and volatile reality was at play.

It started, as it ended, with the Syrian prisoners. At approximately 3.45, one of them attempted to hang himself with his own shirt. Although he managed to get one end of his noose around the internal door handle, as he began to lose consciousness he hit the door with his feet, which alerted his jailers. Meanwhile, his neighbour began his own personal war of attrition by screaming in Arabic at the top of his voice.

'Like a sickness' was how one of the older officers on duty that night described what happened next. Although all but the prisoner who had attempted to hang himself were in their cells, there were just not enough members of staff to be able to discover what was wrong with them all and attend. And so the screaming, the banging, the kicking of doors and walls and the terrible wall of noise just went on. Custody staff called for backup, but the incident in Tarlabaşı had tied up dozens of officers, some of whom were eager to deposit suspects from the gypsy meyhane incident in the few empty cells that remained.

Then there was the smoke.

It came from a cell at the centre of the complex and it was thick and black. Fire alarms were activated and officers broke out extinguishers, sand buckets and water hoses. Automatically locked doors sprang open and officers escorted inmates to safety where they could. The fire service arrived. Kitted out in protective clothing and respirators, equipped with professional firefighting equipment, they moved in to search for the seat of the blaze. But as they went deeper into the complex, it constantly eluded them. Eventually the smoke dispersed, as did the noise and the confusion.

But it still took a while for anyone to discover that the old Syrian storyteller had gone.

Lawyer Eyüp Çelik's eyes were enormous and glassy. Either he'd been disturbed in the middle of a cocaine binge, or he was afraid.

'Inspector Süleyman,' he said. 'There are fire alarms going off in this building!'

'In the cells, almost half a kilometre away,' Süleyman replied.

The alarms had sounded while he'd still been outside the

interview room, talking to Gonca, reassuring her he wasn't dead. Once they were married, she'd have to get used to his not being instantly available to her. And he would have to get used to the fact that she knew everything.

'Of course I know about Harun Bey,' she'd snapped when he'd told her about the death of the gangster. He wondered how she had known. If her brother had been with her and not in Tarlabaşı . . .

As soon as the fire alarms stopped, Süleyman looked at Betül Gencer. He said, 'I should like you to confirm your names and your date of birth.'

Çelik said, 'I have advised my client to give only these details to you at this time.'

'Very well.'

He heard her clear her throat.

'My name is Betül Gencer,' she said. 'I was born on the fourth of November 1960 in the village of Gazimurat in the province of Adana.'

'Gencer being your married name,' Süleyman said.

'Yes.'

'What was your name before you married Erol Gencer?'

'Betül Özcan.'

'Hence my request for names, plural. You have a brother, I understand, called Levent Özcan,' he said. 'Is that correct?'

Çelik put a hand on Betül Gencer's wrist and she said nothing.

Süleyman sat back in his chair. 'You responded to the name "Levent" when you were discovered at the home of Filiz Tepe in Yeniköy earlier this evening,' he said. 'Do you want to tell me about that?'

Again he was met with a wall of silence, until Çelik said, 'My client is not answering any of your questions, Inspector.'

'Doesn't stop me asking them. Or indeed Sergeant Yavaş.' He looked at Eylul. 'Please, Sergeant . . .'

'What were you doing at Filiz Tepe's house in Yeniköy?' she asked.

Süleyman smiled. 'A fair question and one I believe *I* may be able to answer, Sergeant.'

'Oh, really?'

'Yes.' He looked at Betül Gencer. 'When Inspector Gürsel and myself confronted you at the house in Yeniköy belonging to Filiz Tepe, you told us when we asked you what you were doing that you were waiting for "her" blood to seep down through the floorboards and into the earth. Can you tell me who you were referring to when you said this?'

Çelik sat forward and shook his head.

Süleyman said, 'Eyüp Bey, I fully understand and appreciate that you have your client's best interests in mind when you interject in order to silence her. But I should make you aware that our scene-of-crime and forensic officers are still at the site, which means that evidence from their investigations will be reaching us imminently. In addition, a post-mortem on the female body that was discovered at Filiz Tepe's house in Yeniköy is scheduled for later in the morning. I should also point out that after we have concluded here, Betül Hanım will be examined by our doctor before being taken to our cells . . .'

'Which appear to be burning.'

'. . . or to the cells of a local station if that is not possible. But from the sound, or lack of it, coming from that quarter now, I imagine that the emergency is at an end.'

Dawn was just starting to break over the golden city on the Bosphorus. Madam Edith shifted achily on the Gürsels' uncomfortable sofa. She'd come over when she heard that there was trouble across the road. Although she didn't know many gypsies personally, she had learned that Harun Sesler had been killed and was anxious in case the ensuing uproar disturbed Sinem.

Kerim walked into the room, already washed and dressed for work.

'What are you doing up, sweetness?' Edith asked.

'I've not been to sleep,' he said. 'But Sinem dropped off about an hour ago and so I got up. Have to be at headquarters at nine.'

Edith patted the sofa beside her. 'Sit down. I'll make tea.'

When he sat, she put an arm around him and kissed the side of his face. 'You OK?' she asked. 'You looked like a ghost when you got in.'

'It was a hard night.'

'Want to talk about it?'

'No.'

She went into the kitchen, where, rather than firing up the samovar, she made them both large glasses of instant apple tea. When she returned, he was staring into space. Edith knew that look; she'd seen it on the faces of trans girls who had been beaten up by their customers – or the police. It was the face of someone who had had enough. She put the tea glasses down on the coffee table and took his hand.

'You know you need to talk, don't you?'

He turned and looked at her. He was a middle-aged man, but Kerim Bey would always be a dear sweet boy to Edith.

Eventually he said, 'When I joined the police twenty years ago, I thought things were improving. I never fooled myself into believing that I personally could change things, but . . .'

'You having second thoughts?' Edith asked.

He sighed. 'No, not really. I've worked hard to get where I am . . .'

'I know.'

'. . . and I love the challenge the job gives me. I love my colleagues, who are good people, but . . .'

He shook his head. She squeezed his hand.

'When will things change for people like us, Edith?'

'I don't know, darling,' she said.

'Even in the West, things seem to be going backwards.' He put his head in his hands. 'I don't know what to do. Do I carry on fighting, or do I give in and become a taxi driver, or a waiter, or a tourist guide?'

She rubbed his back. 'You know as well as I do that you'll stay where you are, Kerim Bey. You've fought too hard not to, and as you say, you love your job. Then there's Sinem and the kiddie . . .'

'But what about Pembe?' he said. 'Do I carry on as if she never existed?'

'In public you have to,' she said. 'But you can talk about her to me any time, and Sinem.'

He looked up. 'Oh no, not Sinem,' he said. 'Not now.'

And a look passed between them that told Edith that poor broken-hearted Kerim was now well and truly trapped.

Chapter 27

It was still early, and the streets had not yet started baking in the fierce sun. When Betül Gencer had clammed up, Süleyman had called a halt to her interview. He had what he needed from her in the immediate term; they would reconvene later that morning.

Now it was 5 a.m. and the sun was rising. He'd maybe slept for an hour, but no more. He'd slipped into bed beside Gonca and become unconscious immediately. When he'd woken, she had still been sleeping soundly, and so he'd got up, showered and dressed. Now he was sitting in her garden drinking coffee and smoking.

He'd not looked directly at the body that had fallen from that first-floor window in Yeniköy, but he'd seen it out of the corner of his eye. When he presented himself at the lab for the post-mortem, he'd see it again, and the thought of it made him go cold. The head had just . . . shattered. Like an egg, or a water-melon. What had been inside had burst out over Kerim, Eylul and the young constable. That they hadn't been in its path was the only mercy here. In the interview with Betül Gencer and her lawyer, he'd seen some bloodied tissue fall from Eylul's headscarf onto the floor. If anything, this had been even worse than the event itself. He hadn't told her.

'Darling?'

He looked up and saw Gonca framed in the French windows. With no make-up and her hair loose to the ground, she looked pale and unremarkable. But he knew that was just because she was tired. He put a hand out to her. 'What are you doing up?'

'When you came to my bed in the middle of the night, I thought you were staying.' She sat on his lap and kissed him. 'Then I wake up and you're gone.'

'I have to be at work for nine,' he said.

She lit a cigarette. 'What was it about, last night?'

He put his arms around her. 'You know I can't tell you. But you will find out later today, I hope.'

'Something involving Kerim Bey? You should tell him to stop taking you away from me,' she said.

She was naked underneath her silk dressing gown. He pulled it down past her shoulders to expose her breasts, which he kissed. He didn't feel in any way like sex, he was far too tired, but he still wanted to make her feel good. And she was pleased, for a while, stretching like a cat and caressing him. But then she said, 'My brother has a problem because Harun Bey died at his meyhane.'

'Rambo didn't kill him.'

'No.'

'It was the mother of some child he was going to marry,' Süleyman said. 'Did you know his bride was going to be a child?'

'No . . .'

Gonca was a good liar, but this time he doubted her. If she had known, would she have told him? It was, he imagined, one of those Romany things he would never be privy to. Could they realistically live together with that between them?

But he wanted to, and knew that was what she wanted too. He held her tight and nibbled one dark, smooth shoulder. Then he whispered in her ear, 'I love you too much.'

She smiled.

Kerim Gürsel's text was interesting. Apparently Betül Gencer was in custody. He'd speak to him about it later. İkmen put his phone in his pocket and was just about to leave his apartment when a voice called out, 'Çetin Bey!'

He turned and saw Patrick standing in his hallway.

'Ah,' he said. 'You are going to the Grand Bazaar with Çiçek today.'

'Yes. Where are you going?' the boy asked.

Poor kid, he'd hardly seen his father in recent days. Passed from pillar to post . . .

'I have to meet my client,' he said.

'Oh. Did you find that storyteller you were looking for?'

'Oh yes,' İkmen said. 'But he turned out to be someone I . . . well, I hadn't noticed. But then that's the thing with magic, you have to be attentive, and I wasn't.'

'Oh.' Patrick looked down at the floor. 'Is my father really going to marry that gypsy woman?'

'I think so.'

'I wish it was Çiçek and not her.'

İkmen put his case down on the floor and went and hugged the boy. Patrick was so much taller than he was, but it didn't matter.

'Ah, Patrick,' he said, 'often things don't work out as we want them to. But Gonca is a wonderful person, I know her well. She has magic.'

'Does she?'

'Lots of it,' he said. 'And more importantly, she loves your father and he loves her. That I would say is probably the best magic she has.'

He left. Çiçek was going to take Patrick to the Grand Bazaar later in the day, where they were due to meet Hülya's husband, Berekiah. He was working on a small crown for a society bride, which hopefully the boy would find interesting.

Rima Al Numan was sitting at a table on the top terrace of the Setustu tea garden in Gülhane Park. Once the playground of the sultans, Gülhane Park was a bucolic place in the twenty-first century. Full of flower beds, ancient trees and, at the far end where the tea garden was, wonderful views of the Bosphorus. In İkmen's youth there had been a funfair here, complete with rickety wooden rides and even a snake pit. He had always mourned its passing.

Rima had already ordered a samovar and two tea glasses plus a basket of pastries. Not knowing that İkmen didn't really eat, she'd ordered enough for two.

'Inspector.'

'Good morning, Rima Hanım,' he said as he sat down.

'You have news?'

She was anxious to hear what he had to say. Her sister's prison sentence could be at stake.

He sat down and she poured him a glass of tea, into which he dropped two sugar cubes. He sometimes thought that were it not for the sugar in his tea, he could well be dead.

'I do,' he said. 'And for you, I think, it will be welcome.'

He told her about how he had found the Bab restaurant in Fatih, how he'd met Abbas and how all of this had been made possible by a Turkish meddah, a woman called Hakikat.

'I can't really say I fully understand how this connection to Ahmad Al Saidawi came about,' he said. 'Maybe you do?'

'I think maybe all Syrian people can relate to him as a figure who stands against oppressors,' she said. 'And the idea,' she smiled, 'that he is not really dead.'

'Hakikat distributes money that comes indirectly from Assad,' İkmen said. 'That has to hurt.'

'Mukhabarat are always everywhere.' Reflexively she looked around.

But no one was near their table. To their left, the view of the vast blue Bosphorus was breathtaking. And as a ferry blew its mournful horn as it came in to dock down at Eminönü, İkmen was briefly transported back to his childhood of smoky skies, ancient wooden ferries and belly dancers in the Gülhane Park snake pit.

'But while your sister's story has, to my mind, been substantiated, the police themselves do not yet have enough evidence to review her sentence or indeed her case,' he said.

'Oh.'

'Hakikat is long gone, and Abbas, I was informed this morning, escaped from the cells last night.'

'Really?'

'There was a fire, or rather there was smoke. He got away.'

'Somebody must have helped him.'

'Maybe.' But İkmen didn't think so. People escaping from the cells was serious, and if he knew his ex-superiors, those custody officers would have been ripped to shreds for what had taken place on their watch. No. Whatever had happened in the cells had happened because Abbas had engineered it. If that had even been his name . . .

'I have written a report for the investigating officer.'

'Gürsel.'

'Yes,' he said. 'Of course there's no doubt that Samira attempted to kill Erol Gencer. But if it can be proven that she wouldn't have done so if she hadn't met Betül Gencer, then that may alter things, especially if that lady confirms that the meeting did actually happen.'

'Which you have found out it did.'

'Unsubstantiated at the moment,' İkmen said. 'But my colleagues will do their best. Betül Gencer is currently at headquarters on another matter, I believe.'

Eyüp Çelik looked much less wired than he had in the middle of the night. Maybe he'd started his day without chemical assistance. His client, however, looked ghost like. Pale and unwashed,

Betül Gencer was almost unrecognisable. Pretty sure that the lawyer was going to continue to advise his client to say nothing, Mehmet Süleyman looked down at the piece of paper Eylul Yavaş had just handed him and said, 'You are Levent Özcan, born the fourth of November 1960 in the village of Gazimurat in the province of Adana. Son of Hakan and Gülizar Özcan, brother to five other males.' He looked up. 'No sisters.'

Betül Gencer, predictably, said nothing. He said, 'But you know this. You also know, because I believe you are an intelligent person, easily capable of deduction, that there are question marks over your DNA tests, the latest of which should be back from the laboratory sometime this morning. Did Filiz Tepe know you were male? Is that why you killed her?'

She didn't flicker. Çelik said, 'You know without doubt that the body you found outside the house of Filiz Tepe is that woman, Inspector?'

Filiz's sister was on her way to the pathology laboratory to identify the body. Apparently this could be achieved by looking for a tattoo. Süleyman took a punt.

'Yes,' he said.

'If that is the case, my client knows nothing about it,' Çelik said. 'My client was inside Filiz Tepe's house.'

'Filiz Tepe had been in her house until just after my colleagues arrived,' Süleyman said. 'Until she fell or was pushed out of a top-floor window.'

'I understand you discovered my client at the back of the property, on the ground floor,' Çelik said.

'Some ten minutes later, yes,' Süleyman said. 'Ample time to get from the master bedroom, from which Filiz Tepe fell or was pushed, to the back door, which by that time was covered by our officers. It is my belief your client was attempting to escape.'

'It is my belief that the arrival of the police made my client panic. You tend to have that effect upon members of the public.'

'We are not always welcome, no,' Süleyman said. 'But when I asked your client to explain her presence in Filiz Hanım's house, she said she was "waiting". Intrigued as to what she might be waiting for, I asked her, and she replied . . .' he consulted his notes, '"For her life to slide out, to drip through the floorboards, onto the dining table . . . soaking into the earth. Like my own. Although not any more, eh?" Now I don't know who, Mrs Gencer, you meant by "her" or what your reference to her life sliding out might have meant. Did you mean Filiz Tepe? And by her life sliding out, do I take it you were referring to her blood?'

Betül Gencer carried on looking at the table.

Çelik said, 'My client came to Filiz Hanım's house in order to talk to her. While sometimes at odds with each other, Mrs Gencer, in the wake of her husband's death, was desirous of making amends with someone who had been her friend in the past.'

Eylul Yavaş said, 'In the middle of the night?'

'My client was distressed.'

'After police pathologist Dr Arto Sarkissian and Inspector Kerim Gürsel went to Mrs Gencer's house yesterday afternoon in order to obtain a DNA sample from her, her house was put under surveillance,' Eylul said. 'In order to evade our team, Mrs Gencer did not use her car when she left the building and, we believe, left in some sort of disguise.'

Süleyman said, 'The clothes you were wearing last night, which have been taken from you for analysis, were of poor quality. You did not have make-up on when we apprehended you and your shoes were flat. I imagine you would have blended in with some of the maids who work in many of the big houses in Sarıyer.'

'My client went to the house of Filiz Tepe in order to talk,' Çelik said. 'She found the front door open and was going to go upstairs to look for her friend when your officers arrived.'

'Mmm.' Süleyman stood. 'Clearly when we have the necessary forensic reports into the scene, and specifically your place in it, Mrs Gencer, we can talk again. At present, I do not see that anything can be gained from pursuing this conversation with your advocate.'

He bowed to them both and he and Eylul Yavaş left.

Once outside the interview room, he said to his colleague, 'I have an appointment with Dr Sarkissian for the PM in an hour. I'll pick up whatever other results they may have while I'm there. We can't rush this interrogation, Sergeant, it's too complex. There are too many unknowns – at the moment.'

'Yes, sir.'

'You know one of the Syrians absconded last night?'

'Yes,' she said. 'Inspector Gürsel and Sergeant Mungun are with the remaining detainees now.'

'All right,' he said. 'I'll see you back here at one p.m., traffic permitting. Hopefully I'll have further ammunition to break her by then.'

'Or him,' Eylul said.

Süleyman shook his head. 'Technically,' he said. 'But Levent Özcan clearly made a choice some years ago now. I want to find out why, and how that pertains, if at all, to the death of the woman in that house – and, as we know, maybe more deaths.'

'You speak Turkish?'

'A little,' the man said. But from Kerim Gürsel's point of view, his linguistic skills were far from minimal. In the wake of the disturbance in the cells the previous night and Abbas's escape, the Syrians who had been brought in from the Bab restaurant were talking.

Ömer Mungun, as translator, asked this man, Farid Badawi, whether he wanted to revert to Arabic or continue speaking Turkish. He opted for the latter approach.

It had been Badawi who had got into an argument with a man they now knew was called Mahdi Jabal in the Bab two nights before. He'd taken out a gun and shot him. Then Jabal had shot himself.

'Why?' Kerim asked.

Badawi shrugged. 'He think he have to do this.'

'Because?'

'Because we get money.'

'From this hakawati you tried to convince us was three hundred years old?'

He shrugged.

'Who turns out to be an enemy of President Assad who distributes money to you from the sale of an artefact stolen from Assad.'

'If this is how you think.'

'With which some of you purchase arms, which is something for which I could have you deported.'

'This person makes living outside Syria possible for some people.'

'But the money will run out,' Kerim said. 'It's not infinite.' He looked down at his notes. 'Now Sergeant Mungun tells me that you claim you were present at a performance by this hakawati in Fatih in April 2018.'

'Yes.'

'This was where two women, one Turkish, one Syrian, met and planned to kill their respective husbands,' Kerim said. 'At the time and subsequently we have tried to find out about this event but have been met with silence. Can you tell me about that?'

'Is Syrian business going on that day.'

'So money was being distributed. Can you tell me about the hakawati? What was he like?'

Badawi smiled but said nothing. Ömer said something in Arabic, but still Badawi kept his counsel.

Kerim, remembering what İkmen had told him when he'd called, said, 'Because we have reason to believe it was a woman.'

Badawi said nothing.

Kerim said, 'Which I imagine means that that was indeed the case. Moving on—'

'Is Ahmad Al Saidawi,' Badawi said.

'No it wasn't.'

Ömer leaned across to Kerim. 'He may actually believe that.'

Kerim Gürsel raised his eyes to the ceiling.

Then Badawi said, 'The wife of Wael Al Hussain was there. But not Wael. The woman is Alawite, but I recognise her.'

Arto Sarkissian hadn't noticed the tattoo at the top of the corpse's right leg. When he'd seen the body for the first time, early that morning, he'd focused on little beyond the catastrophic damage he had to try to make sense of. Then when Filiz Tepe's sister had arrived to identify the body and he'd had to attend to the tattoo, he'd also been obliged to think about what else he might be able to show the poor woman, and what he should withhold.

The tattoo was distinctive – a finely executed rendition of the head of Alexander the Great from the Getty Museum in Los Angeles.

Filiz Tepe's sister, Buska, had explained.

'She had a boyfriend called İskender, many years ago. He died. She never really got over him. It's her. Nobody else has that tattoo.'

And then she'd dissolved into tears. She'd asked, in full knowledge of the fact that her sister's injuries were catastrophic, to see her face, but Arto Sarkissian had forbidden it. Not so now with Inspector Süleyman.

As he pulled away the plastic sheet covering the corpse, he watched the policeman begin to sweat underneath his surgical mask and head covering.

'I find,' the doctor said, 'that the only way to deal with corpses like this is to get the revelation stage over in one go.'

He didn't expect Süleyman to concur. Men like him, even though Arto knew him to be a compassionate person, were heavily invested in their own status as alpha males. He'd fight with everything he had not to show emotion.

The doctor continued. 'Buska Tepe, sister of Filiz Tepe, identified the body as that of her sibling, and so I believe we can now proceed in the safe knowledge that we have a named corpse.'

'Thank you, Doctor.'

Sarkissian consulted his notes, while also occasionally looking up to monitor the shock in Süleyman's eyes. The policeman had seen a lot during the course of his service, but never anything quite this horrific. The doctor himself had rarely seen anything this bad.

He began to read. 'Our subject, Filiz Tepe, is a sixty-year-old woman standing one-point-six-seven metres tall and weighing fifty-seven kilograms. Distinguishing marks include a tattoo of the head of what her sister tells me is Alexander the Great at the top of her right thigh . . .' Then he stopped as he remembered something. 'Oh, and yes, Inspector, that DNA sample I took from Betül Gencer yesterday came back this morning. It is, as we strongly suspected, male.'

It appeared that money from the sale of Assad's golden lamassu was only being distributed to Sunni Muslims and Christians. It seemed to Kerim Gürsel harsh to completely exclude Alawite Muslims just because they shared a faith with the president. Many of them opposed him.

He said, 'You will face trial for the wounding of Mahdi Jabal. You will go to prison.'

Farid Badawi said nothing. These Syrians were hard work. The supposed fire the previous evening had been caused by a police-issue smoke bomb. But of course none of the Syrians knew anything about it. Ömer had put forward the idea that maybe they hadn't had anything to do with it, and perhaps he was right. Maybe these Syrians had had help from someone at headquarters. There would be an investigation, for what that was worth. But at the very least, now Kerim knew he had been right to open up what had been a cursory investigation by Süleyman into the meeting between Betül Gencer and Samira Al Hussain in 2018. He had been proved right, although whether Mehmet Bey would ever get over the notion that he had been wrong was another matter.

He changed tack. 'Did you help the man known as Abbas to escape last night?'

'I know nothing of this,' Badawi said. Just like he'd known nothing about the smoke bomb.

Kerim's phone beeped to let him know he had a message. He ignored it.

'To return to the storyteller, Abbas: he was, I recall, going to perform stories attributed to Ahmad Al Saidawi.'

The Syrian shrugged.

'And what does that mean?' Kerim asked. 'Was he or wasn't he?'

'I do not know.'

Kerim's phone beeped again. Again he ignored it.

Badawi said, 'You have message, Inspector.'

'Yes, I know!'

'So . . .'

Kerim picked up his phone and saw that the message was from Madam Edith. It said, *Labour has started. Sinem and I now at Memorial Şişli Hospital maternity unit. No rush. Will keep you informed. Don't leave town. Edith*

In spite of himself, he smiled. The crack about not leaving town was a reference to what cops had always said to Edith when she used to occasionally get arrested for soliciting.

'You have good news,' Badawi said.

Kerim put his game face back on. This money distribution amongst the Syrians had the whiff of a cult to him. He said, 'What is this hakawati to you, besides a source of money?'

Badawi said nothing.

'It was poorly done,' the doctor said as he raised one of the corpse's arms up for Süleyman to see. 'The wounds are horizontal, as you can see. Deep, I grant you, but considering the arms were fastened tightly to the arms of the chair, limiting the blood supply, not entirely effective. A more efficient strategy would have been to cut up the arms vertically and leave them unbound. But then of course she would have been able to potentially free herself.'

Süleyman said, 'When I detained her, the alleged assailant talked about the victim's life slipping away down onto the floorboards and into the earth.'

'Could describe it. But if – I don't know, I am surmising – the assailant intended to watch the victim bleed out, then that would have taken some while. Some excellent prints were lifted from the masking tape holding the arms and ankles, as well as the rope with which she was tied to the chair, so no care was taken to even try to avoid detection.'

'Was she dead when she fell from the window?' Süleyman asked.

'Given the paucity of blood reported and recorded at the site, I would say no,' he said. 'But I have yet to confirm this. I will have to visit the site myself, and also I have yet to run blood tests and toxicology and investigate the possibility of sexual activity.' He looked down at the body. 'What we appear to have here is the body of a very slim, fit woman in her sixtieth year. Privileged, manicured, good-quality clothing . . . Oh, I should also add that she was gagged, with masking tape. I can see what remains of it in the head.'

'Yes.' Reflexively Süleyman turned away.

'I'd make an educated guess that it was the fall that killed her,' the doctor said. 'She may have been semi-conscious.'

'Do you think she could have moved herself to the window and thrown herself out?'

'Why do you ask?'

'Because Inspector Gürsel and Sergeant Yavaş heard scraping noises coming from the house just before she fell.'

'Mmm. I can't tell you that definitively,' Arto said. 'Not yet. Depends how much blood she lost, depends whether she was drugged, under the influence of alcohol. Her feet would have only just touched the floor, so it wouldn't have been easy. She would have had to rock herself forward and then shuffle with the chair firmly tied to her back. Was the assailant in the room from which she fell when you found her?'

'No.'

He shrugged. 'Then maybe. But then . . .'

'What?'

'If the assailant wanted, as she implied to you, to watch this woman die, then maybe she was there.'

'Or maybe she pushed her?'

'Indeed.'

Chapter 28

Calmly the paşa's wife reached into her sleeve and pulled out a handkerchief. Her husband, still raging, shouted, 'Open that chest now, madam!' From the handkerchief she took one half of a double-nut almond and put it before her husband. 'Philopena, my love,' she said to the paşa.

He looked at her but found she couldn't hold his gaze. Eventually Çetin İkmen spoke. 'So what will happen to your sea silk now, Gonca?'

She'd not told him that the sea silk she'd somehow been getting from Italy had been intended for Harun Sesler's child bride's dress, but he'd worked it out. He'd known for a while that she owed Sesler money.

'I'll find a use for it,' she said as she sipped her tea.

'Or you could sell it,' he said.

She looked at him with venom in her eyes.

'Or not.' He offered her a cigarette, which she took, and they both lit up.

'Any idea who might be taking over now Harun Bey has left us?' İkmen asked.

'I couldn't tell you even if I knew,' she said.

İkmen leaned back in his chair. 'Were I a betting man, I'd put money on young Serkan,' he said, naming the eldest of the gangster's sons.

She didn't respond. Serkan Sesler was a spoiled, overweight

individual who was known for his lack of attention to detail. If he took over the family business, Gonca would probably slip out of view. Not that her debt would be cancelled, but it would most certainly be shelved. The first thing Serkan would have to do if he wanted to stamp his authority on Tarlabaşı was avenge his father's death. Harun's killer, Afife Purcu, was in police custody having confessed to the murder on the spot. But that still left her husband, Hüsnü, her daughter, Elmas, and her eighteen-year-old son, Ali. If they were lucky, the Purcus would simply have to pay money; if not . . .

İkmen said, 'Afife Purcu must have been out of her mind when she killed Harun.'

'You think so?'

'From what I picked up on my travels over to Tarlabaşı, it seemed that she was too far gone on heroin to know or care what happened to her daughter.'

'People change.'

'Maybe.'

'Anyway,' Gonca said, 'what you probably don't know is that Afife was married off to Hüsnü when she was thirteen. She wouldn't have wanted her daughter to go through what she had.'

'If she could remember . . .'

'İkmen, I feel you're trying to tell me something, without actually doing it.'

He leaned forward. 'You went to see her, didn't you?'

'No.'

'Oh it's all right, I think you did what you did in part for Elmas, but I also think you did it for yourself.'

Her eyes narrowed. 'Do you hate me so much?'

'Oh no, Gonca Hanım, I love you,' he said. 'Platonically, of course. And because I love you, I am perturbed to find out you have been meddling in gangland politics like this. I am also concerned because of Mehmet Bey. Curse who you will, lady, but put the boy in the path of danger and you will have me to deal with. Have you told him?'

She put her head down. 'No.'

'Then let us hope he doesn't find out,' İkmen said. 'And don't do it again.'

Still with her eyes averted, she said, 'How did you know?'

'I didn't,' İkmen said. 'I had my suspicions and you just confirmed them. Some call it magic; I call it taking a punt. Just don't tell young Patrick Süleyman. He's absolutely entranced with magic and he's way too young to have his beliefs smashed to matchwood.'

She smiled.

İkmen paused. 'Which brings me to our Syrian friends. Remember I asked you about Syrians . . .'

'What about them?'

Commissioner Selahattin Ozer cast his cold grey eyes over the document Kerim Gürsel had handed him and said, 'This Farid Badawi, you saw him shoot this other man, Mahdi Jabal?'

'It's in my report, sir. The other men at that table, ten in number, were in possession of illegal firearms. Only Badawi can be charged with wounding.'

'Because Jabal killed himself.'

'Yes, sir.'

The commissioner frowned. 'Extraordinary. Do we know why?'

Kerim, his mind half on the time he was spending doing this when he could be supporting his wife, explained about how money from the sale of an artefact that had once belonged to President Assad was being distributed abroad by a woman who told stories.

When he'd finished, Ozer said, 'A Turkish woman, you say?'

'She was Assad's mistress,' Kerim replied.

'Name?'

'None that checks out,' he said.

'And this Abbas character? I am told that ex-Inspector İkmen was allowed to talk to him . . .'

Of course Ozer had known about that. He was no fool, and at the beginning of his tenure he would have gone berserk. But lately he hadn't. Kerim didn't know why and tended to go along with Mehmet Süleyman's opinion that he was gathering intelligence against some of his longer-serving officers. It was well known that those who had been in post during the attempted coup of 2016 could be vulnerable.

'It was Inspector İkmen—'

'Ex.'

'Ex-Inspector İkmen who exposed Abbas's knowledge about the woman,' Kerim said. 'Without him that connection would never have been made.'

Ozer leaned back in his chair. 'And yet,' he said, 'Abbas is still missing and we have a smoke canister situation.'

'Yes, sir.'

He picked up a pen. 'I will authorise an audit as well as an investigation. If there are people who would collude with enemies of the state, we need to identify and detain them.'

'Yes, sir.'

'But,' he looked up at Kerim and actually smiled, 'it would seem that you need to be elsewhere now, Kerim Bey.'

'Yes, sir.'

In her last message, Madam Edith had sounded as though she was beginning to panic.

'İnşallah your child will be born safely,' Ozer said. 'You may leave.'

Kerim just about managed to get out of his superior's office before he broke into a run.

*

'Sir!'

Süleyman saw Ömer Mungun running towards him as he closed the door of his office behind him.

'Ömer,' he said, 'I have to go and meet Sergeant Yavaş. We're back in with Betül Gencer in fifteen minutes.'

'Sir, I have to tell you,' Ömer said.

'Tell me what? Be quick!'

Ömer led his superior to one side of the corridor. 'The Syrians Inspector Gürsel brought in have finally cracked about the story-telling event in Fatih in April 2018. There was a hakawati there and we've got a witness who can identify Samira Al Hussain.'

'Really?'

Of course this was good news, because it meant he could now exert more pressure on Betül Gencer. But it was also bad news, because he had entirely dismissed Samira's story.

'Yes,' Ömer said. 'How did you get on at the PM?'

'Not one I should like to repeat.'

'I heard some of the details,' Ömer said. 'It was—'

'Quite,' Süleyman cut him off. 'But I've a strong case against Mrs Gencer now, I hope. Forensically, it's promising.'

'Oh, and Inspector Gürsel has gone to Şişli,' Ömer said. 'His wife's having the baby.'

'Oh, well that's . . .' Süleyman smiled. 'Some good news, inşallah.'

Ömer, who wasn't Muslim and couldn't ever really get it together to agree that something would happen if God willed it, said, 'Absolutely.'

Gonca said, 'I'll support anyone who battles against oppression. I'm Roma, we've never experienced anything but oppression.'

'I can't argue with that,' İkmen said.

She lit another cigarette but didn't offer him one.

'I swear to you, İkmen,' she said, 'that I knew no names.'

'So you weren't obscuring what you knew in order to protect Mehmet Bey?'

'No!'

'But you knew about Samira Al Hussain and her story about the coffee house in Fatih?'

'I did. I believed it.'

'Did you tell Mehmet Bey you believed it?'

'No,' she said. 'It wasn't my business.' She crossed her arms over her chest. 'Anyway, when that all happened, he was seeing your daughter.'

So she'd not told him what she knew because she'd been jealous. Much as he loved Gonca, İkmen was disappointed. And being who he was, he didn't hold back.

'What you did, or failed to do, was wrong,' he said.

'That woman still tried to kill Erol Gencer.'

'But it wasn't her idea,' İkmen said.

She pulled her legs up underneath her chin and looked miserable.

Eventually İkmen said, 'Gonca, I will say nothing to him. It's not my place.'

'Not even for your daughter's sake?'

'Çiçek and Mehmet were never going to work, you know that,' he said. 'She doesn't worship the ground he walks on. She doesn't do that for any man.'

'Except you.'

He shook his head. 'But if you want to keep him, you have to be honest with him. I know you Roma keep things to yourselves. You've had to in order to survive. But when he becomes your husband, he won't just be your lover. You'll be partners, which means you'll have to let him into your world as he will let you into his.'

'He won't!'

'He will,' İkmen said. 'Not in the sense that he'll share the job with you. We don't do that. But you will have to accept his child as he accepts your children. You will have to be faithful to him as he will be faithful to you.'

'Will he be faithful?' Now she looked anxious.

'Well I hope so,' İkmen said. 'I'm sure you've given him the speech about cursing him if he isn't. If he's got any sense at all, he'll stay on the straight and narrow. But you have to understand what he has given up for you, Gonca. His mother could disinherit him because of you. But he will take that risk, because he adores you.'

'I adore him!'

'It's not a fucking competition!' İkmen said.

She looked down at the ground.

Then he said, 'You should have told me everything you knew about the Syrians and their storyteller; you should have told Mehmet Bey.' He put a hand on her foot. 'God, you're hard to love sometimes, Gonca Hanım. If we two were not so alike, I couldn't and I wouldn't.'

'When did you transition?'

Eyüp Çelik interjected. 'Is this necessary, Inspector?'

Süleyman looked at him with such obvious disgust, Çelik visibly squirmed. This was the man who had threatened Kerim Gürsel.

'Yes,' he said. 'It is. Mrs Gencer?'

He'd given the lawyer and his client the news about the lab having confirmed Betül's DNA as male. She had looked unsurprised, but Çelik had appeared horrified.

She said nothing.

'And yet you call her Mrs Gencer,' Çelik said. 'If she is Mrs Gencer, then she's a woman.'

'Your client has transitioned from male to female,' Süleyman said. 'That is not, as a stand-alone fact, my issue. What does concern me is how it may have had a bearing on evidence we possess that points towards your client having killed people. Mrs Gencer's DNA, which is biologically male, was found in blood on the floor of the kitchen in the apartment rented by the murder victim known as Pembe Hanım in Tarlabaşı. I therefore need her to explain herself.'

There was a moment's silence while Çelik regrouped.

'Inspector Süleyman,' he said, 'my client is a respected and respectable woman. What on earth would she be doing in the apartment of a cheap Tarlabaşı whore?'

'That's what I would like Mrs Gencer to tell me,' Süleyman responded. 'Maybe, who knows, if she deigns to talk to me, I might be able to actually exonerate her from that inquiry.'

Betül Gencer still said nothing.

'With regard to Filiz Tepe,' Süleyman continued, 'we found you at her house, Mrs Gencer. You made a statement about wanting so see "her" life ebb away, and just before Sergeant Yavaş and myself arrived here, we discovered that the fingerprints found on the masking tape used to secure Filiz Tepe to a chair were yours. According to our doctor, an attempt to kill Filiz Tepe by slitting her wrists, thereby leading to her exsanguination, failed. Therefore, whether she managed to ease herself out of her bedroom window or whether you pushed her, the responsibility is yours.'

'You can't prove my client pushed her.'

'I can prove that your client tied her to that chair. I can prove, beyond reasonable doubt, that she slit her wrists,' Süleyman said. 'I can also prove, not just from forensic evidence, but via eyewitness testimony, that someone matching your description, Mrs Gencer, entered Pembe Hanım's apartment around the time of her death.'

'Inspector, I—'

'Inspector Süleyman,' Betül Gencer interrupted. 'I should like Eyüp Bey to go.'

The lawyer looked at her and shook his head. 'Betül Hanım . . .'

'No, it's better this way, Eyüp,' she said.

'But I still haven't got to . . .' He looked away from her and focused his eyes on Süleyman. 'Inspector, if we might talk alone . . .'

'No,' Süleyman said.

Betül Gencer put a hand on Çelik's arm. 'Say nothing more,' she said. 'Leave now and, well, you know . . .'

'I don't!'

'Eyüp, I am asking you to leave because I care about what you've done for me,' she said. 'It has been above and beyond and I appreciate it. But if you stay, that will change.'

Süleyman and Eylul Yavaş exchanged glances. A suspect effectively dismissing their lawyer during an interrogation had never happened to either of them so far. It was shocking, and they both wondered how his strategy might have developed had she allowed him to stay.

Çelik stood up. 'It would seem my services are no longer required.'

Süleyman knocked on the door of the interview room and asked the guard outside to open up. He offered to shake Çelik's hand, but the lawyer said, 'I'd rather not.' Then he walked out, the door clanging with hard finality behind him.

Alone now with Betül Gencer, Süleyman and Eylul Yavaş looked at each other again.

'Mrs Gencer,' Süleyman said, 'would you like us to allocate a lawyer to replace Eyüp Bey?'

'No,' she said.

'You have the right and I would be derelict in my duty if I didn't make you aware of the fact that you would benefit from professional representation.'

She smiled. 'I think it would be a waste of money, Inspector.'

'Why is that?'

'Because all I'm going to be doing here is telling you a story,' she said. 'That my story is real and contains no sultans or odalisques doesn't make it any less interesting, I can assure you.'

'I'm not going to give you a sob story about my brutal childhood in some hellhole village in Anatolia,' Betül Gencer began. 'I had a nice childhood. I have five brothers, we were poor. Both my parents worked on the land, but we all went to school and we never starved. I knew I was different, though. I didn't know how, and so as much as I loved my family, I left them in 1976 to come here to the city.'

'You were sixteen.'

'Yes. Sixteen and very innocent – or so I thought. I, a boy, discovered men. I discovered that men liked me a lot. I made money that way. Of course I got beaten up from time to time, who doesn't, but on the whole I liked living in Tarlabaşı in the 1970s. As time went on, I made friends – mainly gay men, but also trans girls and drag queens. I loved the queens particularly and began to dress like them. But I never wanted to become a woman. What I did was a game, a flirtatious one.'

'Are you telling us,' Süleyman said, 'that your transition happened against your will?'

'Yes – and no,' she said.

Eylul Yavaş frowned.

'I never sought it myself, but I'm glad I did it, if that makes any sense.' She paused. 'Or rather that was how I did feel, once. My gladness became something else.'

'Why?'

'I'll get to that. May I have a cigarette?'

Süleyman gave her one and lit it for her. There was no ashtray in the interview room, as strictly one wasn't supposed to smoke in there, but Eylul let her use her empty cardboard coffee mug.

'I got a job in modelling,' Betül continued. 'Everyone in the industry knew I was a boy, but no one cared. I looked pretty and thin in the clothes I had to wear and I got loads of sex. That was when I changed my name to Betül. I also moved out of Tarlabaşı to Kadıköy.'

'In the name of Levent Özcan?'

'Yes. I needed to be slightly more respectable on the street by this time. I also think that part of me wanted to lead a double life. I think in a way I still do . . . I was Betül when at the end of 1979 I met a TRT reporter called Celal Koca, who interviewed me for a short news piece about my work. He was married with children, he was kind and he loved that I was so pretty and had a cock. He also liked tits, and so I started taking hormones. The tits pleased me too; they grew big and sensitive and Celal was crazy about them.' She looked at Eylul. 'Sorry.'

'Please don't be,' she said.

Betül took a breath. 'Celal Bey got me work on game shows. That was where I met Filiz Tepe. We started as friends, before she became violently ambitious. It was because of Filiz that I enrolled in Erol's psychology classes in 1986. She was so clever and educated, I felt like a fool in comparison. I also, I now think, wanted to know what made her tick. It's always good to know your enemy, isn't it?'

'I imagine . . .'

'Erol and I didn't mean to fall in love,' she said. 'It just happened, truly.'

Was she saying this to justify herself in some way?

'Did he know?'

'Not at first,' she said. 'Then he said he loved me for myself. He was adventurous in bed. It was something he'd never been able to express before. I played into that. Erol was handsome and charming and I wanted him. I even, once he'd divorced his wife, put up with visits from his horrible daughter. I would have done anything for him, and I did.' She looked up. 'We were never legally married. How could we be?'

Indeed. The obligatory blood test would have given her away.

'I didn't know that he had ambitions to be somebody,' she said. 'When Celal Bey started Harem Medya in the nineties, I got Erol a job.'

'What about Celal Bey?' Eylul asked. 'Was your affair with him still current?'

'No,' she said. 'Celal had moved on to Filiz Tepe by that time. He was with her for years. It was OK – then.'

'Did she know about you by this time?' Süleyman asked.

'Yes,' she said. 'We were friends. It was fine until . . .' She paused.

'When Celal Bey began to tire of her, she blamed me. I don't know why, I had no interest in him by that time, nor he in me. Every new girl was fair game for Celal. I felt sorry for her. I was so happy and she was so miserable. When Celal Bey died, I was surprised he left the company in her hands, but then maybe she was blackmailing him. He was married, after all.'

'So you and Erol?'

'Things were fine for many years. Then one day he came to me and said that he wanted a "proper" woman. He was a media star and he was getting older and it was unseemly for him to be with someone like me.'

Eylul said, 'You must have been so hurt.'

'I was! But as I said, I was in love with him. I knew he'd been messing around with young girls, just like Celal Bey, but I still went ahead and did it.'

'What?'

'I had a full sex change,' she said. 'In Italy. As your doctor knows, and I'm sure you do too, I had my penis and scrotum removed and a vagina constructed.' Her face became pained. 'He loved me again for a bit. Then he got sick and everything sexual stopped. May I have a break now?'

*

She cried so hard one would, Süleyman observed, have had to be made of stone not to feel for her. Eylul brought her tissues, tea and some cigarettes, and then they continued.

'I know some people would say it was shallow of me, but I couldn't cope without sex. It's how I had related to people all my adult life. I felt as if Erol hated me. I met Wael Al Hussain one afternoon at the Pera Palas Hotel. I was having tea and cake and he was looking around at the art and the architecture. He was a clever man, and good looking too. I booked a room for that afternoon and we had the best sex I'd had for a long time. I didn't love him, but he satisfied me. Meanwhile, I had learned that Erol was seeing one particular woman. A pre-op trans girl. He told me he missed cock. After what I'd done for him . . .' She shook her head.

'I began to see more of Wael. By this time I'd lost my job at Harem Medya, thanks to Filiz, who still blamed me for Celal Bey leaving her. I wasn't happy. Erol sometimes abused me in public by this time. He wanted out and so did I by then. But how? His public would be expecting a full-scale celebrity divorce, and because we'd never been married, that couldn't happen. We were stuck. Then he made a new will and asked me to look at it. I was to be cut out completely; everything was to go to Hürrem, his daughter. He was still quite ill at the time, and so I tore the document up. In the meantime, Wael was becoming heartily sick of his wife.'

'And so you devised your plan?'

'We did,' she said. 'I've never seen the Alfred Hitchcock film *Strangers on a Train*, but I did read the book by Patricia Highsmith that it was based on, many years ago. I thought it was so ingenious. If we could get Wael's wife to attempt to kill Erol . . .'

'You would have to kill Wael,' Süleyman said.

'But I wouldn't, and didn't.'

Frowning, Eylul said, 'Samira Al Hussain always maintained that her husband beat her.'

'Exactly! Of course she'd do it!' Betül smiled.

And it was here that Eylul and Süleyman requested another break.

Chapter 29

'It was all so understandable,' Eylul Yavaş said as she stood with Süleyman in the car park while he smoked. 'And then, suddenly . . . sociopath!'

Süleyman shrugged. 'Maybe,' he said. 'I don't know whether my ex-wife would concur, but I agree with you that is how it seems.'

'He beat his wife, and Betül, who claims she didn't love him, was prepared to take that on!'

'She's had to fight to survive.'

'By her own admission, she came from a secure background, sir.' Eylul shook her head. 'I'll be honest with you, after last night, I feel drained. It's only curiosity that's keeping me going.'

He smiled. 'You're holding up brilliantly. I hope that doesn't sound patronising; it's not meant to.'

She laughed. Süleyman put one cigarette out and then lit another. As they watched the comings and goings of people in the car park, Süleyman spotted Ömer Mungun and called him over.

Ömer told his colleagues what had been decided about the Syrians, and then he said, 'Kerim Bey's wife is now in labour.'

Eylul said, 'I will pray for her.'

'He's at the hospital,' Ömer said.

Süleyman nodded. 'Sergeant Yavaş and myself are in the thick of what may or may not be a confession,' he said.

'By Betül, or Levent?'

'Yes.'

'Mmm.'

Whether Ömer was disappointed that he was not involved was hard to tell. But Süleyman suspected he was. Ever since they'd basically competed over the traffic cop Barçın Demirtaş some years ago, things had never been quite the same between them.

Berekiah Cohen, Hülya İkmen's husband, could speak English well. Eighteen years working as a jeweller in the polyglot atmosphere of the Grand Bazaar had honed his skills in German too. But what really amazed Patrick Süleyman about Berekiah was not his linguistic skills but his acuity with his tools and materials.

Badly wounded in the 2003 bombing of the Neve Şalom Synagogue, which was opposite the Cohens' apartment in Galata, Berekiah had lost much of the use of his left arm. It had only been because the owner of the shop he worked at had known the Cohens well that he had been given the time and space to retrain himself, using only his right hand, in the art of gold and precious stone setting.

As he applied just the minutest amount of flame from the soldering iron to one of the golden globes that would become a setting for a diamond, Patrick asked him, 'How many of these do you have to do?'

'Fifty.'

'Fifty!'

The process complete for the time being, Berekiah looked up. 'It is only a small crown.'

'God!'

Çiçek laughed. She said to her brother-in-law, 'I told Patrick it's for the wedding of a media star.'

'She's an influencer, I believe,' Berekiah said. 'I expect you know more about that than I do, Patrick.'

'Vloggers,' he said. 'There are loads of them. They make a

lot of money, some of them.' Then he looked serious all of a sudden. 'Çetin Bey told me that my father is still working.'

'Yes,' Çiçek said. 'But you'll see him soon.'

'Mammy asked what he was doing last night.'

Çiçek and Berekiah looked at each other.

'I told her I was having a good time, like,' Patrick continued.

Neither of them asked the boy whether he was covering for his father. His mother still had a lot of anger about her ex, and nobody wanted to raise that particular spectre while Patrick was in Turkey.

Eventually Berekiah said, 'Well, you'll see Çetin Bey later, so you can ask him about it. Those two speak to each other all the time. Now, Patrick, would you like to go out on the roof of the Bazaar like James Bond?'

'Wael told me that he could arrange for me to meet his wife at a meddah performance for Syrians in Fatih.'

'Did you know anything about this performance?' Süleyman asked.

'It's a regular event. His wife liked that sort of thing.'

'It's a cover for the distribution of stolen money to Syrian refugees,' Süleyman added. 'Did you know that?'

'Yes, it was the perfect cover for us too,' Betül said. 'Wael knew that no one would ever acknowledge the event. Samira wouldn't be believed and would go to prison. Then he would be free.'

'Not forever.'

'No,' she said. 'That wasn't the point.'

'So what was?'

'For me? I wanted him.'

'And your husband?'

'I didn't want to hurt Erol,' she said. 'If he died, I would be homeless, I'd have nothing.'

'So why,' Eylul asked, 'did you kill him?'

'I didn't! I was out when he died. I don't know what happened there. Only Wael was meant to die that night!'

'Meant to die?'

'Wael was having sex with *her*,' she said. 'Pembe Hanım.'

Süleyman put a hand up to his head.

Eylul, who felt she had rather more patience than the inspector, said, 'So between the time you set Samira Al Hussain up and her husband's death, you discovered that he was having an affair with Pembe Hanım?'

People often said that İstanbul was the biggest village in the world, where everyone knew everyone. Not for the first time in either of the officers' experience, this had been borne out.

'I deserve better than unfaithfulness,' Betül said. 'After everything I have done.'

Roused from his momentary reverie, Süleyman said, 'To take things back a little, you set Samira Al Hussain up to fail when she threatened to kill your husband?'

'Yes.'

'As I recall, Mrs Al Hussain's testimony detailed how you had allowed her onto your property prior to the attempt. This I imagine was to make sure your neighbours knew her face.'

She nodded.

'OK. So now moving on to Inspector Gürsel's current investigation into the deaths of your husband and Wael Al Hussain, you are telling me that Mr Al Hussain was meant to die.'

'He cheated on me,' she said. 'Erol did too, but I didn't want him to die. If he died, where would I go?'

'Yes, I understand that. What I don't understand is why your husband and Mr Al Hussain were having dinner together the night they died.'

'Because,' she said, 'Erol invited him.'

'Why?'

'Because I told him to.' She leaned forward in her chair, her eyes shining. 'I discovered that Erol and Wael were both sleeping with Pembe, both for the same reason. I told Erol.'

'Forgive me,' Süleyman said. 'You told Erol that you had been sleeping with Wael?'

'No! Of course not! I told him that Wael Al Hussain was sleeping with Pembe!'

'So . . .'

'Do you know what it's like to lose all your dignity, Inspector?' she said. 'Unlike Wael, who did seek to hide his unfaithfulness from me, Erol didn't. He humiliated me in public whenever he felt like it; he didn't even back me up when Filiz Hanım dropped me. He told me he was going with Pembe, and why.'

'Which was?'

'Which was because she still had what he had begged me to have removed,' she said. Tears came into her eyes. 'I had surgery for him and only for him. But then he said he "missed it", which was why he went with her. He spent money on her! I know she was very beautiful, and the one time I met her, she was charming too.'

'When did you meet her?' Süleyman asked.

'When I cut it off.'

'When you killed her.'

'No,' she said. 'When I cut off her balls and her cock. I wanted us to be equals, nothing more.'

Ruya opened the apartment door and smiled.

'Çetin Bey!' she said. 'Do you have your young friend with you?'

'Patrick? No,' he said. 'My son-in-law Berekiah is showing him around the Grand Bazaar.'

She let him in. While he was removing his shoes, she said, 'He's very dextrous, that boy. He should make a good magician.

And once you get beyond the shyness, he has considerable charm.'

'Oh, he's the full package,' İkmen said. 'His mother once told me all about the charm of the Irish, and she was right. That kid has it in abundance.'

He walked into the living room, where Sami Nasi was sitting on the floor apparently repairing a box. When he saw İkmen, he said, 'You!'

Ruya passed a hand across the top of her husband's head. 'Play nice.' Then, to İkmen, 'Coffee?'

'Yes please.'

She left.

'What are you doing?' İkmen asked as he sat down, affecting nonchalance.

Sami sighed irritably. 'This is, although you wouldn't know it, a faulty sawing illusion box. I am effecting a repair.'

'Don't you have people—'

'No! I do not have "people" to do anything for me, except perhaps you, who chooses to act as some sort of inappropriate alarm clock!'

Ruya's voice came out of the kitchen. 'Sami!'

He looked crestfallen, then said, 'Well . . .'

İkmen smiled and lit a cigarette. 'I'm sorry I woke you last night, Sami,' he said. 'I was in a foul mood and blamed you for something . . .'

'Thank you!' Sami stood up.

'. . . for something,' İkmen continued, 'that I admit I don't understand.'

Sami put his tools on the floor and sat down again.

'With some notable exceptions, most people in this city see the Syrian refugees more in terms of an inconvenience than anything else,' İkmen said. 'People moan about how may signs there are in Arabic these days, how you get hit on for money by Syrian beggars, and how so many working girls can't speak Turkish. The war in Syria is far from İstanbul and President Assad is a sort of weird softly spoken bogeyman you occasionally see on TV.'

Sami shook his head. 'And yet I was wrong to keep quiet,' he said. 'When Dad used to put travelling show people up when I was a kid, many of them were Syrian. We spoke Arabic at home sometimes; it was and is part of us. But we're also Vaneck's children, Europeans, civilised – Dad was always proud of that. We lived two lives.'

İkmen smiled. 'Welcome to the Turkish condition, Sami.'

'I mean it!' he said. 'Truly. And if the magic of storytelling was helping to make the lives of Syrians happier, then I wanted in. Yes, I knew. About the golden lamassu, about the distribution of aid, about how that had all worked against Samira Al Hussain. But what could I do?'

'Did you know about Hakikat?'

'The woman? Not until that night you met her,' Sami said. He shook his head. 'I have often fooled myself that what I have done in the course of my life is for the greatest good for the many, but I don't know. A woman sits in prison while I pontificate about the situation in Syria I have never experienced.'

'That woman tried to kill a man,' İkmen said.

'Yes. But the truth was actively hidden,' Sami said. 'And that's a bad road to walk along. That's Assad's road.'

Mehmet Süleyman didn't often sleep that well. But the last few days had been particularly bad, and now he felt punch drunk. The break he'd called in Betül Gencer's interrogation had allowed him to go outside and get some reasonably fresh air, a cup of coffee courtesy of Eylul Yavaş and the chance to make a few phone calls.

Once Eylul had gone, he called Gonca.

'Hello, baby,' she said when she heard his voice.

'I'll be late again tonight,' he said.

Normally she would protest, but this time she could hear the weariness in his voice and said, 'Is it bad, darling?'

'It's hard work,' he said. 'I'm not even sure what, as yet, I'm going to get at the end of it.'

'When you do come back to me, I will make you better,' she said. 'You know I can.'

'I know.'

Then he called an old school friend he occasionally rang, a lawyer called Aytun Kuran. He outlined a theoretical murder case involving a transgender suspect. He knew what Aytun was going to say before he said it, but he had to be sure.

'She'll go to a male facility,' Aytun said.

'So she'll be in a male prison – indefinitely?'

'Yes,' the lawyer said. 'The way things stand.'

Süleyman had thought this would be the case. He wondered whether Betül Gencer knew. She had been very careful not to admit to murder, but did that mean she really hadn't killed anyone, or was she seeking ways to exonerate herself because she knew what would happen at the point of judicial disposal?

'Do with them? I don't know,' Betül Gencer said. 'I was in the kitchen . . .'

'Did you put the oven on?' Eylul Yavaş asked.

She had taken the lead since they had resumed their interrogation. Betül Gencer was still without legal representation, and now it seemed they had hit a roadblock.

'No. Why would I put the oven on? I think I washed my hands and arms and my feet, and then I left.'

'You were bloodied?'

'Of course I was. I'd just castrated . . .' She threw her arms in the air. 'Why would I put the oven on, for God's sake?'

The only place where Betül Gencer's DNA had been discovered was on the kitchen floor in a small sample of blood. She must have cut herself.

Süleyman looked at Eylul, and then he asked, 'You drugged Pembe Hanım, is that correct?'

'I take diazepam. I loaded the rakı I gave her.'

'You didn't drink any yourself?'

'No.'

'Did you know Pembe Hanım?' Eylul asked.

'No. But I'd followed my husband to several of his meetings with her across the city, and I saw Wael both go into and leave her building in Tarlabaşı. I knew who she was. Since Filiz Tepe let me go from my job, I've had a lot of time on my hands. But I didn't kill her. People survive castration. I did.'

'People sometimes survive, but not usually outside a clinical setting,' Süleyman said.

'I didn't mean to kill her!'

'Maybe,' Eylul said. 'But you will have to prove that in some way, and I don't know how that will work out.'

Betül began to sob, and they let her. As her crying subsided, Süleyman gave her a cigarette. When she was composed again, he said, 'Tell us about the night your husband and Mr Al Hussain died.'

She sighed. 'I think back now,' she said, 'and I wonder what I wanted. I'd taken great pleasure in telling Erol that Wael was also screwing Pembe.'

'To be clear, did he know about you and Wael?'

'No, but even if he had, it would have made no difference,' she said. 'Erol didn't love me any more, even though I loved him. I still do.'

'Did Wael know about Erol and Pembe?' Eylul asked.

'I didn't tell him,' she said. 'I don't know. How they died – they must have fought?'

Neither of the officers said anything.

Betül said. 'I was due to go out with my friends, and he invited Wael to our house, on my suggestion.'

'On what pretext? I mean, I assume there was . . .'

'That he wanted to talk to him about his wife,' she said. 'What we could do to maybe help her. The woman was clearly delusional and perhaps we could buy her some treatment. I don't know whether Wael believed it, but he came. I prepared a meal for them and went out.'

Süleyman said, 'Did your husband know you had colluded with Wael Al Hussain to put his wife in prison?'

'I have to say no,' she said. 'But I'm no longer sure. Maybe he did. Maybe that was why his cruelty to me increased over time. Maybe both Wael and Erol knew more than I imagined. I didn't mean for them to die.'

'You said to us earlier that only Wael was meant to die,' Süleyman said. 'You can't have it both ways. Did you mean for Erol to kill Wael or not?'

She stared into space, and then she said, 'I wanted Wael to die because of what he'd done to me with *her*. I suppose I was glad when I knew that he had died. Not Erol, though.'

'Because now you have no home?'

'And I loved him. Did Wael . . . did he poison my husband?'

'We think so yes,' Eylul said. 'But due to the nature of the toxin, Erol must have killed Wael first. They fought.'

'The poison was in your husband's mineral water and present in a bottle of whisky,' Süleyman said. 'None of this substance was found in Wael Al Hussain's body. But we did discover a packet of it in his apartment.'

'I didn't . . .' She teared up again.

'Wael must have known about Erol and Pembe,' Süleyman said. 'Even if you didn't tell him. He went to your house prepared to kill. Erol, on the other hand, had a disagreement with Wael and killed him reflexively, we believe, with a cheese knife. Then he drank the substance that ultimately killed him. Now tell me, Mrs Gencer, about the climax of your protracted act of revenge.'

'About?'

'Filiz Tepe,' he said.

The baby was a girl. They called her Melda, which meant 'slim young girl'. Because Sinem had become quickly distressed during labour, her daughter had been delivered by Caesarean section. As soon as they saw her, Melda's parents were in love.

But Sinem was exhausted after her ordeal, and although she managed to feed Melda almost immediately, she soon fell asleep. Kerim, sitting in a chair beside his wife's bed, held his daughter in his arms and listened to his wife's gentle breathing. Sinem was going to need at least a week in hospital in order to heal, to learn to feed the baby with confidence and to give her doctors time to work out how her pain relief regime might work. He would, he now realised, have to employ someone to help her.

That person should have been Pembe, but of course that was impossible. Madam Edith had volunteered, but she was old and Kerim wondered whether she'd be up to the job. That said, it would have to be someone who understood the Gürsels' lifestyle. He couldn't live through another Pınar Hanım situation. He'd lose his mind.

He looked into Melda's sweet face and tried not to think about Pembe. He had to forget her, and maybe even that life. From now on, his world revolved around this little baby, the absolute love of his life, as well as his wife, who had been his best friend, whom he loved, but who wanted far more of him than she had, even now, admitted.

'And now you can call me a murderer,' Betül said. 'Erol, Wael, Pembe – I didn't mean to kill . . .'

'But in the case of Pembe, that was what happened,' Süleyman said.

She shrugged, displaying the uncaring sociopath once again.

'I killed Filiz because she was a bitch,' she said. 'I'd been Celal Bey's first mistress and she always believed that he'd never got over me. As soon as she got any power in that company, she made sure I had the worst jobs, like that shitty bridal show.'

'Did she know that you were transgender?' Süleyman asked.

'No. Only when I told her.'

'Which was when?'

'Just before I pushed her out of her bedroom window.'

'So can I take it you are confessing to the murder of Filiz Tepe?' Süleyman asked.

'Yes,' she said. 'I actually hated her. I didn't hate the others, I was just tired of being the wrong . . . being not good enough. When I came to this city, I was a gay boy who turned tricks. Celal Bey made me something he thought socially acceptable, and that was fine, I was happy enough. I had a career and it was fun. Then came Erol, who made me change myself still further until he tired of that and took a lover with a penis. Meanwhile, Filiz got her own back on me by ruining my career. Why can't I be what people want me to be? Why do I always seem to do the wrong thing?'

'I don't know,' Süleyman said.

'I've only ever wanted to please, and yet . . .' She shrugged. 'I've always worked hard, but all my life people have ultimately spat in my face. Never right, always wrong. Erol used to ask me why I kept Levent's old apartment on in Kadıköy, and I would say it was because I never wanted to forget him. I realised later that the reason I spoke his name on the night Erol died was because I was in shock. In spite of everything I have done – leaving my family and my village, becoming Betül, my career, my husband, my money – I know that I was only really happy when I was at home. When I was just some boy, nobody hurt me. You have been kind to me, but in the main, men are horrible to women, they're horrible to trans people and to kids. But what offends me even more is that women hate women too. I had to learn that quickly when I became Betül. Filiz taught me that and I never forgave her.'

Later when she had been charged and it was time for her to return to her cell, Süleyman offered to take her in person. Two guards accompanied them, both of whom were keen to cuff her. But Süleyman wouldn't let them. Instead he offered her his arm and said, 'Let me take you myself, Betül Hanım.'

She began to cry, and so he gave her his handkerchief.

'You are so kind,' she said as she returned it to him.

He took it from her and wiped away a smear of mascara underneath her eye.

'There,' he said, 'that's much better.'

Chapter 30

The djinn looked at Çetin İkmen, and İkmen looked at the djinn.

'I'm getting bored with you,' he said as he lit a cigarette while the djinn hissed.

Samsun, who was ironing on the kitchen table, said, 'Welcome to my world.'

Looking away from the djinn, which had now shrunk to the size of a small cat, İkmen said, 'Are you working tonight, Samsun?'

'Not exactly,' she said. 'Drinks in honour of Pembe Hanım.'

'Where, at the Sailors' Bar?'

'Yes,' she said. 'Madam Edith's idea. It's what Pembe would have wanted. Just a shame about . . .'

They looked at each other, neither or them daring to say Kerim's name.

Instead İkmen said, 'I received a text telling me the Gürsel baby has been born. A girl.'

'Maşallah.' Then she said, 'That poor little Sinem. How will they cope, eh?'

İkmen said nothing. The Gürsels had spent a lot of money on Sinem's care. Now they would have to think about care for both the baby and her mother.

'Well, I'm going to go out on the balcony,' İkmen said. 'There's a lot to tell Fatma.'

'As you wish.'

'Oh, and when Çiçek and Patrick come back, let them know

that Mehmet Süleyman is joining us for dinner tonight.'

'Prince Mehmet?' Samsun shook her head. 'You know it's all around the bazaars that he's actually marrying the queen of the gypsies.'

'I believe he is, yes,' İkmen said.

'Does the boy know?'

'Yes.'

'And Çiçek?'

'Her too.'

'Oh well,' Samsun said. 'If you ask me, our girl missed a bullet.'

Süleyman had never really spoken to Eylul Yavaş before, not properly. He knew that when Kerim had first employed her, they'd all had a tendency to treat her differently, not because she was a woman, but because she wore a headscarf. But she was one of them now. She'd proved that.

Back in his office, he offered her a chair and said, 'Sergeant Yavaş, I would like to thank you for your work these past few days. I know it's not been easy. What we all witnessed two nights ago in Yeniköy will sadly stay with us for a long time.'

'I can't pretend to understand what can make someone do that,' she said. 'I know that Betül Hanım explained to some extent . . .'

'Please don't take this the wrong way, Sergeant,' Süleyman said, 'but I have been very impressed by your handling of what has been a very difficult set of circumstances.'

'You mean because Mrs Gencer is transgender?' She smiled. 'Sir, I know you are not a religious man, but we're not all what you think.'

'I didn't—'

'Compassion is the main thing,' she said. 'My faith gives my life meaning and I am so grateful for that. But if I don't use my faith to advance kindness, then what kind of person am I?'

He shook his head. 'I don't know.'

'Anyway,' she said, 'I took my cue in this instance from you, sir.'

'How so?'

'The way you dealt with Betül Hanım,' she said. 'It was respectful. The woman killed people and yet you showed compassion.'

'No one kills for no reason, and sometimes those reasons, while not excusing murder, are valid.' He sighed. 'But a lot of work still awaits us. You, Sergeant Mungun and me.'

'What about your son, sir?' she asked. 'You were supposed to be on leave with him. It was very selfless of you to support Inspector Gürsel as you did, but . . .'

A look passed between them. Did she know? He couldn't even begin to ask her. Private lives in Turkey, in spite of reality TV, had forever been walled.

He said, 'I will come in tomorrow and then, if I am able, I will have the last two days of his vacation with my son. Fortunately I have very good friends who have ensured that Patrick has had a good time.'

There was an awkward moment of silence, and then she said, 'Sir, will Samira Al Hussain's sentence be re-evaluated now.'

'I hope so,' he said. 'I will recommend that it is.'

'Good.' She stood up.

He said, 'I expect you'd like to go home now, wouldn't you?'

'Yes, sir.'

'Yes.' He looked down at his desk. 'We should all go home. Inspector Gürsel has a daughter, by the way. Did you know that?'

'I did hear, yes,' she said. 'Mother and baby are both doing well, I understand.'

He smiled, then rose to his feet. 'You know, when I was a small child I had a nanny. She was Armenian and I loved her very much. She used to tell my brother and me that for every bad thing that happened in the world, there were always two good things to take its place.'

'I've never heard that before, sir.'

He took his cigarettes and lighter out of his pocket and began to move towards the door.

'Probably an Armenian saying,' he said. 'But in the spirit of nanny's old adage, I should like to add to the good news about Inspector Gürsel's baby and tell you that I am to be married.'

'Oh. Congratulations, sir.'

'Thank you,' he said. 'You are the first colleague I have told, so if you would keep it to yourself for a while, I would be grateful.'

'Of course, sir.'

'Come on,' he said. 'Let's get out of here.'

'There are Armenians on the roof,' Patrick told Çetin İkmen.

'Really?'

Çiçek was in the kitchen helping Samsun to prepare the evening meal. İkmen could hear them both shouting at the djinn. He looked at Fatma, whose ghost sat smiling beside the boy.

'They're all silversmiths,' Patrick said. 'They make a lot of stuff for churches. A lot of those silver covers that they put on their icons and chalices and stuff. Berekiah knows them all.'

'Berekiah has worked in the bazaar all his life.'

'But his dad was a cop, wasn't he?'

'Yes.' Poor Balthazar Cohen, who had lost both legs in the great earthquake of 1999 and had been housebound ever since. İkmen tried to get to see him when he could, which wasn't often. The thought of it made him feel mean and ashamed.

Patrick shook his head. 'İstanbul's a lot more fun than Dublin,' he said. 'I wish I could stay here.'

'Well, maybe when you have been to university, you can,' İkmen said. 'You have a Turkish passport. But you will have to learn the language.'

Patrick pulled a face. 'I'm fairly good at French, but shite at Irish,' he said.

'Well make sure you're good at Turkish. Get your mother to help you. When you were little, you spoke it well.'

'Did I?'

'Yes. It's all probably still in your head, you just have to find it.' İkmen lit a cigarette. 'Now, Patrick,' he said, 'your father is coming here for dinner tonight. It would seem that, just like the clever man he is, he has solved a very high-profile murder investigation.'

'The one about the man on TV?'

'Yes,' İkmen said.

'So does that mean I have to go back to the flat with him?'

'It may, but not tonight,' İkmen said.

'Oh.' Patrick paused for a moment. 'So he'll be off to his gypsy woman tonight, will he?'

Teenagers were such strange creatures. Sometimes when Patrick spoke it sounded as if he was about ten, while at other times he seemed to ape a cynical old man.

'It's all right,' the boy continued. 'I know he's marrying her.'

İkmen sighed. 'I expect he will want you to meet her properly.' The boy looked downhearted, so he added, 'But not tonight. Tonight it is just us, Auntie Samsun, Çiçek and your father.'

Kerim Gürsel gave the baby to Sinem, who was awake by this time, and took the call out in the corridor. He thanked Mehmet Süleyman for his good wishes and then listened as he told him about his protracted interrogation of Betül Gencer. And although he didn't say anything, he felt that Mehmet Bey would know it was a tale, of two lives, to which he could relate.

When he had finished, Kerim said, 'So Betül didn't confess to cooking . . .'

'No,' Süleyman said. 'She claims to have no idea what she

did with the body parts. I have requested a psychiatric assessment. It may be that she performed that act in an altered state of consciousness that she now doesn't remember.'

'And she'll go to a male facility.'

'She will. Considering what she did and to whom, I doubt you have feelings . . .'

'Oh I do, but they are confused,' Kerim said. 'Don't get me wrong, if she killed Pembe, I want her to suffer. But to put her in a male facility . . . Can you imagine what they'll do to her?'

There had been a couple of cases of transgender women being imprisoned in male-only facilities in recent years. These cases had revolved around sexual violence.

Because Süleyman didn't answer – he didn't need to; they both knew what went on – Kerim said, 'I know you interviewed my mother-in-law.'

'Pınar Hanım confessed,' Süleyman said. 'But she didn't do it, and I would say that even if we didn't have Betül Hanım in custody. Her confession, whilst surprisingly accurate, was nothing more than a good guess.'

'So what will you do?' he asked.

'Nothing. I will speak to your brother-in-law, Emir, who seems like a reasonable man. I've no doubt Pınar Hanım knew where Pembe lived and bore her enormous ill will, but she didn't kill her.'

'Thank God.'

'Does she know about the baby?'

'I imagine so,' Kerim said. 'I called Emir just after I spoke to my parents. But I don't want her in our lives from now on. She hurt Sinem and I can't have that.'

'Family can be problematic,' Süleyman said.

Later, when Kerim went back into the hospital room to see his wife and baby, he found them both asleep. And so he sat beside the bed just looking at them, marvelling at how he could feel so much love for them. Why had Pembe never told him about Erol Gencer, he wondered? Had he sworn her to secrecy which she took with her to the grave or had she simply been too ashamed to tell him she had more than one regular lover? He would never know and it hurt.

Çiçek İkmen didn't usually cook under instruction. Not since her mother had died. But now she had to defer to Samsun, because what she was cooking was an Albanian recipe.

'More salt! More salt!' she said to Çiçek as she seasoned the lamb for what was called tave kosi – a huge meaty casserole with rice and yogurt.

Çiçek obliged with no comment and then opened the kitchen window wider. It was so hot. If she'd had her way, they would be eating a cold meze, but Samsun wanted to please Patrick, who had apparently told her that tave kosi was rather similar to an Irish dish. Çiçek, who had travelled to Ireland on several occasions, couldn't imagine what. To her knowledge, the Irish were not big on yogurt.

Mehmet Süleyman arrived just after seven and went out onto the balcony to be with Patrick and İkmen. Çiçek hoped her father would give the two of them space to talk alone. Patrick needed to find a way to communicate with his father as a human being rather than some sort of semi-divine and at the same time truly frightening creature.

There hadn't been time to tell her son anything about the death of Harun Sesler when the godfather's own son turned up on Gonca's doorstep. At first Rambo didn't even recognise him.

'Yeah?' he said when he answered the door.

Serkan Sesler was an overweight and allegedly lazy man of forty. Spoiled by his father, it was said he'd never married because he couldn't make up his mind between all the various beautiful call girls his father had bought for him over the years.

'Can I speak to Gonca Hanım?' he asked.

Rambo yelled, 'Mum!'

When she arrived, Gonca invited Sesler in. She sent Rambo to his bedroom to unpack his rucksack.

'My son has just got back from Italy,' she said to the fat man, who waddled after her into her garden.

'Mmm.'

Did he know about the sea silk she had been getting for his father?

Sesler sat down on one of the chairs outside the living room. 'Nice garden.'

'Yes,' she said, before racing to the kitchen to get rakı, iced water and a bowl of pistachio nuts. If proper rules of hospitality were not observed with the likes of the Sesler family, there could be grave consequences.

When she returned, she offered her guest a cigarette and then said, 'My condolences. May God's mercy be with your father, Serkan Bey.'

He nodded. 'Very kind,' he said. 'Very kind.'

Gonca began to feel her face pale. Did he know? Tarlabaşı was alive with rumours, some of which, she knew, were about her. She was talking to her brother again and he had said it seemed everyone blamed Elmas's mother Afife for Harun Bey's death – even those who hadn't seen it happen. But there were also some who pointed the finger at Gonca. And of course she knew why that was. Poor Afife had been far too off her head on drugs to be bothered with her daughter almost since the girl had been born. But some magic and a chat had fixed all that. And some heroin.

'Gonca Hanım,' Sesler said once he'd taken a deep draught from his rakı glass, 'I will come straight to the point.'

'Serkan Bey?'

'I know you were indebted to my father. That was one of the

reasons why he was so happy when you were able to resolve this matter in such a creative way.'

Gonca began to feel sick.

'But sadly, my father will not now marry Elmas Hanım . . .'

'The poor girl must be so disappointed!' Was it too much?

'Yes.' He smiled. He had his father's smile, which was decidedly vulpine. 'And so in commemoration of my father, and also because I have heard a story that you yourself are to be married soon, Gonca Hanım, I would like to make a gift to you from my family.'

Was it death? She made herself smile.

'Please do keep the sea silk you have collected and woven so far,' he said. 'Incorporate it into your own wedding gown. My father would have liked that.'

Gonca thought about how little the son knew the father – or did he?

'Because you see,' Sesler continued, 'I do believe most strongly that you and I can help each other in far more . . . thoughtful ways than you did in the time of my father.'

She frowned. 'Serkan Bey?'

He leaned across the table, his large stomach tilting it a little.

'My father was old, and much of what the old do is childish, don't you think? I, however, have different ideas. I think for instance that it is far better to work with someone like you, hanım, than to work against you. True, you borrowed money from my father, which needed to be repaid, but there are ways and ways of doing that, don't you think? Especially for a woman of your obvious skill . . .'

If he was suggesting some sort of sexual payment, that would be awkward. In the normal course of events she would just close her eyes and do what was necessary. But to be unfaithful to Mehmet was unthinkable. Especially with this man.

*

Mehmet Süleyman told his son everything, apart from the more graphic details of the victims' deaths. Significantly he described what he had done, the leads he had followed and the deductions he had made, rightly or wrongly. When he'd finished, he said, 'I know that doesn't make up for abandoning you, Patrick.'

'I've had a good time,' the boy said. 'I like it here.'

'Çetin Bey and his family are—'

'No! No, I like them, of course, but I mean the city, İstanbul. It's great. Better than Dublin. Stuff happens here, it never gets boring.'

'Dublin can be lively,' Süleyman said.

'If you like a drink, yeah.'

'I like Dublin,' Süleyman said. 'But I am glad you like İstanbul. I hope you will come again.'

They didn't touch and it made Mehmet feel sad. He'd only ever touched his own father to kiss his hands as a sign of respect. They'd not hugged. And now he was doing the same thing with his son. He put a hand on the boy's shoulder and felt him flinch.

'Patrick . . .'

'I know you're getting married,' Patrick said. 'I've seen Gonca.'

'Oh. Yes.'

'With Kemal. He told me she has magic and she loves you.'

He sighed. 'I do not know about the magic,' he said. 'I have no experience with such things.' And yet the thought that she might have bewitched him was in his head. 'But she does love me, and I love her. Patrick, I never sought to do . . . what I did to your mother.'

The boy said nothing.

'I am in many ways a man who is not strong,' Süleyman said. 'You must not follow me in your relations with women.'

'I've two girls who like me back home,' Patrick said. 'Neve and Sophie.'

'Oh, well . . .' Zelfa had told him about them. One was the sister of one of Patrick's friends, and the other girl worked in a shop. 'You are a very . . . you're a good-looking young man and you are clever.'

'Neve works in a chip shop and said she'd go the whole way with me. Said she'd make it a deadly craic.'

In spite of himself, Süleyman laughed. A craic was, as far as he knew, a good night out. A deadly craic was the best night out of your life.

'Oh Patrick,' he said. 'I take it you didn't tell your mother.'

'No.' The boy smiled. Then he said, 'I'm glad you're laughing, Father.'

Süleyman stood up, lifted the boy out of his chair and hugged him close. He said, 'You know, I always called my father "Father" and I longed to be less formal.'

Patrick hugged him back. 'I used to call you "Daddy", but then you said I was too old to do that.'

'Well then I was wrong,' Süleyman said. 'I know that people in Ireland call their father "Daddy" all their lives. I was I think maybe a little too anxious that you behave like me. I am sorry. I am also sorry that I neglected you.'

'Çetin Bey said that you had to help your friend because his wife was having a baby.'

They stopped hugging and just stood looking at each other. Patrick looked so much like Mehmet it almost broke the older man's heart. So much time had passed, and the boy was almost a man.

'That is true,' Süleyman said. 'But it was not as simple as that. Kerim Bey had other problems too.'

In Ireland it seemed it was easier to talk about homosexuality than it was in Turkey, but Süleyman didn't know enough about the country to be entirely confident in bringing the subject up. After all, Patrick did go to a school that was run by Jesuit priests, and they, as his ex-wife had once put it, 'saw sin in a raindrop'.

'Mammy wants me to be a doctor, like her.'

Süleyman looked down at the boy. 'And what do you want?' he said.

He shrugged. 'I get good grades in most things.'

'Which means you can choose, I imagine.'

'I'd like to be a magician like Ruya and Sami,' he said. 'Ruya reckons I've a gift.'

Süleyman nodded. Zelfa would have a fit if the boy became a stage magician, ditto his grandmother. But if Patrick was happy, did it matter? Süleyman had done what he had wanted to do in life in spite of his parents – why could this not apply to his son?

He said, 'Then practise, as a hobby, for now. Çetin Bey has bought you many magic sets and I will send you money for anything you need. If you continue and enjoy this, then why you should not do it, I don't know.' He smiled. 'I have seen an English magician called Derren Brown who combines that art with psychology.'

The sunset call to prayer from the many imperial mosques that surrounded them provided a soundtrack to yet another hug between the two Süleyman males. Mehmet was looking forward to spending the last few days of Patrick's holiday with the boy. He hoped the feeling was mutual. When the call to prayer was over, Çetin İkmen came out onto the balcony and told them that dinner was, finally, ready.

It was nearly midnight when Samira Al Hussain received the news that Betül Gencer had finally admitted that her story about the coffee house had been true. The guard with the acne scars all over her face had told her. What difference it would make to her, Samira didn't know. But she was glad. That bitch had taken her in and made her do something she hadn't wanted to. She'd felt humiliated and dirty ever since.

In part, this resolution had been down to Rima and some ex-policeman she knew. It had also been down, Samira believed, to the abuse of the name of Ahmad Al Saidawi, which had to be punished. Al Saidawi had always championed the oppressed. Had he not prevented the Ottoman authorities from persecuting the people for three hundred and seventy-two nights? And if his spirit had somehow transferred into the body of a Turkish woman who used his tales to keep the light of the Syrian people alive, then that was all to the good.

Samira had never noticed the hakawati on that day. She had been too taken with Betül and what she was saying. Even a man like Wael could become a beast in a world like this, a world where monsters like Assad were allowed to flourish. Just before the coffee house meeting, he had beaten her everywhere it wouldn't show, until she could hardly move. She'd been ripe for Betül Gencer's suggestion. Ripe.

Mehmet Süleyman slipped into bed beside Gonca, who put her head on his chest and said, 'Is it over now?'

'No, but my involvement is almost at an end,' he said as he stroked her hair.

She held him more tightly. 'Good.'

'I see Rambo has come home.' He'd noticed the boy's dirty washing in a pile by the machine when he'd gone to the kitchen to get some water.

'Yeah.' She sat up, her eyes sleepy and sexy. 'Mehmet, are we really going to do this marriage thing? I mean blood tests and everything?'

'Sweetheart, we'll have a Roma wedding, but we'll also have a legal ceremony, which means blood tests. I have to. We must do that first.'

'I know, but . . .'

'Don't tell me you're frightened of a needle?' he said.

'I'm not frightened of anything!'

He smiled. 'I didn't think so. You just need to tell me where you want to get married – a wedding hall, or maybe a hotel . . .'

'Anywhere,' she said. 'Here?'

He laughed. 'If we can arrange for the registrar to come here, then yes,' he said. 'You also need to think about who will come.'

'Everyone.'

'For the Roma ceremony, yes, but we can't have everyone here,' he said. 'Your family is enormous.'

'I have to feed them all and provide rakı,' she said. 'I have to! And if that happens twice, then so be it!'

She laid her head down on his chest again.

These weddings were going to cost him a fortune. But he didn't care. He was in love with this extraordinary woman and would do anything for her. Had she bewitched him?'

As if reading his mind, she said, 'You know it is you who bewitched me and not the other way around, don't you, Şahzade Mehmet?'

He didn't say anything, just held her closer and wondered where she'd hidden the charms with which she had bound his very willing flesh to hers.

'I've told Patrick that he can meet you properly before he goes back to Ireland,' he said.

She stroked his face. 'Bring him here,' she said.

'I will.' He kissed her. 'He loves the city. That makes me happy. He's like Çetin Bey – entranced by the magic and the stories.'

'Stories are magic,' she said. 'A good storyteller is the highest form of magician.'

'That's what Patrick wants to do when he's an adult – be a magician.'

'Then I look forward to tomorrow,' she said. 'Not only is that boy beautiful, he is also clearly a person of substance.'

'Well, hands off,' Süleyman said. He pulled her on top of him, smiling. 'And anyway, you will have to learn English if you want to speak to him easily.'

'Then I will.' She kissed him.

But as she laid her head down on his chest once again, her face turned away from him, she frowned. Serkan Sesler hadn't wanted her body when he'd visited earlier that afternoon. He'd asked firstly for her services as his personal falcı, his fortune-teller, which was fine. But then he'd mentioned something his father had never done: her loyalty. As a Roma woman, and the person who had cursed his father to death, what choice had she had? Because Serkan had known, she'd seen it in every fat-soaked pouch on his face.

She looked up at her Şahzade Mehmet once again and wondered how she was going to keep her happiness with him perfect now that she was in effect leading a double life.

The paşa placed his half of the almond next to his wife's and then stormed out of the yalı. A little while later, the paşa's wife let the imam's son out of the chest. Still shaking with fear, he said to her, 'How am I still alive, my lady?' She laughed and said, 'Philopena is a game of forfeit, my dear. One finds a double almond, takes one half for oneself and gives the other half to one's spouse. When one partner requests something of the other, the word "Philopena" may be called as forfeit. This happened when my husband the paşa told me to open this chest: I produced my almond and called Philopena, ensuring that there was no way in which he could see you in that box. In a small way, my dear young man, this game provides us weak and rather silly little women with a measure of power.' And then she laughed, both at the boy and at her husband the paşa.